VALOR'S
TRIAL

TANYA HUFF

VALOR'S TRIAL

A Confederation Novel

DAW BOOKS, INC.

DONALD A. WOLLHEIM, FOUNDER

375 Hudson Street, New York, NY 10014

ELIZABETH R. WOLLHEIM

SHEILA E. GILBERT

PUBLISHERS

http://www.dawbooks.com

Copyright © 2008 by Tanya Huff.

All Rights Reserved.

Jacket art by Paul Youll.

DAW Book Collectors No. 1442.

DAW Books are distributed by Penguin Group (USA) Inc.

Book designed by Elizabeth Glover.

All characters and events in this book are fictitious.
Any resemblance to persons living or dead is coincidental.

The scanning, uploading and distribution of this book via the Internet or any other means without the permission of the publisher is illegal, and punishable by law. Please purchase only authorized electronic editions, and do not participate in or encourage the electronic piracy of copyrighted materials. Your support of the author's rights is appreciated.

Nearly all the designs and trade names in this book are registered trademarks. All that are still in commercial use are protected by United States and international trademark law.

First Hardcover Printing, June 2008

1 2 3 4 5 6 7 8 9

DAW TRADEMARK REGISTERED
U.S. PAT. AND TM. OFF. AND FOREIGN COUNTRIES
—MARCA REGISTRADA
HECHO EN U.S.A.

PRINTED IN THE U.S.A.

For Mike Glicksohn.

Who has the very first book I ever signed. (I spelled my own name wrong.) Whose friendship has been a constant touchstone for the last thirty years. (Possibly twenty-nine, but who's counting.) Who was pretty much entirely responsible for the Mictok when he requested "death by giant spider."' (Okay, so technically they were only obliquely at fault for Sergeant Glicksohn's death but still . . .)

It's about time he got one just for him.

ONE

"**GUNNERY SERGEANT KERR**! Good to have you back!"

"Good to be back, Sergeant Hollice." Torin thumbprinted the release that would send her gear straight to her quarters and fell into step beside the sergeant as they crossed the shuttle bay. "And congratulations on the promotion." Adrian Hollice had been in her squad when she was a sergeant and then, when she made staff sergeant, her platoon. She'd fast-tracked him onto his SLC and had been pleased to see her decision justified when Command had given him his third hook. Not that she needed reassurance that she'd been right—these days, she needed reassurance that Command didn't have its head so far up its collective ass it was cutting off all oxygen to its collective brain. "The squad have any trouble getting used to it?"

"Not after Ressk and Mashona knocked a couple of heads together. They said I'd been leading them around by the *diran avirrk* for months anyway, I might as well get paid for it."

Torin grinned. The Corps tried to keep combat units together when it could. Familiar faces strengthened both stability and loyalty under adverse conditions, and Marines had their own ways of working through the disruptions promotions brought.

"The captain was a little afraid they were going to send you to Recar'ta HQ," Hollice told her as they stepped onto the lower beltway.

"So was I." After Crucible, after she'd been detanked with her jaw rebuilt, after she'd passed the physical and psych evaluations that followed any major reconstruction, Torin had asked to be returned to Sh'quo Company. They were short NCOs and, as she'd pointed out, she'd be wasted in a staff position. Although the Corps reserved the right to send her wherever the hell it pleased, both points were inarguable and she'd been sent home. It hadn't hurt that the Commandant of the Corps had agreed with her—although *wasted in a staff position* had not been the phrase used.

"The last thing we need around here is someone else who thinks she's always right," had been the gist of the Commandant's observations.

Given the hour, the lower beltway was nearly deserted.

"They've started sweeping our Division." Hollice stood self-consciously erect as they rode toward the heart of the station. "Started at First Recar'ta, of course, so the war could bloody well be over before they get to us at Fourth. Scuttlebutt says they haven't found anything yet."

He tugged at his collar tabs, and Torin hid a smile at the telltale sign. In a poker game, he'd have been bluffing. In a conversation, he was trying to draw her out. This was why he'd come to meet her; she'd been with the recon team on Big Yellow—the alien spaceship that had turned out to be the actual alien, or aliens, the terminology remained uncertain—later, she'd initiated the investigation into why nobody remembered Big Yellow's missing escape pod and had most recently spoken to a collective of the alien on Crucible. Granted, melting her jaw during a last-ditch attempt to override a reprogrammed OpSat had meant she'd been tanked during the initial *There are aliens among us!* hysteria, and she'd missed the development of the search protocols, but she was the closest thing to an authority in the Sector.

"You think they will, Gunny?" Hollice prodded. "Find anything, I mean?"

"Find bits of a polynumerous shape-shifting, organic plastic alien that boots through our security protocols like cheddar through a H'san?" Torin asked him blandly. "One that can separate into submicroscopic pieces to avoid detection and then recombine itself back to sentience when the danger has passed? I very much doubt it." Search protocols and calming announcements from the Elder Races be damned. "Not unless it wants to be found."

"Great."

She had to admire the dryness of his delivery. He'd deserved that promotion. "Not really."

"What does it want?"

"It told me it was collecting data."

"Studying us?"

"So it seems."

"Why?"

"No idea. We may never know." Little pieces of plastic were ubiquitous thoughout Confederation space. The alien could be a part of any of them. It could *be* any of them. It could mimic other materials, and while the parts they'd most recently been in contact with had been gray, Big Yellow proved rather conclusively that didn't have to be the case. The handrail on the beltway could be recording data for the alien—as the alien—while she passed. Torin, by career choice and disposition more paranoid than most, had made a conscious decision not to think about that.

"It could make us all forget it was ever here," Hollice pointed out, his voice fraying a bit around the edges.

"Not all of us, Hollice."

He turned, stared at her for a moment, and smiled. "That's right. It can't mess with your head."

"Took a look inside and was scared off. It wants to get to Sh'quo Company, it'll have to get through me." Which was both the truth and complete bullshit since she had no more way of stopping the alien, singly or collectively, than she had of convincing the Navy that a straight line was the shortest distance between two points. But it was bullshit Hollice needed to hear and bullshit he needed to repeat to his squad. Or maybe it was the part of the statement that was the truth he needed to repeat. Whatever worked.

Technically, it *hadn't* messed with her head. Hadn't adjusted her memories of the escape pod the way it had adjusted the memories of nearly everyone else who'd been involved in the exploration of Big Yellow.

Hadn't and *couldn't* were two totally different things.

✲　　✲　　✲

The shortage of NCOs meant that Torin had only to put in a request to the station sysop to have her old quarters reassigned. The recon mission to Big Yellow had been a temporary posting, but the promotion before traveling to Ventris to brief Command on the Silsviss had destroyed the certainty of a round-trip ticket—integrating an aggressive reptilian species into the Corps would take decades, and she'd essentially been responsible for their willingness to join. That made her, if not an expert on the species, someone whose opinion Command intended to exploit. Fortunately, new information from the Marines stationed at the embassy on Silsviss had pushed her experience out toward the edge of the target. Some of those Marines were trained xenopsychologists rather than a noncom with good instincts and a willingness to kick ass when required, and, more importantly, none of them had been expected to kill a senior officer.

Torin suspected a few people were concerned because they still weren't sure if she'd have gone through with it had General Morris' sacrifice actually been necessary. She supposed it didn't help that when asked directly she'd said, *"As it wasn't necessary, I guess we'll never know."*

Which was the absolute truth; it wasn't something anyone could know until it happened—no matter what they believed themselves capable of.

Her willingness to hack Major Svensson's arm off with an ax hadn't reassured anyone.

When she dialed the door open, her quarters looked just as she remembered them, right down to the Silsviss skull hanging on the wall over her entertainment unit. Weird. When she'd left for Ventris, she'd put everything she wasn't taking with her into station storage.

"Messages?" she asked as the door slid shut behind her.

She'd verbalized, so the station did the same. "One message to Gunnery Sergeant Kerr from Staff Sergeant Greg Reghubir. As follows: "Welcome back, Gunny. We figured the last thing you'd need to do was sort your crap out, so we did it for you. Lance Corporal Ressk says you need stronger encryptions on your storage unit." Greg sounded matter-of-fact, but Torin would have bet hard currency that he'd changed his own unit's setting immediately after he saw what

Ressk could do with an eight-digit code. "Twenty-thirty tonight in the SRM; don't be late, or we'll start without you."

Torin patted the skull fondly as she passed on her way to the shower. It was good to be home.

"There's been a lot of action out on the edge of the sector. Long-range sensors have picked up Susumi portals here, here, and here." Captain Rose touched three points on the star field currently mapped out on the briefing room's HMU and frowned at the resulting red lights. "Navy swears they're not responsible."

Second Lieutenant Jarret's lavender eyes darkened as light receptors opened to give him a better look at the map. "Civilians, sir?"

The captain sighed. "It's always possible some dumbass corporation or university has decided to scout the perimeter—those types always think they're invincible until they find out they aren't and we have to pull their butts out of the fire—but I don't honestly think so. We usually get some kind of a heads up just so we're available *to* pull those butts out of the fire, and, so far, no one's admitting they've gone visiting."

"What about independents, sir?" Second Lieutenant Heerik was brand new, on her first posting with none of her enthusiasm blunted, and more than one of Sh'quo Company's officers and NCOs bent over their slates and hid a smile at the intensity of the Krai lieutenant's question.

"What kind of independents did you have in mind, Lieutenant?"

"Well, maybe civilian salvage operators." Her nose ridges flared. "It was a CSO who found Big Yellow."

And Torin felt the attention of the room shift to her.

"Gunnery Sergeant Kerr?"

Torin had served with the captain long enough to know he was amused her *relationship*—or whatever the hell it was she had with Craig Ryder—had made it into the briefing. Although his reaction was subtle enough, the odds were good no one else could see it. "CSO Craig Ryder found Big Yellow because of a small error in his Susumi calculations." She waited out the murmur of reaction. Small errors in Susumi calculations were usually fatal errors. "Spaced as they are . . ." She nodded toward the lights on the map. ". . . these portals are clearly deliberate. Salvage operators follow rather than lead, and there's nothing happening out there. No debris, no reason for them to be deliberately jumping that way."

"Unless there's something happening out there," Lieutenant Jarret said thoughtfully.

"Unless," Captain Rose agreed. "Which is why the Navy has sent the *Hardyr* out to have a look around. Captain Treis came out of Susumi space here . . ." Another touch on the star map illuminated a fourth portal, this one green. ". . . and is proceeding with due caution to this system, ST7/45T2 . . ." One last touch. ". . . here." The system was equidistant from all three red portals.

"How long is due caution expected to take, sir?" Lieutenant Joriyl wondered.

"You'll likely be headed Coreward before it happens, Lieutenant."

Her pale orange eyes darkened as she smiled. "And not a moment too soon, sir."

Lieutenant di'Pin Joriyl was the senior platoon officer. With her heading into Ventris on course that meant . . .

Torin blinked as she realized that meant Second Lieutenant di'Ka Jarret would be senior. The voice of reason and experience for Second Lieutenant Heerik and an even greener second lieutenant to be named later. It hadn't been quite a year since a very green Jarret had been tossed into a stew of giant lizards and diplomacy gone bugfuk, and suddenly Torin felt old. Life was moving just a little too fast of late.

"Captain Treis will keep Recar'ta Station informed, Recar'ta will keep Battalion informed, and—if we're really lucky—Battalion will let us know what the hell is going on before they ship us out to deal with it. Platoons are nearly at full strength for the first time in a long time, so let's make sure everyone's geared up and ready to go." The star field flicked off. Captain Rose swept his gaze around the room, then nodded once. "Details have been downloaded to your slates; get out there and get ready to save the galaxy's ass yet again. Gunnery Sergeant Kerr, remain behind."

"Yes, sir." Torin stood as the officers and NCOs made their way out of the small briefing room, Jarret throwing her a distinct *we'll get together later* before turning his attention back to Heerik, who continued talking about the best responses to possible foothold situations, unaware of expressions exchanged nearly a meter over her head. Torin had been Jarret's staff sergeant for that snafu of a giant lizard diplomacy trip, and she'd been impressed by the way the young officer had handled himself—both independently and under her guidance. If he stayed beyond his first contract, he'd be a credit to the Corps, and she'd be happy to serve under him again.

When the room emptied, she followed Captain Rose and First Sergeant Siaosi Tutone through the door to the captain's office.

"Opinion, Gunny?" he asked, dropping into the chair behind his desk. Captain Rose's voice had always seemed about three sizes too big for his body, but here, in the relative privacy of his office, he sounded tired. No, weary. Tired of all the crap that came from being a fair distance down the military food chain.

Or maybe Torin was reading too much into it.

"I think three Susumi points definitely indicates the Others are interested in something in that end of the Sector," she told him. "I think the lack of any significant attempt to hide their presence means they're coming through in force. I think the Navy should have sent more ships because if the Others get that force on the ground we're looking at Battalion moving the whole Ground Combat Team out in response. And I think that the music selection in the Senior Ranks' Mess changed for the worse while I was gone."

"That would be my selection," the first sergeant pointed out. His voice was as deep as the captain's although less incongruous, rumbling up as it did from the depth of an enormous barrel chest. Torin was tall, but Tutone topped her by a head and a half—taller even than most di'Taykan—and proportionately broad. His hands were enormous, and muscle strained against the confines of his Class Cs.

"Good choice, First. It's past time I broadened my musical tastes," Torin added, although she wasn't sure whether she was aiming for more or for less sincerity.

Tutone grinned, teeth flashing white against the rich mahogany of his skin.

Captain Rose leaned back in his chair and smiled as well. "Welcome home, Gunny. It's good to have you back."

"Thank you, sir. It's good to be back."

"Recar'ta Station agrees with your analysis, by the way. When the orders come down, they'll come down for the entire GCT. That's why you're here, specifically here with Sh'quo Company when we don't generally rate a gunny. Aman's short, and she's not reupping. Unless we deploy in the next tenday, that'll leave Jura's platoon with a shiny new second lieutenant and Heerik, who's almost as shiny, with a green staff sergeant. We'll move the new staff sergeant in under Jarret, since he's got a whole year of experience . . ." Pale eyes rolled, although for the most part he kept the sarcasm from his voice. ". . . but that's going to leave the company scrambling for experience among the officers and senior NCOs. We need you to be a kind of utility player, coming in off the bench where needed both at the platoon level and keeping the company connected to Battalion."

"Off the bench is a sports metaphor," Tutone offered. "Baseball."

His tone was dry enough that Torin couldn't quite tell if he was being helpful or facetious, so she settled for a neutral, "Thank you, First Sergeant." The league on Paradise had teams on all three major continents, and the year she left to join the Corps, New Alland—a minor continent or large island depending on who was speaking—had petitioned to have their teams recognized as well. According to the news download in the most recent packet from her younger brother, they still hadn't managed it.

"Until we ship out," Captain Rose continued, "you'll base at a desk by First Sergeant Tutone's, your primary duty to liaise with the rest of the GCT as we attempt to get ready for whatever's coming down the fukking pike. Eventually, I expect you'll be at the first sergeant's desk."

New gunnery sergeants were expected to indicate which way they intended their careers to go—to the combat position of first sergeant or to the staff position of master sergeant. After the incident on Crucible, where both the system and the officer in charge had been taken over by unknown alien forces and Torin had led the training platoon of one-twenty recruits while they fought both the system and the aliens to a standstill, Command had made it quite clear which choice they'd prefer Torin to make. Fortunately, it was the choice she wanted to make. Tutone's desk had been her goal since she'd received her corporal's hooks.

"I wasn't planning on going anywhere, sir."

For an instant, Torin thought the first sergeant had been reading her mind, and then she realized he'd been responding to the captain's statement.

"Glad to hear that, First. I was just starting to get used to you. So, Gunny, is it true what Command says, that there's nothing we can do about the microscopic bits of a big yellow alien scattered throughout known space?"

"That's the gist of it, sir."

"Since the search teams haven't found anything, any chance they've buggered off back where they came from?"

"The bit I spoke to told me they didn't have enough information, sir. I expect they're still collecting data."

"Why can't the search teams find them, then?" Before she could answer, Tutone raised a massive hand. "Never mind. The answer is probably that they can't find their anus with both hands and a map, so . . ." He waved off the end of the sentence.

"Any chance that when they spoke to you, they were messing with your head?" the captain wondered.

Given that some of them had just emerged from Major Svensson's head, Torin sure as hell hoped not. "I don't think so, sir."

Captain Rose sat and stared up at the ceiling for a moment. Specifically stared at the ring of gray plastic around the recessed light over his desk. Tutone followed the captain's gaze, but Torin refused to look. "It's like discovering the enemy is an inanimate object," he muttered, dropping his gaze. "Any inanimate object." Then he shook his head and double tapped his desk, blows ringing against the plastic. "All right. Let's get going on a job we can do."

Both NCOs recognized the dismissal, coming to attention and snapping out a "Sir!" in unison.

Rolling his eyes, the captain stroked one hand down the edge of the lower, right side screen. "I'm sending your first problem out to your desk, Gunny. And I know you've got things to deal with, First Sergeant, so let's have a little less smartass spit and polish and a little more work out of both of you. Gunny?"

Torin paused at the door. "Sir?"

"Can we be expecting General Morris to drop by any time soon?"

General Morris had become Torin's personal pain in the brass. He'd sent the platoon out to Silsviss, he'd sent her out to Big Yellow, and he'd been contaminated by the alien. Torin had a feeling he blamed her for the last. After all, if she hadn't blown the whistle, he'd never have known. Or, specifically, no one would have ever have known it about him. Given their history, the thought of him showing up once again at the Four Two made her feel a little chilled. Their time spent together never ended well.

"I sincerely hope not, sir."

"Glad to hear it."

In the outer office, Torin settled in behind her desk—easy enough to identify as it was the one the first sergeant hadn't settled his bulk behind—and opened the file the captain had sent.

"New desk, new job, eh, Gunny?"

She looked up to find the first sergeant watching her. "Same old war, First. Same old war."

He smiled and nodded, but she had a suspicion that he didn't entirely agree with her. She had no problem with that. There were days when she didn't entirely agree with it herself.

"Do you ever get the feeling that there are things the Elder Races aren't telling us?"

"It is worth noting, Gunny, that none of the diplomatic missions sent to the Others have ever included a member of the species doing the actual fighting."

Granted, it had turned out not to have been the Elder Races messing with the memories of those who knew about Big Yellow but Big Yellow itself, and while that was moderately less distressing than the alternative—always better to be screwed over by an unknown factor than an ally—that didn't actually address either question. Were there things the Elder Races weren't telling the Humans, di'Taykan, or Krai who fought their war? And why hadn't one of the three Youngest ever been invited to join the missions sent out to try to end the war? Over a century of attempted diplomacy had resulted in a few thousand dead diplomats, so why hadn't Parliament tried every possible option?

And, most importantly, had she been discussing the Elder Races with Major Svensson or with the alien living in his brain? If the former, was there discontent growing within the Corps? If the latter, did the aliens know something the Youngest didn't?

Too many questions.

Torin wanted to go back to the days when the only question she ever asked was *What do I have to do to get my people out of here alive?* Unfortunately, once the round was out of the barrel, there was no stuffing it back in. Those days were long gone.

"The company will be at full complement when we deploy, Sergeant—three full platoons plus NCOs plus officers." Torin leaned forward just far enough to tap the screen currently showing the potential packet layouts. That leaning forward also brought her well into the transport sergeant's personal space was intentional. "We're short here. And here."

"I've got the whole GCT moving out, Gunny." His nose ridges opened, closed, and opened again. "Not everyone's going to get what they want."

"That's fair. But Sh'quo Company will get what we need."

He started to answer, realized she hadn't actually asked a question, and shut his mouth with a snap of his teeth. Krai teeth could chew through anything that held still long enough, and the sound was intended to be intimidating.

Torin smiled. Human teeth weren't as strong—it was all in the display.

"No, sir. The download is correct and in order, but the count was wrong. Download says we received eight hundred twenty eight, ninety standard-round mags for one hundred thirty-eight KC-7, five hundred fifty-two high impact mags, and thirty-six full packages for the heavies when, in point of fact, we received eight hundred twenty-six, ninety standard-round mags."

The supply officer flashed her laser at one of the automated retrieval drones up near the roof of the armory, adjusting its approach to an upper storage unit, then turned to scowl in Torin's general direction. "You're making all this fuss for two magazines, Gunnery Sergeant?"

"Yes, sir."

"Fine. We'll make them up in the next ship. Two magazines aren't going to make a damned bit of difference."

"Sorry, sir, but we could deploy at any moment; I need it corrected now."

That focused the lieutenant's attention. "You need it corrected now?"

"Yes, sir."

"Because I have nothing better to do?"

Torin caught the lieutenant's lilac gaze and held it. She'd been a lieutenant through Torin's last three promotions and at this point would likely never see her captain's bars. Torin didn't care about that; there were plenty of reasons people were passed over for promotion. Some of them were even good reasons. What she did care about was that someone who'd be a long Susumi jump back of the shooting had no fukking idea just how much difference two magazines could make when it came down to it.

The lieutenant looked away when Torin allowed it. She flashed the laser at one of the smaller drones, and waited, scowling, until it buzzed up and hovered by her elbow. Picking the magazines out of the bin, she tossed them toward Torin who snatched them out of the air, checked their loads, and scanned the serial numbers into her slate to replace the two they didn't receive.

"Happy, Gunnery Sergeant?"

"Yes, sir."

"I don't want to see you around here again."

"And you won't, sir." She paused just long enough for it to be noticeable. "Not as long as the downloads and the counts match."

"Nice grouping, Mashona."

Lance Corporal Binti Mashona lowered her weapon and grinned. "Thank you, Gunnery Sergeant."

The ten rounds hadn't hit the target in a grouping so much as in a single large hole.

"Lance Corporal Mashona was using a standard KC-7, right off the rack." Torin informed Second Lieutenant Heerik's number three squad. "Now she's proven what can be done when properly motivated, why don't you lot come up here again and, this time, try to hit the damned targets. If you're still having trouble, pretend you all qualified on this weapon back in Basic!"

"Uh, Gunnery Sergeant . . ." The private's ocher hair made tentative movements out at the ends of the strands. ". . . we did all qualify back in Basic."

"I know that, Private Leraj."

"I think you're making them nervous, Gunny," Mashona murmured as the squad rushed back into position.

Torin snorted. "I can't see why."

"I'm surprised, I am, truly surprised, that a big hero like you—got the Silsviss to join up all on your lonesome, discovered a new alien life-form, saved a whole platoon of children from a bit of bad programming—I'm surprised you're still willing to drink with us working stiffs."

"He's drunk, Torin."

Torin looked at Amanda's hand on her arm then up at the di'Taykan technical sergeant looming over their table, his lime-green hair spread out in a brilliant aurora around his head. "You think?"

Di'Taykan hair wasn't exactly hair as Humans understood it. It was more like fine cat whiskers, and this, this was a threat display. Used to thinking of the di'Taykan as lovers—where *lovers* meant the most enthusiastically nondiscriminating species in known space—a lot of people forgot why they were part of the military structure. When the Elder Races first contacted them, they'd achieved peace under the umbrella of half a dozen heavily armed Orbital Platforms and had defense satellites in place all the way out to the edge of their system. While it was true that usually, one on one, they fukked before they fought . . . they also fought.

And this technical sergeant, wearing Armored's distinctive lightning bolt and wheel collar tabs, was looking for a fight.

Thing was, fights didn't happen in the SRM regardless of the amount of alcohol consumed—someone with more than two operating brain cells usually put a stop to things. Tonight, no one was stepping forward. There was, instead, a sense of anticipation among the other NCOs in the mess. As more and more of them became aware of the drama playing out in the corner, that anticipation grew.

In each of those instances, Torin had just been doing her job, and everyone in the room knew that; but there *had* been a lot of attention, and that wasn't going to make everyone happy. Add to that the certain knowledge of a big fight brewing but with no clear idea of when, and it was no surprise tensions had risen to a flashpoint.

"I'm surprised the brass hasn't handed you a commission on a plate," the technical sergeant sneered.

"Let it go," Torin suggested wearily. She didn't feel like talking about it, but she had to at least make the attempt before she handed this moron his head on plate.

"Fuk you."

Or . . .

"Sure." She drained her beer, set the glass down on the table, and stood. "Your place or mine?"

He wanted a fight. But he was di'Taykan. Lime-green eyes darkened as light receptors opened and he took a closer look at her—not that physical appearance was ever part of di'Taykan criteria. His hair fell closer to his head and began to sweep slowly back and forth.

Torin raised a single brow, the effect well worth what she'd paid for the ability. "Well?"

The technical sergeant spread his arms and grinned. "Now that's an encounter you're going to lose, Gunny."

Returning the grin, Torin snorted. "You have an interesting definition of the word lose, Sergeant."

Due caution ended up taking almost three full tendays. By the time the word came down that Captain Treis had recorded the Others with numbers approaching full battalion support on the fourth planet of the system—dubbed Estee by the Marines—Sh'quo Company was supplied, supported, refreshed, and ready to move out.

"Little more *anticipation* and I'd have started moving some of them out myself," Torin muttered. "Right out the air lock without waiting for the *Hardyr* to match up."

"You know what the new kids are like." Amanda took her second duffel bag from Torin and tossed it down the chute to the shuttle bay. "Anxious to get out there and win the war." She half snickered as she turned. "Like until they showed up, no one bothered to put any effort into it."

"I'm not sure everyone is."

The staff sergeant's eyes narrowed. "You okay, Torin?"

Torin considered and discarded a number of answers. Amanda was on her way Coreward—two contracts fulfilled, one long and one short—and as soon as Ventris dealt with her data dump, this would no longer be her war. She'd been a good Marine, a good staff sergeant, and good friend; she'd survived everything the Others and the brass could throw at her, and Torin suggesting she question all that would only throw shadows over what should be a celebration. "I'll be fine," Torin told her, "as soon as they give me something to shoot."

As a response, it had the added benefit of also being true.

Amanda snickered, as Torin intended. "At least Command delayed Lieutenant Joriyl's course. The last thing you needed was two green twoies and Lieutenant Jarret as senior going into a knockdown fight. And, although I'm happy you'll be taking care of my kids, it sucks you're back in charge of a platoon."

When Torin raised an eyebrow, she sighed. "Not what I meant. It's a step back for you."

"But they're still paying me more. And, until I can be in charge of the whole company, it suits me better than running the captain's errands."

"Gotta do the shit before you can do the shine, Gunny."

"Truth." Torin watched Amanda take a last look down the corridor, saw her note a scuffed section of wall she could put a punishment detail to buffing out, and she smiled. "You're going to miss it."

"I am. And I need to go while I still will." She frowned. "Still will miss it."

"I got that." Good-bye seemed depressingly final, so instead: "Stay safe."

Amanda rolled her eyes. "Why wouldn't I be? As long as you're out there."

"Isn't this kind of fast?"

Torin paused, twenty meters of rope looped over one arm, and actually looked at the screen. "What do you mean fast?"

"I mean *fast?*" Craig Ryder sat back in his pilot's chair and crossed his arms. That put his face farther from the pickup but allowed Torin to see more of his upper body, so she figured she came out ahead. Not that he didn't have an attractive face—blue eyes, slightly crooked nose, and dimples bracketing a self-assured smile currently visible without the on-again, off-again coverage of a scruffy red-brown beard—but she had a special fondness for the heavily muscled arms and the set of shoulders so broad they threw things out of proportion, making him look shorter than he actually was. "I mean, sure, the bad guys are jumping in pretty much right up your lot's arse, but don't you need more time to get ready?"

"No."

"Yeah, well you could definitely use a little more good oil on what you'll be facing. I mean, fuk, they're deploying the whole GCT out of Four Two and you've got almost no intell."

She smiled then, mostly at his sudden switch into military jargon. "We've got almost no intell *you're* aware of." Civilian Salvage Operators worked the edges of battles. They knew where those battles were, or more precisely where they'd been, but they didn't know much more.

"So you know more than: Oh, look, one fuk of a lot of Others in our space—let's go kick butt?"

"I don't actually need to know more than that."

"No . . ." He sighed and reluctantly returned her smile. ". . . I guess you don't. You know how long you'll be gone?"

"Until we win."

Neither of them mentioned the corollary.

"If it lasts long enough, then I expect I'll rock up."

If there was debris enough to make it worth his while. Debris meant dead pilots. Dead crew. Dead Marines. They didn't talk about that. Safer to talk about the recent repairs to his ship. Torin stowed the rope in her pack while Craig went over the modifications he'd planned for *Promise*'s living quarters to accommodate the possibility of a second person. As her continued silence moved him from not quite ready to acknowledge possibilities into more general gossip, she moved to the desk and opened her med kit. The contents provided a little more than first aid and, odds were good, a little less than what she'd likely need.

"Hey! Are you even listening to me?"

"I am." She liked hearing his voice in the background as she got things ready. It was—gods help her—comforting. It didn't matter what he was actually talking about.

"So what do you think about it?"

Turned out she hadn't been listening closely enough although she was fairly certain he'd been telling her about a military rumor now making the rounds of the general public. Which would make the safest response: "I doubt it'll happen."

Craig shrugged. Torin watched the movement appreciatively. "I don't know, Presit seemed sure your R&D guys could reverse engineer her pilot's trip behind the *Berg* to Big Yellow."

Presit a Tur durValintrisy, reporter for Sector Central News, had wanted the story of the unidentified alien ship badly enough that she'd bullied her pilot into locking onto the tail end of the *Berganitan*'s Susumi signature, basing his own equations on information received from riding the sweet spot in the warship's wake. It was amazing piloting, and Parliament had declared the stunt too dangerous to be repeated without further study. A lot of further study.

The reporter still had no time for Torin but considered Craig one of hers. One of her *what* Craig wasn't willing to say, although the Katrien were a matriarchal species, so the chances of him being embarrassed by the details were high.

"If your lot can dummy a way to follow the Others home," he continued, "then won't you be able to take the fight to them?"

"We will." Torin shoved her med kit into her pack. "And then there'll be more fighting."

"I thought that was what you did."

It wasn't a question, so she didn't answer it. Wouldn't have had an answer to it had it been a question.

"So . . ." The chair creaked as he shifted his weight. ". . . one of my salvage tags seems to have gone walkabout."

"You probably stuffed it into the junk drawer." No probably about it—she knew he'd stuffed the tag in the junk drawer because that was where she'd taken it from. It was currently tucked in between her breasts, hanging around her neck on a length of braided cord.

He shook his head and grinned. "The buggers are chipped, Torin."

"I know."

"I run the codes and I can find it."

She looked up then. She'd taken it on impulse, wanting to carry something of his with her and ignoring the fact that she never did *anything* impulsively. On the shuttle ride to the station, turning it over and over, she'd found a weird sort of comfort in knowing that as long as she held on to it, he could find her. Provided he was close enough. Her military ID had a stronger signal, but he'd be more motivated.

She hoped he'd be more motivated.

She'd almost sent it back to him twice. Almost.

Finally she said, "I know."

After a moment, Craig reached out and touched the edge of the screen. "This must be costing you big bikkies."

"A few." Full squirt with no discernible time delay was expensive, but they wouldn't have another chance to talk until she got back to the station. No way of knowing when they'd be together physically, and the thought of that made her ache in ways she found just a little disconcerting. It wasn't the sex—there was always plenty of that to go around—it was him.

"Why?"

That got him her full attention. It was the same tone he'd used during their *we're going to damned well discuss a future whether you like it or not* conversation. She hadn't liked it. And he hadn't backed down. And damned if they weren't likely to have a future together. Some day.

"Why what?"

"Why spend so much to say good-bye?"

"It isn't . . ."

He snorted and she paused.

"Fine. You mean that much to me. Okay? Happy?"

"Yeah."

His smile made her fumble a rolled pair of socks, and she called herself a sentimental ass as she bent to pick them up.

"Happy unless," he continued as she straightened, "you've got a bad feeling about this fight and you think this may be it."

She flicked an eyebrow in his general direction. "I'm going into combat. Of course this may be it."

"Damn." One corner of his mouth twisted, turning the smile into a parody of itself. "I wasn't expecting you to agree with me."

"Don't worry." She stopped herself before she could touch her fingertips to his on the screen, knowing that whatever the impetus for the cliché, no matter how much Craig would appreciate the gesture, she'd hate herself for it later. "I'm not that easy to kill."

He snorted. "Everyone's easy to kill, Torin."

Moving a full GCT of fifty-four officers and 1,178 enlisted Marines from the station out through the lock tubes and into their packets on the *Hardyr* called for split-second timing and some inventive profanity. As all three GC companies, the recon platoon, and the engineers waited to board, the masses of black uniforms surging back and forth across the main loading bay looked, at best, like barely organized chaos. The chaos was unavoidable, but Torin had made damned sure that Sh'quo Company's part in it at least was organized. Their armory had been loaded, their packets checked, their mess adjusted—Supply had its collective head up its ass if they thought Marines could survive a four-day Susumi jump and an indefinite time fighting on their idea of coffee rations.

Slate in hand, she watched as C'arden Company moved its first squad over the lip and into the tube and grinned as Sergeant Perry, a distinct *enough of this shit* tone to his voice snapped out, "Double time, people! I'll be right pissed if we miss the rest of the war!"

First squad in set the pace, and double-timing half a kilometer with full gear should be no one's idea of a rough time. They might even get all three companies loaded before the Marines on the short-list claimed their contracts were up.

With Captain Rose and First Sergeant Tutone huddled up with their counterparts, Torin calmed Second Lieutenant Heerik, who was not handling the waiting well, broke up a shoving match between a pair of heavy gunners by threatening to link their exoskeletons to a dance biscuit, and joined Sergeant Hollice watching Corporal di'Merk Mysho repack her pack.

"She says fussing kills time," Hollice said without being asked.

Torin shrugged as Mysho smacked Sam Austin's hand away from a bag of high-calorie chews. "She's right."

"She also said fukking would kill time."

"She's right again."

"Except that we're in ranks and I wouldn't excuse her."

"Bastard."

Hollice snorted. "Yeah, I'm pretty sure she expressed an opinion on my parentage, too."

"You need to learn more di'Taykan, Sergeant."

He snorted again. "Safer not to know, Gunny."

"Is Private Padarkadale praying?" His eyes were closed and his lips were moving, and a circle pendant dangled from one pale hand.

"Probably," Hollice allowed, rolling his eyes in the greenie's general direction. "But we needed a religious one to complete the set."

Mashona was asleep, head on her pack, KC-7 cradled against her chest like an infant, long, dark fingers gently cupping the sniper scope. Boots off, slate held in prehensile toes, Ressk worked the screen with both hands—nose ridges clamped shut, lips drawn back off his teeth. Whatever he was working on, he was finding it a challenge. Given that he'd broken through station security so cleanly they'd remained unaware of the breach for almost six tendays, Torin told Hollice to check him out and continued circulating.

Sh'quo would be the last of the three GC companies to load. Most of the Marines had their slates out playing a game biscuit or writing one last message home; a few, like Mysho, were going through their gear, fewer still were sleeping. There were a couple of quiet conversations, a couple of louder conversations, and another shoving match broken up by their teammates before Torin could get across the floor.

The engineers would load after Sh'quo and then Recon—last on, first off.

"Gunnery Sergeant Kerr!"

Torin knew that voice. She turned, slowly, figured what the hell, and smiled at the dark-haired young woman currently trying not to smile at her. "Private Kichar. I see you've gone into Recon."

Dark eyes narrowed over a prominent nose. "How . . ."

"Collar tabs."

Kichar flushed slightly but didn't glance down at her tabs. Point for her, Torin acknowledged. "I just wanted to say it's an honor to be serving with you again, Gunnery Sergeant."

"I can't say I'm unhappy about it either, Kichar." And she meant it. The battle on Crucible had knocked the stick mostly out of Kichar's ass—the creases pressed into her combats indicated she was still an annoying overachiever, but there'd be plenty of battles to knock that out of her, too.

"I didn't ask to be posted to 4th Recar'ta 1st Battalion after training," Kichar explained.

"She doesn't want you to think she's stalking you, Gunny." The Krai corporal's teeth were showing as he detached himself from the crowd and moved into their space. "Even if all she does is fukking talk about you."

"You don't think I'm worth talking about?"

He snorted. "I don't know, Gunny. What've you done lately?"

Kichar's eyes narrowed further, her weight shifted forward, and she was clearly about to do something she'd just as clearly regret about five seconds after doing it. Torin closed a steadying hand around her arm. "It's okay, Kichar. Lance Corporal Werst was with me on Big Yellow—although he was a private then."

"And I'd be one again if they let me give the fukking hook back," Werst grunted.

Torin grinned. She'd bet serious credit on him ending up career Marine. "I'm sure you can figure out a way to lose it."

Although she managed to keep from grabbing the much shorter Krai, Kichar's hands kept opening and closing. "You never said you served with the gunny before."

Werst shrugged, a Human gesture both the di'Taykan and Krai had adopted. "So? Dursinski's here too, Gunny. Still bitching."

That was a surprise. The lance corporal hadn't seemed to be enjoying her time in the Corps. A bigger surprise that she'd remained in Recon given the attrition rate. "She reupped?"

Werst shrugged again. "Said it beat looking for a real job."

"That's not," Kichar began, paused and frowned. "You were kidding?"

"Not me," Werst told her, nose ridges pinching shut. "Dursinski might've been."

"Gunny, I need to . . ."

"Ask the corporal what she meant?" Torin interjected into the pause. "Go ahead."

"Fuk, she's annoying." Popping something in his mouth Torin was just as glad she couldn't identify, given the Krai were as indiscriminate in their eating habits as the di'Taykan were about sex, Werst nodded toward an argument among the engineers. "You going to deal with that?"

The trio of specialists seemed to be disagreeing on who'd be carrying what equipment. Before Torin could work up enough interest to care, a Human technical sergeant broke it up, smoothly separating the combatants and bending quickly to catch something that looked like a metal spider before it hit the floor. As he straightened, he met Torin's eye and nodded before handing the spider back to the Marine who'd dropped it.

"Looks like it's under control," she said. Across the loading bay, Captain Rose raised a hand. "And I'm needed. Be seeing you, Werst."

"You can join us out in front any time, Gunny."

Gunnery sergeants did not need the approval of lance coporals, but Torin was Human enough she appreciated the thought all the way back across the bay.

"It's like supervising a kindergarten class," the captain sighed as she joined him. "Tutone's just gone to broker a deal with Captain Yun's First concerning pudding cups."

"Pudding cups, sir?"

"Yun thinks their mess got too many vanilla cups." He scratched at a patch of old scar tissue on his jaw and sighed. "We don't wait well, do we?"

"No, sir. But we'll snap to once the fight starts."

"Gunny!" Captain Rose leaned in so close she could feel his breath hot against her cheek. The only way to be heard over the Others' artillery and their own answering it. "Any word from Heerik's number three squad?"

"No, sir!"

"Should have sent a runner when the PCUs went."

"Yes, sir!" A lot of "should haves" got missed with the company pinned down under small arms and artillery fire while attempting to take an entrenched position. Blasted communication units made the list even longer.

"I have to know . . ."

They ducked together as something impacted against the other side of their hastily thrown up earthworks and blew with a *whomph* that rattled Torin's teeth.

Coughing and spitting out mouthfuls of finely pulverized dirt, the captain glared at her with bloodshot eyes. "You think they knew we were coming?" he bellowed as the dust settled.

"Seem to have baked a cake, sir."

He spat again and rubbed dirt off the readout in his sleeve. The various items actually woven into their combats were pretty much the only wireless tech working; even their slates were down. "God fukking damnit, I'm not directing an air strike down on my own fukking Marines. Find that squad, Gunny! And when you find it, move it back!"

"Yes, sir."

Balancing safety and speed and concluding she had no time for the former, Torin raced toward the squad's last known position. They were out front, every one knew that, but no one knew how far out front and where they'd gone to ground. If they'd gone to ground. If they were still alive.

She jumped a body, got cursed out by the corpsman working on a slightly more intact body beside it, recognized the pale orange hair, and froze momentarily as another mortar hit. The Others were blowing nothing bigger than their own Em223s. Small stuff from the firing position, significantly bigger boom for those at the other end of the trajectory.

As soon as the earth stopped moving, she started running again.

"Gunny!" One of the new recruits. "What are we supposed to do?"

"Wait for air support," she snapped without breaking stride.

And right on cue, three Marine 774s screamed by with two of the enemy's planes in close pursuit.

Torin half heard the whistle, shouted, "Down!" with no hope of being heard, and hit the dirt as at least half a payload landed a little too close. The earthworks shuddered as the blast wave hit, then slowly toppled inward. Torin tried to scrabble clear and got tangled with a warm body. She managed to get her arms over her head to make an air pocket as the dirt rained down.

Fuk!

Rocks in the mix slammed against body parts not protected by her vest. She took a hard hit to the calf, then strong hands grabbed her ankle and began to haul her clear. Digging in elbows and knees, she gave what help she could.

"You okay, Gunny?"

"I'm fine, Anderson. Thanks," she added as the heavy gunner set her on her feet. Fortunately, the exoskeletons had been unaffected by whatever pulse the Others had hit them with. Half turning, she saw another heavy drag Lieutenant Jarret out from under the collapsed barrier.

"We've got to stop meeting like this, Gunny . . ." He coughed and spat out a mouthful of mud. ". . . people'll start to talk."

Torin's lips caught against the dirt on her teeth. "Let them talk, sir."

He returned her grin. "What's your heading?"

"Lieutenant Heerik's three squad is up front." New bruises were rising, but everything essential still worked. "We need to place them so the captain can call in coordinates for the air strike."

The lieutenant glanced at the Marines working to rebuild the blown section, his lilac eyes dark. "Call in on what? Nothing's working!"

"We've had word that Signals are running filament. Should be out our way eventually."

"And until then?"

Gunnery sergeants did not ever admit they didn't know. "Smoke signals, sir."

He blinked, then he grinned again and nodded. "Stay on thirty-seven degrees. If she proved to have half a brain and stayed put, you'll find Heerik."

"Yes, sir!"

"Keep your head down, Gunny."

"Count on it, sir."

She didn't find Heerik, but she found her other two squads. "God damn it, Doctorow, don't tell me you've lost your lieutenant already!"

The staff sergeant rolled his eyes. "She went up to find three squad.

"She went herself with this lot sitting on their fine Marine asses getting fat?"

The Marines close enough to hear suddenly found something to look at over the barricade.

"Said it was her job. Wouldn't listen to me. Slipped away when I was dealing with . . ."

Screaming.

". . . that. Damn it, Huran," he whirled and glared at the corpsman. "Knock him out if you can't shut him up."

"We've been through this, Staff. His religion says he can only lose consciousness naturally."

Padarkadale. Or most of him.

Torin held up her right arm. "See all these hooks? They say my religion trumps his. Dope him!"

"Gunny, I . . ."

"Do it!"

"That was intolerant of Padarkadale's beliefs," Doctorow muttered as Huran bent back over his patient.

"Yes, it was," Torin told him as the private stopped screaming. "His god can talk to me about it later. Which way did Heerik go?"

"That way—one hundred and eleven degrees from Marine zero."

Torin lined up on the way he was pointing and checked her sleeve. "How far?"

"Shouldn't be more than a klik and a half." He snorted. "Could be anywhere in hell's half acre."

Another set of 774s roared by. Higher this time.

"They'll start dropping by eye any minute now," Doctorow noted, glaring up into the sky.

"They've started."

"Oh, fukking joy."

One hundred and eleven degrees took Torin over the barricade . . .

". . . through the woods and to grandmother's house we go," she muttered, slapping a filter over her mouth and nose. That took care of breathing, but with all the dust in the air, she could hardly see. Running bent almost double, KC-7 in her right hand, left arm out in front to maintain her bearing, she concentrated on keeping the readout in the green.

From the sound of it, things were getting interesting in the lower atmosphere.

Interesting was seldom good for the Marines on the ground.

At a klik and a half, during a miraculous pause in both artillery and the air show, she thought she heard voices. Two hundred and fifty meters more, another pause, and she was sure of it.

"Lieutenant Heerik!"

"Gunnery Sergeant?"

No mistaking the Krai lieutenant's voice. There just weren't that many female Krai in the infantry.

Five meters more and Torin slid down into a crater, riding a ridge of dirt to Sergeant Hollice's side. A quick count gave her all twelve members of the squad and Second Lieutenant Heerik. Mashona lifted a hand in a remarkably sarcastic wave, but Ressk kept his gaze locked on the lieutenant.

"Captain would like your three squad back behind the barricade, sir."

"I came out to bring them back in, Gunnery Sergeant . . ."

More planes screamed by. Theirs. Others. Torin frowned as something broke the sound barrier. Navy?

". . . we were just about to leave." She had her boots off and scrambled up the crater wall a lot faster than anyone but Ressk was likely to manage.

No, not Navy.

"Sir! Get down! Now!"

Torin had no idea which side had dropped it, or what it was, but on impact it distinctly went BOOM.

BOOM was never good.

The lieutenant turned, lips drawn back off her teeth, and looked startled as the top half of her body blew across the crater, spraying blood onto the uplifted faces below. Her legs swayed for a moment, then slowly crumpled. As they slid back down the slope, each individual mote of dust in the air picked up a gleaming white halo.

The halos joined.

The ground rose.

Torin's knees slammed into her chest, and she tasted blood.

The whole world went white.

Then black.

TWO

"**N**o."

"I are being sorry, Craig, but Gunnery Sergeant Torin Kerr are . . ."

"No." Hands flat against the control panel, Craig leaned in closer to the screen. "She isn't dead."

Presit pulled off her dark glasses and arranged her features in what she probably thought was a sincere expression—*something furbearing species sucked at,* Craig sneered silently. "I are knowing you are not wanting to believe, but . . ."

"You said there's no body."

"The blast are having melted her position. I are having seen the raw news feed, there are being no hope of bodies. There are barely being hope of DNA resolution."

"The *news* . . ." He didn't bother hiding his disdain. ". . . has been wrong before."

Dark lips drew back off very white, very pointed teeth and, within the black mask of fur, Presit's eyes narrowed. But all she said was, "True."

"And the military doesn't know shite half the time."

"That are being also true."

"They haven't told me . . ." He stopped then, unsure if they would tell him. He didn't know, had no way of knowing, if Torin had added him to her notification list. If she hadn't, if Presit hadn't spotted Torin's name in the data stream coming into Sector Central

News for rebroadcast, he would never have known. He'd have just kept waiting and wondering until finally there'd be no question and then . . .

His fingers curled against the warmed plastic. "She isn't dead."

Presit shook her head, the motion sending a visible ripple through her silver-tipped dark fur, the highlights too artfully natural to be real. "Saying it are not making it true. No one are surviving that attack."

His laugh sounded off, even to his own ears. "It wouldn't be the first time Torin's beaten the odds."

"A direct hit by a missile fired from orbit that are melting the landscape to slag are being large odds, even for Gunnery Sergeant Kerr." The reporter sighed, her acerbic tone softening. "She are not being invincible."

Yes, she is.

"No." Craig had no idea whether Presit took his soft denial as agreement or disagreement—mostly because he wasn't sure himself—but she clearly accepted it as the end of the conversation.

"I are not liking her much," Presit admitted, muzzle wrinkling, "but I are being sorry for your sake that she are being gone. If you are wanting company?"

It took him a moment to realize what she was offering. The last thing he needed was Presit a Tur durValintrisy in his face while he was griev . . .

While he was . . .

While . . .

"No. Thanks. I'm fine."

Presit's snort spoke volumes as the signal faded.

He got no signal off the salvage tag, but ST7/45T2 was damned near to the edge of known space. Too far to read. Too far to go himself with no certainty of salvage on the other end although he ran the Susumi calculations just because.

Then he returned to the job, working the edges of the debris field left behind when the Others slid a pair of battle cruisers into a system already claimed, scooping up the wrecked pieces of Navy Jades because, well, he had to breathe and oxygen wasn't free although he had been thinking that if things went well, he might invest in a converter since *Promise*'s arms would do just as well capturing chunks of the small ice asteroids littering known space and with two people in the cabin . . .

Sweat trickled down his sides as he stepped out of the air lock, faceplate polarizing in the unfiltered solar radiation.

Torin hadn't been ready to leave the Corps and he hadn't been ready to push, but they'd both known where they were heading, sooner or later, and it wasn't like he couldn't do the job on his own because he'd been on his own since he started, but it'd be fukking pleasant to have some backup when the only thing separating his bare ass from hard vacuum was a twelve-year-old Corps surplus HE suit and a bit of luck. A second pair of eyes would . . .

Craig locked the last piece of twisted metal and plastic in place, DNA residue flagged. DNA turned up in the strangest places. Once he'd found Human residue on wreckage from an enemy fighter. Navy had found the body months earlier and no one had any idea how those few cells had wandered. Once, he'd found a pilot, or most of one, in the crushed remains of her Jade. The Others had fried every system on her ship, and the commander had been nothing more than meat in space. The Navy couldn't find her without a signal. He'd only found her because finding the small debris, too small for the military to waste time and money recovering, was how he lived, and he worked on instinct as much as equipment.

"And what would I be doing while you're using these well-honed instincts of yours?" Torin had asked as she pulled on her tunic.

"Same thing you're doing now," Craig had said, tossing her a boot. *"Keeping your people alive. Fewer people,"* he'd added grinning, *"but better job perks."*

She'd matched his grin as she'd snagged her first then her second boot out of the air. *"You think?"*

"You haven't complained."

"Too polite."

"Bullshit."

He checked the pod configuration before he headed back into the air lock, loading the dimensions into his slate. The data went automatically into *Promise*'s memory, but having survived one Susumi miscalculation, he had no intention of pushing his luck. Careless pilots were dead . . .

Were dead.

As the door cycled closed behind him, he clawed at the shoulder catches and dragged his helmet off the moment the telltales showed green, suddenly unable to breathe within the confines of the suit. Hands braced on his thighs, he sucked in deep lungfuls of air and forced his heartbeat to slow.

Fukking irony that the panic attacks he used to have at the thought of sharing limited space and resources were now being caused by the realization that . . .

No.

If there was one thing Torin excelled at, it was staying alive.

She wasn't dead.

He opened the inner door, stripped out of his suit, and hung it precisely in its locker, tank snapped up against the remix valve. Next time he needed it, *Promise* would see that it was ready.

A quick visit to the head; he never hooked up the plumbing in the suit if he didn't absolutely have to. A visit to the coffeepot to start the whole cycle up again.

And then there was no way of avoiding the message light blinking on the control panel.

Turned out he was on Torin's notification list after all.

The Confederation Marine Corps had two levels of notification. Level one included a trip into the Core and Ventris Station where the details would be explained and counselors both military and civilian would be on hand to deal with the emotional maelstrom that came with the loss of a loved one. Figuring that any maelstrom was his own damned business, Craig hadn't planned on taking them up on it until he found himself working out the Susumi equations.

Hands above the controls, he paused. He didn't need some counselor telling him how he felt.

He did, however, need to sell his salvage, and Ventris was as good a place as any. Particularly since the notification had come with a code that granted him a free berth and hook-in. No reason not to do what he could to broaden his limited profit margin.

And while he was there, as long as the Corps was paying for the privilege of his company, it wouldn't hurt to find out what the fuk they thought had happened because the whole thing sounded damned shonky to him.

"*Civilian salvage vessel* Promise, *this is Ventris perimeter. State your reason for approach.*"

"Salvage license tango, sierra, tango, five, seven, seven, nine, tango. I have cargo." Craig sent the details of his load and then stared out at the bulk of Ventris Station, covering a quarter of his screen even at perimeter distance, and ignored the way his hand was resting beside the pressure pad that would transmit the notification code.

"*Roger,* Promise. *Delta yard has docking available. Stand by for . . .*"

"Wait." One finger moved to the pressure pad. "And I have this."

"*Roger,* Promise." The dispassionate tone hadn't changed although he knew there was a person of some species on the other end of the link. "*Salvage must be unloaded and cleared before you can proceed to the station. Stand by for coordinate download. Docking master will take control in three, two, one . . . mark. Docking master now in control.*"

He sat back as the program ran and his ship surged forward. He'd been expecting . . . more.

A reaction.

Condolences?

Someone he could tell to fuk off, that Torin wasn't dead.

Apparently, enough Marines died it was business as usual.

"Well, fuk you, too," he muttered at no one in particular.

"No, *you* don't understand . . ."

One foot raised to step over the hatch, Craig put it down again and eased back into the corridor. The voice filling the room he'd been about to enter was male, the tone frustration heading toward anger. He was, himself, just here for information, he didn't want to intrude on another man's grief.

". . . I have all the information you lot are willing to give me and I'm not here to talk to a counselor; I'm here to talk to talk to someone who doesn't have their head up their ass about this . . ."

Obviously, the man hadn't spent much time dealing with the military. In Craig's experience, head up the ass was the default posture.

". . . my daughter isn't dead!"

A thousand daughters in uniform.

More. So many more.

And more than a thousand fathers who'd refuse to believe.

There was no reason, absolutely no reason that this overheard conversation had anything to do with Torin. Except that Craig's code had directed him here, to this anteroom off the docking bay, an area barely inside the station, awkward civilian interactions kept at the edge of things military. Three dozen doors along this corridor—he'd counted them while wondering what the hell he was doing there, pacing past other men and women who seemed to have a lot fewer questions. Three dozen doors and the notification code brought him to this one.

He stepped into the room.

The Krai corporal behind the desk looked up, his nose ridges flaring. Or maybe her nose ridges—secondary sexual characteristics were subtle and Craig never had been able to tell the Krai apart. Since it had never been an issue, he didn't worry about it much. "I'm sorry, sir, I'll just be a moment."

Ignoring her—or him—Craig crossed to the man standing by the desk. He was big—not just in contrast to the meter-tall Marine behind the desk—and the patchy red-brown of his tan said he spent most of his time outside in actual atmosphere. Before the Marine could speak again, Craig held out his hand. "Craig Ryder."

Deep-set eyes narrowed, creases pleating at the outside corners. Recognition dawned, and he nodded, once. Craig always figured Torin had picked up the gesture in the military. Maybe not.

"John Kerr." Torin's father had one hell of a grip, his hand hard and callused.

"Drink?"

"You know how to find a bar in this tin can?"

"Mate, I can find a bar in Susumi space."

"Yeah? Well, I don't have the faintest idea what means . . ." He scratched along the edge of his jaw, nails rasping against rough skin where the depilatory had begun to wear off. ". . . but if you can find a bar, I'll buy."

"Sir. Sirs," the corporal amended as they turned together. "The Corps will deal with your needs while on Ventris."

"The Corps can," John Kerr began. Stopped. Drew in a deep breath. And pointed one large, scarred finger across the desk. "I'll be back."

"Torin liked this bar."

"Yeah." Their notification codes hadn't got them onto Concourse Two; that had been Craig's not entirely legal schematic of the nonsensitive parts of the station, a little bullshit to an actual live Marine at a checkpoint, and the taking of the Commandant of the Corps' name in vain when asked for his authorization by the station sysop at the last hatch. There were plenty of bars on Concourse One, the area reserved for those just passing through. Craig knew and liked a number of them, knew and avoided a couple more, and didn't want to see the inside of any of them. Not now.

Torin had liked *Sutton's*.

Half a dozen second lieutenants had pushed two of the small tables together over in the corner, a couple of Krai NCOs sat at the bar watching cricket on the vid screen and occasionally commenting in their own language, but other than that the bar was empty. The Corps ran on a 28-hour clock, but 1530 seemed to be an off hour.

John took a long swallow and set his glass back on the table. "The beer's good."

Craig raised his own glass in acknowledgment and drank. They hadn't done a lot of talking on the way and now . . . "You don't think she's carked it." At John's blank expression, he shook his head. "Sorry. Died. You don't think she's died."

"I don't. They hear it all the time, you know: *My* kid's not dead." His hand tightened around the base of the glass. "There's no body. They haven't found anything that resembles her fukking DNA. Give me a body. Give me something." His eyes were a darker brown than Torin's, but the intensity was the same. "I'll believe when I have proof but not until."

"The force of the blast melted rock." Presit had been right. Nothing could have survived it. "The whole area was slagged."

"I saw the vids."

The vids had come in a packet with the notification code. Craig had always suspected these sorts of things were sterilized for public consumption—the last thing the Corps needed to do was expose the grieving to the ugly reality of war. In this case, there'd been nothing to sterilize because the enemy blast had done the job too well. Over thirty square kilometers of battlefield had been turned to a rippled sheet of gray green. Shining. Lifeless. A helpful X marked Torin's last known position.

"She was too far from the edge to have been thrown clear." Far enough from the edge that being thrown clear would have killed her.

One dark brow rose. "My daughter tells us you're a bit of a gambler. Guess you have to be," he continued without waiting for a response. "Doing what you do. You want to bet on a sure thing, you bet on my daughter having survived."

"I don't . . ." Craig drank a little more beer if only because it forced him to unclench his teeth. "I didn't believe it when I first heard, but . . ." Then the notification. Then the vids. Then Ventris. Then sitting down in a bar on a military station with Torin's father. That last, he realized—feeling as though the station had just vented into space, feeling steel bands tighten around his chest, feeling his lungs fight for air—that was when the verb changed.

Torin was dead. And only a galah would, could believe different.

He might have said it out loud. He wasn't sure.

A large hand closed around his wrist, and Torin's father said, "No."

"No what? No one could have survived that." How the fuk did he get here . . . here trying to convince a man he'd just met that his daughter was dead?

John's grip returned to his glass. "Saying it doesn't make it true."

Craig frowned. Hadn't Presit said that to him? Hadn't she been arguing the other side?

"Mr. Ryder."

He recognized the voice. When he looked up at the Commandant of the Corps, he also recognized the pissed-off expression on the face of the colonel standing behind her. "High Tekamal Louden." Then, because he didn't what else to say and she was obviously waiting for something, he nodded toward the other man. "John Kerr."

"Yes, of course," she said as he stood and held out his hand. "I'm very pleased to meet you, Mr. Kerr, and wish it had been under better circumstances."

"High Tekamal? That's . . ."

"High Tekamal Louden is the Commandant of the Corps," the colonel pointed out.

John Kerr shot him a disinterested glance. "And you're not," he said dryly. Dismissing the man with an ease that caused the corner of the commandant's mouth to twitch, he indicated the table's third chair. "Join us for a drink, Commandant?"

"I'd like to, yes. I'm sure you have things to do, Colonel."

Too well trained to react, the colonel managed a neutral, "Yes, sir."

Sure money he'd be waiting when she left the bar, Craig thought as he turned and walked stiffly away.

"You're here, both of you, because you were notified about Gunnery Sergeant Kerr," Louden said as the bartender sent over a glass filled with a lager significantly paler than the ales the two men were drinking. Either she came in here a lot, or every bar on *Ventris* had Commandant Landen's preferences on file. Given the demands on her time, probably the latter.

"And you're here . . . ?" John prodded. "Not that I don't doubt my daughter was an exemplary Marine, but from what I hear, you lose a lot of those every day."

"Too many." She raised her glass slightly before she drank, and the men drank with her. "But most of those," she continued after the glasses returned to the table, "don't have a . . ." Eyes the same pale gray as the station walls swept over Craig and back to John. ". . .

friend who uses my name to access sections of the station off limits to casual civilians."

The snort was deeper but similar in every other respect to the sound his daughter made. "Is he in trouble?"

"No. We, the Corps, indeed the entire Confederation, owe Mr. Ryder a debt . . ."

She wasn't, Craig realized, going to explain what exactly that debt was. Probably not a good idea to remind civilians about the infiltration of the military by molecular-sized bits of intelligent plastic.

". . . and he's taking advantage of that."

John nodded. "And you like him."

A network of fine lines bracketed the pale eyes when she smiled. "And I like him."

"Good. The Corps was everything to my daughter for a long time. We always figured that when she finally met someone, they'd be a part of that. When he wasn't, we were curious. But you, for all intents and purposes, you are the Corps, so if you like him, well, that's another point in his favor."

"The gunny didn't tell you much about him, then."

He took another drink. "Torin was never one for passing on details of her personal life."

"Thank fuk for that," Craig muttered into his beer.

"I need to know what happened to my daughter, Commandant." The tip of one finger rubbed a pattern into the condensation on the tabletop. "I can't go home and tell them that the Corps doesn't know."

She died. Craig thought. He could barely hear Louden's answer over the roaring in his ears.

"Gunnery Sergeant Kerr died while performing her duty as a Marine."

"You've got no evidence of that."

"We have no evidence she survived either. We're no longer receiving a signal from her ID, and she couldn't possibly survive anything able to destroy that chip."

John Kerr shrugged broad shoulders. "Chip could have been removed and destroyed."

"Mr. Kerr, we lost seven hundred and thirty-eight people in the attack that took your daughter. Another twenty-seven died in other actions during that same battle and we had three hundred and twelve wounded. We took . . ." Both her hands tightened around the base of her glass. "We took catastrophic losses that day and I would give anything to believe that even one of those seven hundred and sixty-five people survived, but I can't."

"I can."

"How?"

A good question and one Craig wanted the answer to as well. He wanted his belief in Torin's invincibility back.

"This whole thing could be a ploy by the Others. They could have cleared the battlefield before they destroyed it, before they destroyed the evidence." He held up a calloused hand. "I know what you're going to say, the Others don't take prisoners—but they could. They could be covering their tracks. Could have been covering their tracks from the beginning. Every body you never found could have been a result of the enemy scooping up your people, questioning them, learning about the Confederation, using them for slave labor, hell, using them for food.

The High Tekamal sighed and shook her head. "I'm sorry, Mr. Kerr, but we learned early on in this war that if you surrender to the Others, you die, even when it's in their best interests to keep you alive. We don't know why, but we do know that they don't take prisoners."

Based on her initial experience, Torin had to say that the afterlife truly sucked. Her entire body ached, her mouth tasted like she'd been licking shell casings, and she had a headache centered over both eyes that pounded on and on like a silent artillery barrage in her skull.

No noise, just the kind of pounding that shook teeth free.

No.

Not quite *no* noise.

A soft scuffling.

Bare feet on rock.

To both Krai and di'Taykan, the Human sense of smell was limited, but she had no trouble identifying the sharp, old-cheese scent of unwashed flesh.

Holding her breath, she waited until the first tentative touch, then grabbed about ten centimeters back, wrapped her fingers around a warm cylinder of flesh, and slammed it to the ground. By the time she had her knee pressed against the familiar ridges of a bowed spine, she had her eyes open.

Krai. Problem, but not a bad one. Krai bone was one of the toughest substances in known space, but joints were, as always, the weakest part of the design, and a spine was essentially a long line of joints. She'd have been in trouble had she not managed to flip . . . *him,* Torin guessed from the size and the pattern of mottling on the nearly hairless scalp, but as it was, all she had to do was hang on.

And hope she hadn't taken down a medic come to check on her condition.

That would be embarrassing.

And not the first time.

Although medics were usually cleaner.

"Arshantac chrick!" she barked as he struggled. The approximate translation: Yield or be food! Historically, Krai battles became banquets with astonishing speed although, even had she been Krai, Torin doubted she'd have made a meal of her captive. To begin with, the smell was distinctly off-putting, but more importantly, he wore a Marine Corps uniform, and the Corps had worked very hard to instill the belief that Marines did not eat other Marines.

Impossible to read his collar tabs while she had him flat on his face on the . . .

Floor of the cave?

Looked like a natural pocket in the rock off what was definitely a constructed tunnel if the lights she could see hanging from the rough curve of the ceiling were any indication.

The Marine under her knee had neither the leverage nor the strength to move her, but he gave it his best shot.

Torin appreciated that even as she blinked away new pain from where the side of his fist had connected with her cheekbone, impact creating a counterpoint to the pounding that continued in her skull. "That is *enough,*" she snarled, at the end of her patience. She was not surprised when he stilled. There were theories that a senior NCO could stop artillery fire using that tone. Shifting her weight back onto her heels, she stood, dragging him to his feet and spinning him in place to face her.

He tensed to bolt.

"Don't."

He didn't.

Private first class. Not surprising given his youth. In spite of the smell, he didn't actually look too bad. Combats were designed to repel dirt and, given the filth of his exposed skin, his had obviously been fully tested. The fit of his uniform suggested he'd been eating, if not frequently at least regularly. He stood with his weight almost entirely on his left foot, only the outside edge of his right touching the rock.

Physically, she'd seen a lot worse. Emotionally, though . . .

There was desperation in his eyes that made her think of a whipped dog. He wanted to move toward her, he wanted her to make it all better, but pain and terror kept him away.

Torin arranged her face into its best *every Marine in the Corps is mine* expression. "Name, rank, and unit number, Private!"

Muscle memory attempted to bring him to attention. "Kyster . . ."

The Krai had family names that went on for hours and could not be shortened.

". . . Private First Class . . ."

Not surprising given his youth.

". . . 6th Division, 2nd Recar'ta, 1st Battalion, Tango Company!"

Name, rank, and unit number spilled out as one long word—a drilled response rather than a conscious reply, his voice rough as though he hadn't been using it enough over the last little while to wear down the edges. Years of practice slotted the breaks in, and Torin frowned. Sixth Division? Interesting. Same Defensive Sector as Torin's 7th Division but, given the distances involved, not exactly right next door. They'd never fought together, that was for damned sure. "How long have you been here, Kyster?"

"Don't . . . can't . . ." He frowned, struggling to find the right the word. ". . . remember . . ." His gaze flicked to her sleeve, as he struggled to stand straight. ". . . Gunnery Sergeant."

"Kerr. Gunnery Sergeant Kerr. Sit down before you fall down."
She nodded toward a reasonably flat-topped chunk of rock. "There."

The downside of Krai bones was that if they broke they took a long
time to heal. Kyster had broken at least one bone in his foot—maybe
two; she'd need a closer look to be sure. They'd healed unset, but
they were healed. Given that he'd clearly been on short rations and
just as clearly had been using the foot, Torin figured it had been at
least twenty-five tendays since the break. Minimum.

As he settled, his gaze never leaving her face, she checked herself
for injuries and found nothing more than the bruising she'd already
been made aware of and the headache that was beginning to fade.
Atmosphere was clear breathable. Gravity . . . She flexed her knees.
Gravity was approximately Human norm. Maybe a little less. Station
norm, not dirtside. With muscle and bone developed in Paradise's
heavier gravity, that gave her a slight advantage although against what
was still to be determined. She was in her combats with vest and boots,
but her helmet and her slate were missing. She still had two filters—
she remembered using one just before all hell broke loose—all three
stims, a packet of wet wipes, and a tube of sealant. Her KC-7 and
grenades were gone as was the knife from the sheath in her boot—no
big surprise that her weapons had been removed. Both sleeves were
blank, so she had to assume that the tech in her uniform was dead.

Unsealing her vest, she slipped a hand inside and smiled.

Kyster bolted.

"Not a threat," she snapped, grabbing the back of his collar and
reapplying his ass to the rock as carefully as circumstances allowed.
"Just happy they missed something." Two somethings actually, but
she wasn't going to think about the salvage tag still hanging between
her breasts, not right now. Not until she knew she could control her
reaction. "Hold out your hand."

There were pinkish-gray scars on his palm and a half-healed sore
between thumb and forefinger. His weight hadn't dropped much, but
nutrition levels were low enough his body wasn't diverting much to
nonessentials like minor wounds. That, at least, she could do something about.

Part of an organization with the best support system in known space,

Marines carried everything they needed into combat, fully aware that supply lines could be cut. A burden in the beginning, eventually, and sooner rather than later, the pack—food, first aid, coffee, dry socks, porn—became another appendage like an arm or a leg or a KC-7. But packs could be lost or destroyed, and everyone kept something tucked into his or her vest.

Torin, responsible since her promotion to staff sergeant for a minimum of forty Marines, kept three strips of food tabs—one for Humans, one for di'Taykan, one for Krai. They were supplements only, but since living off the land meant sweet fuk all if even one essential amino acid went missing, they could easily mean the difference between strong-enough-to-fight and roll-over-and-play-dead.

When she dropped a tab on Kyster's palm, he stared at it as though he'd never seen it before.

He probably hadn't. Given the impressive parameters of the Krai digestive system, supplements for their species were considered almost an oxymoron. Torin carried them because of that *almost*. If she had to guess, given that they were clearly underground, she'd say the odds were good Kyster's diet had been limited as to selection.

"Eat it," she said.

Air whistling past the mucus plugs in his nose ridges, Kyster obediently licked the tab off his palm.

Torin nodded once in approval and took a look out into the constructed tunnel. At some point, and not recently given the way the edges had lost the look of raw stone, there'd been a rockfall about three hundred meters to her right. The broken pile plugged the tunnel, spilled out about nine meters and left the last light dangling in pieces although the wire apparently continued unbroken. To the left, the tunnel ran about half a kilometer and then curved. No more than two meters at their widest point, the walls were rough and rounded, floor and ceiling only barely flattened. It looked like the work of a mining bore—an access shaft to the work face. Darker shadows suggested other natural alcoves like the one she found herself in.

It smelled too much of Kyster for her to identify any other scents, and the absolute silence told her nothing at all.

In a war that spanned both centuries and galaxies, time and space, there were three absolutes: the Navy had better food, the Corps left no one behind, and the Others didn't take prisoners.

When she turned, Kyster was staring up at her as if he expected her to have all the answers.

Good thing that was part of her job description.

"All right." Moving back inside, she sat facing the young Marine and gentled her voice to keep him from trying to bolt again. "What the hell is going on here?"

"Here, here?" His gesture included her and the small cave.

"Start here."

"Must've been a battle."

He paused, so she nodded. Heerik and number three squad and 744s dropping by eye and the brilliant white light . . .

"After battles, people in little caves. Marines. Sometimes."

Torin forced herself back to the here and now, filling in the missing words. "Marines show up in the little caves? How?" she demanded when he nodded.

"Don't know."

She looked around the cave, stood, ran her hands over all of the rock she could reach, and methodically moved everything that could be moved. With her sleeve light out and only the dim spill from the tunnel, it was possible she missed a hatch or some other entrance, but she didn't think so. Kyster stayed where she'd put him, never taking his eyes off her.

"All right. Fine." She sat down again. "Where are we?"

"Underground."

Succinct, but a bit obvious. "Where?"

"Don't know."

An underground POW camp, then. All right, she could work with that—she didn't like it, but she could work with it. "Where're the other Marines who've shown up in the caves?"

"By the pipe."

"Why aren't you by the pipe?"

"Didn't want me." He thrust his right foot forward and took a deep breath. "Said I was a waste of food 'cause I came with my foot busted."

Some of the words ran together, and some of the pauses between them went on a little too long, but it was an actual sentence.

"Who said?" Torin asked, pleased to see Kyster's lips curl back off his teeth. The kid had taken the rejection as a challenge. That attitude had likely kept him alive.

"Calls himself Colonel Harnett. Not!" His nostril ridges flared wide. "More like a . . . a *beranitac!*"

A large predator on the Krai home world. They formed packs, and the alpha male ruled by tooth and claw—both of which they had in abundance. There were theories that the *beranitacs* were one of the main reasons that the Krai hadn't bothered coming down out of the trees until they'd developed the necessary weapons tech to deal with them. There were very few wild *beranitacs* left.

"Is he a Marine?"

He nodded. "All Marines here."

And this Marine had said Kyster was a waste of food because of his injury. And other Marines had allowed it. Corps structure didn't break down that rapidly on its own. It had been broken.

"Dumped in the tunnels, away from food. I . . ." He seemed to fold in on himself and wouldn't look at her.

"You survived," Torin told him, struggling to keep her growing rage from her voice. The last thing she wanted right at this moment was for Kyster to think she was angry with him. He'd survived. Alone. All those tendays while his foot was healing. No wonder he was having trouble talking. "I suspect only a Krai could have."

"Marines don't eat other Marines."

And that answered the question of *how* he'd survived. A limited diet indeed. "Were they dead?"

"*Chrick* . . ."

When he didn't go on, when he stared down at his misshapen foot, lips still off his teeth, his whole bearing a combination of abject misery and defiance, she nodded and said, "But one of them was very badly injured." Kyster had been scooped injured off a battlefield; it didn't take a genius to figure it wasn't the only time it had ever happened. "So you sat with them until they died, and then you ate them. They were *chrick*. Edible. Is that what happened?"

"Yes, Gunnery Sergeant."

"Well done, Private."

The words jerked his gaze up onto her face.

"Under these circumstances," she continued in a tone that left no room for argument, "those Marines would be proud to have kept you alive. And when we haul ass out of here, they'll be going with you because they're a part of you now. You've seen to it that we don't leave them behind."

He didn't quite believe her.

"If I'd died," she said, reaching out and gently grasping his shoulder, "I'd have been honored to have you eat me."

Kyster made a noise somewhere between a whimper and a wail and, shaking like a leaf in a high wind, began to slide off his rock.

Torin caught him before he hit the ground, held him while he sobbed, and murmured what Krai words of comfort she knew. He was very young, and he'd been through one hell of a lot, and they needed to get this breakdown out of the way so that she could get on with kicking Colonel Harnett's ass—currently holding top position on her to do list.

Kick Harnett's ass.

Escape.

Let the relevant parties know that the Others fukking well *did* take prisoners.

It wasn't a long list.

Kyster was too worn out to be embarrassed when he managed to hiccup his way to quiet, and Torin would have loved to have given him time to recover, but they'd barely touched on the information she needed.

"Let's go back a bit," she said as he rubbed his nose ridges up and down either side of his bent knee. "Who's running this place?"

He looked up at that. "Harnett."

"No, who's running the prison? If we're prisoners," she continued when he frowned, "then this is a prison and someone has to be running it."

"Stuff comes down the pipe."

No point in asking who put the stuff into the pipe; the poor kid had been stuck out away from things trying to survive. He wouldn't know if all twenty-eight species of Others showed up every afternoon at 1730 and led an hour's PT.

"All right, then. How did *you* get here?"

The story emerged in bits and pieces. Sometimes he had to be gently prodded to speak out loud. In the end, what he knew was that he'd been pinned down with his platoon on Sa'tall Three, defending a mining station from a snatch and grab by the Others—"Sometimes want raw materials, you know?" His squad had taken a hit from one of their fliers, and a chunk of the big mine bore they'd been sheltering behind had come down on his foot. He thought he'd maybe passed out for a minute. Next thing he knew, he'd woken up in one of the little caves just the way Torin had, although he'd been a lot closer to the pipe, so one of the colonel's hunting parties had found him almost immediately. "We're way far out here. Almost to the end. Safer. Hunting parties don't come this far."

"Glad to hear that. Tell me about them."

There wasn't much to tell she hadn't already assumed. A goon squad was a goon squad no matter what it was called. They "hunted" the Marines that landed in the little caves. Stripped them of whatever gear they'd kept before they'd recovered enough to defend themselves. The injured were left to die or helped on the way. The healthy were taken to the pipe and assimilated into Harnett's fiefdom.

Years of practice kept her feelings from her voice. Kyster didn't need to deal with that on top of everything else. When she saw him staring at her hands, she managed to uncurl both fists. "And the pipe, what's that?"

The pipe was an actual pipe in the middle of the big open area where a number of the tunnels met. The food chute was there, and water, sometimes even hot water. The colonel and his staff lived right up beside it.

Control the food, control the population.

Kyster had no idea how many people Harnett controlled, but he knew there were at least four hunting parties of three Marines each. "No Krai." He was proud of that.

Torin didn't explain that the Krai were good fighters and good Marines but, at a meter high, not exactly physically imposing. "He keeps at least some of people he trusts around him at all times, doesn't he?"

"His staff."

"A goon's a goon, Private. Is the colonel's . . . group, the only group down here?"

He was pretty sure there were others; the tunnels extended for kilometers in every direction—Kyster had no idea how far—and once he'd watched a hunting party returning after having clearly been in some kind of a fight. If they'd found something that could beat them, he wasn't going anywhere near it. Besides, it was safest to avoid the places the hunting parties went.

"Never come out here. Never been a Marine dropped out here since I came."

"Then why are you out this far?"

"Water."

The moment he said it, the inside of her throat felt as though it had been lightly sanded.

She stood, stiffly, and stretched, bracing her hands against the rough rock of the ceiling. "Lead on, Private. The day I've had, I could do with a drink."

He turned to the right once out of what she'd come to think of as her cave. Just before the rockfall, he turned right again and slipped through what had probably once been the entrance to another small cave. The spill of rock had turned it into a dark, rough-edge wedge in the tunnel wall.

Brows up, Torin took a mental measurement, turned sideways and slid her right arm through. She was in shoulder-deep before her reaching fingers felt the other side. The spread-eagled crouch required to distribute height and bulk wasn't going to be fun, but she could do it.

Breasts and buttocks compress, but skulls don't, and she was bleeding from a scrape along her right cheek before she popped out into a space that from the sound—and the closeness of Private Kyster—was about a quarter the size of the one she'd originally appeared in. With the spill of light from the tunnel cut off, it was too dark for even di'Taykan eyesight.

"Don't stand." Kyster's fingers closed around her arm as she began to straighten. "Low ceiling, Gunny."

She went to one knee instead.

"Water's . . ."

She could almost hear him thinking in the pause. Trying to dredge up words he hadn't used in all the long days he'd been alone.

"Water's forty-five degrees to your zero," he continued, swallowed, and added, "about a meter five away. Dribbles from a crack in the wall. Pools at the floor."

Torin shuffled forward cautiously. Her outstretched fingers touched moisture. The actual *dribble* was a little to the right. She followed it down to a shallow pool that seemed no bigger than her two cupped hands. "There's not much here."

"It's steady. Been here lots of times and always water there." The water was his, and he was proud of it. "You can drink."

She'd feel a little better if she could have put it in her canteen first—any parasite or bacteria that survived the protections the Corps built into their canteens deserved a chance at the inside of a Marine—but her canteen had disappeared along with ninety percent of the rest of her gear. One hand braced against the wall, she lowered her head toward the ground, pursed her lips, and touched them to the water.

It was lukewarm.

And tasted slightly metallic.

Odds were high it was a cracked pipe rather than a natural spring.

The tunnels clearly continued on beyond the rockfall. Torin wondered if the Corps did.

Kyster was right; it didn't take long for the puddle—pool, she decided, was too grand a description—to refill. She emptied it three times and then moved back out of the way.

"How far to *Colonel* Harnett's pipe," she asked as Kyster drank.

His swallow sounded unnaturally loud. "Day."

"And this is the closest water?"

"*Only* other water, Gunny. This. His at the pipe."

She settled with her back against a relatively smooth rock. "How did you find it?"

"Running from hunting party . . ."

Running and hiding, Torin filled into the pause. She could hear the detail in the way his voice had quavered slightly, in the sound of his hands rubbing together in the dark. *Terrified and alone, you panicked and ran until you couldn't run any farther. In this case, the tunnels ended before your strength and, still panicked, you threw yourself into a hole in the rock to hide.*

"I saw the cave," he went on after a moment. "Knew they couldn't follow me—too big."

Of course they were. Harnett had recruited for an ability to intimidate.

If we band together, we'll make sure we get our fair share.

If we control the access to the food, we control the tunnels.

Make an example of anyone who stands against us.

If you want food and water, you have to do what we say.

What I say . . .

Torin could understand how it had happened, the strong banding together to rule the weak. The strongest, the most ruthless rising to rule. That it had happened within the Corps, however . . .

Hidden in the dark, her hands curled back into fists.

"Time is against us," she said calmly. "We have water but no food. Recon would mean nearly two days without food, and I need to be at full strength when I confront that bastard. I'd rather have a little more information before going in, but we're going to have to play this by ear."

She heard Kyster turn, then felt him grab handfuls of her uniform. "You can't go there. You can't! They'll take you, and they'll . . . they'll . . ."

"They won't," she told him, cutting off the rising panic.

After a moment, he released her, slowly, and she knew that because she believed it completely, he'd started to.

"He kills you if you try to stop him," he said so quietly she could hear the trickle of water behind his voice. "Killed everyone who tried."

"He *won't* kill me." Privates did not question that tone. The whole purpose of the tone was to keep the junior ranks from questioning.

The sound of his breathing changed as his nose ridges flared. "Promise?"

Promise you won't leave me.

"I promise." Reaching out, she wrapped a hand around his ankle—he'd moved as far from her as the cave allowed—and gentled her voice. "We'll sleep here tonight and start for the pipe at your best speed first thing tomorrow."

"Me? With you?"

"Yes."

Wiry muscle tensed in her grip. "He threw me away."

"His mistake. Now, he pays for it."

If Harnett killed her on sight, he won, but Torin was willing to play the odds that power had made him cocky. It was a good thing Kyster couldn't see her smile. He was Krai and he'd know a show of teeth for what it was.

THREE

THE TUNNEL COMPLEX SEEMED TO have been laid out completely randomly. The pattern of turns and cross tunnels leading toward the pipe made no logical sense and more than explained Kyster's difficulty in sketching her a map, rock against rock, on the tunnel floor.

It was alien.

Random, therefore, was no real surprise. One species' random was another species' logical progression.

Any contact the Confederation had managed to have with the Others over the long years of the war had resulted in either dead diplomats or combat situations. Neither allowed for the kind of familiarity that would give Torin any insight into how they built prisons. Particularly since, until yesterday, she'd believed they didn't take prisoners.

That belief was either a lie by politicians who didn't want to commit the resources necessary to retrieve said prisoners—for varying values of *retrieve*—or the Others were a lot slicker than anyone in either branch of the military had ever given them credit for. Following Kyster through the tunnels toward the pipe, Torin decided that the second option was the better choice. She had no emotional investment in the enemy being smarter than anticipated, but believing her own government had thoroughly screwed over their military would make her so furious she wouldn't be able to think straight, and dealing with *Colonel* Harnett would require a clear head.

If things went well, she'd have a go at cursing the government later.

Kyster paused at the next corner, and Torin dropped to one knee, putting her head by his—a necessary move given the height difference. "Hunting parties come out this far," he whispered pointing across the t-junction.

Recon glyphs. Torin's lip curled. The last hunting party had passed this point two days before. Nothing found.

"They don't go careful," Kyster continued, looking up and locking his gaze on hers, trying to convince her of the importance of his words. "You hear them, you get into the closest cave and climb up. Be out of sight."

The small caves had been dug out of the tunnel walls at random intervals—or the pattern was too large for her to recognize it. "Don't they check all the caves for incomers?"

"Yeah." The edges of his mouth curled up. "But they never look up." On a Krai, what looked like a happy smile added *the stupid serley fukkers* to the statement.

Torin's answering smile said much the same thing.

She'd woken that morning just before he had. The cave remained dark, but something told her the lights were back on in the tunnels—a subliminal hum of power, perhaps. Although planetborn, she'd spent enough of her adult life on stations and ships that she found comfort in the background noise of things actually working—things like lights and air scrubbers. During the night, Kyster had moved close, tucking his hand up under the edge of her vest and hanging on, his grip desperate enough she couldn't break it without waking him. Young as he was, he was still a Marine and being caught exhibiting that kind of need, no matter how justifiable given what he'd been through, would embarrass any of the three species in the Corps. So she waited, her own comfort the salvage tag clutched so tightly that the edges pressed into her palm on the edge of pain.

Pain was good. It meant she was alive.

Craig would have been told she was dead.

Her family had always believed the Corps would kill her—but not

Craig. In spite of what he'd said about everyone being easy to kill, he expected her to come back to him.

He'd react the same way she'd react if she got the news he'd been killed on a salvage run. He wouldn't believe. Couldn't believe. Not at first. He'd demand answers from the Corps, and they'd give him the only one they had: The Others didn't take prisoners. If there was no body, it was because there was no body. Both sides had weapons big enough to vaporize rock let alone flesh. They'd tell him she was dead again and again until eventually he believed it.

She'd just have to get out before *eventually* happened.

The tag cracked inside her fist and she eased off slightly as Kyster stirred, feigning sleep until he reassured himself she was still there and then for a few minutes more while he pulled himself together.

They drank until their bellies sloshed with liquid, then set out for the pipe. Torin had paused a moment at the rockfall, strangely certain, with absolutely nothing but instinct to back that certainty up, that this was the way out. She'd lifted a rock a little larger than her fist off the pile and set it to one side, a promise to return after she'd dealt with Harnett and his shit, then she'd turned, nodded, and they'd started walking. Kyster had limited mobility in his bad foot—Krai feet were damned near hands—but by rolling his weight along the outside edge, he set an impressively quick pace.

The unchanging light in the tunnels made it hard to judge time, but Torin doubted they were more than an hour away from the hunting party's glyphs when the unmistakable sound of an argument stopped them two strides from one of the cross tunnels. Kyster scrambled into one of the small caves so quickly an impartial observer wouldn't have believed he had a crippled foot. Torin lingered in the tunnel for a moment, sifting sound.

Three of them. A di'Taykan and two Humans.

Just around the corner. Just having crawled out of one of the small caves.

"Fukking bleeders," one of the Humans snarled. "Fukking hate them. Blood all over his fukking gear."

"And if we'd been ten minutes later," the second Human snorted, "he'd have been fukking dead already, and I wouldn't have gotten sprayed when I took off his vest."

"Looks good on you!"

"Ass!"

"Bastard!"

The muffled thud of a fist against muscle. "Don't fukking talk about my parents like that, you fukker."

Boots rang against stone as they headed for the corner.

Kyster was right; they didn't go careful.

Torin slipped into the cave, bending nearly double to fit through the entrance, and calmed Kyster's panicked grab for her arm with a touch. After everything he'd been through, he had the right to be twitchy for a little while longer. When the voices made it clear the hunting party was nearly right outside, the two of them climbed up into the rough arch of the ceiling. Even with only three working appendages, there were plenty of edges for Kyster to hold and Torin's height made bracing herself nearly effortless.

A silhouette halved the spill of light and a tousled head poked in through the low opening. Both Marines froze, breathing shallowly through their teeth. Di'Taykan hair was fully capable of feeling a change in the small cave's air currents. After a long moment, which probably lasted no more than five or six seconds in real time, the head withdrew.

"Nothing."

"Could be worse," one of the Human's answered as they moved away. "Could be another fukking bleeder."

They were making more than enough noise to cover Torin and Kyster returning to the ground. Making more than enough noise riffing about how they'd left a Marine to die.

Torin indicated that Kyster should remain where he was. His eyes wide, his nose ridges open as far as possible, he covered his teeth and took a step away from her, his reaction to her expression better than a mirror.

The hunting party had their backs to her as she slipped out of the cave and headed for the cross tunnel, moving quickly rather than silently, counting on their overconfidence to cover any sound she might make as she followed the bloody bootprints back to where they'd left the Marine.

The prints overlapped at the entrance to the cave, devolving to a sticky smear of red brown.

Inside the cave, a naked male body lay crumpled where it had fallen, pale skin streaked with drying blood, one hand reaching toward her, his face turned away. Whoever he was, he'd been brought in when she had. Whoever he was, he had probably been in the same battle.

He was Human. Not Jarret.

He was white. Not Tutone. Hell, Tutone would make two of him.

It could be Hollice. Or Captain Rose. Too much blood had spilled from the gash over his temple to see hair color.

The skin of his throat was still slightly warm. Too cold for the living. Not quite cold enough for the dead. The flesh still gave under the pressure of her fingertips.

No pulse.

Gently, she turned his face toward her.

No one she knew.

His eyes were green, truly green and not hazel or gray. Torin brushed them closed with the edge of her hand. He had a dusting of freckles over the bridge of his nose and more on the right side of his chest, the side that hadn't been ripped open by something harder and sharper than muscle and bone. Not young. Not Kyster young anyway.

No one she knew except . . .

She knew him. Had arrived with him on the shuttle at Ventris and watched him take his place beside her on the yellow line. Had learned to march and shoot and survive with him. Had crammed into a VTA beside him, KC-7 held close, hearts pounding together as they slammed through atmo. Had gone drinking with him after, toasting those who'd made it, remembering those who hadn't. She'd given him orders. Or taken orders from him.

Known him.

He'd been alive when the hunting party had found him.

Torin backed out of the cave and straightened. She drew in a deep breath. And then another. The air in the tunnel coated the back of her throat with the taste of iron.

She could hear the hunting party around the corner. They hadn't gone far.

Removing the gear from live Marines and then using it to subjugate those same Marines . . . to the strong go the spoils. Torin didn't like it, but she understood it. Removing the gear from dead Marines made perfect sense.

Removing the gear from a dying Marine, allowing that Marine to die . . .

The hunting party—two big Humans and a di'Taykan—had stopped two caves from where Kyster hid on the opposite side of the tunnel, all three facing the low entrance. One of the Humans, bare arms glistening, held a weighted club, a hunk of rock tied to the thicker end. Torin couldn't see what weapons the other two carried, but overconfidence had left their hands empty. Certain nothing in the tunnels could touch them, they stood around a bloody bundle of fabric and argued about whose turn it was to check the cave. Finally, the di'Taykan threw up his hands and bent down.

With her first step, Torin heard her boot come up off the rock, the blood that coated the sole half dried and adhesive. Second step, second boot, more blood. She closed the last couple of meters at full speed, spun the woman with the club around and slammed the heel of her hand up into her nose—the bone shattering as the momentum of her approach met the momentum of the spin. Torin grabbed the club one-handed as it dropped from nerveless fingers, ducked inside the other Human's wild grab, and jabbed her elbow into his throat. As the di'Taykan backed out of the cave, she brought the club down first on the bow of his spine to knock him flat, then back around to crush his skull.

Two dead. One with bone fragments from her shattered nose driven up into her brain, one with his brain spread out over the dressed rock. One man choking on his own blood, heels drumming on the floor of the tunnel as, thrashing from side to side, he grabbed at his beard and tried to pull air in through his crushed larynx. Torin swung the club again and he stilled.

As she knelt by his side to be sure, she heard a small sound from back the way she'd come, and she looked up to see Kyster staring.

"So fast," he stammered.

Torin blinked. Let the world rush back in. Found her voice. Barely recognized it. "Can't give the enemy a chance to think," she told him, bending to remove the stone knife from the dead man's boot. Lingering adrenaline kept her heart thrumming, but her breathing had begun to slow. The knife was obsidian, its edges flaked to an unexpected razor edge.

"They died so fast." He waved his hands as he limped closer. "In vid fights, people get pounded and pounded, and they don't fall."

It was one of the longer sentences he'd managed since he found her.

"This wasn't a fight." Blood had turned the di'Taykan's pale blue hair a streaky lavender. "It's only a fight when both sides are involved. This was . . ."

Up on one knee, she froze, one hand on the di'Taykan's knife, the other resting on his thigh, on the leg of his combats. Her fingers were outlined in blood, dark against the gray on gray.

These were Marines. Had been Marines.

This was . . .

Revenge. For a Marine stripped and left to die, his blood pumping out to pool on the rock floor of an impossible prison.

Reaction. To what she'd heard about Harnett and what she knew her only option would be when she reached the pipe. Harnett had three fewer goons standing beside him now.

Execution. For crimes committed against the Corps.

Here and now, her decision to make, and she'd stand by it. Her job to keep her people alive, and sometimes that meant removing those things that would keep her from doing her job. Remove the things that were killing her people.

She could live with that.

And she could live with having killed in anger because she had every Goddamned right to be angry about a young man who'd bled out while they joked about the mess.

Torin looked at the dead, at the people she'd killed, really looked at them, remembering their faces. The Corps left no one behind. She'd carry them out with her, too.

After months in here, she wondered, bending to brush the blood from the dead woman's eyes so she could close them, *will I be them? Did they think they were doing the right thing when they started?*

It didn't matter how it had started, what mattered was where it ended up.

"Kyster."

"Gunny?"

"If I become that," she shoved the di'Taykan back into the small cave, "find someone to kill me."

He ran one hand back over his mottled scalp, eyes locked on her face. "Who, Gunny?"

Torin sighed as she shoved the second body into the cave. "Improvise, Private."

"Yes, Gunny!"

As she moved the third body, she became aware of the way Kyster's gaze never left it. Marines didn't eat other Marines. The Krai had a long history of devouring the bodies of their enemies. "You hungry?"

She heard him swallow, the sound wet and wanting. "Yes, Gunnery Sergeant."

"Eat in the cave, then, and make it fast."

As eminently practical as it was, she couldn't bring herself to watch. No way to avoid the crunch of tiny bones, though. No way to avoid the thought of fingers as she used a wet wipe to clean the blood from her hands.

Torin's ears alerted her to the closeness of the pipe before her nose did—and the fact he'd maintained control over basic sanitation was the first positive piece of information she'd received about Colonel Harnett. Granted, he'd probably maintained control with a club, but things hadn't degenerated to the point that people were shitting where they lived. Of course, since he lived there, too, it was in his own best interest, but it was still a point in his favor, and it gave her another piece of the man who was running the node like his own private fiefdom.

He had a practical side.

She'd expected more than a low murmur of sound. No one seemed to be shouting or laughing or screaming. No screaming was good.

Kyster tensed up the closer they came, his limp becoming more pronounced until he stopped in the center of the tunnel. When she turned to face him, he stared up at her in mute entreaty, his right leg visibly shaking. He wasn't going to say he couldn't go closer, she realized. He was afraid to say he couldn't go closer.

She weighed having to protect him against the use she could make of him.

"I'm going to need you in there," she said quietly.

Nose ridges opened and closed, air whistling through the half-blocked passages. That wasn't what he'd expected. "Can't fight like you."

"Of course not." She kept her tone matter-of-fact. "I'm a gunnery sergeant, you're a private. I've had years more training and years more practice."

He glanced back down the tunnel although the bodies were over half a day's travel away. "You going to kill him? Harnett?"

She should try to take him alive; bring him before a military court, allow him to face his accusers and mount a defense, trust the Corps to see that justice was done. Except . . . until she got rid of Harnett, she was the Corps, and if a single person hoped to remove a brutal regime, she couldn't afford to be subtle.

"Yes."

The word hung between them for a moment.

Kyster thought about it for a moment longer, then he pushed the fear aside and, although his right leg still trembled, his lips curled up off his teeth. "What can I do?"

Torin nodded, once, allowed her pride in him to show in the gesture, and said as his chin rose and his shoulders squared, "You can say, *Yes, Gunnery Sergeant!* promptly and loudly where required."

He looked confused. "What good will that do?"

"It'll remind these people that they're Marines." Torin leaned in slightly, caught Kyster's gaze and held it as she smiled. "A Marine can get through a full contract and never have any contact with an officer above captain, but gunnery sergeants are a known quantity. *Aren't they, Private Kyster?*"

"Yes, Gunnery Sergeant!"

The response was instinctive.

Torin waited until she saw that he understood, then she straightened, turned on one heel and started toward the pipe. "Let's go, then." After a moment, she heard Kyster fall into step behind her left shoulder.

They left the club and the di'Taykan's knife in the next cave they passed, but Torin kept the Human's knife in her boot sheath. It fit well enough; the material was forgiving. She'd have liked Kyster to take the other knife, but without boots it seemed like a bad idea to walk in with him so visibly armed. Given the difference in height, a knife sized for a di'Taykan hung from a Krai's hand like a short sword, and nothing was likely to set off the people she had to face faster than a subliminal game of *mine's bigger*. Particularly since it was a game Torin intended to win.

Provided she'd been slapped in stasis directly after the explosion, and a complete lack of any memories regarding transport suggested she had, it had already been over thirty-eight hours since she'd last eaten. The combat she'd been pulled out of didn't allow for a lot of reserves, and the fight in the tunnel had used up nearly all she had left. The longer she waited to deal with Harnett, the more the lack of food would affect both her judgment and her strength. As the colonel controlled the only food source, the more it placed her under his control.

That wasn't going to happen.

"Around that corner, Gunny," Kyster said at last. "Then it's about a ten-meter walk to the place where the pipe is."

No individual voice rose above the muted hum. Either Harnett had everyone thoroughly cowed or it was nap time. Maybe both.

Torin pulled one of the three stims out of her vest and tucked it under her tongue, where it dissolved into a fizz so bitter her eyes watered and her nose ran. The taste was intended to discourage addiction—with her system tagged, a second stim within eighty-one hours would taste even worse.

After a moment, the world shifted into a sharper focus.

"Let's do this. Remember, Private," she continued as Kyster hesitated, "you've got two things those people in there don't. A belly full of meat and me." She rubbed a bit of dust off one toe cap, twitched her vest down into position, and rounded the corner.

There was a trick to making boots—the same boots worn to slip silently up behind the enemy—ring against stone. As she wouldn't be able to slip silently up behind *Colonel* Harnett, Torin announced her presence with authority. It was less efficient but a lot more fun.

The tunnel opened out into a chamber that wasn't actually circular but seven-sided with a tunnel in the middle of each of the walls she could see—a sort of a nexus or node in the tunnel system. The ceiling was a broad cone, about three meters high at the edges to easily five times in the center where a smooth pipe dropped down to . . . possibly the floor, the billowing walls of crude tents hid the lower two, two and half meters. Torin assumed the tents were Harnett's command center.

Striding forward, she had time to see that most of the Marines present were sitting or lying on pallets. The faces turned toward her were uniformly gray, the Human males easily distinguished by their beards, depilatories long since worn off. Torin had stridden barely two meters from the tunnel mouth when the first of Harnett's people reached her, the di'Taykan staring at her with a combination of fear and disbelief, violet eyes dark as her gaze flicked between her face and her collar tabs.

There was an old joke in the Corps about a man who'd gone to his eternal rest in the Garden and, while he was sitting by the gate, he saw one of the newly dead welcomed by three acolytes and a small child throwing flowers.

"I didn't get a welcome like that," he complained to an acolyte near him.

"Ah," said the acolyte, "but this is the High Exalted of the Church of the Red Star's Light."

And that satisfied the man until the next day when he saw another of the dead welcomed by a dozen acolytes, half a dozen small children, fireworks, performing animals, and a full brass band. As he watched, mouth open, he saw the Gardener walk over to greet this new arrival in person.

"The High Exalted arrived yesterday," he reminded the nearest acolyte. "Who the hell is that?"

"That," said the acolyte proudly, "is a gunnery sergeant. We've never had one of them before."

Torin made sure that every millimeter of her said, *this is a gunnery sergeant.* Given the situation around the pipe, she was willing to bet they hadn't had one of those before. She locked her gaze on the di'Taykan.

Who slowly straightened. Her head rose. Her shoulders went back. Her feet shuffled out into parade rest. Odds were good she didn't even know she was doing it.

Torin glanced down at the club, essentially identical to the one she'd left back in the cave, and raised a single brow—the ability worth every credit she'd paid for the download.

The club came up to shoulder rest.

Torin waited.

Violet hair began to scribe short jerky arcs in the air.

"I assume you've been sent to find out who I am, Private . . ."

"Di'Ferinic Akemi, Gunnery Sergeant!"

Torin waited a moment longer. She could hear the background noise falling off.

The violet eyes darkened and lightened, and Akemi's gaze flicked to Torin's face and away. "Ah . . ."

"Identify . . ." Torin prompted.

"Identify yourself and state your business!"

Torin's voice filled those parts of the node the background noise had vacated. "Gunnery Sergeant Torin Kerr. I'm here to see Colonel Harnett." She had to force herself to use the rank, but she managed it. No need to force herself to sound impatient. Every moment she had to spend on Harnett was one more she wasn't spending on escape.

Akemi shook herself, as though trying to wake up, and managed to bark out, "Why?" in a voice that only proved how shaken she was.

"*Why* is none of your business," Torin snapped. She nodded toward the half dozen watchers. She'd have thought that the monotony of imprisonment would have pulled more of them toward a change in their routine, but it seemed only the closest cared enough to make the effort of rising off their pallets.

They were thin, uniforms hanging loose, and the three di'Taykan standing remained in constant physical contact, a sure indication of distress. Shoulders slumped, their faces wore a patina of dirt and hopelessness.

Looking at them, Torin saw only Marines.

One by one, they began to straighten.

Then a swaggering Human, a good half meter taller than Torin's 1.8 and burly to near beefiness shoved one of the watchers hard enough to knock him off his feet and stomped forward to glare down at her from barely an arm's length away. She'd been keeping half her attention on his approach while talking to Akemi. His red-blond beard actually bristled; she'd never seen a beard do that before, and she'd seen Craig's beard do some fascinating things. Like the woman in the tunnel, he'd removed his sleeves—an impressive bit of tailoring since the construction of Corps combats was definitely Marine resistant. The watching Marines drifted away, Corporal Bristly Beard's presence negating any interest they had in what was going on.

"You tell me your business with the colonel, or you don't come any closer." He snarled so broadly, she could see bits of food stuck between his teeth.

The brow rose again.

He frowned, realized where she was looking, and stopped snarling, cheeks flushing self-consciously.

"My business with the colonel is need to know, Corporal . . ."

"Alejandro Edwards, Gunnery Sergeant." He drew out her rank, his tone mocking.

"Corporal Edwards . . ." *Her* tone suggested she hadn't quite decided if he was worth the time it would take to bring him up to Corps standards, but the odds were against it. The difference was subtle, the biggest difference that Torin's words slipped in under the skin, their edges so sharp the immediate damage remained unnoted.

"Fine." He sounded a little sulky now. "You want to see the colonel? I'll take you to see the colonel."

The final statement was clearly intended to be a threat. Torin didn't give a half-eaten rat's ass what his intentions were. "Thank you, Corporal. Lead on."

He scowled past her. "Akemi! Check out the fukking tunnel. See if she's got friends out there."

"And do what if she does?"

Edwards opened his mouth to say something, saw Kyster standing at parade rest behind Torin's left shoulder, and snarled. "Who the hell is he?"

"He's with me."

The corporal visibly weighed his options. His gaze dropped to the knife in her boot and hazel eyes widened slightly as he recognized it. Bullies were often cowards. Not always, but in Torin's experience often enough. "You're responsible for him," he muttered at last.

The look Torin shot him said that was too stupidly obvious to merit a response.

He turned, suddenly anxious to get moving. "Right. Follow me."

"Let's go, Private Kyster."

"Yes, Gunnery Sergeant!"

Textbook response. Muscles tensed across Edward's broad shoulders, and Torin hid a smile.

A rough estimate of the node's area put it between 200 and 250 square meters. Unless there were a lot of people hiding in and on the other side of the tents, she put the number of people at around a hundred. Three platoons worth of Marines, the usual ground troops mix—even numbers of Human and di'Taykan, ten percent Krai. Their feet weren't made for boots, so Krai who joined the Corps rather than the Navy usually headed into Armored or Air Support.

Mostly the captive Marines lay on pallets arranged in rows starting about two meters in from the outer walls. A few of them sat up as she passed. A whisper followed her, spread out, and rippled around the node. The sibilants made at least one of the words obvious.

Silsviss.

So some of these Marines had arrived after the tales of the mission on Silsvah had made the rounds. A single platoon of underarmed Marines, trapped in a barely defensible position, had defeated several hundred of the giant lizards. Her own part in the story had involved defeating one of those giant lizards in single combat and showing the willingness to kill a two-star general had it been necessary in order to bring the Silsviss into the Confederation as allies against the Others. Both parts of the story had grown in the telling, and she'd had to endure the embellishments and speculation for months. It looked as though she was about to reap the benefits.

The ripple lifted a few more Marines onto their feet, and as they began to move closer to try and get a look, the movement lifted a few more.

The area between the pallets and tents had been kept clear, a demilitarized zone easy to patrol, except . . . just as the curve made determining the details difficult, she could see a body staked out. A small body. Krai.

"New guy," Edwards snorted without prodding. "Tried to rush the communal food. Can't have that, can we, Gunnery Sergeant? We'll leave him there until he's hungry enough to see reason."

Until he was too hungry to fight back.

Behind her, she could hear Kyster's teeth snapping rhythmically together. She'd been reminded earlier that Krai teeth had no trouble with Human bone. It seemed Edwards didn't need the reminder.

"Make him stop," he snarled, two spots of color high on each cheek above his beard.

Torin's eyes narrowed. "You were taking me to Colonel Harnett," she said.

Another long moment of weighing his options, then Edwards turned on one heel muttering, "Yeah, the colonel'll stop him."

At the entrance to the tents, he shoved a flap of fabric aside and spat, "Wait here." Before he could turn, she caught his gaze with hers and held it. When he added a reluctant "Gunnery Sergeant," she let him go.

Harnett kept her waiting.

Good. The longer she stood, sweeping her gaze over the pallets, the more Marines dragged themselves onto their feet and shuffled toward her with the short careful stride of those afraid of losing an already precarious balance and, should they fall, not entirely certain they could rise again. In a remarkably short time, a decent-sized crowd, a full platoon's worth at least, stood at the edge of the demilitarized zone. When pressure from the rear pushed a few forward, they scuttled back into the pack.

She saw no one she recognized, but then she was careful not to see individuals, just Marines, because her belief that these *were* Marines was the only reason this was going to work.

"All right, you can . . . What the fuk? Go on, move!" Edwards charged a couple of steps toward the crowd, and they scattered. They didn't scatter far, Torin noted. By the time Edwards returned to her side, muttering under his breath, they were already shuffling back.

"Colonel says to bring you in." A jerk of a bristling chin at Kyster. "He stays out here."

Where more Marines would gather to look at him and note he had been recently well fed. Starving people—and if this lot wasn't starving, they were close to it—maintained a very specific focus.

"Private Kyster."

"Gunnery Sergeant!"

"Remain here until I return."

"Yes, Gunnery Sergeant!" His anger over the staked Krai had added a carrying edge to his voice, banishing the last of his fear.

Torin flashed her teeth as she passed, a promise as she followed Edwards into the tent.

She saw no supports—the fabric clearly had some kind of tech woven in—and the rooms were open to the sky. To the roof. Edwards led her to the right, through three narrow passages, and into another open area around the center pipe. The pipe was a lot bigger up close than she'd originally thought. Maybe three meters in diameter, it ran from the ceiling down into the floor. At the two-meter level or just above, a variety of pipes emerged hanging over niches pressed into the metal. Food, she assumed. And water. The smell of unwashed flesh was weaker here and the smell of waste stronger. The latter was an interesting observation she'd have to take the time to figure out later.

Standing by the pipe with seven—no, eight—goons, spread out to his right was the alleged Colonel Harnett. He stood a little taller than Torin with brown hair and a red-brown beard and no indication he'd been missing meals. More the opposite. A slight paunch strained against his combats, but Torin wouldn't make the mistake of thinking a little belly fat had made him weak. A weak man wouldn't have been able to maintain the kind of control he had. He knew how to fight and would do it ruthlessly. The fact that his goons were armed and he wasn't just drove that point home.

He could have been any age between thirty and seventy—impossible to tell and irrelevant anyway.

He retained his sleeves, but his collar was missing.

No surprise that.

Not a colonel, then.

The goon squads meant he didn't do his own dirty work. That sounded like an officer. But he appeared to have no clear delineation between himself and the goons who carried out his orders. Officers learned early on that removing themselves by the distance of at least one NCO from the more unpleasant orders was more than a good idea; it was virtually a necessity if they were going to command.

She watched him watch her as she closed the distance between them. His eyes lingered on her collar tabs and narrowed slightly in resentment.

A staff sergeant, then.

Probably passed over for promotion.

Torin would have bet her pension that Harnett's belief he knew best had first slowed and then stopped him, keeping him off the promotion list entirely in spite of the war and need for experienced replacements as Marines were lost. Senior NCOs didn't think they knew best, they knew the Corps did and, as the voice of the Corps, that omnipotence *then* devolved onto them. It was a fine distinction but a necessary one.

An officer in charge would have created a situation she needed to deal with for the sake of the Marines his ego had fukked over. For the sake of the Marines left to die in the caves. For the sake of the Marines slowly starving to death under his command. The crap going down in the node was a more extreme example of abuse of power than usual, but finding a solution would still be part of her job description.

A staff sergeant, though . . .

It still came down to doing what was necessary to keep her people alive, but that, that made it personal. Only the thought that it would make it harder to get them around Harnett's throat kept her from curling her hands into fists.

Two meters away, she came to parade rest, and waited. Gunnery sergeants didn't speak first, colonels did. It took Harnett a moment to remember that.

"So, Gunnery Sergeant Kerr, is it?" His smile was broad and false. He didn't seem to recognize her name, but from the reaction sweeping through his goon squad, at least a few of them did. "What brings you here?"

"Reporting to the commander of this area, sir." She'd have liked to use that *sir* to tell him what she thought of him, but it seemed wisest to keep her tone ice and iron. He'd have her opinion on things soon enough.

Pleased by what he heard as deference but clearly confused, Harnett frowned. "How did you get past my guards?"

"I was challenged."

"Not the purple idiot!" He'd clearly heard what had happened just after she entered the node. "The guards in the . . ." Torin almost saw the lights go on. "You didn't come from the other pipe, did you? You woke up in a small cave," he continued, answering his own question. "Last day or two."

"She's got the tunnel rat with her, Colonel Harnett, sir," Edwards told him before Torin could answer. He spoke quickly, eagerly, currying favor with information. "The Krai. The one with the fukked foot. I knew he was still alive. I told you, remember? She left him outside. And that's not all, the rest of them, they're all up and crowdin' the fukking line. Waiting to see what the . . . what she's going to do."

"Crowding the fukking line?" Harnett's smile twisted. "Well, get your ass out there and *discourage* them from crowding the fukking line. Take Bakune and Maeken with you. Let's show the gunny we can maintain discipline."

"Yes, sir, Colonel Harnett." Edwards grinned so broadly he could barely get his lips around the words.

When Edwards left, he took two of the three di'Taykan with him, lowering the odds to six to one. No one moved into his place behind her. And while the six remaining goons had moved closer, not one of them moved to cover Harnett's left. When this was over, she'd have a few words to say about proper security measures.

"Colonel Harnett, sir. Look at her boot."

His eyes flicked down to the knife and up again to her face. "So you did run into some of my guards."

Torin let nothing show on her face. "I believe the three persons were referred to as a hunting party, sir."

"Were?" This new smile told her he finally understood what was going on and was happy his world made sense again. "Well, yes, I believe they *were*. The question becomes, what are we going to do with you, Gunnery Sergeant Kerr?" He spread his hands, and, still smiling, slowly turned.

Clearly, there'd been coup attempts before.

For a moment, Torin thought about making the bastard work a little harder for it, but she'd had about as much of Colonel Harnett as she could stomach, so she took her cue.

They expected her to go for the knife in her boot. That was one of the reasons she wore it. Ignoring the knife gave her a two or three second jump on a reaction.

He expected her to try and stab him in the back.

When he whirled to face her, she was two seconds closer than expected and already on her knees sliding under his kick. Up on her feet inside his guard, one hand went to his chin and the other to the back of his head. Once again, momentum, his and hers, added force as she straightened her inner arm.

He was already sagging when she felt a knife slam into her vest, and although it didn't have a hope getting through the body armor, the impact pushed her from cold rage to full fury. Bending her knees, Torin let the late colonel fall across her back, hoisted him up, and heaved him at the goon squad. Paradise, her birth planet, had a gravity 1.14 Human norm. It was a small difference, but added to adrenaline, it came in handy. She had her knife out by the time he stopped bouncing, and when she blocked the next blow, she didn't block it blade to blade but blade to hilt.

As she'd already noticed, the flaked edge was sharp.

Three fingers fell. She cut the scream off in his throat.

They obviously hadn't fought anyone who hadn't been starved or beaten in months. Forty hours ago, Torin had been in combat.

One of the women approached and got a boot to the side of the knee. The body armor in the vest was inert, but it depended on tech in the combats and all tech was down. As the joint cracked and she crumbled, Torin ducked in, grabbed her, turned her as a shield toward the whistle of a descending club. The stone sent teeth flying. Impact loosened the wielder of the club's grip, and a second later Torin used his own weapon to smash in his throat. Soft tissue was *always* the safer shot.

Three down.

The other three stared at her over the body of Colonel Harnett.

If they decided to rush her together, Torin wouldn't stand a chance. Even one at a time, the odds weren't in her favor, not having to adjust for both Human and di'Taykan physiognomy.

So she smiled and said, "Don't."

And like the hundred Marines who'd been ground under the heels of maybe two dozen goons, they didn't.

It was all a matter of perception.

They believed she could win.

The man with the crushed throat had died, heels drumming. The woman with the smashed mouth and the broken knee should have been alive—none of her injuries were fatal—but lips were blue and one hand still clutched at the collar of her combats. If Torin had to hazard a guess, she'd say the dead woman had choked on her own teeth. Had she lived, the pain from her knee would have been intense and the shattered bones in her jaw couldn't have been re-built without tech. She'd have complicated what had to be clear and simple.

The three remaining members of the goon squad still standing by the pipe stepped back as Torin stepped over the body.

If there was a moment of savage pleasure taken in their fear, Torin didn't let it show. "Weapons there!" Out in the open where they couldn't retrieve them unobserved. "Then get these walls down."

"But . . ."

"Now!"

From the time she walked into the tent to the time the walls began collapsing gracefully to the floor, no more than fifteen minutes had elapsed.

Colonel Harnett had a storeroom of gear taken off dead and dying Marines. *Colonel* Harnett had what passed for opulent personal quarters. *Colonel* Harnett had three of the youngest Marines in a room by his quarters. While not as well fed as his fighters, they were less thin than the general population and the scraps of clothing he'd left them made it obvious what he used them for.

They wore twisted fabric collars and cuffs.

"What the fuk is going . . ."

Sweeping Edwards' feet out from under him, Torin yanked his left arm over his head and slammed the stone knife into his armpit, grinding it through his ribs, and driving it into his heart. The silence as he hit the ground was absolute. Fighting her way back from a blind rage that would have seen every one of Harnett's people dead by her hand, she could hear nothing but her own blood pounding between her ears.

The fabric walls lay in drifts around her. She could feel the weight of a hundred pairs of watching eyes from the other side of the demilitarized zone and six pairs watching from a lot closer. It was dangerous to gain a reputation for uncontrollable rage, no matter how justified. Edwards' death would just have to be fuel for another story then.

"That," she snarled, bending to wipe her blade on Edwards' hip, "is why you don't cut the sleeves off your uniform." As she straightened, the two di'Taykan who'd been with Edwards took a step toward her. She let them see what she was thinking, and they backed away. "Private Kyster!"

"Yes, Gunnery Sergeant Kerr!"

"Release the prisoner."

"Yes, Gunnery Sergeant!"

"You!" The finger she pointed toward the youngest of the surviving goons was only metaphorically not dripping red. "Name!"

"Private di'Nurin Jiyuu, Gunnery Sergeant!" He looked a little surprised by the vehemence of his reply.

"How many still out in the tunnels?"

"There's two and a runner in tunnel seven, Gunnery Sergeant," Jiyuu told her quickly. Time under Harnett had clearly taught him to suck up to power. "Three in tunnel four. Tunnel two hunting party has already checked back."

If there'd been only two hunting parties working, then the three in tunnel four had already checked out. Torin could see Akemi standing just back of the assembled Marines, closer to the tunnels than the pipe. If she decided to run and turn the five goons still out in the tunnels into a strike force, there'd be trouble.

"Private Akemi!"

She visibly started at the sound of her name, her hair flipping back and forth.

"Get over here. Double time."

There was absolutely no reason Akemi should obey. There were a hundred starving Marines between them, no way Torin could get to her in time should she decide to run, and it was clear—even at a distance—that she was considering it. Had any of the survivors standing unsecured behind Torin said anything . . .

No one did. Although Bakune shuffled back from the spreading puddle of Edwards' blood.

Torin snapped out, "That wasn't a request, Private."

Decision made for her, Akemi pushed her way through the crowd, jogged across the open area as though expecting a shot in the back at any moment, and rocked to a stop an arm's length away.

"Weapons there," Torin pointed. "Then join the rest."

The violet eyes darkened, as she took in the bodies, gaze lingering for a moment not on Harnett but on the three severed fingers. "Are you . . . ?"

"Let's move, Private, we've got a lot of work to do before dark. Mind the blood," she added. "You track it around, you clean it up." She waited until Akemi's weapons hit the pile, then drew in a deep breath and faced the mass of gray and brown. "Sergeants and above, fall in. Three ranks!"

A hundred pairs of eyes blinked.

Torin's eyes narrowed. "Now!"

In the end, there were eleven of them. They locked their eyes on the far wall; none of them looked at her. She could have said she expected more of them, but she hadn't been here, she hadn't been starved and beaten, so all she said was, "Who's senior?"

A staff sergeant with a pale beard and a missing front tooth stepped forward. "Staff Sergeant Kerin Pole, Gunnery Sergeant."

"Get those kids taken care of, Staff Sergeant. Get them clothes and medical attention if they need it." She shouldn't have had to specify but none of this should have happened, so . . . "Then have the lower ranks divided into groups of ten to fifteen so that we can see about getting them fed. We'll set up actual platoons later."

"What about them?" His gaze flicked past her at the remains of Harnett's six still standing where she'd left them. They were uncertain, confused, but Edwards had been an object lesson the way Harnett hadn't, and what they'd become proved they weren't the type to sacrifice themselves on a fool's chance.

"They're not our problem, Staff."

"But . . ."

"You have your orders."

After a long moment, he nodded and she walked away, turning back to the staring eyes. She took a deep breath and let only calm expectation shape her voice. "Would the senior officer please meet with me here."

She almost thought she'd have to ask again, but finally, after feet shuffling and muttering had run its course through the group, two di'Taykan emerged. A major and a lieutenant who was clearly supporting a good portion of the major's weight.

Torin came to attention. "Major . . ."

Face and voice both showed no emotion. "di'Ree Kenoton."

"Major Kenoton," she spoke to the major but loudly enough to be heard, "Gunnery Sergeant Torin Kerr, 7th Division, 4th Recarta, 1st Battalion, Sh'quo Company. What are your orders, sir?"

The lieutenant's eyes flicked from light green to dark so quickly it must have hurt.

The major merely stared, his eyes a mid-range blue. It looked as though he didn't understand. He had to understand. This was crucial.

They had to become Marines again, or she'd just replaced Harnett as their keeper.

After a long moment, his hair moved, just a little. "My orders?"

"Yes, sir."

After a longer moment, she began to be afraid this wasn't going to work.

Then the major, blinked, wet his lips, and said, "Carry on as you have been, Gunnery Sergeant."

"Yes, sir!"

FOUR

"**WHAT TOOK YOU SO FUKKING** long, Gunny?"

Torin turned toward the familiar voice and smiled. This time, her expression meant nothing more or less than how it appeared. It felt good to see a familiar face. "Fuk, Werst, if there was shit disturbing going on, I should have known it was you."

He didn't look bad, all things considered, but his natural mottling couldn't hide the bruises, one eye was swollen almost closed, and Kyster had definitely been supporting him as they moved toward her. She could see abrasions on one wrist and knew there'd be a matching set on the other wrist and both ankles. He hadn't just lain there after he'd been staked out, he'd fought the bindings. A bloody scab weighed down one corner of his mouth, but his lips still rose up off his teeth. "Harnett?"

"Dead."

"Edwards?"

"Also dead."

His grunt suggested he found the news of Edwards' death disappointing. Torin assumed that was only because he'd had plans to take care of it himself. "How many total?"

"Seven. Eight including Harnett."

Werst's good eye widened. "How many with you?"

"Private Kyster found me and brought me in."

"Not what I meant."

"I know."

His nose ridges opened and closed. "I landed in this *serley* hell hole yesterday, so unless you came in earlier . . ."

"No."

". . . you're saying you killed eight armed shitheads today."

Since that wasn't a question, Torin didn't answer it.

"Okay." He very carefully covered his teeth when he smiled. "I guess it's a damned good thing they didn't piss you off, Gunny."

"Gunnery Sergeant Kerr?" Major Kenoton's voice pulled her back around toward him. "You know this Marine?"

"Corporal Werst and I served together on the Big Yellow expedition, sir. A Recon mission to an alien ship," she expanded when the major stared at her blankly. Obviously, he'd been here for a while.

"The ship was of an unknown alien construction, sir," Lieutenant Myshai put in, the movement of her hair speeding up. "The Others were exploring it as well, and our Recon team had to fight its way to the air lock. They wouldn't have gotten off except for the CSO who'd discovered the ship." Her eyes darkened as she glanced up at Torin, and she nearly grinned before returning her attention back to the major. "He came and got them and packed them into his cargo pod. Gunnery Sergeant Kerr captured the survivors of the Others' Recon team, but the Others sent vacuum jockeys out to kill them before they got to the *Berganitan*."

The lieutenant had, just as obviously, been here for some months less and had seen all the vids. A few of the amateur remixes made di'Taykan opera look sedate, and the Corps had attempted to keep them out of circulation without much success.

"I see," said the major. He didn't. But it didn't matter. "I'm pleased to see you took no significant damage, Corporal Werst." Torin wondered how much of the low rasp was a result of his voice deteriorating as he starved. There was a certain detachment to it she found just a little unnerving. More significantly, the color of his eyes never changed; for a di'Taykan, that was either frighteningly detached or evidence of significant vision loss. She almost hoped for the latter. "The gunny's going to need support," he continued, "until the rest of us get a little steadier on our feet."

The gunny was also going to need Marines she could count on

as part of her escape team, but this didn't seem the time to bring that up with the major. Torin swept a critical gaze over the Marines. Most of them were sitting while the strongest in each group joined the line at Harnett's food stores. Staff Sergeant Pole seemed to have things under control, and if her name was being used to maintain discipline when starving Marines would rather surge forward and fight for whatever food they could get, well, that's what it was for.

Still, they were probably lucky that most of those waiting were physically incapable of surging forward.

Harnett's goons had been put to work gathering up the fallen fabric panels. There was a trick to folding them without activating their internal tech, forcing the job to be much less a mindless activity than it could have been. And that was good. Keeping Harnett's goons busy was a significantly better idea than letting them stand around and consider their situation. Besides, from the way they were being watched, their situation was under consideration by pretty nearly everyone not currently shoveling food into their mouth.

Food in hand got one hundred percent attention.

"Gunnery Sergeant."

"Sir."

"Have you eaten?"

"I'll eat after everyone else has eaten, sir, just in case there isn't enough to go around. It hasn't been as long for me," she added before he could speak. "Private Kyster."

"Yes, Gunnery Sergeant!"

The corners of Werst's mouth twitched up.

Torin leaned in, just enough to acknowledge what they'd shared. "You can dial the volume back a little now, Kyster."

"Yes, Gunnery Sergeant."

"I need you to go get food for the major and the lieutenant." The other five officers, two captains and three second lieutenants, were sitting together, one of the sergeants seeing they were fed. Eventually, the second lieutenants would lead platoons and the captains would become part of the major's staff, but for now they were fine where they were.

"One moment, Private Kyster."

He stopped at the major's command but glanced at Torin for confirmation.

Torin appreciated the major ignoring that as he declared, "Like you, Gunnery Sergeant, we'll eat when the rest have eaten."

"Yes, sir. From the look of things, that'll be about when the private returns with your food. The NCOs are just getting their food now."

"Then the private can also return with your food."

"I think I should deal with the rest of Harnett's people first, sir. There's still a hunting party out and three more at the guard station."

"You can eat first."

This wasn't going to work if she argued with every word out of the major's mouth, and the last thing she wanted him to do was make his desire an order. "Very well, sir."

"Good." He took a deep breath, as though the argument had exhausted him, and turned his attention back to Kyster. "Bring enough food for Gunnery Sergeant Kerr and for Corporal Werst, Private."

"Yes, sir."

Werst knew better than to glance at Torin. "I'll go with him, sir."

"Are you able?"

"Wouldn't have off . . ."

Torin cut Werst off with a raised brow.

"Yes, sir."

"Go on, then."

"Yes, sir. Come on, kid," Werst wrapped a hand around Kyster's arm and turned him toward the stores. "We have a job to do."

As the two Krai moved away, Major Kenoton murmured, "I think I'd best sit now, Myshai. It won't look good if I smack into the floor with my face."

"Everyone will understand, sir." Myshai gracefully folded to the floor beside him, guiding his collapse but somehow making it look as though they sat in unison. "They know what you've been through."

"What they know and what they see are two entirely different things." At his gesture, Torin also sat, although less gracefully. "Aren't they, Gunny?"

"Yes, sir." Chain of command had to be reestablished. The major had to be seen to lead. She was grateful he realized that—there were officers who wouldn't have, and had she been stuck with any of them, they'd have made her job a lot harder.

"The private didn't arrive with you, did he, Gunnery Sergeant?"

Kyster and Werst were at the food stores now. "No, sir, he's been surviving in the tunnels since Harnett decided his injured foot made him not worth feeding."

"*How* did Private Kyster survive in the tunnels, Gunnery Sergeant?"

"He's Krai, sir." The emphasis in the major's question made it clear he knew what that meant. She rubbed the hand he couldn't see over the floor of the node, fingernails skimming over the smooth gray rock making sure it was actually *rock*. A sentient polynumeric molecular species that was essentially organic plastic really ratcheted the paranoia up a notch or two.

"We can't have that, Gunnery Sergeant."

The major's delivery remained detached but the subtext was obvious. *Marines don't eat other Marines.*

"No need for it anymore, sir."

"There's nothing in the tunnels to eat," the lieutenant said suddenly. Her hair stilled. "Nothing except . . . *Vret ter yeinan kell,* Marines!"

"*Sa minek ple,*" Torin snapped, her di'Taykan more than up for this exchange. "He'll be taking those Marines home, Lieutenant. They're a part of him now."

"I don't care how you spin it, Gunny, it's disgusting." She stared down into the cradle of her legs, apparently unable to cope with the thought.

"Lieutenant Myshai."

Unable to stop herself from responding to Torin's voice, the lieutenant looked up.

"Any of those Marines would have been happy to know they didn't die in vain. That their deaths meant something. That with their deaths they kept another Marine alive."

"You don't know that, Gunnery Sergeant." Her eyes were so light Torin knew she could barely see. That was all right, she didn't need to see; she needed to listen.

"I do know that, Lieutenant."

"But . . ."

"Enough." The major's soft rasp cut her off. "It's over and done, and we won't speak of it again. Gunnery Sergeant?"

"Yes, sir."

"Lieutenant Myshai?"

"Yes, sir." The lieutenant's agreement was a little less definitive.

Torin understand her problem—the ingrained reaction to eating sentient flesh had a strong pathological basis originating back when each sentient species thought they were the only sentient species, and eating the dead led to some very nasty diseases. Unless, of course, it was Krai eating Krai. The Krai gut was the most efficient in known space. When the Elder Races approached the Krai to join the fight against the Others, they were just lucky the Krai had been willing to surrender at least a part of their cultural heritage—while they still ate each other during the privacy of their own rituals, they didn't usually eat anyone else.

Given that the Krai preferred Human flesh over . . . well, over damned near everything, Torin was more than happy to return to the default rules. She just wasn't going to put up with the lieutenant thinking less of an injured kid thrown out on his own like so much trash who'd done what he had to in order to survive.

"It seems Harnett had enough food put by to give everyone in this hole two generous portions," Werst announced as he tossed Torin a brown plastic bowl a little larger across than her fist.

"Hard to believe that's all." The major's fingers looked even thinner against the curve of a similar bowl he'd pulled from inside the front of his combats. Safest place to put it, Torin realized as the lieutenant followed suit, and they'd lost enough weight there was certainly room. All the bowls were identical, and she only just resisted the urge to put her bowl on the floor and wipe the feel of the plastic off her hands.

"Looks like he and his crew ate the rest. There were a bunch of these." Werst held up a long curved jug made of the same material as the bowls, his fist shoved through the handle in its back. "And they stored the rest in sleeves tied off at both ends."

Torin had to acknowledge it was a creative storage solution.

"So, this is how they told me it's done, Gunny. Water first." Carefully, Werst filled everyone's bowls—beginning with the major's and finishing with Kyster's. "We drink."

The major and the lieutenant had already emptied their bowls.

The liquid beaded up on the surface, the beads joined and ran, and not a drop was wasted.

"Then . . ." Werst took a second jug from Kyster. ". . . we fill the bowl with the Marine chow . . ."

The jugs were marked, Torin saw as he poured. Each line representing the volume of one of the bowls, each jug held ten servings. Torin tried to remember which of the species fighting for the Others had five digits on each hand. *First figure out who created this place, figure out who exactly was holding them; decide later what to do with that information.* She thought maybe the crazy little guys who rode the quadrupeds had five though the quadrupeds themselves had four. Three thick fingers, one opposing digit—thumb for lack of a better word.

The pellets were a dark red brown, about the size of Torin's smallest fingertip. They had a strong, almost meaty odor, but they looked like formed grain of some kind.

". . . and add more water."

Water turned the pellets into a rough porridge. The major and the lieutenant used their first two fingers to scoop the mush up to their mouths. It was lukewarm, probably some kind of chemical reaction, a bit gritty, and tasted like the yeast paste Craig liked to spread on his toast although it was entirely possible it tasted completely different to each species. Most food did. Who could have anticipated the way the H'san overreacted to cheese?

"What do you think it is?" she asked the corporal as he ate.

He shrugged. *"Chrick."*

"I was hoping for a little more than edible."

He shrugged again and kept eating. Torin wondered if he couldn't say or he wouldn't. Werst was contrary on a good day and this—well, they'd both had better.

The surface of the bowls repelled the mush much as it had the water; the Others appeared to have mastered self-cleaning dishes.

Torin approved. It meant they understood what bacteria could do to their prisoners and had taken steps to prevent disease. She thought about the supplements tucked inside her vest and decided to wait on mentioning them for now. Harnett hadn't seemed to be suffering from any lack of nutrients, so it was possible the appalling condition of the rest of the Marines around the pipe could be blamed on lack of calories.

"Second helping now or later, Gunny?" Werst asked, setting his bowl to one side.

"Major?"

Kenoton stared into the dark curve of his empty bowl as if he expected to find the answer. Torin could see the order he wanted to give and was impressed when he said, "Later. It would be good to sleep without hunger."

She rocked up onto her feet. "I'll let Staff Sergeant Pole know, sir." Kyster bounded up beside her, and Torin hid a smile as she pulled him away from the two officers and Werst. "I need you to stay here and be the major's legs for him. He's going to need to stay on top of things, but if he goes ass over tip . . ." One of Craig's sayings. She banished both it and the unexpected pain that came with it. ". . . if he falls, it won't look good. Any running that needs to be done, you do it for him. Understand?"

Kyster glanced down at his bad foot then back up at her. "You want me to run around for him?"

"Yes."

"But I . . . I'm . . ."

She could read *broken* off his face. "You're not going to be able to program a slate with that foot, but you obviously get around on it just fine. Does it hurt?"

"No."

"Good."

"Gunny, I want . . ."

He wanted to stay with her. That was obvious. "Corporal Werst will be here with you."

She gave him credit for not turning to look at the other Krai, and, gradually, his breathing slowed. "If the major wants to move around?"

"Look eager. Respectfully remind him you've been kept out of things and you want to help." Kyster's youth and the major's apparent good sense should do the rest. "If he's going to keep command, it's important no one knows how physically weak he is." Which was both the truth and total bullshit since everyone—including Harnett's goons—knew exactly how weak the major was.

"I can . . . I . . ." He ran a hand back over the bristles on his scalp and finally settled on the one answer he knew she wanted. "Yes, Gunnery Sergeant."

Pole wasn't happy about waiting for the second helping, but he understood. "Evening meal's never enough," he told her, struggling to stand.

Torin indicated he should stay seated and squatted beside him. "How often do they feed you? Us."

Pole ignored the slip. "We line up for a bowl of this shit night and morning—bowl's are filled to the point seven five, but I'm guessing that's because that bastard Harnett was skimming—and two biscuits in the middle of the . . ." He frowned. ". . . the day I guess you'd call it. While the light's on. Bowl of water every time."

That was a liter and a half of water plus the water in the kibble. Not a lot, but enough when the day's activity consisted of lining up to be fed and then sitting on a pallet waiting for the next meal. Two fair-sized bowls of food, though, plus biscuits—Torin hadn't eaten in almost forty hours and the mush she'd just eaten left her feeling, if not full, satisfied. Of course, it had been a nearly full bowl and it hadn't been all she'd been eating for months, but still, if Harnett had only skimmed off two full meals' worth plus extra for a dozen goons . . . it didn't quite add up to starvation.

"What about Harnett's guards, Gunny?"

"I expect they've been eating regularly; they can wait until the next scheduled meal."

"Not exactly what I meant. Point is, they're Harnett's." He nodded toward the six survivors. "Right now, this lot's shitting themselves every time they look at you, but that won't last forever." When Torin raised a brow, he grinned. "All right, maybe it will, but eventually they'll realize they have the advantage of numbers, and they'll try to take you down. Try to get back what you took from them."

"Won't happen."

"There's three more out guarding his barricade—I have no idea from what," he answered before she could ask. "But something kicked the shit out of one of his hunting parties, and he built the barricade right after that. You've got a couple of days before you have to deal with them, though. There's six still out in the tunnels, and they're due back any minute."

"Three."

"Three?" He glanced down at the knife in her boot. "Ah. Three out there and five here. You had an impressive day. But you can't kill them all."

"I can." That could never be brought into question. "But I don't intend to."

"You're thinking of using one of the small caves as a prison, then? Won't work." The fingers of one hand scratched hard under the edge of his beard. "There's no way of knowing where new Marines are going to end up. One ends up in with them, and they've got leverage."

"True. But Harnett wanted followers, people who would obey his orders without question. That's an appalling description of a Marine, and he scraped the bottom of the barrel to find them, but we can use it. Now they'll obey Major Kenoton without question."

"They'll obey you," Pole snorted.

"It amounts to the same thing."

"Because you'll obey Major Kenoton."

"Of course."

He laughed then. It sounded rusty, jagged, a little as though he'd forgotten how. Several heads turned, expressions suggesting they, in turn, had forgotten the sound. "Well, I'm convinced, Gunny. You might actually manage to pull this whole shitty thing as far out of the crapper as it'll come. You want platoons formed?"

"I do." She trusted the sergeants to group their people wisely.

"No one's got enough strength to march around."

"Pull the pallets into ranks, then." She didn't help him stand, but it was close. "We can use the fabric to create a communal area for the di'Taykan."

Pole shook his head. "Only Harnett's people know how the tech works."

"Then they'll teach the rest of us what they know."

"And lose the leverage, Gunny? Not likely."

Torin smiled. "I said I didn't intend to kill them, Staff. I didn't say I was against cracking a few heads together."

"Well, the di'Taykan will appreciate it once they're fed up enough to regain interest. Which brings us to your other problem; what happens when everyone's fed up enough to regain interest and what they're interested in is taking all the shit they went through out on Harnett's goons?"

"By then, they'll remember they're Marines."

Pole's smile was a little sad as he closed a thin hand around her arm. "Marines are just people, Gunny, and there's nothing more petty and vicious than people. When you give them a uniform and a weapon, you don't change that."

"We don't just give them a uniform and a weapon, Staff Sergeant. We give them a uniform, a weapon, and something to believe in." She swept a gaze over the faces turned toward them and nodded as weakened bodies sat a little straighter. "They'll believe in it again."

"Believe in what, Gunny?"

She looked at him then. Staff Sergeant Pole was taller, but his captivity had curled him in on himself until they were eye to eye. "Believe in us, Staff Sergeant. You and me and everyone else who accepted the responsibility of leading them. We do our job, we take care of our people, the rest falls into place."

"And it's just that simple?"

Her turn to snort. "Fuk, no. It's the hardest Goddamned job in known space, and we were fools to take it on. But now we're stuck with it. Get those pallets divided by platoons; I'm going to have Harnett's lot clear out the bodies."

The bodies were still lying where they'd fallen. Torin stared down at them for a moment, rolled the meat that had been Edwards onto his back away from the blood with the side of her boot, and then beckoned Harnett's survivors over. "All right, let's move this lot out of here."

Arms folded, a Human female curled her lip and snarled, "Move them where, Gunnery Sergeant?"

Torin smiled gently at her, a smile usually directed to those with head injuries and impaired brain function. "To where the bodies go, Private." There were no bodies piled up in the corners; there were no Krai in Harnett's organization and no way in hell Harnett would feed any of the Krai he was oppressing; there had obviously been deaths. Therefore, there had to be a place where the bodies went. Jailors who provided self-cleaning dishes wouldn't leave something like that to chance. "Two to a corpse."

One corpse left over.

"Gunnery Sergeant Kerr? Staff Sergeant Pole said we should help."

The two Marines were thin but not quite over the line to emaciated. Torin assumed they were the last to arrive before her and Werst.

"And you two are?"

"Lance Corporal Divint and Private Sergei, Gunnery Sergeant. Seven, two, two, Delta Company."

Torin frowned, trying to remember where she'd last heard that designation. Someone she'd run into in the SRM on Ventris. Someone on course . . . "Staff Sergeant Arklan was with seven, two, two, Delta."

The lance corporal nodded. "Don't know if he survived the battle, Gunny, but he's not down here with us."

Divint had a scar on his cheek, still red on the pale skin just above the line of his dark whiskers. Sergei had a single honey-blonde braid hanging down her back and a triangular tear in the right shoulder of her combats. As she still had a right shoulder, Torin made a mental note to find out what had happened. They didn't look like they could even lift a di'Taykan body, let alone carry it to the disposal site, but if Pole thought they could do it, and they thought they could do it, she'd let them try.

Rest stops wouldn't matter to the dead.

"All right, then." She nodded toward the smallest corpse—relatively speaking—and was pleased to see they had sense enough not to be insulted by the choice.

The Human female, on the other hand, wasn't happy to find herself standing over Edwards. "He's too heavy."

Akemi, waiting at Edwards' feet, flicked her eyes through dark to light and back again, the di'Tayken equivalent of an eye roll.

"Suck it up, Private . . . ?"

"Terantowicz, Gunnery Sergeant." Only three words, but dripping with attitude.

Of the six surviving goons—ignoring for the moment the three still in the tunnels—Terantowicz would be the one to instigate a coup. The first to say, *There's just one of her and there's still plenty of us and we can be on top again.* Torin could see it in the way she kept glancing around as if she didn't quite believe what had happened. She burned with the kind of ambition that needed an outlet. The odds were good that somewhere barely acknowledged in the back of her mind, she'd had plans to replace Harnett. She hadn't been chosen because she'd blindly follow orders—Torin was willing to bet she'd volunteered.

"Gunnery Sergeant Kerr!"

"Corporal Werst." Torin turned, brow raised.

"Major Kenoton told me to join you." *Not my fault I'm here,* said the subtext.

Torin wanted to ask if Major Kenoton expected Werst to help "guard the prisoners." Since she couldn't, she took her own advice and sucked it up.

It turned out there was a latrine trench at the base of every other wall. Covered with a substance that allowed as little surface adhesion as the bowls, the trench angled off steeply under the cut rock.

"How far does the slope go?" Torin wondered as they passed.

"About two meters, Gunnery Sergeant," Private Jiyuu told her quickly, tone and delivery saying *see how useful I can be,* "then it falls at ninety degrees. Doesn't get any wider, though."

"How did you know we measured it?" Terantowicz demanded,

hands shoved under Edwards' armpits, breathing heavily as she carried most of the weight.

"Harnett was exploiting a hundred Marines with sixteen goons." Torin indicated that Akemi should put just a little more effort into it. "Therefore, Harnett had all options covered."

"You talk like you knew him," the younger woman sneered.

"No one's entirely unique, Private Terantowicz. And some people are less unique than most."

She chose to take that personally but switched her protest to what could be more easily understood. "Yeah, well, we weren't goons!"

"Really? Because you sure as fuk weren't Marines."

"But now *you're* here?"

"That's up to you, isn't it?"

Terantowicz's expression suggested that if it were up to her, Torin's head would be doing a full three sixty sometime soon.

The position of the latrines explained why the scent of waste was higher in Harnett's tents. He and his, too good to walk across half the diameter of the node to take a leak, had likely used pots that someone else emptied for a little bit more food. The three Marines he'd been keeping as playthings had certainly not been allowed out to use the latrines.

Given a chance to do it over, she'd have killed him more slowly. And enjoyed it.

At the base of the wall designated Wall One—Jiyuu helpfully numbered each of the walls and their corresponding tunnels—was a circular pit a little better than a meter and a half in diameter. The trapdoor seemed to be made of the same metal as the central pipe, Torin realized as she bent and opened it, leaning it against the wall.

When you get a moment, she reminded herself, *you need to examine that pipe.*

It could wait. The pipe was a constant. She needed to deal with the variables first. She couldn't work on leaving until they'd been brought into line, until she knew Kenoton and Pole together had things under control.

About six centimeters thick, the trapdoor was lighter than it looked like it should be. The pit itself had the same slick lining as the latrines.

Without a direct light source—and habit had her slap the light in her cuff, which continued not to work—Torin couldn't see the bottom.

"No idea how deep it is, Gunnery Sergeant," Jiyuu said apologetically, and she barely stopped herself from reacting with violence. *This* he chose to be sorry for? "We could never get a read on it. Easiesr to show you why."

Torin stopped him before he and Maekan could slide Harnett's body into the pit. "Strip him first. Strip all of them."

"To the victor goes the spoils," Terantowicz muttered as Edwards' body hit the floor.

Torin turned just far enough to catch her gaze. And hold it.

Terantowicz grinned. Her gaze flickered up and over Torin's left shoulder.

Torin's expression never changed. When Bakune charged her from behind, clearly intending to sweep her into the pit, she leaned away from his rush, grabbed the front of his uniform and directed his momentum.

They'd never measured the pit because matter entering it set off a charge.

Bakune managed a sound that might have grown into a scream had a flash of light and the sharp tang of ozone not cut it off as his head passed below the lip of the pit. One hand closed around the edge with a desperate grip, then the fingers spasmed and slid free.

There was surprisingly little smell.

"Too bright to see what actually happened, Gunny," Werst reported from the edge. "But I'm betting the body was destroyed."

"Odds are good," Torin acknowledged, finally allowing a visibly shaken Terantowicz to look away. "I'm not happy about losing the tech the Corps built into Bakune's combats. Just because it's not working now doesn't mean it can't be repaired."

The other bodies were stripped with impressive speed.

"Waste of meat," Werst murmured beside her as Harnett's corpse was slid feetfirst over the edge.

"Take it up with the major, Corporal."

He snorted. "Pass, Gunny. You notice there were no Krai among Harnett's *gertiv*."

She wasn't familiar with the word, but the context sufficed. "Not a lot of Krai in the infantry, Werst, so don't get smug. He was choosing for size."

"If I was di'Taykan, I'd have a response for that."

"If you were di'Taykan," Torin admitted, "I wouldn't have said it."

"So, Gunny, about that guard post Harnett had out in the tunnels." When she looked down, his nose ridges were opening and closing in a slow, rhythmic wave from top to bottom. "What are they keeping out?"

"Something that beat the crap out of one of his hunting parties. That seems to be all anyone knows. Kyster saw them go by; doesn't know what did it, though."

"It'd be like the Others to drop a few surprises in here with us."

"Can't see why," Torin muttered. "It's not like the Others to take prisoners."

Werst snorted. "They'd better take prisoners, Gunny. Because if this is the afterlife, I'm feeling a little fukked over."

"Yeah, you and me both." Later, she'd have to find the point where the tunnels intersected the lava flow, where Harnett had been mining his blades and . . . A sudden realization cut the thought off. "Where did the wood come from for the handles of the clubs?"

"It's not wood," Jiyuu told her, shuffling closer. "It's the mush."

Only years of experience kept Torin from reacting. "The mush?"

"If you form it when it's cooled but still wet and let it dry, it's almost unbreakable. You'd think that after eating it, you'd be shitting literal bricks, but you don't."

That was good to hear.

"The leather ties came out of the pipe, though," he continued before Torin could ask, "Sometimes it drops weird crap, Gunnery Sergeant. Like the fabric and the ties and once, once it dropped four black rubber balls. Harnett grabbed it all. The stuff he didn't use, it's all in where the food was."

"There was stuff," Werst acknowledged at Torin's look and added, "You're quite the ass kisser there, Private Jiyuu."

The di'Taykan shrugged. "I like to be helpful. I can be very helpful."

No mistaking the emphasis on the last word, particularly not when his hand rose toward his masker. Torin really hoped he wasn't stupid enough to think a shot of pheromones would make everything all better.

"Touch that masker, I'll have Corporal Werst take your hand off at the wrist," she said calmly. Jiyuu might be a suck-up and no older than Kyster, but he'd been one of Harnett's goons, and she wasn't underestimating any of them, not when it came to blatant self-interest at least.

"How . . ."

Werst snapped his teeth together.

Jiyuu's eyes darkened and his hand dropped. "The hunting parties will be returning soon," he offered, ignoring the black look Terantowicz shot him.

"Party," Torin corrected. "What tunnel?"

His smile was about fifty-fifty ingratiating and unnerved as he realized what that had to mean. "I'm guessing one of the tunnels you didn't come out of."

Terantowicz growled something under her breath.

Torin raised a hand to cut Jiyuu off and snapped, "What tunnel, Private Terantowicz!"

"Tunnel two, Gunnery Sergeant!" Eyes wide, she all but slapped a hand over her mouth when she realized what she'd done. Training had kicked in, and she'd responded instinctively.

"And tunnel two is where?"

Reluctantly, she pointed.

"Thank you, Private. All right," Torin raised her voice slightly. "Terantowicz, Jiyuu, Maekan, Akemi, and . . ."

"Phillips, Gunnery Sergeant."

". . . and Phillips, go to Staff Sergeant Pole, have him assign you to platoons."

"Platoons, Gunnery Sergeant?"

"Got extra food stored in your ears, Phillips?"

"No, Gunnery Sergeant. But aren't we . . ." He looked around at other four survivors. ". . . your prisoners?"

"No, like everyone else in this node, you're my responsibility. Most days, there's a difference. Now move. Lance Corporal Divint and Private Sergei, if you could see that they get there safely . . ."

"Yes, Gunnery Sergeant."

"What in this shithole is any danger to us?" Terantowicz muttered as they began to walk away.

"A hundred Marines you helped screw over," Divint told her.

Torin read the realization of just what that could mean from the sudden stiffening in all five backs. There were only three platoons, but the di'Taykan, likely to be shunned by the rest of their species, would need to be kept together anyway. As for the hunting party still out and the two goons plus a runner at the barricade, well, six more would mean two more in each platoon—easy enough to keep apart and still under the minimum number necessary for them to begin to feel comfortable enough to plot. With so few Krai in the infantry, there'd been a lot of research done by the wetware squad into how many of a species were needed for them to feel secure. Right now, Harnett's group was essentially another species.

"You going to hit the hunting party before they get home?" Werst asked, falling in beside her as she started for tunnel two.

"That's the idea."

"Not going to clear it with the major first?"

She should.

Before she could answer, Werst grunted a noncommittal addendum. *Never mind, stupid question,* probably came closest in translation.

If she waited to face the hunting party in the node, there was always the chance one of them would be smart enough to yell for reinforcements. Terantowicz, at least, would be right there. Stopping them out in the tunnels kept it between the four of them. Five, if Werst had to get involved although she hoped he wouldn't—these were her lives to carry out. With any luck, the hunting party would accept there'd been a change in the chain of command, and no one else would die. Torin wouldn't bet her pension on it, but a little optimism never hurt. Optimism backed by kickass hurt a lot less. Hurt *her* a lot less anyway.

Tunnel two looked exactly like tunnel four, the tunnel she and Kyster had entered the node through—ten meters with no small caves and then a corner. The corner seemed like a good place for an ambush; cut the hunting party off just out of sight of home.

As they reached the corner, the sound of six bootheels hitting rock told her she was just in time. They weren't in sight, not yet, thanks to the drunken worm layout of the tunnels, but they were very close.

"Stay here," she told Werst.

"And if you need backup, Gunny?"

"I'll yell."

His nose ridges flared. "Really?"

"Really. I've had a long day," she added when he didn't seem to believe her. As he snickered, she rounded the corner.

The boots rang louder.

The sound was intended to strike fear into anyone listening.

Or would when they got close enough to the node for anyone to hear it.

It definitely sounded less cheesy when she did it.

This hunting party consisted of two females and one male although once again two Humans and one di'Taykan. Twice as many Humans out in the tunnels explained why there seemed to be a disproportionate number of di'Taykans with Harnett in the node—not that Torin really gave a shit about species, but she preferred to have that kind of discrepancy explained. They all wore knives. Two of them had clubs. One of them had removed her sleeves.

Pity she hadn't been around to see Edwards prove why that was a really stupid idea.

They were talking about their patrol, about how boring walking the tunnels was when they found no new Marines, about the things they wanted to find on the next new Marines they found.

"I would fukking kill for a pouch of coffee."

"What, again?"

They didn't see Torin until she moved out from the tunnel wall and when they did, they stopped laughing. If she'd needed a reminder of why Harnett's people deserved to die, they'd just given her one.

"Who the hell are you?" the Human female snarled.

"I am Gunnery Sergeant Torin Kerr." Her lip curled as she noted their collar tabs. "Who the hell are you, Corporal . . . ?"

"Honisch."

"I'll have something to say about the state of your uniform later, Corporal Honisch."

Honisch glanced at her bare arms, opened her mouth . . .

"Later," Torin repeated, cutting her off. "Right now, I'm here to tell you that there's been a change in command at the node."

"Colonel Harnett . . ."

"Staff Sergeant Harnett is dead, Private . . ."

"Thurman, Gunnery Sergeant!" His cheeks flushed above the edge of his beard as he snapped out the trained response. Then he shifted into a more belligerent stance. "So you think you're in charge now?"

"Major Kenoton is the officer in charge."

Honisch snorted. "Major Kenoton is . . ."

The di'Taykan's hand on her bare arm cut her off. She stepped forward, looking young and uncertain, ocher eyes dark and locked on Torin's face. "I had a *thytrin* on Silsviss with you, Gunnery Sergeant Kerr."

Torin waited. She lost sixteen of her people on Silsviss.

"Corporal di'Merk Mysho."

Mysho had made it home.

"I saw her just before we shipped out to Gantry Three and then . . ." A graceful gesture managed to include the tunnel, the node, the entire concept of captivity. "She said no one would have survived the slaughter if it wasn't for you. She said you would have been willing to take on every giant lizard on the planet if it meant getting your platoon out alive. She said you were *der heen sa verniticna sa vey.*" Her companions stared as she drew in a long breath and came to attention, her eyes never leaving Torin's face. "I am Private di'Hern Darlys, Gunnery Sergeant. I surrender to your authority."

Torin held out her hand. "Your weapons."

"Hey," Thurman began as Darlys handed over first her club and then her knife, but Torin silenced him with a look. It had become quite clear from the moment Darlys realized who Torin was, it was no longer three goons to one gunnery sergeant but even odds, and the type of people willing to follow a man like Harnett wouldn't think much of that.

"Go to Staff Sergeant Pole; tell him I said you're to be put into platoons. No di'Taykan will be left alone," she added, answering the question before Darlys asked it. "Honisch! Thurman!" Her tone froze them in place as they started to follow the di'Taykan around the corner. "Weapons!"

"We're not giving . . ." Thurman's protest trailed off when he realized he was making it alone.

"Corporal Werst."

He strode around the corner like a Marine off a training vid. "Gunnery Sergeant Kerr!"

She handed over Darlys' club and knife. "Take charge of their weapons."

"Yes, Gunnery Sergeant!"

Neither Thurman nor Honisch were happy about it, but they obeyed the order, and that was all that mattered. The whole lot of them had been just a little too happy for just a little too long.

Torin let the three walk far enough ahead of her she could watch their body language while keeping close enough they couldn't plot without her being aware of it. Not that there was any plotting going on—Darlys hushed both her companions when they tried to speak.

"What did it mean, Gunny?" Werst asked when the hunting party was safely with Staff Sergeant Pole and no longer immediately her problem.

"What Corporal Mysho said?" Eyes narrowed, Torin watched as the three platoon sergeants came forward to claim their new people. Pole had the di'Taykans grouped under a Human sergeant. Smart move. "Roughly, that I was fit to start a family."

His nose ridges flared as he looked up at her. "That's it?"

"Roughly."

The grunt suggested he'd ask around later, and that was fine with Torin; she hadn't lied to him.

"All right . . ." She ran a hand back through her hair. ". . . that's thirteen taken care of, fourteen counting Harnett. Three to go."

"Like you said, Gunny, busy day."

"Not over yet. Kyster!"

He limped over so quickly he'd clearly been waiting for her call.

A quick flash of his teeth at Werst, then he moved between them. "Major's sleeping, Gunny."

It seemed that most of the prisoners were. Given their condition, the extra food and shuffling about into platoons had been enough to exhaust almost everyone. A quick sweep over the pallets showed mostly Krai sitting up, more or less alert. Had the Krai been supplementing? If it was even partially organic, they could digest it. The pallets of the dead, maybe?

She'd work it out later. "Who was in the hunting party that got attacked?"

Kyster glanced toward the tunnel then back at her. "Don't know, Gunny."

It took her a moment to realize that he was confused about which hunting party she meant. "The one you saw out in the tunnels. Before I arrived."

"Edwards." His teeth snapped together. "Dark pink di'Taykan."

"Jiyuu."

"And a di'Taykan with pale blue hair. Male."

There were no di'Taykan with pale blue hair among the surviving goons. "He was in the hunting party we ran into this morning?"

Kyster frowned, considering it. Finally, he said, "Yes, Gunnery Sergeant."

That left Jiyuu the only one still alive.

"Go get Private Jiyuu, Kyster. Bring him here."

"Yes, Gunnery Sergeant."

"Fuk, Gunny, good thing your body count wasn't one higher," Werst snorted as the younger Krai scurried off.

Torin raised an eyebrow in his general direction.

"If you'd offed Jiyuu, too, we'd be facing tunnel trolls with our heads up our butts."

"Tunnel trolls?"

He shrugged. "Good a name as any."

Jiyuu's eyes, when he looked at her, were so dark they'd lost nearly all their fuchsia. With all the fallen di'Taykan together, Darlys had clearly used the opportunity to pass on her *thrytin's* opinion. Jiyuu was staring at her the way the H'san stared at cheddar.

She snapped her fingers in front of her face and his focus slid in. "I need to know what attacked you out in tunnel seven, Private. What's that guard post watching for?"

"It was Edwards' fault we got beat!" Both hands rose to defensive positions. "He was an idiot. He thought they'd crawled out of the caves and come together."

"What had come together?" Jiyuu was going to need that defensive position if he didn't start making sense.

"Incomers."

She didn't need to turn, she felt Werst's expression change. Not tunnel trolls, then. "Marines?"

"Yeah, Marines. But these weren't incomers." Hair flipping back and forth in choppy fuchsia arcs, he leaned closer and lowered his voice. "They were exploring from another pipe."

Torin raised both brows, experience adjusting astonishment to look like disbelief. "Another pipe?"

"They were going to do us, Gunny!"

"Why?" Then she realized there could be only one reason. "They came on you just as you left one of the small caves. Just after you stripped a Marine of anything useful and left him to die."

"Would have died anyway." Jiyuu muttered the protest as he slid quickly back out of reach, then took two quick steps to the left as both Werst and Kyster snapped their teeth.

Forcing her fingers to uncurl, Torin took a deep breath and let it out slowly. "Have they ever come back?"

"They tried once, but we drove them off." Fingers clasped together up by his chest, Jiyuu sidled another step left. "They never came back since."

Why the hell not? Torin wondered. The Marines had to have reported what they'd seen. Their CO knew something was wrong on the other side of the barricade—how could they have allowed it to continue? "So there're three people out there, standing guard?"

"Yes, Gunnery Sergeant."

Why hadn't the other Marines attacked the barricade in force? Overwhelmed the guards, continued through the tunnels to take out Harnett? Why hadn't they dealt with this mess so that she didn't have to?

"It's about a day's walk away," Jiyuu continued ingratiatingly. "We take enough food for five days, eat one day's on the way, then we're relieved after three and have food for the walk back."

So the barricade was out about as far as Kyster's water hole and the collapsed tunnel. Since Kyster had seen the aftermath of the attack and had clearly not cut back through the node to return to the area he claimed as his, there were cross tunnels and, somewhere out in the deranged nonpattern, there was a way to get from point A to point B. Either Harnett knew the tunnels well enough to put the barricade on the far side of the cross tunnel or he'd been one lucky s.o.b. Evidence suggested the latter.

"How long before the three out there now are relieved?"

"Relief team needs to leave tomorrow morning, Gunnery Sergeant. Team that's there now, they'll be back here evening after that."

Very little time to decide what to do about it and not her decision anyway. She wished she'd had time to learn how Major Kenoton thought before presenting him with something quite so far up the scale of *could turn into a situation that's totally fukked.*

"Gunnery Sergeant Kerr? Darlys said, you were *der heen sa verniticna sa vey.*"

"What of it?"

"I've never . . . It's just you have . . . Well, it explains . . ." He took a deep breath. "What are you going to do now?"

"I'm going to send you back to your platoon and then, not that it's any of your business, I'm going to take this information to Major Kenoton."

"No. We need to maintain the barricade."

"Sir?"

"What if the other node is run by someone like Harnett, Gunnery Sergeant? Granted, you descended on this place like an avenging *nartar,* but should they attack us, there's no guarantee your luck will hold a second time."

Nartars were spirits that in Taykan mythology watched over the righteous. Translated into Human terms, the major had just referred to her as an avenging angel. Torin wasn't entirely certain how she felt about that. Kind of depended on whether *nartars* ranked gunnery sergeants.

"My luck, sir?"

"Gunnery Sergeant Kerr, you have killed eight armed insurgents today, survived a coup attempt and killed a ninth by throwing him into the disposal pit, and been proclaimed *sa verniticna sa vey*, which allowed you to take the weapons from the remaining three armed insurgents without a fight. Luck had to have something to do with that."

"Luck is nothing more than taking advantage of a situation, sir. Although, I will grant that, as I had nothing to do with it, Private Darlys' declaration was lucky."

"Indeed."

However the rank and file reacted, Major Kenoton seemed less than impressed, his eyes still not changing tone. Lieutenant Myshai, on the other hand, kept glancing over at her as if Torin were about to start a family right then and there.

"Yes, sir. However, given the reaction of those behind the barricade to Edwards and his hunting party stripping a Marine and leaving him to die, I doubt we'll have another Harnett to deal with."

"And if they were merely upset that Edwards stripped the incomer before they could?"

Torin had to admit that was a possibility.

"As I have no wish to trade the attentions of one psycho for another . . ."

It took Torin a moment to realize she was neither of the two psychos referenced.

". . . we will, for now at least, maintain the barricade."

"Yes, sir." The major had a point; it wouldn't hurt to leave the barricade staffed until they were sure. On the other hand, there was only one way to be sure. "Request permission to be part of the relief party, sir. I can do a little recon and . . ."

"No. Until we are all stronger, you're needed here."

"Sir . . ."

"No, Gunnery Sergeant. Remember, you'll have to subdue the three out there now when they arrive. Make sure they don't connect with the rest of the survivors. Make sure it doesn't . . ." His voice trailed off.

Make sure it doesn't happen again.

"Yes, sir." Once again, he had a point, and more, she should have thought of it. She wanted out so badly—and she was going nowhere until the Marines at the other pipe were dealt with one way or another—that she was losing sight of the job. "If we send three out, sir, then fifteen servings of the extra food will have to be sent with them."

Lieutenant Myshai looked a little panicked at the thought, but the major merely shrugged. "Take the loss out of every bowl. No one will notice."

"Doesn't mean fit to start a family, it means you've been named a progenitor."

Shifting through the odds and ends Harnett had tucked away in his storeroom—inventory was a time-honored military way of avoiding hard decisions—Torin snorted. "Same thing, Corporal."

"Matter of degree, Gunny. While you were getting your orders from the major . . ." Werst's tone stayed just close enough to the edge of sarcasm that Torin could ignore it. ". . . I had a little chat with Jiyuu, and I learned that being named a progenitor is the highest honor a Taykan can get."

To be able to begin a new family had sociopolitical implications that cut to the heart of the Taykan culture.

"Don't know if you noticed Werst, but I'm not a Taykan."

"They don't seem to care. And here I thought that with Private Kichar nowhere around only Kyster thought the sun shone out of your ass."

"Illumination is just part of the job, Corporal." She lifted a stack of pale blue felted paper and saw it wasn't blue all the way to the bottom. It was a third pale blue, a third pale pink, and a third pale yellow. Something about those colors . . .

"So, Gunny . . ." He squatted beside her and rubbed at the cuff of bruises around one wrist. "Harnett's asswipes aren't prisoners?"

"No. You and I are the only two Marines in here not likely to fall on our asses if attacked, so we'd be doing the guarding and we've got other things to do."

"Yeah, but if they're not prisoners, the rest'll see there's no punishment for being general all-around bastards and general all-around bastardness will increase."

"That's the major's problem."

Werst snorted.

Torin raised her head just far enough to glare at him. "Do not do that again."

"Sorry, Gunnery Sergeant." He sounded like he meant it. "You should've killed them all when you had the chance."

It would have simplified things. But she'd never admit that out loud.

Among the supplies, Harnett had managed to put together a fairly extensive first aid kit. He'd probably convinced the prisoners to hand over the few things that had come through with them for the good of the group—where convinced meant took it regardless and the good of the group referred to him and his goons. Even if every Marine in the node had only come through with one or two bits of kit, it added up.

Torin had her filters and . . .

She pulled the supplements from inside her vest. Human supplements were pale blue, di'Taykan pale pink, Krai pale yellow. She ripped off a small square of the pale blue paper, about the size of the tab she carried and let it dissolve on her tongue.

"Uh, Gunny, isn't unsupervised tasting dangerous for you lot? I mean, Humans?"

"It's supplements."

"What is?"

She flapped the paper in his general direction. "This is. That's why everyone's in such bad shape. There isn't quite enough food, but there's more than physiological deterioration seems to indicate. The Krai are in the best shape on the same amount of food, but your gut's the most adaptable."

"Harnett was hoarding."

"Yes, but the numbers don't add up. He wasn't keeping everyone weak through lack of food but through the absence of trace nutrients the food didn't have. He was denying everyone but his supporters the supplements. Add some of this to everyone's food and, provided the Others keep supplying it, they'll be back up on their feet in no time."

Werst looked around at the surrounding gray on gray of Marines on pallets and snorted. "Yay."

FIVE

THE SOUND FILLED THE NODE. It wasn't loud or unpleasant, it was just . . . omnipresent. For the approximately twenty seconds it sounded, it was impossible to think about anything but the sound.

"It's the warning for the evening meal," Staff Sergeant Pole told her in the sudden, welcome silence. Torin hadn't heard him approach. "Same sound as the morning meal. You'll get used to it after a while."

"If you say so," she muttered, resisting the urge to rub at her temples. Behind him, the sergeants had pulled two Marines from each squad and sent them to line up at the pipe. Two lines: one with two jugs to a Marine for water, one with a single jug for kibble.

It hadn't taken much to reinstate the structure of the Corps. Torin would have been happier about that if the structure hadn't crumbled so completely in the first place.

A closer look and she could see that each of the three newly formed platoons had sent one of Harnett's survivors toward the pipe.

"They're the only ones who know what to do," Pole said when she pointed it out. "Harnett's people brought the jugs out to the edge of the DMZ. No one ever went into his tent." His gaze flicked over to one of the young Marines who Harnett had been using as a plaything. "Not voluntarily anyway."

Torin fought to keep any accusation from her voice. "How are they doing?"

"Physically, superficial injuries. Nothing that won't heal, especially as they're a little better fed than the rest of us. Mentally . . ." He shrugged. "Hell, I'm not sure how the rest of us are doing mentally—in all the sitting around and waiting to starve to death, we forgot they were in there. I could remember every festival meal my mother had ever cooked, in detail, and I could lovingly linger over the memory of barbecued ribs and baked yams with syrup, but I forgot about those kids the moment the tent closed up behind them." His mouth twisted up into something that in no way resembled a smile. "You got an answer for that, Gunny?"

"Time."

"Yeah. Heals all, they say."

"Mostly they're full of shit, but about the starving to death . . ." Toirn held up the pastel pages of felted supplements. "These need to be divided into the bowls."

"What . . . ?"

"Blue to the Humans, pink to the di'Taykan . . ."

"Yellow to the Krai," he finished, reaching for them. "Supplements?"

"It looks like you've been getting enough calories . . . almost enough," she amended remembering how Harnett had been skimming the kibble. "But not enough nutrients."

The pages bent in Pole's grip. "Marines have died without these. Starved to death with enough food in their bellies. And the living lost their grip on what it meant to be Marines. On what it meant to be alive. Harnett . . ." He took a deep breath and growled, "You should have killed him slowly."

"Trust me, if I had it to do over, I would. At the moment, I'm wishing I'd put the boots to his body a few times before we dumped it." When Pole's brows rose, she grinned. "I know, would have meant nothing to him, but it would have made me feel better."

"You got to kill him," the staff sergeant reminded her pointedly. "I'll distribute these."

As he left, Kyster limped up carrying all three of the jugs they'd used for the extra feeding. "I have your bowl, Gunny," the young Krai told her, moving in close. "Major says we eat with him."

She glanced over at where the major sat in a cluster of officers.

The NCOs had their platoons, but the officers had gathered around Major Kenoton and Lieutenant Myshai. The second lieutenants, at least, needed to be assigned. If the major didn't get to it soon, she'd see that Pole suggested it. Meanwhile, she was left wondering why the major didn't want her eating with the NCOs, and the best reason she could come up with was that he wanted Kyster and Werst to go for the officers' food and the two Krai were considered hers. There were worse reasons, including a couple that slid right past paranoid to *highly* paranoid, but she decided to give him the benefit of the doubt.

"Werst."

"I'm on it, Gunny." He took one of the jugs and shoved Kyster toward the pipe with his free hand. "Move it, kid."

Time to check out the pipe.

The sound returned for a three-second count just as she reached the front of the line. Three seconds after that, a stream of kibble clattered down one of the chutes and into the first jug. Phillips went to pull it away with one portion still to be filled, but Torin closed her hand on his shoulder.

"Not anymore," she said, pitching her voice to carry along the line. "All the way to the top."

His shoulder tensed in her grip and the Marine behind him made a noise she probably wasn't even aware of making.

At the next chute, another Marine pressed the edge of his first jug to what looked like a contact point, and it filled with water. The water stopped when the jug was taken away. Although the kibble poured constantly, there were never more than one or two pieces lost in the changeover, and they were quickly claimed.

It seemed to help that she was standing there—maybe because the prisoners had been conditioned to connect food to power, maybe because they were standing in what had been Harnett's inner sanctum—so she stayed. Werst and Kyster filled their jugs last. After she checked that was, indeed, the end of the kibble, she followed them back to the major, scanning ceiling and walls of the node.

Water. Kibble with water. It tasted exactly the same as it had earlier.

"Would it have killed them to flavor the supplements?" Lieutenant Myshai wondered as she watched a pink piece of felted paper the size of her thumbnail dissolve into the mush. "I am so bored with this."

Chewing hid Torin's smile. If the lieutenant could complain about the food, things were definitely looking up.

"So have you decided who to send to the barricade, Gunnery Sergeant?" Major Kenoton asked as he slowly and methodically emptied his bowl.

"I'm still working on it, sir." Finished eating—she was less methodical and therefore faster—Torin set her bowl to one side. "Our jailers, whoever they are, are watching us."

Fingers paused, then began to rise and fall again a heartbeat later. Food continued to trump all else.

"How do you figure, Gunny?" one of the captains asked at last.

"There was exactly enough kibble dispensed—one serving per Marine present."

"Convenient," the captain allowed. Heads nodded.

Torin frowned. Convenient? Well, yes, as far as the food went, but if the Others were watching . . .

"Nothing we can do about it, Gunny," Myshai pointed out.

Granted, but . . .

She scanned the roof and walls one more time. "I haven't been able to work out *how* they're watching."

"No one's expecting you to," a second captain snorted.

Except they should have been. Still frowning, she stood and held Kyster at Werst's side with a gesture. He scowled, but he stayed. "I'd like to check out the pipe, sir."

The major looked up, his hair moving slightly but his eyes still the same mid-blue. "I'll want your suggestions before dark."

"Yes, sir."

"Take Staff Sergeant Pole with you to the pipe," he added. "Harnett kept everyone away, but he'll know more than you do."

"Sir, the staff sergeant . . ."

"Not an option, Gunnery Sergeant Kerr."

"Yes, sir."

"I wouldn't mind a closer look," Pole agreed when Torin passed on the major's orders. He started to stand, swayed, and collapsed back onto his pallet. "I'm good," he muttered, eyes closed and one hand raised to hold Torin in place. "Busy day."

Torin snorted. "Tell me about it. We can check out the pipe tomorrow. It's not like any of us are going anywhere."

He peered up at her from under dark blond brows. "I thought you had to send a party out to the barrier?"

"Fine, no one's going anywhere except for three Marines to be named later."

"It has to be three of Harnett's." Pole pulled the material of his combats out from what was left of his thighs. "No one else could walk that far."

"Divint and Sergei?"

"Not that far."

"I could."

"You're needed here."

"Werst or Kyster . . ."

"No way Kyster'd leave you, and Werst, well, you don't want your only backup out in the tunnels. And," he added while Torin considered that, "you'd still have to send two of Harnett's people with him, putting him in an unenviable position if they turn on him when they reach the barrier of five against one."

"He's Recon."

"So four to one would be no problem for him. But five?"

Werst was a tough s.o.b., but the three at the barrier would be armed.

"I'll send three of Harnett's di'Taykan. I have it on good authority that they think the sun shines out of my ass."

Pole leaned forward just enough to bring the major into his line of sight. "All of them?"

"Some of them are officers and thus blinded by the sun shining out of their own asses."

"Did you just say that?"

"Yeah." She offered him her hand. "Get over it."

His palm was cold and dry in hers, and he weighed so little she had to be careful not to haul him up onto his feet too quickly.

"You okay?"

He took a deep breath and let it out slowly. "I can fake it."

Torin let him set the pace between his pallet and the pipe, not entirely happy that Major Kenoton had insisted the staff sergeant go with her.Harnett hadn't let anyone near the pipe, so Pole wouldn't know much about the particulars. If she wanted a native guide, she'd do better with one of the surviving goons, and Jiyuu would certainly spill fast and furious, progenitor hero worship adding to his natural inclination to suck up. Not to mention, she could perform an inspection a lot faster on her own.

So why had the major wanted her to take the staff sergeant along?

It was possible, given what he'd been through, he was afraid of her gaining enough information to take Harnett's place, particularly with the lower ranks of di'Taykan thinking she could do no wrong. She'd have been insulted by his concern except that had their positions been reversed, had she experienced the privation he had, she'd have been worried about the exact same thing.

She also noticed she seemed to be analyzing every order the major gave. Picking it apart to find out how it pertained to her. Personally. That wasn't good.

Will alone seemed to be keeping Pole on his feet by the time they reached the pipe. He didn't look any worse, but then, he'd started out looking like crap. His hands had curled into fists, and his breathing came short and shallow through clenched teeth. Harnett had used extra pallets folded in thirds as chairs and Torin dragged one behind the staff sergeant's knees as he began to crumble.

From a distance, it must have looked as if he'd sat down when the option had been offered. Torin kept him from toppling backward with a hand on his shoulder, removing it when he gave her a quick nod.

"So for breakfast and supper, kibble comes from here," she said, closing the two meters between Pole and the pipe. The chute was about four centimeters in diameter, centered in the middle of an indent in the pipe clearly designed to take the jugs. It had no charge screening it, but since there were a limited number of things available to stuff up a four-centimeter-wide hole, that wasn't too surprising. "You notice we got exactly enough kibble?"

"I did."

"You know that means we're being watched."

He shrugged, a minimal movement that barely raised the sharp peaks of his shoulders inside of his combats. "Nothing we can do about it, Gunny."

"That's exactly what Lieutenant Myshai said."

"Doesn't make it wrong."

"True." Didn't make her any happier about hearing it again, though. Still, they'd only just started getting the supplements. "So the kibble comes out here, what about the biscuits at lunch?"

"No idea. Harnett's goons brought jugs of them out to the DMZ." Head cocked, Pole leaned forward and squinted into the indent, then made a circle with the forefinger and thumb on his left hand, a circle about four centimeters across, and put the first two fingers of his right hand up through it.

Torin raised a brow.

"Biscuits fit in the chute," he explained, repeating the motion.

"I can never keep up with the new slang," Torin snorted and moved on to examine the water delivery as he snickered.

This second indent looked essentially the same as the first except there was a pressure point on the back curve. Frowning slightly, Torin set her thumb against the pad. Cold water poured over her wrist.

"Did Harnett tell you that this was only active while the food was being dispensed?" she asked, watching the water drain away through pinprick holes.

"He didn't tell us anything, but that's the only time we got water."

Torin pushed the pad again. The same thing happened. "There's water available whenever we want it."

Pole shook his head. "Just because it's on now . . ."

"No, it was on while we ate the first of the stored food." She flicked drops off her hand, noted the darker gray-on-gray pattern the splatter made on the floor of the node. "You're all conditioned to water with food, so you didn't make the connection."

"So we can drink whenever we're thirsty?"

The staff sergeant sounded so amazed Torin spent a moment imagining killing Harnett slowly before answering. "Yeah, looks like."

About a meter farther around the pipe was a larger indentation, essentially an alcove—two and a half meters high, two thirds of a meter deep. There was a raised ring the same color as the pipe in the top of the alcove, and along the front of the bottom was a ridge about five centimeters high. It looked like . . .

"Staff, how was personal hygiene handled?"

Pole snorted. "Handled? Harnett's lot would come out with jugs of hot water, pick a few prisoners, strip 'em and sluice 'em down. But then, you don't get real dirty when you're sitting around starving to death."

"I think this is a shower."

"You think?"

Gunnery Sergeants didn't think; they knew. "Only one way to find out."

Pole hauled himself up onto his feet. "You calling for volunteers, Gunny?"

"Since I trust the Others about as far as I can spit a rat, no." She dragged over a rolled pallet, rolled it tighter, and set it in the alcove. The floor gave under the weight, exposing a drain along the back edge, while the ring pushed farther out of the ceiling and began to spray water. "Smell's off," Pole noted as Torin caught some of the water in her palm.

She touched her tongue to it. "There's disinfectant in this."

Approximately a minute of disinfectant, a minute of rinse. Then it shut off. The pallet had absorbed none of the water, drops beading up off the surface when Torin tossed it out onto the floor and let it unroll.

"Two-minute showers. Every platoon could go under say, once every three afternoons. Officers and NCOs in the mornings. We could set a piece of that smart fabric up like a screen . . ."

Torin could see Pole drawing up schedules in his head, and she smiled as she moved around the pipe. As the prisoners regained their strength, both physical and mental, they'd need things to do, and lining up for showers was a long-standing tradition of the Corps.

Bitching about lining up for showers had been going on for almost as long.

The next alcove was about the same size but had no pressure plate and no showerhead. She could almost get her fingernail into a crack around the outside of the alcove ceiling so assumed this was the place where pallets, the smart fabric, and the other odds and ends Harnett hoarded had dropped from.

The remaining arc of the pipe was smooth, unmarked metal. Torin ran her fingernails over it just to be sure. Metal. Not plastic. Past experience had taught her not to trust that particular shade of gray. Remembering that the hatches leading out of Big Yellow's replica of the dirtside warehouse had looked and felt like metal didn't help.

"Gunny?"

"Just feeling a little paranoid, Staff."

"Part of the job."

"That's what they tell me." Turning away from the pipe, she could see the stack of pallets where Harnett had slept. Fortunately, there were four of them, so there'd be three for her and Werst and Kyster with the top one left over—none of them would have to sleep directly on the same pallet Harnett had.

There was little available to make his private quarters opulent, but he'd done what he could. Besides the bed, there were two other pallets folded into chairs, two water jugs—one of them clearly for pissing into—and a scattering of things that had to have been taken off incoming Marines.

"Son of a fukking bitch . . ."

"A little hard on his mother," Torin heard Pole murmur as she ran for Harnett's quarters. She hadn't been mistaken. It was a slate. Impossible to tell whose or what it had on it but she felt better just holding it in her hand and, as much as she hated to admit it, she completely understood why Harnett had kept it close.

"None of the tech works," Pole reminded her, sinking down onto one of the chairs, breathing heavily. "It's all been completely drained of power, and there's no way to get it running again."

Torin just barely managed to keep herself from stroking the housing as she snapped the slate onto her vest. "If all we need is power, then there has to be a way to recharge."

"Because you say so, Gunny?"

"Because the lights are running on something."

Pole glanced up at the high ceiling. "Can't reach the lights."

"We can in the tunnels."

"All right, you can touch the lights, maybe even tap their power, how do you use it to recharge the slate?"

"I have no idea," Torin snorted. "I'm no tech. But there's a hundred Marines gathered around this pipe; odds are good there's one with the skills we need."

"A hundred Marines out of the hundreds of thousands available and you think those are good odds?"

She smiled at him then. "I've had worse."

"Okay. But speaking of your power source, we need to get that second extra feeding started if we're going to do it tonight. The lights won't stay on much longer." He stood, stepped forward, swayed, and would have fallen had Torin not caught him.

Strange to hold a man with so little flesh on his bones, to feel the ridges of his spine, the blade of his hip. Craig was . . . muscular. Burly even. Heavy, working muscle she could test her own strength against. They'd have told him she was dead. They—everyone—believed the Others didn't take prisoners.

"Gunny?"

She hurriedly schooled her expression. Pole's tone had been too kind; her thoughts had to have been showing on her face. "Sorry."

"Not a problem." His hands closed around her wrist, and she realized she still had an arm around his waist. "But we're going to have to stop meeting like this or people will start to talk."

"Start?" Torin found a fairly believable laugh as she carefully released him. "I can't get people to shut the fuk up . . ."

"There are not being much of a story there." Presit speared a piece of fruit out of her drink and popped it into her mouth. "The Others are having used a big weapon, and our side are having lost," she continued after swallowing when Craig remained silent. "I are having seen the military vids, and the ground are being flat and glassy. Flat and glassy are not looking exciting on vids."

"And you think that's all there is to the story, then?" Craig asked, using his beer bottle to make interlocking circles of condensation on the tabletop. "So the military word is dead set to you now; you never used to believe them."

The reporter shrugged, the motion sending highlights rippling once again through her dark fur. "The law are insisting they are giving full disclosure. So unless you are knowing a reason they are hiding something . . . ?"

He didn't. He looked around the bar, kept dim because of the number of Katrien at the tables and in the booths, and saw no reasons there either. "You used to believe they were always hiding something."

"I are knowing what you are doing," she sighed. "You are wanting to go and be seeing where Gunnery Sergeant Kerr are dying . . ."

"I'm not . . ."

". . . but the military are not allowing civilians to the site. Full disclosure laws are meaning they are not keeping me away, so you are coming to me." She speared another piece of fruit and paused with it halfway to her mouth. "I are owing you a little bit . . ." Thumb and forefinger on her other hand were close enough together that the silvered claws nearly touched. ". . . for the story on the gray plastic alien, and I are willing to do this for you if you are finding me a story there. So far, you are wasting my time." The piece of fruit disappeared behind sharp white teeth with a bit more emphasis than Craig thought was merited.

"Parliament has sent in a team to do DNA testing at the site . . ."

"No one are wanting to watch DNA testing."

". . . to identify the remains . . ."

"There are being no remains. Remains are interesting."

". . . before the Others return."

"There are being a chance the Others will return?"

He had no idea. He just needed to see the place where Torin had died. "That was the impression the Commandant of the Corps tried not to give me when I was on Ventris."

"Why are the Commandant of the Corps talking to *you*?"

Clearly, breaking the story on the gray plastic aliens hadn't been enough for Presit to gain further access to High Tekamal Louden, and it was pissing her off a bit. Not that it was particularly difficult to piss Presit off. "I used her name to access sections of the station off limits to visitors. She tracked me down to tell me not to do it again."

"Ah." Presit sat back in her chair and ran her claws through her whiskers. "And then you are all being friends and she are giving you privileged information?"

"We were talking about Torin. Her father—Torin's father—he was there, too."

"And there are being drinking? Of alcohol?"

"There are . . . was."

"Humans are talking about everything when they are drinking alcohol. I are noticing that in the past." She combed her whiskers again. "A chance to be getting actual footage of the Others invading while there are only helpless scientists attempting to be bringing closure to the grieving, that are being something I can use."

Craig found it amazing that it hadn't occurred to her she'd be just as helpless as those scientists in case of an attack, but since he needed her to get the coordinates for the Susumi equations from the military, he didn't point that out.

"You are wanting to be my crew?"

"I've done it before, haven't I?" No point in adding that since the camera did most of the work, it wasn't exactly a difficult job. Presit, yeah, she was difficult. The job, not so much.

"And you are offering your ship for transport?"

"I'm sure as shit not leaving her here." Hiring her out to Sector Central News would cover his costs.

Black lips curled up off Presit's teeth. "And you are realizing I are being your boss for the duration?"

He lifted his bottle and tried not to think of a planet's surface melted like glass. "I can cope if you can."

Torin sent Darlys, Jiyuu, and Akemi to the barricade carrying sleeves of kibble skimmed from the morning feeding, a canteen each, and two eight-liter jugs of water hanging off a yoke made from the smart fabric.

The major had seemed resigned to her choices.

The two biscuits in the middle of the day tasted a bit like the jerked yeast she'd had in the barbecue place next to the recruiting station high above Paradise. She hadn't thought of that place, or the recruiting station, in years.

"You don't want to know, Gunny," Werst snorted when she asked him what he tasted. "You really don't."

Something in his tone convinced her she didn't.

That afternoon, she sent Werst and Divint, Kyster and Sergei out into the tunnels to check the small caves for new Marines. Tunnel three was nearly a direct route to a wall of obsidian, the remnant of an ancient lava flow, but the other six had to be covered.

"Colonel Harnett had a schedule based on the pattern of arrivals he'd observed," Terantowicz sneered. "Should've thought of that before you killed him."

"I'd have killed him if he'd had a foolproof plan to get us all out of here," Torin told her with a smile.

She blanched and backed away.

Torin spent a moment regretting that Terantowicz had convinced Bakune to attack her at the pit rather than doing it herself.

New supplement sheets dropped out of the pipe the next morning. Torin suggested they station a Marine at the pipe with one of the clubs, ready to jam the hatch open the next time something dropped. Major Kenoton seemed less than enthused but allowed her to give the order to Pole.

"Can't see Harnett not having tried this," Pole pointed out.

"He may have," Torin allowed, "but that doesn't mean we can't."

The next evening Torin met the last three of Harnett's goons out in the tunnels. Two Humans and a di'Taykan who stared at Torin as though he were trying to figure out if it was true—where *it* could mean only one thing. The Humans just stared, one of them trying to figure out if they could take her.

"No, you can't," she told the younger woman wearily.

"I wasn't . . ."

Torin raised a brow, and Private Malan fell silent. So far, things were going well.

Which was, of course, when Lance Corporal Zhang Yadong, the second Human, charged her. Torin twisted, grabbed his arm above the elbow, and continued his forward momentum into the rock wall. Her desire to kill him was so strong it frightened her a little—a long time since anything had done that—and she barely managed to make sure his skull impacted with less than lethal force. When he flipped over, blood streaming into his eyes, Torin put a boot on his throat before he could rise. "Stay down!" she snapped.

He could have grabbed her ankle and taken advantage of the way she stood, balanced with her weight on one foot. She would have. But he stayed down.

Malan was staring with her mouth open in shock—or awe, it was hard to say—and the di'Taykan had a visible erection.

"Private Waturu." Experience kept her from adjusting her clothes. She'd been a lot more uncomfortable for the same reason.

"Yes, Gunnery Sergeant!" He leaned toward her, lime-green eyes dark.

"Turn up your masker."

"It's at the regulation mark, Gunnery Sergeant."

"Then you're obviously overpowering it. Turn it up."

"It's not my fault; you're *der heen sa verniticna sa vey.*"

With a Human, Torin would have moved into their personal space. Di'Taykan, particularly di'Taykan as aroused as Wataru seemed to be, were likely to take that the wrong way. Teeth gritted, grateful she was female, Torin growled, "Does it say progenitor on my collar tabs?"

"No, Gunnery Sergeant!"

"I don't give a rat's ass whose fault it is; turn your masker up!"

His erection looking suddenly less visible, he did as commanded. Malan looked grateful.

Torin nodded down at Zhang as she lifted her foot from his throat and stepped back. "On your feet, Corporal. It's almost time for evening mush, and I get cranky if I miss a meal."

"I'm bleeding."

"But you're alive, so I'd say the cup is half full. Hand your weapons to Corporal Werst . . ." He rounded the corner on cue. ". . . then go and get your platoon assignments from Staff Sergeant Pole."

"And that's it?" Malan asked suspiciously as she handed Werst her stone knife.

"As far as *I'm* concerned," Torin told her.

"So you're in charge?"

"Major Kenoton is in charge." Torin stepped aside to let her pass. "Try to stay out of trouble."

"That's not it," Werst muttered as they watched the last three of Harnett's survivors head into the node.

"Tell me something I don't know, Corporal."

"Di'Taykan tastes like chicken."

"Didn't *need* to know that."

The noise in the node had changed in just two days as more and more Marines shook off the listlessness that had kept them lying silent and gray on their pallets. It wasn't the supplements, not in only fifty-six hours. It was, Torin believed, the normalcy of routine, of organization they understood, of a visible chain of command. And all that would go to hell if she had to save them again. At some point, people had to start saving themselves.

The next morning, they found Staff Sergeant Kem Takahani dead on her pallet.

"She was pushing seventy," Pole said quietly as he rose carefully to his feet. "Heading toward becoming one of those grizzled old sergeants who'd found their niche and had every intention of staying there until retirement forced her out. She was one of the first taken, and I'm a little surprised she lasted this long. She had a broken face and was pissing blood when I got here," he explained as Torin raised a brow. "Couldn't stand straight—something with her spine. She fought Harnett and paid for it." He glanced down at the body, one cheekbone flatter than the other, her hands so thin the veins stood out under the skin like blue-gray cord, and he smiled. "She used to lie there and mutter over and over, *bastard'll get his*. When you brought his walls down, and there he was, lying dead, head on backward, she said, 'I told you so.' " He frowned. "I don't remember her speaking again. That may have been the last thing she said."

"As last words go, they're not so bad." Torin glanced across the node at the knot of officers. "I'll tell the major."

The warning for the morning meal came as they were sliding Sergeant Takahani and her pallet into the pit. Torin touched the pockets on her vest where the capsuled remains of her Marines should go and tried not to grind her teeth.

"I half expected you to bitch a bit more after the funeral about the waste of food."

"No point, Gunny," Werst grunted. "What the hell do you think the kibble is made of?"

Torin paused with a fingerload of mush halfway to her mouth. "There hasn't been enough . . ."

"No. But it's in there, and in the biscuits. Can't miss the taste."

Torin glanced over at Kyster, who nodded as he chewed. "And the Krai who've been here all along?"

"They know," Werst told her. "No way they couldn't know. But they're not going to say anything. You lot are touchy about meat."

"We're touchy about being considered meat," Torin corrected. "And if this was what I didn't want to know, why tell me now?"

"Kyster told me what you said out in the tunnels. How this is a way to carry our people out with us. Very Krai for a Human. I was impressed. And . . ." He licked a bit of mush off his fingers. "There's no way of knowing what information is necessary to break out of here, so it's best you have all of it."

"I'm planning a breakout?"

"Aren't you?"

Wasn't she?

"It's been a busy few days. Can I have a minute to catch my breath?"

Werst snorted. "The Staff Sergeant Kerr I know would have been out of here by now." He set his empty bowl aside and grinned at the other Krai. "You should've seen the gunny when she was a staff sergeant, Kyster. Now that was a Marine."

Kyster's lips curled up off his teeth and his nose ridges clamped shut. "I think she's amazing," he snarled.

"You're young."

"Kyster!" Torin's tone sat him back down so quickly his teeth snapped. "It's all right, Corporal Werst is just being a pain in the ass. Ignore him."

"But he . . ."

"All he said was that when I was a staff sergeant I was a good Marine. He didn't say I wasn't a good Marine now."

"But . . ."

"Let it go."

After a long moment, Kyster covered his teeth. "Yes, Gunnery Sergeant."

The thing was, Werst was right. She'd been so caught up in the drama, she hadn't thought of escape in days. Sliding her hand into her vest, she touched the salvage tag. That had to change.

"What the hell is going on here?" Torin grabbed the corporal by the collar of her combats and yanked her back. Maybe, given their relative conditions, she was rougher than she needed to be, but she was pissed.

"This doesn't concern you, Gunny." The corporal staggered but managed to stay on her feet. "This is a fireteam matter."

"Really? Because I could have sworn I heard you call this Marine a whore."

"He was fucking for food, Gun . . . nery Sergeant." Torin's expression made the diminutive a bad idea. "That makes him a whore in my book."

"Was it his choice?"

The Marine in question, young enough that his auburn whiskers were sparse on his cheeks, closed hazel eyes, eyelashes lying in a thick fringe against his cheek. He still had bruises around both wrists and a band around his throat turning purple and green where the collar and leash had been.

"He didn't fight. Just like he's not fighting now." Like Staff Sergeant Pole, the corporal was missing teeth. A common enough result of malnutrition. Torin fought down the urge to knock out a few more.

"Use the brains the gods gave you and look at his hands. He fought." The knuckles were swollen and bruised, a couple probably broken. Torin shifted her grip to the front of the corporal's combats and dragged her so close they were breathing in the same hot, stale air redolent of mush. "There were seventeen of them, and the bruising on his body says they beat him for fun." She didn't need to add what else had happened *for fun.* "Seventeen to one odds—how well would you do, Corporal? I see a hundred to seventeen odds, I see one hundred of you and three of your own being tortured, and you didn't do a Goddamned thing, so before you say another fukking word to this Marine, you make sure there aren't a few choice words he could call you."

The corporal's pupils were dilated, and she was breathing in short, terrified bursts.

Torin shook her one more time, hard enough for her to flop within her combats like a rag doll, and released her. "We will *not* have this conversation again."

There was the sudden, sharp smell of urine as the corporal pissed herself in fear. Torin ignored it, turning to touch the young private gently on the arm. His head ducked down as if he were bracing for a blow, but he opened his eyes. "Walk with me, Private . . . ?"

"Graydon, Gunnery Sergeant, 6th Division, 3rd Recarta, 2nd Battalion, Sierra Company." His voice had been roughened by the pressure on his throat, the vowels softened by a soft drawl she couldn't place.

"Private Graydon . . . we need to talk."

He was taller than she was, broad shoulders, much of his height in his torso rather than his legs. Like Craig, she realized and forced her thoughts in another direction. He walked with a limp, curled in on himself, trying to make his size seem less of a threat. He was so damned young it hurt her to look at him. "You came off Crucible, your unit was deployed, and you were taken in your first fight?"

"Yes, Gunnery Sergeant." He sounded surprised. Not the question he'd expected.

"You need to bring the surviving Marines who served Harnett up on charges."

"I what?"

"I killed them to stop them from doing what they were doing, but I can't just kill them because of what they did." Although she found herself wishing she'd slammed Corporal Zhang's skull into the rock so hard his brains had painted the tunnel. "We're all Marines here; we have to remember that and, when Marines do what they did, they're dealt with by the Corps. You, and the others, bring them up on charges, and Major Kenoton will see that they're dealt with."

"Why can't you do it?"

Her hands were curled into fists so tight that, within them, her fingers ached. "I wasn't here."

They walked halfway around the node, slowly, quietly. Graydon was thin, flesh skimmed over bones, but he'd clearly been getting at least some supplements.

"I'd have to tell what they did," he said at last.

"Yes." It wasn't a question, but Torin answered it anyway.

"It was easier when the di'Taykan turned their maskers down."

She'd never heard of a di'Taykan taking an unwilling partner, but she supposed there were bastards in every species.

Something of the thought must have shown on her face because Graydon gave a short, humorless bark of laughter. "You're not unwilling, then, and you enjoy it. We were grateful to the di'Taykan."

"But they weren't always there."

"No." His turn to answer what wasn't a question.

"It wasn't your fault."

"And I'd tell you it wasn't your fault either, Gunny, but we both know you'd believe that here . . ." One hand pressed against the fabric over his heart. ". . . as much as I do."

"Charges, Gunnery Sergeant?"

"Yes, sir."

The major shifted slightly on the folded pallet as though searching for a spot where he still had enough flesh to cushion his tailbone. "And when they are found guilty, how do you expect me to punish them?"

Torin took the moment she needed to keep from saying, *You could drop them in the disposal pit* and said, "That's not for me to say, sir."

"As I just asked, I think it is."

"You could begin by reducing their rank."

"I'm sure that will make a huge difference while we're imprisoned."

"Yes, sir."

"Don't be deliberately obscure, Gunnery Sergeant, it's annoying. Say what you mean."

"Marines have a clearly defined rank structure, sir. If we're Marines while we're imprisoned, then to knock Harnett's survivors down to the bottom of that rank structure is at least a beginning."

"But where do we go from there, that's the question." Major Kenotan sighed, and his hair swept languidly from front to back. "Still, it will give everyone something to focus on, something to keep us from slipping back into . . ." The pause extended almost too long. ". . . bad habits. Captain Allison was a lawyer before he got his commission. I'm sure he can convene a disciplinary court."

"You might consider asking the three Marines who'll be laying the charges what they'd consider a suitable punishment, sir."

The major looked up at her, and for the first time since Torin had handed over the command, his eyes changed color, darkening slightly as he studied her face. Not for the first time, Torin wondered how much he could actually see. "You think I might consider that?"

"Yes, sir."

He drained his bowl and very nearly smiled. "You're an extraordinarily bloody-minded individual, Gunnery Sergeant."

"Yes, sir."

"The question now becomes: What do we do with you?"

She'd been half expecting this.

"Although Corporal Werst seems to have a fairly balanced

opinion—and whether that's in spite of or because of your history I have no idea," he continued—"the Krai seem to be following young Kyster's lead. Most of the di'Taykan . . ." A quick glance toward Lieutenant Myshai, who wasn't even pretending not to hover just beyond eavesdropping range. ". . . expect you to begin that family line here and now. As far as the Humans are concerned, well, you're one of theirs. And, over all, you're Gunnery Sergeant Torin Kerr—you defeated the Silsviss, you outwitted Big Yellow, you exposed a new alien threat, and you marched in here and single-handedly saved us from starving to death under Harnett's gentle care."

He hadn't known about Big Yellow or the new alien threat three days ago.

"I've been hearing stories, Gunny." His eyes lightened again although the difference was minimal. "There's quite the cult of personality developing around you."

Force of personality had put Harnett in power.

The warning came through loud and clear.

"I think we need to get you out of here, Gunnery Sergeant." More than anything, he sounded weary.

"Yes, sir." Torin was one hundred percent behind getting out. "There's a rockfall out the end of tunnel four. We need to find out what's on the other side of it."

The ends of his hair flicked back and forth, the movement dismissive. "More tunnels."

"That's possible, sir. But my gut tells me it's also the way out."

"Your gut tells you?"

Maybe not the best body part to bring up to a man who'd just been more than half starved. "Yes, sir."

"Are you planning an escape, Gunny?"

"Yes, sir." Although, so far, there wasn't much of a plan beyond clearing the rock away.

"Not what I meant when I said we need to get you out of here." The major stared down at the back of his left hand for a moment, watching his right thumb stroke across the loose skin. "These are your orders, then," he said when he finally looked up. "You're to go out to the barricade with the next group. As part of the next group," he amended before she could speak. "Food for three is quite enough to skim."

"Sir?"

"Go beyond the barricade," the major continued as though they'd been discussing a trip to the barricade all along. "Make contact with the other group of Marines. If they're in the situation we were in, well, you can use your overabundance of personality to save them. If, however, they're having as pleasant a time as is possible under the circumstances, let them know that our situation has changed. I will want to speak with their CO; however, there's no rush. It's not as if either of us are going anywhere. Return with your group if you can, if not . . ." He shrugged.

"Sir . . ."

"Yes. Your escape plan." He went back to staring at his hands. "Who knows, they may have escape plans of their own. Or," he added quietly as the skin folded under his caress, "you can refuse a direct order and do what you want. I'm sure Corporal Werst and Private Kyster and all of Harnett's surviving di'Taykan will go with you to help clear rocks." It didn't sound as though he cared.

The question was, did Torin?

"I'll leave for the barricade in the morning, sir."

Apparently, she did.

Torin fought the urge to tell Werst that he was in charge while she was gone. Not because she didn't believe Staff Sergeant Pole was doing his best, but because Werst was carrying a lot less baggage than anyone who'd been in the node under Harnett's care—although starvation-induced lethargy seemed to be keeping a lid on what should have been a powder keg.

"Why take Kyster?" Werst demanded as she adjusted the rope holding the sleeve full of kibble on her shoulder.

"Fuk you," Kyster muttered, close enough to hear.

"Fuk you, Lance Corporal," the older Krai corrected smugly. "What about his foot, Gunny?"

"Didn't slow us down walking here."

"You think he'll follow you if you don't take him?"

Kyster's body language made it obvious that was exactly what he'd do.

"He'll follow you over the fukking barricade," Werst pointed out.

"I'll deal with that at the barricade." It was a long walk; she had a whole day to come up with something.

Harnett had assigned six of the eight two-liter canteens he'd retrieved off incoming prisoners to the hunting parties on the barricade. Torin had found the other two in Harnett's stores, both bloodstained but intact—four liters meant two days out, two days back. She had twelve biscuits tucked into the pockets of her vest, traded for the biscuits she'd be missing while she was gone.

"So why do you have to go?" Werst asked.

"Major's orders, Corporal." Torin looked out over the prisoners—Marines—and shook her head, although at what, exactly she wasn't sure. "And if I don't, well, I'm just a little concerned I'm going to kill someone."

His nose ridges opened and closed, and his expression suggested that her killing someone would be no surprise. That was one of the things she was concerned about.

"Still plenty who need killing," he reminded her.

"It might not be one of them."

That was the other.

"Ah." He stood quietly for a moment, arms folded. "Why not me?"

"You were one of them, if only for a short while, and besides, Terantowicz will likely try something the moment I'm gone. You can . . ."

"Wer tayner chrick ca keeteener amick."

She snorted. "If you can find a nice red sauce, go for it."

They left just after the morning meal, Watura and Kyster to remain at the barricade while she went on. In another three days Divinit and Sergei might be strong enough to make the trip, but for now she was still forced to rely on Harnett's di'Taykan.

Who had been complicit in the abuse of three Marines.

Just like the hundred who did nothing, her subconscious insisted on adding. Intellectually, she understood why force of numbers didn't apply. There had been thousands of Silsviss surrounding that supply station. Thousands of Silsviss against most of one platoon and half a dozen diplomats. Numbers had not given the Silsviss the victory. Emotionally, however . . .

In an effort to keep her thoughts from circling around and around like scavengers over a battlefield, she worked out the logistics of clearing the rockfall. Worked out how much food she'd need if she used Harnett's survivors in shifts. Manual labor was a traditional Corps punishment.

She'd consider conscripting a few heavy gunners had they come through with their exoskeletons, but with nothing plugged into their implanted contact points, they were no more capable of moving rock than any other Marine.

Traveling through the tunnels screwed with Torin's time sense. The light never varied, and the rock had very little gradation in color. Number seven tunnel had fewer of the minor caves than number four, and she mentally mapped them against the positions of the equally smaller number of cross tunnels. Watura and Kyster had a small argument at each cross tunnel concerning where it went and how it got there. About half the time they were unable to come to an agreement, and Torin sided with Kyster. Survival was a better teacher than the occasional patrol.

Otherwise, they didn't talk much; Kyster had grown used to keeping his own counsel, and Torin didn't feel like chatting. Watura was either too much in awe of her progenitor status to attempt conversation or, hopefully, smarter than he looked. Since he didn't seem to be in awe, she reluctantly granted him the second option.

They ate mush when Kyster said it was midday. When Watura demanded to know how he knew, Kyster showed his teeth and said, "Half the light is gone." Since they had no other way of judging time besides their bellies, and bellies were notoriously inaccurate, Torin took his word for it.

A couple of hours, give or take, after mush and Watura waved at a cross tunnel. "Last one, Gunnery Sergeant Kerr."

" 'Swhere I saw the hunting party come back. Beaten," Kyster added cheerfully.

"Tunnel goes straight after this," Watura continued, ignoring him.

"So the prison is set up as two separate territories with a link between them. Maybe more than two," Torin corrected thoughtfully. "There could be an infinite number of nodes strung out like beads on a necklace." The string had broken at the rockfall by Kyster's water supply. Were there more nodes beyond? "Why did Harnett send you out this far?"

"He was extending his perimeter to the limits of the canteens— one liter for the day out, one for the day back. Edwards said they got jumped on the second day. Other than that, I don't know. I wasn't there."

Didn't matter, Jiyuu was at the barricade, and if she needed more details than he'd already spilled, she had no doubt the youngest di'Taykan would be happy to oblige.

"How long ago did it happen?"

"Damned if I know, Gunnery Sergeant." Watura raised his left arm with its dead cuff. "My calender's completely fukked."

"Kyster?"

"More than thirty days, Gunny. Less than sixty."

He sounded so definite she didn't smile at the thirty day margin of error. "The other group only approached the barricade that one time?"

"Yeah, just once." Watura's hair flipped back and forth. "Some say they've seen people moving in the distance, but I never have. It's pretty fukking creepy at night, though."

The barricade had been made of rock pulled from the smaller caves and piled across the tunnel. More of a territorial statement than a deterrent against a determined assault—particularly when the only missile weapons were more rocks—it was waist-high on Torin, a little lower on the di'Taykan, and about eye level for Kyster. He peered over it, grunted, and backed up to sit against the tunnel wall and rub his bad foot.

Darlys, Jiyuu, and Akemi seemed pleased to see her and would have included her in the welcome they gave Watura had she not raised a warning hand.

Later, over bowls of mush and supplement, she looked toward

Jiyuu tucked up tight against Watura's side, jerked her head over the barricade, and said, "I want a full report on what happened the day you met the others . . ." She frowned. "The other Marines. I want the details. Everything you remember."

"I told you . . ."

"Your report was short on detail."

He sighed and turned his bowl between his hands. "We stopped just past here; maybe another hour, it's hard to tell." His eyes lightened to pale pink as he glanced around the tunnel and shrugged. "It all looks the same. After dark, we decided not to get entirely naked because Edwards . . ."

Torin raised a hand. "Skip those particular details."

"But . . ."

Her patience had frayed beyond allowing for species idiosyncrasies. "You know how to give a sitrep, Private. Stop screwing around."

The hair of all four di'Taykan momentarily stilled. When Jiyuu began speaking again, his voice had lost some of its ingratiating tone.

"Next morning, Edwards figured we should go a little farther before we turned. Even if we got caught in the dark, we'd be nearly back to the node and we could easily go the rest of the way without light."

Possibly but not easily; not unless they'd reached that last ten meters of straight tunnel.

"We got just past where the tunnels started to twist again . . ."

On the other side of the barricade, the tunnel looked like it ran straight for about a kilometer.

". . . and at the first small cave . . ." Jiyuu paused, his hand rising to his masker.

"Lower it," Torin snapped. "Making me horny won't make me any less angry about this. At the first small cave you found a new Marine."

"We heard moaning," Jiyuu admitted. "Edwards went in, and a while later he came out wiping his hands . . ."

"Killed him or robbed him. Left him to die," Kyster growled when the di'Taykan paused again. "Not too fukking gentle about it, neither. I found some of the guys you left. I *was* one of the guys you left!"

"We didn't leave you . . ."

Kyster snapped his teeth together, and Akemi jumped. "Fukking dumped me!"

Darlys shook her head, ocher hair spreading with the motion. "If we hadn't done what Harnett said, someone else would have."

"Do not give me that crap." Torin's voice slapped the di'Taykan's hair flat, even as she closed her hand around Kyster's arm and held him in place. They stared at her, all four of them breathing hard, their eyes dark. "Let's be clear about this. There are no excuses for what you did. Young and stupid isn't an excuse. Fear isn't an excuse. If I had killed you all when I took the node back from Harnett, I would be feeling no remorse." She took a deep breath. "You did what you did. All you can do now is take responsibility for it."

"Der heen sa verniticna sa vey." The Taykan phrase pushed Darlys into formal cadences. "We are truly sorry for what we have had a part in."

"Because a progenitor caught you at it or because it was wrong?"

She spread her hands, hair spreading out again. "Were it not wrong, it would not matter that you had caught us at it."

"You shouldn't have needed me to tell you it was wrong. You were complicit in the death of fellow Marines. You were complicit in the abuse of fellow Marines. You were complicit in the slow starvation of fellow Marines."

"We didn't know about the supplements, Gunnery Sergeant," Akemi protested.

Torin realized she was still holding Kyster's arm, released him, and scrubbed a hand over her face. What a fukking mess. Maybe she *should* have disobeyed Kenoton's order and headed straight for the rock wall because the only thing that was going to fix the mess was getting her people out.

All her people. Every fukking Marine down here.

And that put her right back at the barricade.

"Gunny?"

"Just trying to keep from beating my head against the wall. You'd got to the point where Edwards had come out of the cave," she prodded Jiyuu. "Go on."

Jiyuu looked down at the last of his mush and pushed it across to Kyster—who pushed it back. Offering food to a Krai had—could have—ceremonial significance. Torin didn't know Jiyuu was aware of it, but from the way his hair flattened, she suspected he was. She appreciated the attempt but had no sympathy for the rejection.

"Edwards came out with a first aid kit. Just a combat kit, but we hadn't had one of those in a while, and he knew Harnett would be pleased, so he decided it was time to head back. We hadn't gone more than thirty meters when four . . ."

"Marines." Torin dropped the word into the extended pause.

"Yes, Gunnery Sergeant. Four Marines came up on us from behind. We never even heard them coming."

Torin raised a brow, and his hair flattened again.

"We were making a bit of noise, joking around."

About a fellow Marine they'd just left for dead.

"They didn't have weapons—I don't think they had weapons—but there were four of them and only three of us."

Kyster snorted

"Edwards yelled they were just incomers who'd banded together. They had an officer with them, a lieutenant. He told us to surrender, but Edwards told him to fuk off. And he kept telling them to fuk off until they started beating the shit out of us. When we ran, they didn't follow us. We got back and told Colonel . . . Staff Sergeant Harnett, and he ordered the barricade." The flip of his hair reminded her she knew the rest.

Anything else she needed to know, she'd have to find out from the other Marines.

Darlys turned her bowl around and around, the movement oddly similar to the way the major had rubbed at his hand. "What are you going to say if you find them, Gunnery Sergeant?"

"That depends on who I find."

When the lights went out, the di'Taykan made themselves comfortable on one side of the tunnel while she and Kyster bedded down on the other. Later, when soft noises made it obvious what they were doing in the dark—although Torin gave them points for keeping the noise down—Kyster said quietly, "You could forbid it."

She could, but they weren't on watch, and the tunnel was so dark it couldn't be said they were showing interspecies insensitivity. But mostly she didn't forbid it because it would be petty behavior on her part, and that was a line she wasn't ready to cross.

Deadly behavior, not a problem.

Petty was an entirely different thing.

"You could join them, Gunny."

"So could you." The di'Taykan were firm believers in the more the merrier.

Kyster snapped his teeth together. "I'd rather eat my own *dirr* on a bun."

"Well, I wouldn't go that far, not having a *dirr*, but I'm not joining them either."

Waking with the return of the light, Torin found Kyster holding her wrist with his good foot and pulled gently free without rousing him.

The breakfast mush tasted sharper. She wondered if the flavor changed as it aged.

"Straight back to the node," she told the three di'Taykan before they left. "Debrief immediately with Staff Sergeant Pole."

"Yes, Gunnery Sergeant."

Darlys paused, half turned. "Be careful, Gunnery Sergeant."

"I always am."

Not one of them, including Kyster, looked as though they believed that. Torin didn't know why.

She didn't bother watching the di'Taykan until they reached the first curve but stared out over the barricade. "Private Kyster, you're to wait here with Private Watura. That's an order."

His teeth were showing, just a little, and he frowned as he searched for the right words. "If you're not back before we're relieved, Gunny?"

"Then you can send one of the new Marines to the node in your place."

His nose ridges opened and closed. After a moment he said, "I wait?"

"You wait."

"But if you need me . . ."

"I need you to wait here."

"But if . . ."

"Private Kyster, you are to wait here until I return. That's an order."

Reluctantly, he nodded.

It wouldn't hold him for long. Hopefully, it wouldn't have to. Carrying two canteens and twelve biscuits, she jumped the barricade and started walking.

Torin could feel their eyes on her until she reached the first turn, knew they were still watching even though at that distance it was unlikely they could see her—gray against the gray. The absence of their attention made her feel suddenly light.

She hadn't been thinking clearly since getting rid of Harnett. The aftermath had been clouded in ways the Corps never was for her. Never had been for her. One hand slid inside her vest and touched the salvage tag. She was tempted to blame Craig and whatever it was between them, but this wasn't his fault.

Achieve the mission objectives and get her people out alive.

Everything else was baggage.

She didn't look in the first cave as she passed it.

After a while, after her stomach insisted on a biscuit, Torin realized that the tunnel exactly matched the tunnel they'd taken from the node to the barricade. Like all Recon—or ex-Recon—she mapped constantly. Comparing the area she'd just left to these new tunnels and cross tunnels, the similarities were unmistakable. If she hurried, it should be possible for her to reach a second pipe—if there was a second pipe, before dark.

Turning a corner, she walked right into a group of four Marines. Almost literally right into them, rocking to a stop no more than a meter away from the older Human male at the head of the group. She just had time to see his collar tabs when the lieutenant's gaze dropped to the stone knife in her boot, and he took a swing at her.

It would have been easier had she wanted to kill them. Unfortunately, trying to cause nothing more than minor injuries meant fighting handicapped. Fortunately, they weren't armed.

More fortunately still, it seemed they didn't want to kill her.

✿   ✿   ✿

Torin didn't think she'd lost consciousness for more than a minute or two, but she definitely regained it when she was dumped onto the floor and rolled over with a boot to the shoulder. If she'd been carried to the second pipe, this one was a lot noisier than the one she'd come from. There seemed to be a lot of yelling going on.

"Begging your pardon, Lieutenant, but are you fukking insane? That's Gunnery Sergeant Kerr!"

And that sounded like Binti Mashona.

SIX

TORIN ACCEPTED THE BOWL OF water with a grateful nod
and frowned at the technical sergeant who'd handed it to her.
Brown hair, brown eyes; his depilatory hadn't yet begun to wear off,
so he hadn't been here long.

He grinned. "Mike Gucciard, Gunnery Sergeant. We've never actually met. I have, of course, heard all about you."

"Of course," she snorted. She drank a little water, mostly because it
was there, not because she thought it would do much for the lump on
her head or the ache in her left knee or the various bruises she could
feel rising. The four Marines who'd brought her into the node hadn't
been particularly gentle, but neither had they been as vicious as they
could have been, all things considered. She spared another glance for
Gucciard, still on one knee beside her, and finally connected the dots.
"I saw you in the shuttle bay while the GCT was loading for Estee;
you broke up that fight."

"Yeah, that was me." He had an attractive smile and remarkably ex-
pressive eyebrows. At the moment, they managed to convey pleasure,
relief, and anticipation pretty much simultaneously. Torin figured
the pleasure for being remembered, the relief that they didn't have
to go through the litany of "I served with so and so at the battle of
such and such" that defined the parameters between members of the
Corps, but the anticipation she couldn't figure. He was staring at her
as though he'd been eating that damned kibble for months and she
were a steak dinner. Real steak. Not a sculpted slab of soy protein.

"So the slate, does it work?"

Ah. Not staring at her, then. Given the look in his eyes, that was a bit of a relief. Like almost every other species in the Confederation, she'd carried a slate for most of her life—the weight of it on her vest had been so familiar, she'd forgotten it was there. "No, it's as dead as the rest of the tech." Unsnapping it, she passed it over, hiding a smile at the obvious control Technical Sergeant Gucciard was managing to maintain. Eyes locked on the slate, he clearly wanted to snatch it from her, but he allowed her to place it on the palm of one large hand before he closed his fingers around it and let out a breath Torin doubted he even knew he'd been holding.

"Yours?"

She didn't bother hiding her smile any longer. His attention on the slate, blunt fingers moving with surprising delicacy over the screen, Gucciard had partitioned as little of his attention as possible off to deal with things like conversation. "No. It was one of the things Harnett had collected."

Harnett's name—or probably the way she spat it out—actually drew his attention back to her face. She could see him wondering if he should ask, saw him decide it was less important than what he held in his hands, and saw him turn his attention back to the dead piece of tech.

"No visible damage, just like the combats. If it's only the power source, if whatever brought us here drained it, then there's a chance I can charge it."

"The lights in the tunnels?"

He grinned at her again, clearly pleased she'd already gotten there. His thumbs gently rubbed the casing while he spoke. "I can use the inert tech in a pair of combats to create an interface that'll let me charge not only our combats but the slate as well. Once it's running again, I can reboot the operating system out of the partitioned memory and then start pulling programs up."

"Provided the memory hasn't been completely wiped."

He shrugged broad shoulders. "If I've got working tech, I can program in what I need."

Torin blinked. "From scratch?"

Gucciard actually removed one hand from the slate long enough to tap his head. "Wetware predates software, Gunny." Halfway to his feet, he paused, frowned. "That is if I can use your slate . . . ?"

"You were clearly the reason I picked it up, Technical Sergeant. Knock yourself out."

"Probably won't come to that. I have no idea what's actually powering those lights, but that's why I'll be using the combats as an inter . . . You didn't mean that literally, did you?" Before she could answer, he frowned at a group of three officers heading her way and held out a hand. "You're going to want to face these guys on your feet, Gunny. Officious," he explained in answer to her silent question as she stood, keeping as much weight as possible off her left leg. "Lieutenants," he added as though that should explain things, and it pretty much did. "They're a little wrapped up in running a *tight* ship."

Interesting emphasis. "Directly?"

"Too many officers, not enough NCOs."

"Oh, joy."

"Second Lieutenant Teirl, Lieutenant Cafter, Lieutenant O'Neill. The other two aren't bad on their own, but they take their cue from O'Neill, and he's a pain in the ass," Gucciard continued, his voice a rough burr by her ear. "Seems to think he should have made captain by now."

"I'm not seeing a lot of chance for promotion down here."

"He is."

Officious seemed like a good description as the three approached.

"Technical Sergeant Gucciard." Lieutenant O'Neill's acknowledgment suggested to Torin that while officious might do, inert carbon rod stuffed up their collective asses might have been more accurate. "You are not required. Have you no work of your own to do?"

"Yes, sir. Gunnery Sergeant Kerr has provided me with a slate."

"Is it functioning?" Lieutenant Cafter demanded, dark orange hair fanning out around her head.

"No, sir, but there's a chance I can power it back up."

"How?"

"Power conduits in the tunnels, sir."

Her lip curled. "If there's anything left in there, you'll fry it."

"Not if I run the power through a set of combats first, sir."

"And you think Lietenant McCoy will issue you a set of combats."

So, not only too many officers but too many lieutenants; it seemed every pipe had its problems. Fortunately, Torin had been dealing with lieutenants for about as long as Second Lieutenant Teirl had been away from his *sheshan*.

She'd known Gucciard for about ten minutes, but the tension across the technical sergeant's shoulders was easy to read. He was about one more snide comment away from showing the lieutenant where the actual power in the Corps rested. Given his trade, he probably hadn't so much dealt with lieutenants as worked around them. "I haven't spoken to Lieutenant McCoy yet, sir."

"Then get to it, Sergeant."

"Yes, sir." A quick nod to Torin—wry amusement and commiseration combined—and Gucciard pivoted on one heel and set off across the node.

"Gunnery Sergeant Kerr." O'Neill's tone suggested he was taking control of the situation back from Lieutenant Cafter.

"Lieutenant O'Neill." Torin's tone, in turn, reminded him that he was a lieutenant. And that she wasn't.

He shifted in place, frowning slightly, clearly sensing he'd been slapped down but just as clearly uncertain of how. "Colonel Mariner will see you now."

The name sounded vaguely familiar, but then space was big, and each species seemed to have a limited number of names in rotation.

Torin dipped her head once, in acknowledgment. "Thank you, sir." And then she waited.

After a moment, Lieutenant Cafter's hair began to flip back and forth. "If you'll follow us, Gunnery Sergeant."

"Yes, sir." But her voice said, *Aren't you a good officer, then*. All three of them reacted to it—shoulders went back, heads went up.

The area around this pipe was physically identical to the one she'd come from. The hunting party, or whatever they called it here, had dropped her by one of the outside walls without the latrine trench. Colonel Mariner had his command center in a familiar place by the central pipe—although the fabric had been used for the di'Taykan enclosure instead of as a tent to hide his command decisions.

The biggest difference was that the Marines here weren't just lying around on their pallets watching her go by. Pallets were stacked by what Torin assumed were platoons, given the numbers and their positioning. She frowned at the lines of small rocks laid out on the floor delineating different areas. In one area, some of the Marines were doing calisthentics, watched by an officer. In another, some of them were obviously in a class of some sort, led by an officer. A few were still lined up for the showers; an officer stood at the end of the short line. The rest were *standing* around watching her go by.

Except for the gray sameness that came from being locked underground for an extended period of time, they looked reasonably healthy. Beards had been made as tidy as possible and hair, once it had grown long enough, was tied back.

She heard a familiar whisper ripple out from her passage. *Silsviss.* The moment she got back to civilization, she'd have to send a message to Cri Sawyes thanking his people for adding what had become a useful layer to her reputation. He'd appreciate that she appreciated being considered slightly psychotic.

Most of the fabric had gone to the di'Taykan's enclosure, Torin amended as she drew closer to the command center. Colonel Mariner had used at least one sheet of it as a desk, folding it in thirds and then folding the ends of that thickened fabric rectangle at ninety degree angles before setting the tech.

He sat behind his desk on a folded pallet, hands flat on the fabric in front of him, her knife in front of his hands. Two majors and a captain stood to his left—the captain was one of the rare Krai infantry officers—two captains and an artillery major to his right—this major's beard had barely begun to curl out from his chin. He hadn't been here long. Binti Mashona stood to one side at parade rest, the fingers of her right hand tapping against the palm of her left, the motion safely out of sight behind her back.

He'd used a sheet of smart fabric to make a desk? That was . . . different.

And then she remembered where she'd heard Colonel Mariner's name. Almost a year and a half ago, the Others had attacked a colony on the Edge during a diplomatic visit from Parliamentary representa-

tives. Torin had no idea what idiot thought a diplomatic visit to the
Edge was a good idea—there might have been an election in the
offing; not her Sector, so she didn't really care—but the Parliamentary representatives had a military escort. Colonel Mariner had commanded it. His body had never been found.

Torin really hoped there weren't politicians tucked away in here
somewhere.

Colonel Mariner was a staff officer, not a line officer. Which made
very little difference, given their current location, but she'd have to
remember to use a more delicate touch when dealing with him. The
time spent on Ventris debriefing what felt like half the staff officers in
the Corps now seemed to have become, in retrospect, a useful learning experience.

Within a forest of beards, he was clean shaven, and the dome of
his head gleamed. Permanent depilatory. Torin vaguely remembered
the style from around the time she'd joined the Corps and figured the
colonel was lucky it suited him. It was also a fair indication that he
was a man who made up his mind and never changed it.

She came to attention—because he expected it—and snapped out,
"Gunnery Sergeant Torin Kerr, 7th Division, 4th Recar'ta, 1st Battalion, Sh'quo Company, sir!"

"At ease, Gunnery Sergeant."

She dropped into parade rest and stared just past his left ear.

"Corporal Mashona has told us a bit of your history until you were
captured by the Others and dropped here with us . . ." *And I believe
less than half of it*, added the subtext. ". . . and I'd like to hear the rest
from you. And when I say *the rest,* I mean I'd like to hear how you
came to be wandering the tunnels in such a way as to be picked up by
one of my patrols."

"Yes sir. It will require some background on the situation as I found
it, sir."

"Excellent. The present cannot be judged without an awareness of
the past. Do you know who said that, Gunnery Sergeant."

"No, sir."

"Shirree Sataan. One of the great H'san philosophers. The only one
ever translated into Federate."

"Isn't ze also the one who said, the cheese stands alone, sir?"

"Ze adopted that from a Human philosopher, Gunnery Sergeant." He leaned forward, shifting the highlight higher up the shiny curve of skin. Torin squinted slightly, and the major with the short beard bit his lip. "The background details, Gunny?"

So she told them about how Harnett had taken control. "That was the situation in that node when I arrived."

"Good God!" Mariner's cheeks had flushed nearly purple. "He called himself a colonel? The man has to be stopped. Our policy of nonintervention as long as his people stayed on their side of the barricade has to be changed."

Torin fought to keep her opinion of nonintervention from showing on her face. "He's been taken care of, sir."

"Taken care of?"

"Yes, sir."

The young major and the Krai captain seemed to have figured out the ending. The others were looking appalled, outraged, and a little nervous. Upon reflection, Torin decided the nervous major may have also figured out the ending.

Mariner began to relax slightly. "The Marines rose against him."

"No, sir. I killed him." She kept it matter-of-fact. She might have been reporting on the toilet paper inventory.

"They rose against his goons."

"No, sir. I killed about half of them."

"About half?" The colonel was no longer even a little relaxed. He looked as though he'd twang if flicked with a fingertip. "How many, precisely, is about half?"

"Precisely seven, sir. Sorry, eight." She'd forgotten about tossing Bakune into the disposal unit. "And Harnett makes nine. And then I returned command to Major Kenoton."

"So you're telling me that on your own recognizance, without orders, you killed nine Marines?"

"No, sir, on my own recognizance, I killed half the people who were starving a hundred Marines to death."

"And Major Kenoton approved of this?"

"He preferred it to starving to death, sir."

Safely out of the colonel's line of sight, the young major bit his lip again.

"And it never occurred to you to approach Major Kenoton and place yourself and your skills under his command so that due procedure could be implemented in the removal of Staff Sergeant Harnett from his position?"

It wouldn't have surprised Torin if some sort of due procedure existed for exactly that situation. There were officers on Ventris who did nothing but come up with due procedures without ever considering how to implement them in the field. "No, sir. Harnett would have kept me from approaching the major until I was too weak to stand against him."

"I think you overestimate how much of a threat he'd have considered you, Gunnery Sergeant Kerr."

The Krai captain leaned forward. Given that Colonel Mariner was sitting, that put his mouth right at his CO's ear. "Sir, she killed ten Marines who'd been handpicked for size, general badass attitude, and a willingness to crack heads. A few of them *must* have seen her coming."

"And your point, Captain Diir?"

His nose ridges opened and closed. "My point, sir, is that I doubt Gunnery Sergeant Kerr is overestimating anything."

Mariner shifted uncomfortably on the pallet. "Yes, well . . ." He looked down at the knife then back up at Torin. "Now we know how the situation stood when you arrived, perhaps you'd best fill me in on the details of how you resolved it."

"Yes, sir."

So she told him about meeting Kyster and the hunting party, about gaining the knife, and, eventually, about dealing with Harnett.

"You just walked in? Bold as brass?"

"Yes, sir."

"What were you *thinking*?"

"That there was only one way to resolve the situation, sir."

"But to kill . . ." His voice trailed off as though he still couldn't quite believe it.

Suddenly weary, Torin closed her teeth on a sigh. The Corps had taught her to pull the trigger, to divorce what had to be done from what she was actually doing. Killing Harnett and his men was no different from killing the Silsviss who had her platoon pinned down or any of the Others she'd faced over the years. It all came down to getting her people out alive. For all his lethargy, at least Major Kenoton had understood that.

Mariner's brows, particularly emphatic because of the lack of other hair, drew in. "And yet you barely fought when Lieutenant Schmid's scouting party discovered you."

"I didn't want to hurt anyone, sir."

"There were four of them, Gunnery Sergeant."

The young major snorted and hurriedly covered the noise with a cough.

"Given the way your people responded when they met Harnett's people in the tunnels," Torin continued, drawing the colonel's attention back to her, "I knew this area had maintained discipline."

"Discipline is at the heart of the Corps," he said, nodding approvingly. Although who or what he was approving, Torin had no idea. "But you were carrying one of their weapons." A nod was redirected toward the obsidian knife. "Lieutenant Schmid assumed you were one of them."

"A valid assumption, sir."

"So," he fixed her with what he likely assumed was a piercing glare. "Why are you here, Gunnery Sergeant?"

"My orders were to assess the situation in this area and to determine what plans had been made toward escape so as to prevent duplication of effort."

He laughed at that, a short, sharp sound that held no humor. "There is no escape, Gunnery Sergeant. When you've been here a little longer, you'll realize that. Well, you've certainly given my staff and me plenty to discuss. Corporal Mashona."

Mashona snapped to attention so perfectly she might as well have flipped him the finger. Fortunately, Torin was the only NCO around to see it. "Sir!"

"You will liaise with Gunnery Sergeant Kerr while she is with us."

"Yes, sir!"

"Gunnery Sergeant."

"Sir."

"I expect you to keep a lower profile than you're in the habit of while you're under my command."

The young major bit his lip.

"Yes, sir. I will need to report back to Major Kenoton, sir. Soon."

"You won't get back to the barricade before dark, Gunnery Sergeant, so you'll be with us for tonight at least." Mariner patted the knife. "I'll hang onto to this. Dismissed."

"Liaise, Gunny?"

"Keep me from killing anyone."

"Is he fukking kidding?"

Torin grinned and gripped Mashona's shoulder for a moment. Underground prisons apparently made her sentimental. "Don't worry, Corporal, I have every intention of staying on the colonel's good side. And I suspect he mostly just wants you to show me how to get fed, where to sleep."

"He couldn't just say that?"

"Takes all types, Corporal." She studied faces as they walked. "Anyone else here we know?"

"No one from Sh'quo Company, but Major Ohi came in the same time as Technical Sergeant Gucciard and me. He's the young guy who kept trying to not to laugh. He's artillery. Seven, two, four Fan'tal Company. I don't know about the other area, though—rest of the fukking company could be there."

"There's another area?"

"Yeah." She pointed toward the tunnel opposite to the one Torin had arrived by. "That way. Two day's walk. It's just like this one only with a lieutenant colonel as the ranking officer, so hopefully the stick up her butt is one rank smaller."

"Mashona."

"Sorry, Gunny."

A familiar tone filled the node.

"There's chow," Mashona said when she could be heard again. "You got a bowl?"

"I do."

The bowls here were the same shade of brown, but the kibble was slightly lighter. Torin wondered if that was because this node put more officers into the mix. It tasted the same, though, and she figured she'd best keep the thought to herself.

"I never thought I'd miss field rations." Mashona scooped a double fingerful of mush up to her mouth and swallowed with minimal chewing. "That's some great knife you came in with, Gunny. No one here's got one."

"The surrounding tunnels don't cross the lava flow, then."

"Captain Yonvic is going to love it. She's a . . ." A wave of her hand spattered a bit of mush onto the polished stone floor. ". . . rock person. She's always poking around the small caves. You won't believe this, Gunny, but she found two stones you can smack together to make fire. Well, sparks since nothing down here burns."

"The captain found flint and steel?"

Mashona snorted. "Doesn't look like steel. Looks like two rocks. There's a whole bunch of one, though, and not much of the other. Scouting parties going out are supposed to keep an eye out for it." She used her thumb to clear the last of the mush from the bowl, polishing the plastic clean. "So, Gunny, you really killed nine people at that other pipe?"

It was almost not a question, and Torin could tell it hadn't been prompted by disbelief. "Yeah." She swallowed the last mouthful of her own mush. "I really did."

"You okay with it?"

She was the first person to ask.

Torin had done what she had to do in order to get the job done and, given the job, she'd long since learned not to second-guess the tough decisions. She regretted Edwards, not because he was dead but because she'd killed him in anger. His death was a little too close to the line between soldier and killer. The rest? If they'd had a couple dozen MPs and a stockade, things might have been different, but since they didn't . . . nine dead and their deaths her responsibility measured against over a hundred alive and their lives her responsibility, too. "Yeah, I'm okay with it."

Mashona nodded as though she'd heard both halves of the response. "All right, then. So, you really got a plan to get out of here, Gunny?"

"Beginning of one."

"This lot . . ." She flicked long dark fingers in the general direction of a hundred or so Marines all concentrating on a plastic bowl. ". . . they just laugh when you talk about escape, you know? Like you're so new you don't know it can't be done."

"Hasn't been. Doesn't mean it can't be."

"That's what I said."

Any of the Krai would have recognized Torin's smile. "Yeah, but they'll listen to me."

"And thank the gods for that." Legs crossed at the ankle, Mashona rocked up onto her feet. "Let's get you a pallet. Hope you don't mind bunking by me and the tech sarge, Gunny. We're all that's unassigned.

"After nearly a tenday?" Torin stood a little more slowly, still favoring her left knee.

"All six platoons want us, so the colonel is taking detailed request things." One long fingered hand sketched the word in the air. "Starts with a *dee*."

"Depositions?"

"That's it."

"And Major Ohi?"

"He was added to the colonel's staff pretty much immediately so that the colonel could get all the new buzz. Me and the sarge were a bit less thoroughly debriefed."

Torin spared a moment's sympathy for the young major as they approached one of the areas delineated by the lines of rock. There were no automated retrieval drones, but quartermaster stores never looked like anything but what they were regardless of the situation.

"Lieutenant McCoy? Gunnery Sergeant Kerr needs a pallet."

The lieutenant scowled up at Mashona then over at Torin, then backed up a few steps to lessen the kink in her neck. It was a maneuver Torin had often seen from the Krai; she'd never seen a Human use it before, but the lieutenant was tiny. "Can't the gunnery sergeant speak for herself, Corporal?"

"The colonel said I was to liaise, sir."

"I see." But she didn't look happy about it. "I only have two spare pallets right now."

Quartermasters were like quartermaster's stores—true to type. Although their job was to supply the Corps, they hated actually releasing any of their inventory.

"I only need one, Lieutenant."

Dark eyes narrowed. "I'm aware of that, Gunnery Sergeant."

Torin waited, gaze locked on the lieutenant's face.

"All right, fine, you'd best get it then before the lights go out. Follow me." She led the way across to the opposite imaginary wall and gestured at the two rolled pallets. "Take the one on the left and sign for it."

"Sign for it, Lieutenant?" Torin followed the pointing finger and looked down. On the floor next to the pallets was a drawn rectangle enclosing a list of names scratched into the rock. Next to the rectangle was a slightly paler rock, just smaller than her fist. "Ah. Sign for it. Yes, sir."

Technical Sergeant Gucciard glanced up when Torin dropped her pallet down beside his and grinned. "I see you've met Lieutenant McCoy."

"I appreciate gung ho as much as the next Marine," Torin muttered as she shoved the ends of the pallet flat with her boot, "but that was a bit . . ."

"Surreal?"

"That's just a little more polite than I was going to go with."

"Fukking surreal?"

Torin returned the grin. "That's it." She sat and nodded toward the pair of combats spread across his lap. "So, Gucciard . . ."

"Mike."

"Mike . . . you still think you can get that slate up and working?"

"I'll let you in on a secret, Gunny . . ."

"Torin."

"Torin." He nodded toward the spill of fabric. "Once I set my mind on something, failure is not an option."

She watched for a while as his large hands teased the tech free of the fabric at an access seam. Given the size of those hands, he had a surprisingly delicate touch. "I take it you can't just plug into the diagnostic points?"

"Is it ever that easy?" he asked as he exposed another millimeter of tech. "The diagnostic points can hook up to other combats and to the slate, but for the hookup to the power source, I'm going to have to improvise."

Torin had to admit he looked like he knew what he was doing and, over the years, she'd developed good instincts for who was faking it.

The announcement that it was ten minutes to lights-out finally freed Mashona from the three lieutenants who had her cornered. She jogged over to her mat and dropped down with a heavy sigh. "They want to know how long you're staying, Gunny."

"Not long," Torin told her, voice pitched to carry over orders to retrieve pallets and the sounds of a hundred Marines doing just that. She hadn't noticed before how much the smack of a pallet hitting the rock sounded like a body going down for the count.

"You got people who'll come after you?"

"Very probably." Kyster definitely. "How do they know how long until lights out?"

"Colonel's got people assigned to count."

"Count?"

"One, H'san like cheese. Two, H'san like cheese." Mashona folded her arms behind her head. "You can use whatever spacer you want, but you go to a thousand and then pass it off to the next guy. Forty-two thousands in a day," she added anticipating Torin's next question. "Give or take."

Torin did the math. "Roughly a twenty-eight-hour day."

"Station norm," Mashona agreed. "If you're here long enough, you'll get your own place in the queue."

"Colonel Mariner needs noncoms; he's going to want to keep you," Mike put in, looking up from his work.

"No, I don't think so." Torin grinned. "I make him nervous."

The technical sergeant snorted. "Can't think why."

"She killed nine mutineers single-handed back at the other pipe. What? Was that supposed to be a secret?" Mashona asked as Torin turned toward her. "Sorry, Gunny."

"I can see how that would make the colonel a little nervous," Mike admitted. "If it's true."

Torin sighed. "It's true. Although aren't mutineers Navy?"

"Damned if I know." He shook his head. "No Navy around to ask. So you took out nine? In that case, you should be gone by . . . shit."

Like everywhere else she'd been in the underground complex, the lights didn't dim. They just went out. There was a fair bit of swearing for the first few minutes—for the sake of swearing mostly. As far as Torin could see from where she was sitting, nearly all the Marines had been on, or right beside, their pallets.

"That's enough, people." The voice rose to fill the space, the tone proof there was at least one senior NCO in the node. "Settle down, get some sleep, get ready for another glorious day in the Corps."

The volume level dropped to muttering and the muttering fell off sooner than Torin expected. Sleep was something to do, at least. There were other things being done as well, and not only in the tent with the di'Taykan where sex was a given.

"I heard the colonel tried to stop this lot from so much as having a wank after lights out. I heard his staff talked him out of it. I wonder if he has hair on his . . ."

"Corporal Mashona, go to sleep."

"Yes, Gunny. Sorry, Gunny, it's just . . ."

"I know." It was just seeing a familiar face. Having someone there who knew her, who tied her to her past. Torin had felt much the same way about Werst. Now, however, her head hurt, her left leg ached, and she was more tired than she could remember being. Which was weird, because she'd certainly been awake longer and done more. One hand slipping inside her vest to close around the salvage tag, surrounded by the comforting sounds of a hundred Marines, she closed her eyes and slept.

✿　　✿　　✿

"I've sent messengers to the barricade and to Lieutenant Colonel Braudy." Colonel Mariner attempted to lock his gaze with hers, failed, and stared at his hands folded on his desk instead. Torin continued looking just past his left shoulder. "I believe it is necessary for you to tell your story to the lieutenant colonel yourself, Gunnery Sergeant. I see no way she'd believe it if it came to her secondhand. I will inform your Major Kenoton that you are remaining here for further debriefing and that as soon as he is physically able, I shall expect him to report to headquarters."

"Headquarters, sir?"

"Here, Gunnery Sergeant. Or have you missed the fact that I am the ranking officer in these tunnels?"

"No, sir."

"Structure of the Corps must be imposed. Staff Sergeant Harnett's abuse of power is a prime example of what happens when that structure is ignored."

He hadn't asked a question, but he seemed to be waiting for a response. Torin spent a moment considering an honest answer but she really didn't need to deal with the fallout so she stuck with a bland, "Yes, sir."

Highlights gleamed as he settled back, satisfied. "As you will not be remaining permanently, I see no reason to assign you to a platoon. Technical Sergeant Gucciard seems to think he can get that slate of yours up and running; it might be best, the least disruptive anyway, if you kept yourself busy assisting him until Lieutenant Colonel Braudy arrives."

"Yes, sir."

Mike gazed up at Torin from under brows nearly meeting in a vee at the top of his nose. "You know anything about working with tech?"

"I know how to use it, and I know how to delegate when I need something done with it."

"Nothing personal, but what kind of help does the colonel think you're going to be?"

Grinning, she held out her hand. "I can pick you up when you touch a live wire and get knocked on your ass. I can field dress any injuries that happen when you're flung backward and your head connects with the rock. And I can do CPR if the power surge stops your heart, although you'll probably stay dead since, as I understand it, your lungs will have filled with liquid and you'll have drowned."

He snorted and put his hand in hers, allowing her to haul him back up onto his feet. "Yeah. You're going to be a big help."

"It are looking now we are being here, live, remarkably like it are looking in the vids," Presit said, the dry wind ruffling her fur. "Imagine that."

The battlefield, the battlefield where Torin had died, looked like a rippled sheet of gray-green glass. Shining. Lifeless. Craig went to one knee, reached across the seam where melted rock met dirt and rapped his knuckles against the glossy surface. Felt like glass, the kind tourists to backwater worlds picked up as "a primitive remnant of precontact culture" without ever realizing it was mass-produced at a filthy factory down streets a little less quaint.

"Artisans," Presit said suddenly.

Craig twisted to look at his reflection in her mirrored sunglasses, his position putting them eye to eye. "What about them?"

"There are being a seven hundred and thirty-eight dead mixing into this glass. I are thinking those who are mourning would be liking a piece of it."

"No." He straightened.

"It are being presented tastefully," she argued. "Could be having piece of glass set in metal enclosure for garden or be cutting flat and are using for patterns in windows."

"No," Craig repeated, a little louder.

Presit sighed. "You are being the only one who are getting closure, then?"

He didn't answer that, just as he didn't respond to the number of the dead. The difference between seven hundred and thirty-eight and seven hundred and thirty-seven was the difference between hope and despair. He hadn't come here because he believed Torin was dead.

He hadn't come here because he hoped she was alive. He just needed to see. Shouldering the camera, he stepped onto the glass. "Let's go find those scientists."

"Based on the coordinates the military has given us, we know that Captain Gordon Rose was standing right on that spot . . ." The Niln scientist half turned away from the camera to point. ". . . when the attack occurred. Captain Rose's DNA becomes, in effect, our control. We have his pattern on file; we know where it should occur within the melt. Once we can develop a way to pull a clear reading out, we can use the same techniques across the battlefield to bring closure to the families of the other Marines."

"Closure are being important." Presit's left ear tip flicked pointedly toward Craig. "So if I are understanding you, *Harveer* Umananth, you are not having the techniques to be getting the captain's DNA out yet."

The *harveer's* nictitating eyelid flicked across both eyes but whether in reaction to the dry wind or the question or to Katrien syntax, Craig wasn't sure. "Whatever weapon the Others used to do this, it had an effect like nothing we've ever seen. Strictly speaking, it didn't melt the ground; it reformed everything in this immediate area—where immediate area refers to everything within 38.172 square kilometers—at the molecular level. Essentially, it took it apart and put it back together again as something new."

"So you are saying you are not having the techniques to be getting the captain's DNA out yet," Presit repeated, smiling toothily.

Harveer Umananth sighed, the tip of his tail making lazy figure eights by his right leg. "Yes, that is what I am saying."

"And how long are you being working on this new technique until you are successful?"

"There's no way of knowing. We could work it out today. It could take years."

"Years? And when the Others are returning, what are you doing then?"

The young Niln's tail snapped out straight as he hissed. "The Others are returning?"

Presit's species was omnivorous. Her smile suggested otherwise. "This are being a front line and there are being a war on. Also . . ." She waved at the undulating hectares of glass. ". . . there are being Others *reformed* in this, are there not? I are having seen the last recorded battle positions, and they were definitely being within 38.172 kilometers. Are you being sure that this are being caused by one of the Others' weapons?"

Craig shifted position to stare around the camera at Presit. She hadn't mentioned any of this to him.

"We have data from the Navy that indicates the weapon was deployed from one of the Others' ships," Umananth insisted.

"On friend and foe alike?" Presit combed her whiskers. "That are being very careless of them, and I are imagining someone are catching trouble for it. If I are being them, I are definitely returning to analyze results."

"Logically I suppose, but . . . you have no actual *data* on the Others returning?"

"I are having no actual data on the Others staying away."

"Yes, right." His tail scribed agitated figure eights in the air. "Well, I should get back to the team. You may, of course, wander around, but please remain outside the tagged area. We don't want your DNA to mix with that of Captain Rose." He bobbed his head and turned to go.

"You are thinking you might be mixing up my DNA with DNA of Captain Rose?"

Keep going, mate. Craig thought at him. *You can't win this one.*

The *harveer* paused and almost reluctantly faced the reporter again. "Captain Rose is Human. We could never mix your DNA."

"Then why are we being kept outside the tagged area?"

Katrien syntax was usually so scrambled that those times it matched up with Federate always came as a bit of a shock.

"Are you hiding something?" Presit continued.

"No! We just . . ."

"Full disclosure laws are allowing me full access."

"Yes, I know, but . . ."

"If I are not allowed full access, I are thinking you are being up to no good."

"But you have full access."

"Except to the tagged area."

"It's barely three square meters! And that camera . . ." He waved a green-gold hand in Craig's general direction. ". . . can zoom to practically microscopic levels. I assure you, we are hiding nothing."

"Well, good, then." She smiled.

He blinked.

Craig sighed and jerked his head toward the group of scientists clustered around their equipment. It took Umananth a moment to realize what he meant, then his tail went up and he hurried back to the safety of the group as Craig asked Presit about an editing function on the camera and didn't bother listening to the answer.

The scientists had set up their equipment on the back of the big hoversled—maybe so they wouldn't contaminate the site, maybe so they could make a fast getaway if the Others did return. He may have pulled the possibility out of his ass in order to get Presit to agree to the trip, but she was right, there was nothing that said the bastards wouldn't return. They were standing on the front lines, and there was a war on.

Craig watched *Harveer* Umananth scramble up onto the sled, talking and pointing back their way. He was well within range of the microphone on the camera—all Craig had to do was put the ear in and he could eavesdrop on conversations up to 500 meters away. Well, not eavesdrop exactly since the moment the software analyzed the distance it would apparently do *something* to prevent sentient beings being recorded without their consent. He had no idea of what. Or how it knew if it had their consent. Or why it was restricted to 500 meters. He suspected the latter came out of the same laws that kept official media recording equipment large enough to be seen, resulting in a camera that held—as well as two separate recording devices—a full editing program, broadcast ability, the personal game, music, and vid library of the operator with room left over inside the casing to pack a change of clothes and some snacks.

Hell, given that the *harveer* had already spoken to the press, it was possible that anything further he said in range of the pickup could be considered recordable. But Craig liked him—he spoke plain Federate without sounding as though he'd dumbed things down for his audience—so he kept the recorder off. He supposed that if Umananth had made *harveer* so soon out of the egg, he was smart enough he didn't have to keep proving it by confusing people.

"We definitely are being shooting the tagged area," Presit said, one small hand on his wrist, the ambient heat making her touch seem cool. "And then you are setting the camera on a tripod and I are interviewing more scientists because I are a glutton for punishment, and you are going that way . . ." She pointed. ". . . and are finding Gunnery Sergeant Kerr."

He was suddenly finding it hard to breathe.

Nothing marked the spot, but he bounced a signal off *Promise*—she was hooked to the cruiser that had brought the science team across space, locked together in a geosynchronous orbit over the battlefield because the downside of a Susumi drive was the loss of VTA capability— and stopped walking when the little red dot that was him matched up with the little green dot that was Torin's last recorded position.

She was in a dip in the melt, as if she'd been taking cover in an artillery crater when it happened.

Craig turned that thought over as he dropped down to one knee and realized that a year ago, while he'd have been able to figure out "artillery crater" from context, he sure as shit wouldn't have spent any time considering the implications of diving for one during battle.

The glassy surface was warm under his hand, but that was hardly surprising given the height of the sun and the lack of cloud cover. If he swept his hand around, would he find a cold spot? Torin's feet were always freezing, and she was flexible enough she could tuck them up under the warmest parts of his body.

"What the bloody hell do you think you're doing!"

"Warming up."

"Yeah?" Hand wrapped around her ankle, he hesitated before turning it into a wrestling match he'd probably lose. "And if they freeze and snap off, what then?"

Her smile was wicked. "I'll warm them up before it comes to that."

His knuckles were against the ground now although he didn't remember his hand clenching into a fist.

He didn't know what he'd expected, but she wasn't here.

Not, she wasn't dead—he'd pretty much come to believe that. Mostly.

He uncurled his fingers and pressed only the tips against dirt and rock and flesh and blood and clothing and weapons and everything else that the ground had been before it had been reformed.

She wasn't *here*.

"Listen to what I'm saying, Private! Gunnery Sergeant Kerr is fine!"

Watura closed his hand around Kyster's shoulder, his eyes darkening as he tried to get a better look at the four Marines who were shouting at them from down the tunnel. "They've got no reason to lie to us," he said quietly.

"They've got no reason to tell us the truth," Kyster growled, but he let the di'Taykan hold him in place up against the barricade even though his hand was close enough to bite. He wanted to charge toward this new hunting party even as he wanted to run from it. It seemed safest for the moment to stay where he was.

Someone in the new hunting party started shouting again. "Colonel Mariner has ordered her to remain and debrief Lieutenant Colonel Braudy when she arrives!"

Kyster shook his head—although he knew they probably couldn't see the motion given his height and the height of the barricade. "Why should we trust you?"

"Sir!"

"What?"

"Why should we trust you, *sir*?" the someone yelled back.

Watura snickered. "Second lieutenant."

Kyster's nose ridges opened and shut. "No shit." He shook himself free of the di'Taykan's grasp. There'd been something so stupidly normal about that exchange it made him feel the way Gunnery Sergeant Kerr did, like he belonged again. "Sorry, sir, is that what we report to our CO? That Colonel Mariner ordered her to remain and debrief Lieutenant Colonel Braudy?"

The distance was too great for them to hear a sigh, but the lieutenant's tone carried the same effect. "Yes, Private, that's what you're to report to your CO."

"Ouch, sarcasm," Watura snorted quietly.

"You're smoking again."

"It's from the last time."

"You sure?"

Mike's grunted response sounded fairly positive, so Torin let it go. He'd fried a bit of the tech in his own combats when his sleeve had brushed against the exposed wire and had taken that as a sign he was on the right track. It wasn't actually wire, of course, not as Torin understood the word, but since *long, narrow, alien power conduit* was a mouthful, they tended to stick with the technically inaccurate descriptions they recognized.

The evening kibble had been served, so Colonel Mariner's orders had to have reached the third node by now. If Lieutenant Colonel Braudy started back with the corporal who'd run those orders over, she'd be here by the next evening kibble. A day to go through the sitrep one more time and Torin could head back, report to Major Kenoton, and begin doing something approaching useful by clearing that rockfall.

Arms folded, her back against a smooth spot on the tunnel wall, she wondered if Mariner would let her have Mashona. The most recent arrivals seemed to be the only ones who gave a shit about getting out. Maybe it was something in the food. Maybe after a while it caused complacency. Complacent prisoners would make life a lot easier for their wardens. Kyster's willingness to consider escape seemed to support that. He'd been around for a while, but he hadn't started eating the kibble until recently.

She'd like to have Gucciard with her, too, but figured there was no way in hell Mariner would ever give up the tech sergeant.

"Hey, Mike, have you ever heard of the Others taking prisoners?"

Standing on a hunk of rock they'd carried from one of the small caves, leg of the combats in his teeth, both hands still working the wires, he grunted a negative.

"No. Me either." Torin frowned. Three pipes. Approximately three hundred Marines. That was a tiny fraction of the number of MIA since the war had begun. Logically, that meant there were a lot more places like this. Except that logically, if all those MIA Marines had been taken prisoner, someone would have seen something. Rumors would have started. The Corps was like a fukking high school when it came to gossip and rumors.

She couldn't figure out what the hell the Others were up to, and it was driving her nuts.

As Lieutenant O'Neill came around the corner, Torin pushed off the wall and fell into an easy parade rest. She could play the game. It gave her something to do.

"As you were, Gunnery Sergeant. Carry on with what you're doing, Technical Sergeant Gucciard."

Since Mike was completely ignoring the lieutenant, Torin figured that last order was a given.

"The colonel wants to know what progress you've made."

"The power source has been isolated, and the technical sergeant is now adapting it for use in our equipment. Sir."

"And how much longer will it take?"

"Hard to say, sir. Sergeant Gucciard is creating an interface with alien technology."

"I know that, Gunnery Sergeant."

"Yes, sir."

"The colonel believes that powering up the combats should be a first priority. Because of the . . ." Lieutenant O'Neill gestured at his left cuff. The color high on pale cheeks made it clear he wasn't entirely in accord with his CO's beliefs. ". . . clocks. The colonel feels the count is never entirely accurate."

He relaxed slightly when Torin responded with a neutral, "Yes, sir." She wondered what he'd been expecting her to do—head back into the node and snap the colonel's neck because he thought clocks were more important than a functioning slate? There were easier ways to save the ranks from the idiot orders of the brass, well, not easier but definitely more acceptable to the smooth running of the Corps. It was, in point of fact, a large part of her job description.

"Did you hear that, Technical Sergeant?"

Teeth still clenched around fabric, Mike grunted out a two-toned affirmative that could have just as easily been "Fuk you," as "Yes, sir."

Lieutenant O'Neill seemed to realize that. He stood staring up at Mike, brows dipped in, for a long moment. Then he glanced over at Torin who was wearing her best *nothing to see here* expression. "All right, then," he said at last, "Carry on."

"Yes, sir." She'd been at this game long enough to let her approval of his decision show in her voice without it being either overt or patronizing.

Cheeks flushed, he pivoted on one heel and stepped out smartly down the tunnel toward the node—the martial effect only slightly marred by both hands rising to scratch at his ginger-colored beard as he turned the first corner.

"The combats?" Torin asked when the lieutenant's footsteps had faded sufficiently

"Clocks!" Mike spat the leg out of his mouth, and pulled the exposed tech away from the cable to fray a little more of the charred fabric. From the ground, it looked as if he were trying to fuse the shoulder seams together. "Can't power up the combats until I have an interface working. Just burn them up otherwise. Once I can run power safely, I can power a slate in next to no time compared to powering up a hundred or so combats."

"So doing it your way is the best way to obey the colonel's order."

He grinned down at her. "Isn't it always?"

"Pretty much, yeah."

"Once I get the slate powered, anyone who knows where the diagnostic points are in their combats—and that had damned well better be everyone down here—can use these . . ." A brief wave of the exposed tech. ". . . to charge themselves, and I can concentrate on accessing the contents of the slate's memory."

"Think there might be something in there that can help us escape?"

Both brows rose. "You planning something, Gunny?"

She let her shoulder blades hit the wall again. It wasn't quite a plan. Not yet. "I'll tell you this much, I'm not planning on staying here."

"You and me both." He lifted the combats to the conduit again. "You noticed that those who've been down here for a while seem to have lost their drive?"

"I have." The rock was cool against her back, a welcome point of sensation.

"Something in the food?"

"Probably."

"Clocks," he snorted.

Which was when the lights went out.

Turning carefully on the spot to face the pipe, Torin kept her right hand against the rock, stretched her left out into the tunnel, and carefully shuffled sideways out away from the wall until her right arm was nearly straight and the palm of her left hand bumped against Mike's hip. Maintaining contact so as not to wander off into territory she didn't know him well enough to explore, she moved her hand up slightly and snagged the fabric at his waist.

She felt him relax at the contact.

"Perhaps," he sighed, "an accurate way to tell time isn't such a terrible idea."

"Sleeve lights wouldn't hurt either," Torin pointed out.

SEVEN

"**SO, THIS STAFF SERGEAN HARNETT WAS** withholding supplements to keep the Marines in his sector weak so that he could do what he wanted?"

"Yes, sir."

Lieutenant Colonel Braudy rocked back on her heels, dark eyes never leaving Torin's face. "And what he wanted involved abuse of power, abuse of personnel, and actions leading to the deaths of incoming Marines in his sector?"

"Yes, sir."

"And no one tried to stop him until you arrived?"

"In the early days, before the lack of supplements began to take their toil, there were attempts. They didn't succeed." Where didn't succeed translated as being beaten to death and, in at least one case according to the conversation she'd had with Pole, dumped down the disposal pit alive, but at this point the colonel wasn't looking for details.

"But you did. Succeed." One of Braudy's brows rose, and Torin wondered if she'd also had the ability downloaded. And if she honestly thought Torin would quail at the expression. "You succeeded where every other attempt failed."

"Yes, sir."

"And is there any particular reason we should believe this story, Gunnery Sergeant? Besides our belief in your personal integrity?"

Behind the colonel's back, Binti Mashona, Ressk, and Miransha

Kichar stiffened. The latter two had been part of the party that had accompanied the colonel from the third pipe, brought along because they'd been serving with Torin and scooped up in the same battle—a second and third opinion that Torin was who she said she was. Braudy's attitude while listening to Torin tell the story of Harnett's defeat, yet again, suggested she'd gotten an earful about Torin's earlier adventures during the journey between pipes. Kichar—hopefully over her earlier crush—would have covered the Crucible incident, and Ressk would have filled the colonel in on the Silsviss. Too bad Major Kenoton had gotten Werst—with someone available to tell her the details about Big Yellow, Braudy would have had the hat trick.

Thrilled to see Ressk and pleased to see Kichar alive, Torin had had no chance to speak to either of them, but Ressk and Mashona's reunion had been enthusiastic enough to make up the lack.

"Not that I'm questioning your personal integrity, Gunnery Sergeant," Braudy added, her tone edged.

"My report is easy enough to check, sir."

"Of course. We send—or you take—a small party to that sector." Her gaze flicked down toward the stone knife lying exposed on Colonel Mariner's desk. "A sector with a distinct weapons advantage." Her eyes narrowed. "And how do we know the plan is not to ambush us in an attempt to begin the takeover of the remaining two sectors?"

"You'd have to count on my personal integrity, sir."

"I don't find you amusing, Gunnery Sergeant." There was a bitterness just below the surface that had probably started as anger and was looking for a reason to be anger again.

"I'm not being amusing, Lieutenant Colonel."

"Gunnery Sergeant Kerr seems to think we should be working on escape plans." Colonel Mariner's punctuating snort made his opinion plain.

Braudy seemed to share it. "And what would be the point in an escape, Gunnery Sergeant, when there is no way out?"

"There's a rockfall in Major Kenoton's sector, sir. I plan to search beyond it."

"There'll be nothing beyond it but more tunnels," Braudy snorted.

"I don't think so, sir."

"What? You have a gut feeling?"

"Yes, sir."

"And we should trust your gut?" Her lip curled. "Apparently, we've all just waiting for the great Gunnery Sergeant Kerr to show us the way."

"Apparently," Torin agreed blandly.

Off on the other side of the pipe, one of the lieutenants called cadence and boots slammed down on the rock floor. Someone filled a jug with water at the pipe. Two voices, one of them probably Lieutenant McCoy's, rose above the background noise.

"I think," Braudy said at last, "that you . . ."

The lights flickered.

For a heartbeat, two, the silence was so complete Torin doubted anyone was even breathing.

"All right, you lot!" It was the same voice that settled the troops after lights out. "No one told you to stop marching!"

"Gunnery Sergeant Kerr." Braudy pitched her voice to carry over the relieved return of the background noise. "As you seem to have energy to spare. Deal with that."

Lieutenants Teirl, Cafter, and O'Neill got into the tunnel before her. Hardly surprising as they'd been remaining as close to Mike's workstation as Colonel Mariner had allowed.

"Gunnery Sergeant Kerr!" Teirl's hair spread out from his head in a pale pink cloud, the ends waving slightly. "He's done it! Technical Sergeant Gucciard has done it!"

"You sound surprised, Lieutenant."

"Oh, come on, Gunny. He not only interfaced a pair of combats with alien tech, but he programmed them to work like a surge suppressor while he used them as a big floppy charge cable." He grinned, his eyes lightening. "I'm not surprised, I'm astonished! I'm impressed! I'm . . ."

"Acting like a child," O'Neill declared, turning just far enough to fix Teirl with a disapproving sneer. His right arm raised, his right cuff was in Mike's care. "Try to remember you're an officer."

"Try to loosen up," Teirl told him. "You're witnessing a fukking technological miracle!" He lifted his gaze past the fuming lieutenant. "Technical Sergeant, if we were back in the real world, I'd suggest that you get a commendation for this! As we're not, I'm more than willing to show my personal appreciation anywhere, anytime!"

"That's not necessary, sir. Just doing my job."

Only Torin recognized the amusement in his tone as *they're so cute when they're young.*

Teirl—and his hair—bounced. "And you're doing it damned well!"

"John! Your display!" Cafter pulled O'Neill's left arm out from his side. Just up from the cuff, numbers flashed against the fabric. Twelve seconds later, by Torin's silent count, every readout on the sleeve flashed zero twice. "Full charge, Technical Sergeant! Disconnect!"

"Disconnecting."

After a moment, O'Neill lowered his right arm while everyone in the tunnel stared at his left. Without a signal lock, the clock began running data from the last saved time. "Air pressure, temperature, and mix are all fairly close to station default," he said after a moment. When he looked up, his eyes were gleaming. "The colonel needs to see this immediately."

"Wait until I'm done," Cafter told him, shoving him out of the way and thrusting her right arm up. "We'll go together."

"The colonel needs to see this now," O'Neill snorted, spun on one heel, and ran off.

"Yeah, like the colonel's going anywhere," Cafter muttered. "What a kiss-ass—and I don't mean that in a good way." Realizing there were two noncoms in her audience, her eyes lightened.

Neither of them smiled.

Second Lieutenant Teirl, safe behind the bar on his collar tab, snickered.

"Any problems, Technical Sergeant?" Torin asked as the two junior officers pointedly ignored each other.

He shrugged. "Eyebrows are overrated."

By the time Colonel Mariner, Lieutenant Colonel Braudy, and those officers they considered their staff arrived in the tunnel—the delay no doubt due to O'Neill having to deal with every link in the chain of command—Cafter and Teirl were gone and Torin's combats were nearly charged. When Torin'd suggested Mike do the slate while he had the chance, he'd grinned and said, "Did it first. Well, second." His cuff, slightly charred in the incident that removed most of his eyebrows, insisted the time was either 0001 or 1000 depending on the blink.

"Technical Sergeant Gucciard!" Colonel Mariner was not happy. "I should have been notified the moment you fulfilled your mission objectives!"

"Yes, sir."

Torin hid a smile as, somewhat taken aback by the bland agreement, Mariner remained speechless for a full seven seconds. She'd never expected to be so damned happy about knowing exactly how much time had passed. Lowering her arm, she worked the stiffness out of her shoulder, noted that she'd been scooped out of the battle at 1543, and said, "Would you like to be next, sir?"

"I should have been first, Gunnery Sergeant!"

"No, sir, you shouldn't have." Mike took the colonel's wrist in one hand and effortlessly turned it eighty degrees. "Command gets new tech only after it's been thoroughly tested."

"That's not," Mariner began. He paused. And frowned. "What the hell happened to your eyebrows, Technical Sergeant?"

"Got a little scorched, sir. No need to worry," he added as the colonel tried unsuccessfully to jerk his hand away. "The power surges are under control."

Braudy had brought five Marines with her—three of her "staff" as well as Ressk and Kichar. There was exactly enough kibble to feed six more mouths plus Torin.

"Proof we're being watched."

Ressk shook his head. "Easy enough to set up a sensor to do a body count, Gunny. Hook it to an automatic feed bin and no one needs to be within light-years of it."

"Food for Harnett's hunting parties still dropped even if they were out in the tunnels," Torin told him, frowning. "Although not for the three at the barricade."

"Then the sensors extend into the tunnels and the numbers cross over at the halfway point."

She had to admit that made more sense than the Others pulling warm bodies out of the fight to monitor the minor relocations among their prisoners.

Ressk swallowed another double finger of food, then used those fingers to point in the general direction of her face. "Shouldn't you be happier about not being watched, Gunny? Given the whole planning to escape and all?"

"Yes." She should be. But she'd been looking forward to kicking some ass on the way out. Making someone pay for giving a bastard like Harnett the opportunity for abuse. More importantly, making someone pay for the way Mariner, Braudy, and every Marine who'd been captive for any length of time accepted this as their lot. Losing the fight was one thing, having it taken away . . . that was something else again. Turning off a sensor wouldn't give the same visceral satisfaction as feeling flesh compacting under her fists.

The curve of her bowl began to bend in her grip.

Torin took a deep breath and looked up to see Ressk staring at her as though he knew what she'd been thinking.

His nose ridges opened and closed slowly. "If you don't mind my asking, Gunny, how much of a plan do you actually have beyond clearing that rockfall?"

"I plan on getting out."

He studied her face for a long moment, grinned when she lifted her upper lip, and said, "I'm in."

"And me!"

Only Torin bothered to hide her smile at Kichar's enthusiasm. "I didn't call for volunteers."

Mashona chased a last bit of mush around the bottom of her bowl. "Looks like you've got them anyway, Gunny."

No one bothered to mention that there were no guarantees either Mariner or Baudry would release the Marines under their respective commands. No one bothered because a gunnery sergeant was as close to a guarantee as the Corps provided.

"So, just us, then?" Ressk wondered.

"No. There's another two back at Major Kenotan's sector. Corporal Werst . . ."

Kichar started at the familiar name and, when Torin nodded, made a noise they all knew she'd deny later. Mashona reached over and squeezed the younger woman's shoulder.

". . . and Private Kyster. Kyster survived on his own in the tunnels long enough for a broken bone to heal."

"But how," Kichar began, frowned, and glanced over at Ressk who calmly finished his mush. "Oh."

"Tough kid," Mashona noted neutrally.

"Very." Torin agreed.

"I notice there's no di'Taykan in your escape group," Ressk pointed out, tucking his empty bowl into the front of his combats.

"Unless there's other sectors, no di'Taykan came in when we did."

"So Lieutenant Jarret, Mysho . . . ?"

"Sar?" Kichar added.

It was possible, and they all knew it, that the four of them and Werst were all that was left of an entire battalion. That not only the di'Taykan were dead but every other Human, every other Krai. Everyone they'd served with, fought with, drunk with, laughed with . . .

Torin shook it off. "If we want to know what happened to them, we'll have to get out of here." She set her bowl to one side and met each gaze in turn. "Let's think of it as incentive."

"Incentive for what?" Bowl in one hand, slate in the other, thumb working the screen, Mike dropped down beside Torin.

"To get out of here."

"Good. When?"

"As soon as Colonel Mariner releases us."

He took enough of his attention off the slate to raise what remained of his eyebrows in Torin's general direction, the expression very clearly pointing out that Colonel Mariner would release them when Torin arranged it.

"Tomorrow," she acknowledged. "Early enough that we make the barricade before dark."

"Give me time enough to finish setting up Mariner's tech crew. You lot . . ." He used the bowl to gesture at the three Marines, realized he was carrying food, and set the slate carefully down in the cradle of his crossed legs to eat. ". . . we'll charge you three as part of their training and leave right after that."

"Coming with us, Technical Sergeant?"

"Well, I don't plan on staying here, Gunny." He set the bowl, mush barely touched, to one side and picked up the slate again, cradling it in his left hand while the fingers of his right danced over the screen. "Don't know if you've noticed, but after you've been here a while, you stop caring you're here. You start living your life like this—the tunnels, the pipe, the mush, the inane marching about in patterns—is your life."

"I've noticed!" Kichar flushed as four sets of eyes locked on her. "Well, I have."

"So have I," Torin told her. "The technical sergeant and I think there's something in the food that causes complacency," she added, expanding her attention to include the rest. "Kyster's been down here as long as many of them, but he hasn't been eating from the pipe. He's still willing to challenge the status quo."

"Given that we're stuck with the kibble, all the more reason to get out before it dulls us, too." Mike reached out for a fingerful of mush, glanced at the screen, frowned, and flicked the mush to the floor. A quick swipe of his fingers against his combats and they were back on the screen. "And I want the slate out of here before the colonel realizes he can keep the minutes of his staff meetings on it." His fingers actually paused in their patterning when he looked up. "He made a *desk*."

"Uh, Sarge?" Ressk reached out a foot—toward Mike's bowl Torin thought at first and then realized his eyes were locked on the slate. "If you need any help reprogramming . . ."

"Know what you're doing?"

"I do. I've . . ."

At that point the sentence slid into jargon, and Torin didn't bother trying to make sense of it. She knew as much tech as she needed to do her job and was fully confident she could do her job with no tech at all. Mike had already proved himself capable of miracles, and Ressk was personally responsible for the latest security upgrade to the Navy's sysop. It wasn't long before they were shoulder to shoulder peering down at the screen.

"Mike." Torin dropped his nearly full bowl in his lap. "You need to eat while there's food available."

Something in Torin's tone actually got through Mike's programming haze. "You expecting food to not be available?"

"We don't know what's on the other side of that rockfall," she reminded him.

"I can keep working on the slate while you eat, Sarge," Ressk offered eagerly, fingers and toes flexing.

He looked from Ressk to the slate to his bowl and reluctantly passed the slate over. "But you stay right here!"

"Not going anywhere, Technical Sergeant." Ressk's nose ridges were fluttering. Clutching the slate with his right foot left the fingers of both hands free to dance over the screen.

"I get it back when I'm done eating."

"Of course, Technical Sergeant." Noting with some amusement that Mike never took his eyes off the slate, Torin picked up the bit of discarded mush and rolled it between her fingers.

"What you seem to be forgetting, Gunnery Sergeant Kerr, is that you are not running an independent command."

Behind Colonel Mariner's left shoulder, Major Ohi was trying so very hard not to roll his eyes he might as well have surrendered to the expression.

"If Major Kenoton plans on allowing this ludicrous escape plan of yours to be carried out, Technical Sergeant Gucciard *will* be going with you."

"But, sir . . ."

"No arguments, Gunnery Sergeant, you're not going to change my mind. As he is already accompanying you back to Major Kenoton's sector to train technicians in the charging of combats, it only makes sense for him to continue on. Not to mention the fact that with the combats charged there is no job remaining in the known sectors suitable for a man of his rank and ability. He may be the only chance of success for your harebrained plan."

"Yes, sir." In that particular instance, Torin's agreement was sincere.

"Now, then, about the slate . . ."

"Sir." Major Ohi leaned forward. "It's just more useless tech without the sergeant."

Colonel Mariner stared at his hands lying flat on the desk. "Fine," he said after a long moment. "He might as well take it with him, then."

"Thank you, sir." But she wasn't speaking to the colonel.

"You're very good."

"It's just a different kind of programming." Torin grinned as she handed Mike a full canteen and began filling another. "And, in all fairness, the colonel wasn't at the top of his game."

"I feel a bit sorry for Major Ohi."

She took advantage of her position to rest her forehead against the pipe, the smooth metal cool against her skin. "Yeah, me, too. Bright side, it won't be long until he starts thinking of this as his life."

"How long?"

They'd all been scooped up from the same battle. They'd all shared the same timetable. They'd already been in the tunnels for fourteen days. Did she care less now about getting out than she had? Did she care about caring less? The pipe made a surprisingly loud, unsurprisingly hollow thunk as she bounced her forehead off it.

"Torin?"

"We need to get the hell out of here."

"No." Sitting on top of the barricade so that he was eye to eye with Yvonne Sergei, Kyster bared his teeth. "I'm not going. Gunnery Sergeant Kerr said to wait for her here and that's what I'm doing."

"She's not your CO," Sergei insisted. "Major Kenoton is."

"Did he send orders for me to leave the barricade?"

"No, but . . ."

"Then I'm staying." He watched Sergei pace away and then back and then glare at Divint leaning against the barricade absently chewing on a mouthful of biscuit. He'd have stayed even if Major Kenoton had sent orders, but Sergei didn't need to know that.

"A little help here!" she snapped.

"Makes no fukking difference to me if he stays," Divint drawled. "Why do you care?"

"Because it's not what's done. Three Marines come out. Three go back. Not three come out and one goes back with two of the ones who are already here!"

"It's been done once," Divint reminded her, reaching into his vest pocket and breaking off another piece of biscuit.

Kyster stopped listening. The argument didn't actually have anything to do with him; they were arguing for the sake of having something to talk about. Humans sucked at sitting in silence. So did di'Taykan, but they usually found a quieter way to pass the time. He spent a while wondering what a Human would have done out in the tunnels all alone—besides die—and figured they'd have ended up arguing with themselves.

And then . . .

"Shut up!"

"Fuk you! You can't just . . ."

He turned far enough to snap his teeth uncomfortably close to Sergei's chin, and she shut up.

He could hear voices, just at the edge of hearing, and he thought, maybe, he could see a shifting of patterns in the gray distance. If he *could* see patterns, then he'd been hearing the voices for a while but assuming they were just more of the sounds his head made when he was alone.

When Divint shifted, sleeves whispering against the rock, he growled.

By the time Sergei started to say, "I don't think . . ." Kyster was over the barricade and doubling it down the tunnel. He'd heard a sound he knew.

"Yeah, but, Gunny, you convinced Lieutenant Colonel Baudry to transfer us to your team because we were troublemakers, and Kichar here couldn't make trouble if it was marching in front of her wearing a target."

A Krai, older than him. Werst's age probably. The sound had been his bare feet slapping against the rock.

"I can make trouble if I have to!"

Human. Young and female.

"You were troublemakers by association, people; unfortunately, the colonel didn't take to me."

Gunny. Gunny. Gunny.

"Gunny. Incoming."

"Where, Mashona?"

If she could see him at this distance, one small figure moving quickly and close to the tunnel wall, the one called Mashona had good eyes. And not just good for a Human either. Actually good.

They stopped talking then, but they kept moving. Maybe a little faster, Kyster couldn't be sure. He couldn't seem to slow down.

She stopped the others and came forward alone to meet him. Caught his shoulders, brought him to a stop close enough he could feel the heat coming off her body. Catch her scent. He wanted . . . he wanted to climb her. Find refuge in her branches. Be home.

"Hey. It's all right. I'm back."

The only place he wasn't trembling was under her hands. "I waited, Gunny."

"So I see. Sitrep?"

Sitrep. He could feel the heat rise in his face. She needed to know what had been happening while she was gone. He took a deep breath. "Divint and Sergei are at the barricade. I sent Maeken back with Waturu."

"You sent?"

He shrugged, an awkward mimicry of the Human motion. "He went."

"Good job, Marine." She released him as she turned but moved a step closer. He would have closed the distance between them if she hadn't. "Private Kyster, this is Technical Sergeant Gucciard . . ."

Human, male. Older. He looked competent. His eyesbrows looked . . . scorched?

". . . Lance Corporals Ressk and Mashona . . ."

They measured him, Krai and Human, their expressions weirdly identical given their species differences.

". . . and Private Kichar."

The young one. Dark hair, dark eyes, nose like a bird of prey; she stared at him like she wanted his place beside the gunnery sergeant. His lip curled up off his teeth. Ressk noticed, but Kyster didn't care. Not when he felt Gunny's hand close on his shoulder.

"They'll be leaving with us," she said.

Us.

Balanced carefully on the edge of his bad foot, he stood a little straighter.

"Why not have them tear the barricade down and head back with us, Gunny?"

"Not my call." Torin watched Kichar back out of one of the small caves and emphatically signal all clear before moving on. She'd put the young Marine out on point to give her something to do away from Kyster. Kyster believed he'd won their snarling match because he was still walking by Torin's side. Kichar believed she'd won because she'd been given the job of checking the caves. Torin expected she'd have to physically knock their heads together at some point.

"It smelled like a latrine," Mashona continued, rubbing her hand under her nose although the smell in question was half a day's fast walk away.

"Hardly surprising," Torin pointed out. "I'll give Major Kenoton the details, but the decision is his." She didn't care about the barricade. At worst, it was a symbol of Harnett's control. At best, it gave the captive Marines something to do.

And those were valid reasons for not caring.

She wasn't not caring just because she didn't care.

How long did they have before the additive in the food sapped their ambition and trapped them in the tunnels until the end of the war?

"Let's pick up the pace a bit, people."

"Forty minutes before the evening kibble." Mike checked Ressk's sleeve as they turned onto the last straight section of tunnel before the node. "We made good time."

"Forty minutes if the areas are in sync," Torin pointed out, indicating that Kichar should fall in behind with the other three. "Because I'm going in first," she said as the private passed.

Kichar blinked. "I wasn't going to ask, Gunnery Sergeant."

"You were thinking *why* so loudly it was setting up an echo." She ran a hand back through her hair and sighed, turning just far enough to sweep a gaze over all five of her . . . team? Squad? "Odds are good they won't care, but the Marines at this pipe have reason to be paranoid. If they see me, they shouldn't overreact." She turned again to stare down the tunnel. "If they react at all."

Major Kenoton listened without comment to Torin's report, his hair nearly still. When she finished, he visibly roused himself and said, "Colonel Mariner?"

"You know him, sir?"

The major's eyes lightened slightly. Torin thought they'd gained some variation in shade during the eight days she'd been gone, but she couldn't be certain. "I know of him, Gunnery Sergeant—a staff officer lost while accompanying a diplomatic mission to the Edge. And he's the senior officer in here?"

"Yes, sir."

"Bet that's up Baudry's ass," he muttered, then raised his voice to add, "I read the lieutenant colonel's file on the battle of the TriVor Stations. She reminds me a lot of you. When does Colonel Mariner want to see me?"

"He didn't say, sir. I expect he'll send a runner. It's how he communicates with Lieutenant Colonel Baudry."

Sitting on one of the folded pallets with his back braced against the pipe, the major stared at her for a long moment. "Colonel Mariner could have sent orders with you, but it seems he just wanted you and your . . ." His gaze flicked over her shoulder to where the others were waiting. ". . . team gone. Why is that, Gunnery Sergeant?"

"I got the impression he didn't want to delay the escape attempt, sir." Torin had no qualms about using Mariner to overrule any of the major's objections and she was running out of time to be subtle.

"The escape attempt?"

"Yes, sir. Through the rockfall."

"The rockfall." The ends of his hair flicked back and forth as he frowned. Just as Torin thought she'd have to remind him about the rockfall, he said, "So Colonel Mariner has approved your plan, has he?" He sounded like he didn't believe her. Fortunately, he also sounded like he didn't care. "All you'll find is more tunnels, Gunnery Sergeant. Waste of time. Still, it's not like we don't have time to waste and speaking of time . . ." He tapped his left sleeve. ". . . Lieutenant Myshai tells me your tech is up and running."

"Yes, sir." Torin brought her arms out from behind her back and showed him that her cuff believed it was 0917. "Technical Sergeant Gucciard has developed a way to use a pair of combats as a buffer and recharge off the power lines in the tunnels."

"He's worked out a way to interface the combats with alien technology?"

"Yes, sir."

"I'm impressed. Lieutenant!"

Lieutenant Myshai hurried over, hair swaying against her movement. "Sir?"

"Tell Staff Sergeant Pole that Technical Sergeant Gucciard is to have whatever he needs."

"Yes, sir!"

"Maybe we'll get lucky," he said thoughtfully as Myshai led the sergeant away, "and someone stored some decent music in their inseam. When do you plan on leaving, Gunny?"

"As soon as possible, sir."

The twenty-second tone delayed his answer. As sergeants began sending two Marines from each squad to the pipe, Kenoton smiled. "I have a good idea of what you'll need from me, but I'd like to hear you say it."

"I'd like to take Werst, sir."

"Not what I meant, Gunny."

The supplements had put some color back in his face, but the major, like everyone else at this pipe, was still painfully thin. She hated to ask, but if she'd intended to live doing only what she wanted, she'd never have joined the Corps. "If we could pull half the biscuits tomorrow and half the next day as well as filling a couple of sleeves with kibble, we'll have . . ."

"You'll have to find another food source." He didn't sound like the loss of the biscuits bothered him much. Apparently *not giving a shit* had trumped *nearly starving to death*. "Even at only three biscuits a day, you're looking at five days. Maximum. Or two and a half out, two and a half back. You won't get far."

"If we each have a sleeve . . ."

"An extra two days."

They could cut rations further if they had to; let the Krai forage. Even starting from the rockfall with full canteens, water would be the problem.

"It's still worth attempting, sir."

"If you go alone, you'll get a lot farther."

That was true enough and Torin had lain awake in the dark at the base of the barricade, ignoring Kyster's grip on her sleeve, working the numbers over and over, knowing that every Marine with her meant one less day in the tunnels. But, bottom line, for whatever reason—imprisonment, the kibble, Craig—she didn't have it in her to carry the weight of three hundred Marines she couldn't see or hear or fight for. Make her responsible for the lives of six Marines who were right there, right in her face, and she didn't give a rat's ass how she personally felt or what the Others put in the food, she'd get them out. She'd come back for the rest.

"Hey, Gunny, my combats won't fukking charge."

Torin looked up from tying off a sleeve of kibble. "Technical Sergeant Gucciard say why?"

Werst shook his head. "Said he could find out if Ressk managed to pull the diagnostic program up on the slate."

"And Ressk said?"

"He'd have better odds of getting H'san opera."

With the tech up and running, they had the time, environmental conditions, medical readouts, and a few of the actual physical functions. The body armor was iffy at best. She'd have to talk to Staff Sergeant Pole about vests.

Some Marines arrived in the small caves with vests, some didn't. As far as she could tell, it was completely random. She'd arrived with one, so had Mike, Ressk, and Kichar. Werst, Kyster, and Mashona hadn't.

None of the Krai had come through with boots. None of them seemed too upset about it.

"SpaceCops?"

Pole grinned as they skirted two dozen Marines grouped around one gesticulating di'Taykan. "Nermci has the first three seasons damned near memorized. Every afternoon, he does an episode—most of the dialogue and some of the action even."

"How much do you figure he's making up?" Torin had been a bit of a *SpaceCops* fan herself, and she couldn't remember that particular gesture.

"Does it matter?"

"I guess not."

"Point is, it's giving people something to do. Something to look forward to." He snorted. "Hell, not even the di'Taykan can fuk all the time."

"News to me." Torin stopped walking, forcing Pole to turn and actually look at her. "Staff, this place is . . ."

"Safe," he said quietly. "Now. Thanks to you. There's nothing out there but more tunnels, Gunny." One hand rose to scratch at an ingrown hair on his throat. "You do what you have to, but my responsibility is with these Marines right here."

"And if I find a way out?"

He shrugged carefully as though his uniform still rubbed against bone too close to the surface. "We'll reassess then."

She nodded. There wasn't really another response available. "While I'm gone, Staff, the small caves need to be searched."

"We'll maintain the patrols for incomers, Gunny."

"Good, but we also need to find the way the Others are bringing the new Marines in."

Pole's eyes narrowed. "We?"

"You."

"Seems like something you could stay around for."

"A way in doesn't necessarily mean a way out, Staff, and my gut says escape is on the other side of that rockfall."

"Rockfall will still be there after the caves have been searched."

"I know, but . . ." Torin looked around the node. At the pipe. At the Marines. At the place where Harnett died. At the episode of *Space-Cops* which had definitely not included *that* gesture. Had she started feeling like she belonged there? ". . . I don't have that kind of time."

"Fuk, Gunny," Pole snickered. "All you've got is time."

Torin still had most of the supplements she'd been carrying but pulled another three sheets for each species from Harnett's stores. The only tube of sealant she could find was the one she carried, and the stores were skint of pain killers entirely, but there were enough filters that everyone who'd come through in a vest must've been carrying. That seemed like a sign to Torin, so since neither Kenoton, or, more importantly, Pole cared, she made sure that all of her people had the full set of three.

No one tried to stop her when she claimed the knives and clubs Harnett's men had carried.

Ressk and Kichar had hung onto the canteens they'd been given for the two-day trip between Baudry's and Mariner's pipes. Before leaving, Mike had somehow managed to talk Lieutenant McCoy out of one; Kyster still had the one he'd carried out to the barricade . . .

"Not the same one, Gunny. Traded with Maeken when I sent him back."

. . . and Torin had made damned sure she'd left Mariner's pipe carrying all three of the canteens she'd walked in wearing. One to Mashona, one to Werst; that left only one extra.

"Gunnery Sergeant Kerr?"

Jiyuu. Torin handed Werst the tied-off sleeve of kibble and turned.

Not only Jiyuu but Darlys and Watura as well. All three di'Taykan were in vests and carrying canteens—the three canteens that were to go out with the relief to the barricade, Torin assumed, and slung over Watura's shoulder was another tied-off sleeve.

"We want to go with you."

"Why?"

Jiyuu glanced over at Darlys. Her hair flattened and she said, "You are *sa verniticna sa vey*. We need to atone for the evil we committed under Harnett. If we remain here . . ." She shook her head. ". . . it will be forgotten."

Unable to stop herself, Torin searched out Private Graydon and found him standing, arms wrapped around his torso, at the edge of a group of Marines. "I don't think so," she growled.

"Perhaps not by everyone," Darlys admitted, ocher eyes so dark they looked almost brown, "but Akemi and Maeken are sleeping communally and only Terantowicz speaks of taking power again."

Behind her, Werst snarled, "Terantowicz doesn't know when to fucking quit."

No one argued.

"You want me to punish you?"

"We want to work toward your forgiveness."

It might have been what Darlys wanted. She had a fanatic's attachment to that whole progenitor thing and was well on the way to making it a personal religion. Since Torin had considered herself the voice of God pretty much from the moment she made sergeant, she didn't have a lot of trouble with that in theory, but she'd be damned if she was going to give any of Harnett's people a way out.

"No."

"We can be useful, Gunnery Sergeant." Jiyuu's hand rose toward his masker, but at Torin's glare, he snapped it back to his side.

Jiyuu was doing what he'd done with Harnett, sucking up to power.

"I said, no."

"You have no di'Taykan on your team," Watura pointed out. "According to the Parliamentary regulations pertaining to the Corps, all three species must be proportionally represented in any maneuver."

She didn't have the faintest fukking idea what Watura was up to although the way he was standing protectively behind Jiyuu suggested he was there only because the other di'Taykan was. How sweet. And it didn't matter. "What part of no don't you understand, Privates? You are not going with us to find forgiveness. You are not going with us because I'm the scariest thing left down here. And you are sure as shit not going with us because the Parliament that keeps fukking insisting that the Others don't take prisoners wrote you a fukking note!" She was right up in Watura's face, nerves singing with the proximity and more than willing to turn the low-level lust into violence.

"Gunny."

Mike's voice, closer than he'd been, his voice held understanding and warning about equally mixed.

Torin stepped back, took a deep breath as soon as she'd gained some distance, and forced her fists to uncurl. She seemed to have been doing that a lot since she'd arrived in the tunnels.

Watura swallowed and wet his lips. He was visibly shaken, but only his hair gave it away. His voice remained steady. "Major Kenoton sanctioned our request to go with you."

"He *sanctioned* it?"

"Yes, Gunnery Sergeant."

"Did he make it an order?"

Darlys would have lied to force Torin's hand—Torin could see that on her face—but she let Watura answer.

"No. . . ."

"Then you're shit out of luck, aren't you?" She pivoted on one heel and scooped up her canteen. "Let's go, people. I want to get as far as we can before the lights go out."

"Gunnery Sergeant Kerr . . ."

She indicated that the others should keep moving—Mike looked dubious but snapped the slate onto his vest and waved Kichar out on point—then she turned just far enough to growl, "When I say no, I mean no."

Terantowicz gave them a one finger wave good-bye as they left the area. "You're going to die out there," she said cheerfully.

"If I was certain of that, Private, you'd be coming with us," Torin told her in exactly the same tone.

Her expression twisted and Torin could read *like to see you make me* as clearly as if she'd spoken the words out loud. That she hadn't proved she was smarter than she looked.

"Ten to dark, Gunny."

Torin acknowledged Mashona's observation but kept her team moving.

There was a red-brown stain on the smooth rock floor outside one of the small caves and the smell that spilled out into the tunnel coated the back of the throat with the taste of decay. All four Humans were breathing through their teeth.

"What is it?" Kichar fought to keep from gagging.

"Rot," Torin told her shortly, a little surprised given the constant temperature and lack of moisture that the smell lingered over a ten-day later. She figured it was likely the lack of other smells that made it seem so potent, and if it wasn't . . . well, she wasn't crawling into the cave to find out.

"Marines that Harnett left to die, Gunny?"

"Not exactly." When Kyster glanced up at her, Torin shook her head. The story didn't need to be told. "Five minutes should get us to the next t-junction and around the corner. Air'll be fresher there."

It was—although given that they were still underground "fresher" was a relative term. The air had the same recycled flavor as air on a station or ship—familiar enough to be disregarded—and Torin wasted a moment wondering where it was coming from. She hadn't seen any vents. Up by the top of the pipe where the lights made it impossible to get a good look at the "ceiling"? Probably.

Around the corner, one small cave cut into the left wall in the approximately twenty meters of straight tunnel. For thousands, maybe millions of years caves had meant security to early Humans, and Torin could feel herself responding to that racial memory. She hadn't even thought to question spending that first night in the cave with Kyster, so maybe she'd been more shocky than she'd thought because now, training took one look at a single, tiny entrance and screamed "trap."

"Kyster."

"Gunny?"

"Anything in this place but Marines?"

"No, Gunny."

"No tunnel trolls?" Werst grunted.

Kyster stared at the older Krai, nose ridges slowly opening and closing. "Tunnel troll?"

"A troll that lives in tunnels." The *you idiot* was silent but clear.

He glanced over at Torin, who shrugged. "We find a med-op down here to patch you up and you may try to kick his ass. Until we do, attempt to get along." She checked her sleeve. Three minutes to dark. The question now became did they keep moving with the cuff lights or did they bunk down for the "night." Six hours until the tunnel lights came back. A Marine could get by on a lot less sleep, and all of them had, but eventually fatigue impacted on decision making. Balance that against the need to get out before the kibble melted their will. Add in the potential for getting lost as it became harder to identify the correct turns and cross tunnels.

One minute to dark.

"We're stopping for the night, people. Pick a spot up against the right wall."

"Gunny, the cave . . ."

"Has no back door." Torin cut Mashona off. "And we're against the right wall," she continued before one of them could ask, "because if anything comes out of the cave in the night, it'll orient itself along the left."

"What's going to crawl out of the cave, Gunny?" Kichar asked, dark eyes wide.

"Who the hell knows? We do know that since the incoming Marines appear in the caves, the Others have access. So piss against the left if you're going to." She sat back against the side of the tunnel, club cradled in her arms like her KC-7, and stretched out her legs. She had a job to do, she had no officer to interfere with her doing it; if she'd been carrying her actual weapon, she'd have been relatively happy.

Kyster settled in on one side while Mike propped himself up on the other, using the last minute of light to work on the slate.

The sudden darkness was no longer entirely absolute. The circular beams of four cuff lights danced over the opposite wall.

"Lights out, people."

"I'm just going to work a little longer," Mike murmured, head down, face illuminated by the screen. "I've almost accessed the index."

"And?"

"And then I can start recovering programs."

"We," Ressk muttered quietly from along the tunnel.

"We," Mike amended, his smile shifting the shadows.

Torin slid along the smooth rock until she was lying flat, club along her right side.

"Gunny?" Kyster's head was practically on her shoulder. "You know they're following us, right?"

Past Ressk, Mashona snorted.

"I know," Torin told him. The three di'Taykan had been careful but not quite careful enough, not when they were the only other movement in the tunnels. "Now get some sleep, we have a lot of rock to move tomorrow. Technical Sergeant Gucciard, remember the dark lasts only six hours . . ." It had seemed longer until they could time it. ". . . and we move out with the light."

He snorted. "I never sleep much without my own pillow anyway."

"Well, maybe by tomorrow you can call home on that thing and have it delivered." She slipped her hand inside her vest, closed her fingers around the salvage tag, and closed her eyes.

The rocks in the fall were flat, brittle, and felt just a little greasy. Rubbing her fingertips together under her nose, Torin could pick up an oily scent that reminded her of low-tech machinery. It matched the puddle's flavor. Odds were evening out that the crack had exposed a natural vein of water rather than a broken pipe.

"Shale," Mashona offered, tossing another onto the pile behind her and rubbing her hands on her thighs. Settled on new worlds, Humans had taken the labeling of oldEarth with them and concentrated on similarities—differences carefully cataloged and then ignored by almost everyone.

"Slate," Torin corrected. "Started as shale but went through some high heat; it'll shatter before it crumbles." She glanced down at the stone knife in her boot. "Question is, was it changed by the volcano or by whatever the Others used to make these tunnels?"

"Does it matter?" Werst snorted.

"Everything matters in the end, Corporal." Torin reached up and carefully began to ease one of the medium-sized slabs free. "You never know what information you'll need to win the war."

"And I'm sure this'll be useful, Gunny, if we're ever up against a battalion of geologists."

Torin grinned down at him. "Who's to say we haven't been? They threw rocks on Simunthitir." She braced her legs and shifted her grip as the stone started to move. "Stand clear—when this comes out, we're going to get another spill."

Small rocks slid into the holes left by the removal of the larger rocks. This time they kept spilling in and over the space, edges whispering against each other until Torin was standing ankle-deep in shards of rock, boots protecting her from minor injuries. She twisted, handed the larger rock she still held off to Mashona and studied the rock face as she freed herself. If anything, it extended a bit farther out into the tunnel.

"Get the feeling the whole planet's going to slide down here given half a chance, Gunny?"

"If it does," she grunted, reaching for another rock, "it'll make it easier to get to the surface."

"Don't even know if there's an atmosphere," Werst pointed out.

"I'd put prisoners in a moon." Ressk glanced up from the slate. "Make it harder to escape from."

"Gunny, what if there's no atmosphere?" Waiting her turn at the rock face, Kichar sounded a little desperate.

"Well, that depends, Private. How long can you hold your breath?"

They started with three Marines at the rock face, either Technical Sergeant Gucciard or Ressk working on the slate, two hours on, two hours off. On her first break, Torin walked back to the cave she'd been found in and swept her sleeve light over the walls.

She'd meant everything she'd said to Pole about a way in not necessarily meaning a way out, but she was here . . .

"What're you looking for, Gunny?" Kyster hadn't quite pressed up against her leg.

"The way out. If the Others dropped me here . . ." She glanced down at the top of his head. ". . . and we both know they did, then there has to be an access hatch." Atmosphere, air pressure, gravity; according to her sleeve, it was exactly the same in the cave as it had been in the tunnel. Rough in places, and smooth in others, the walls, ceiling, and floor were solid. Her sleeve light threw cracks into high relief, but none enclosed an area large enough to move an unconscious body through. "You found me soon after I arrived; how did you know I was in the cave?"

"I heard you moan. No noises but me," he added at her silent suggestion. "Makes not me noises really loud."

Being back in this cave wasn't doing Kyster any good, devolving his speech patterns to near where they'd been at Torin's arrival. Since that was all being in the cave was accomplishing, Torin waved him out and followed close behind. The Others had to have a way in—they weren't just pushing Marines in through solid rock.

Still feeling a solid surface under her feet, she couldn't change her position. The pressure against her lower body was so slight it couldn't possibly be holding her in place. But it was.

What had been the floor was now up around their waists.

Then the floor touched her chin. It felt cool. She couldn't smell anything but the smoke she'd inhaled before she got the filter on. . . .

Torin reached out and touched the tunnel wall for reassurance. Definitely rock. Still, there was nothing that said there couldn't be a patch of organic plastic in the ceiling of one of those caves. It would feel like rock to the touch—Big Yellow had felt like all of the substances it had appeared to become—and without the scanners in their helmets, they'd never find it. And that could explain why no helmets had come through.

She could find it. All she had to do was run her hands over every square millimeter of every cave and every tunnel. Crucible had proved that the alien reacted to her—to her and to Craig back on Ventris—probably because of the way they'd been deep scanned.

From what she'd seen, Big Yellow—well, the component parts of

Big Yellow, and that was still easier to say than polynumerous molecular sentient polyhydroxide alcoholydes with an agenda—was certainly capable of setting up this kind of a system, but it seemed like an awfully complicated load of rubbish to go through just to . . . what? Study a few hundred captive Marines?

No. Her father had never thought much of the Corps or her joining it, but the two of them—her father and the Corps—had shared a few essential beliefs, the relevant one being that the simplest answer was usually the right answer.

Why would unknown aliens bother to set up such a complex scenario when they'd proved they could observe the entire Corps with no one the wiser? And not only observe but make them dance?

"Twenty-seven percent of the polyhydroxide alcoholyde in the major's arm has migrated—primarily to his nervous system . . . I suspect the alien entity is probably observing the major from the inside."

It didn't make sense.

Prisoners of war did. They'd been at war for a long time.

But the Others didn't take prisoners.

Except they did.

"Gunny?"

Bottom line, it didn't matter who was holding them. They were leaving.

"Come on, Private. Let's move some rock."

By midafternoon, they'd switched to three at the rock face, three carrying the debris back out of the way. By early evening . . .

Torin turned away from the face, wiping her sweaty forehead on her sleeve. The sides of the tunnel were closing in, and work was slowing as the three Marines carrying had to move farther and farther back. "That's enough of this shit," she snarled and raised her voice. "Darlys! Jiyuu! Watura! Turn your maskers to maximum and haul ass! If you plan on going through after us," she added as the three di'Taykan appeared a little better than five hundred meters away at the first bend in the tunnel, "you can damned well help haul rock! Double time, Privates! Move!"

"I thought you didn't want them with us?" Mike murmured as the three small figures began to run.

"I don't," Torin growled. "But I'm not wasting the time to drag them back to Staff Sergeant Pole, so if we're stuck with them, they might as well make themselves useful."

"You brought supplements for all three species."

She turned to glare at the tech sergeant, who gave her a blandly neutral expression back. "Force of habit," she said at last.

By dark, although the rockfall looked no different, Jiyuu swore he could smell a change in the air up near the ceiling.

" 'Cause stink rises, you fukking ass kisser," Werst snarled. "And only Gunny here is still smelling like *heritaig.*"

"If I didn't know that was a type of meat pie, I'd be flattered." Immediate area around her illuminated by the light in her sleeve, Torin chewed a mouthful of biscuit. "We're not setting off the kinds of slides we were," she said thoughtfully after she swallowed. "We work in shifts through the dark and we should get through tomorrow."

By midday, no more rock slid down to replace rock removed. By midafternoon, they were making significant forward progress. By evening, a slide opened the fall up to the other side, both the di'Taykan and the Krai swearing they could smell a change in the air.

Standing on Mashona's shoulders, her hands gripping his ankles to hold him in place, Kyster twisted his body through the space, arms stretched out in front of him. Broken rock snagged the sleeves of his uniform, and jerking his head away from the line of pain as a protruding shard scored his scalp only drove the opposite temple into a point rather than an edge.

"You okay, kid?"

He tightened his grip with his good foot and muttered, "Not a kid." as his fingers butted up against a barrier of loose rock. The little light that managed to seep around his body told him nothing, so he squirmed a little closer and shoved, swearing as the rock spilled through to the other side and a piece from the side of the narrow passage fell loose and smacked against his cheek.

"Kyster!"

Nothing else seemed to be falling, but he could feel . . . not a breeze but movement in the air against his face. "I'm okay, Gunny! We're through!"

"What do you see?"

He twisted to let a little more light through from behind him, but it barely pushed the gray out past the ends of his fingers. "Feels like open space, but it's dark.

"Use your light!" Mashona barked, whacking him in the calf with the side of her head.

His light. He'd spent so much time in the dark, his uniform doing nothing more than covering bruises, he'd forgotten that most of the tech was back on-line. Glad that Gunnery Sergeant Kerr couldn't see him flush, he tapped his left cuff and peered, eyes watering, along the beam. No mistaking the curved walls or the light dangling from the ceiling or the darker patch of a small cave.

"Gunny! It's more tunnels!"

EIGHT

AS THE ONLY HUMAN MALE, TECHNICAL Sergeant Gucciard
was the bulkiest, so they sized the break to the new tunnels for
him.

"He's tech, he's not a fukking tank," Torin sighed, stopping Watura
from dragging out one of the larger rocks. "You remove that and you'll
start another slide. Just make sure he can get his shoulders through;
everything else is compactable."

Another time that would have been more than a di'Taykan could
resist, but here and now none of them were comfortable enough
around her to make the obvious comment. That didn't bother her
much although, to those used to serving with di'Taykan, the innuendo
was conspicuous by its absence.

Stomachs sloshing with water—the easiest way to carry another
couple of liters—they went through: Krai, di'Taykan, Human, one
representative of each species at a time. Facing the unexpected, it
was smartest to have the strengths of all three species available as
quickly as possible. Torin went through after the first three, an extra
Human, safe enough to leave her people in the tunnels behind where
she knew there was no threat, needing to be with those facing the
unknown. Wanting to be first but well aware that leading from that
far out front wasn't smart.

The passage added new bruises to old ones turning green under
her combats. The width of the rock fall was the only thing that made it

even relatively stable, and, at that, the exit into the other tunnels was less a controlled descent than a function of gravity and loose rock.

Torin rode boots and ass to the floor of the new tunnel, rising, club in hand, only when stability was assured. Gunnery sergeants did not go slip sliding away. It was in the manual.

Moving away from the fall to give the rest of her team room to come through, Torin played her light over the walls. The shadows took over before she could determine the lay of the land, but it looked exactly like the tunnels they'd come from—exception, the lack of lights with just over three hours to go before dark. The only thing she could smell was the faint oily odor of the rock dust they were disturbing, and the only thing she could hear was the slide and clatter and profanity of the rest of her team coming through.

The nearest small cave was empty and skewed slightly as though the force that had brought the section of tunnel down had twisted it off center. Torin ran her fingertips over the cracks in the rock by the low entrance—rough, smooth, rough again—examined the residue on her skin with more paranoia than it probably merited, then headed back to the fall.

Mike had chosen to come through last and seemed to have paused, stretched out along the broken rock. Torin could just see the top of his head as he squirmed around until he was lying on his back. Given the tight fit she'd experienced and the width of his shoulders, that was some serious compression going on. "You still with us, Technical Sergeant?"

"Yeah." He shifted, sending a piece of loose rock down the slope.

"Thought so. Power cable."

"What about it?"

"I've got one."

Jiyuu murmured something obvious in the background as Torin said, "I'm missing the significance, Sergeant."

"I might be able to give us some light. Ressk! You got a dangling cable down there?"

Torin turned to look as Ressk did.

"Not dangling, Sarge, but loose. The light's hanging off the one-eighty end and here at zero the cable's dropped a belly."

"Give it a tug!"

Ressk glanced over at Torin, who nodded. At best, multiple cuff lights created variable patterns of light and dark and, given a choice, she preferred a few less shadows for an enemy to hide in. And they'd find enemies eventually; they were Marines, that's what they did.

Reaching up over his head, Ressk wrapped his fingers around the bottom of the bell and tugged. With a soft hiss, the cable pulled out of the ceiling. The watching Marines moved respectfully back against the wall, no one wanting to be the casualty who discovered the cable was live.

"Got a dangler now, Sarge."

"Pass it up."

"You'll come up a bit short," Torin noted as she waved Ressk forward.

"Empty sleeve'll work as a temporary patch," Mike grunted. Half a dozen smaller rocks slid free as he worked a hand back and out past his shoulder. "Same principle as using the internal tech as a conduit," he added before Torin could ask.

"Okay. Jiyuu, get Ressk up on your shoulders, that'll put him close enough to help if needed. You have a time frame on this fix, Sergeant?"

"I'm repairing alien tech with a *sleeve*, Gunny."

Torin glanced down at her cuff. "So, ten? Fifteen?"

"Fifteen."

"Good enough. Werst, Kichar, give me five out into the tunnels, mark, and head back."

"Yes, Gunnery Sergeant!"

Werst rolled his eyes at Kichar and slapped the end of his club lightly into his left hand. "My light's not working, Gunny."

"Kichar's is."

"And if we run into a troop of tunnel trolls?"

"Don't engage. Get your asses back here and report."

Torin didn't hear Kichar's question, but Werst's answer rang out loud and clear as the recon team moved out. "Yeah, well no one believed in the Il'san either, not until they showed up in our *serley* orbit."

He had a point. "Everyone else, stay ready to pull Technical Sergeant Gucciard clear should the slide collapse."

Without a light actually on her face, Torin couldn't see Mashona's expression, but she could hear the amusement in her voice. "You expecting a collapse, Gunny?"

"The technical sergeant is repairing alien technology with a piece of torn uniform—I'm expected the Goddamned tunnel to blow up."

"Ressk's helping." Mike's voice sounded muffled.

"And that makes all the difference," Torin snorted.

"Ah, come on, Gunny, have some faith."

"It's still alien tech and a dirty sleeve, Ressk." Feet spread to shoulder width, weight evenly distributed, she cradled her club in the crook of her left elbow—a position she could hold indefinitely. She wanted to walk down the tunnel and crawl into that cave. Crawl, because the twisted entrance was low enough even Kyster would have to duck. But if she checked that one, rubbed her palms over every nook and cranny waiting for a response, torn between hoping something would or something wouldn't, then she'd have to check them all and the walls of the tunnels, and that would help no one—because who was to say that if Big Yellow was involved, it couldn't move the entrance as it pleased? Walking down the tunnel to that cave smacked of obsession, and she had no time for that sort of shit if she was going to do her job. *So stop fukking thinking about it.*

Ten minutes of Mike swearing softly to himself and once or twice not so softly to the tunnel at large, then Werst and Kichar were back.

"Nothing out there, Gunny." Werst was senior by a considerable margin, but Torin could tell he was making the report because Kichar wanted to. "Tunnel's the same, though. Same curves, same caves." He grunted and amended: "Same *lack* of caves for the most part. More rocks on the floor of the tunnel, some continuing damage from whatever caused this shit." A nod toward the fall. "Looks stable, though, and if the pattern holds, we'll hit another pipe."

"It's dark," Watura snorted, waving his cuff light until Torin's expression snapped his arm back down to his side. "How can you tell the pattern's the same?"

"They're Recon," Torin reminded him. "It's what they do."

"We took a look inside the two caves we passed, Gunnery Sergeant." Kichar's need for Torin to notice her won out over protocol. "They were empty of everything except, well, rocks."

"Marines never come in this far on the other side," Kyster reminded her.

"Gunnery Sergeant Kerr did."

"She was *chosen*," Darlys announced breathily.

Torin felt the muscles in her jaw clench independent of any conscious action. "She is the H'san's mother, Private." It was something Staff Sergeant Beyhn used to say.

Darlys' hair stilled. "Sorry, Gunnery Sergeant."

The pause lengthened, Ressk's background muttering about power flux capacitors louder than it should have been.

"So . . ." Mashona flicked her light up into Kichar's face. ". . . did you check *under* the rocks."

The young Marine stared from Mashona to Torin under the arm she'd thrown up to cover her eyes. "Should we have checked under the rocks?"

"No, we shouldn't have," Werst muttered, shaking his head.

"Gunny . . ."

She turned in time to see Kyster's nose ridges flare as, eyes squinted nearly shut in Torin's cuff light, he looked up toward the top of the rockslide.

". . . cooking!"

"Like meat," Werst agreed, moving until he stood shoulder to shoulder with the younger Krai. "But not."

Torin stepped forward until she was standing next to Jiyuu. "Technical Sergeant?"

"What!"

Not exactly the correct military response. Ass-deep in a problem, it seemed Technical Sergeant Gucciard got a bit terse.

"What's cooking?"

"Not me." Still lying in the gap, he sounded more amused than hurt so Torin took his response at face value. "The kibble is conductive."

"I'm more thrilled to be eating it than ever," Torin muttered. "You almost . . ."

All three di'Taykan swore as the lights came up. The multiple tiny light receptors in their eyes had probably been a fraction of a second too late slamming shut.

"Cuff lights off, people. Let's get Technical Sergeant Gucciard on solid ground."

"You weigh a fukking ton," Jiyuu muttered as Ressk climbed down off his shoulders. He twitched a bit as Watura came up behind him, then settled back into the other di'Taykan's touch. "Feels good," he sighed as long fingers dug into his back.

"At least wait until the lights are out," Mashona snorted. "We don't need . . . Ow!" She aimed her light at the floor. "Fukking rock hit me in the ankle!"

"Fall's shifting!" Leaping forward, Torin wrapped one hand around Mike's right wrist. "Mashona, grab his other hand and get him the hell out of there!"

They managed to drag him free as the rockfall collapsed, dancing back as he belly surfed the wave of rock. When the dust cleared, they were ankle-deep and his lower legs were buried.

"Guess we're not going back," Ressk noted thoughtfully.

"Good thing that was never the plan," Torin grunted, moving one of the larger pieces just far enough for her to free her right foot. "You all right, Sergeant?"

He peered down at his sleeve. "Impact seems to have fixed my clock."

"Glad to hear it. Darlys, Watura, dig out the technical sergeant, and let's get moving."

"Kilometers to go before we sleep, Gunny?" Mashona asked, arms flailing as she fought her way free.

"Farther than that," Torin grunted.

With the lights on, even Watura had to agree that the tunnels they were traveling were the same pattern as the ones they'd just left although these were marked with cracks and fissures.

"Looks like whatever brought the tunnel down ended at the rockfall," Torin noted, stepping over a rock that had clearly dropped from the ceiling.

"How do you figure, Gunny?"

She shrugged. "No damage on the other side."

"Could have *started* at the rockfall," Mike offered, reaching up to poke at the ceiling and stepping quickly aside as a two-centimeter-thick slab the size of his hand dropped and shattered. "But all the force was expended in this direction."

"So, not natural?"

"Couldn't tell you without more intell, but the universe is a big place and *natural* means what you want it to."

"Uh-huh." Here and now, Torin didn't really care what had caused the damage. "Let's go, people! Sing out if you smell or hear anything in the caves. Otherwise, we're making time. Let's remember this is an escape, the Others are definitely monitoring the pipes, so sooner or later they'll know we're on our way out."

"Do we expect a fight, Gunnery Sergeant?"

"We always expect a fight, Private Kichar. We're Marines; it's what we do."

They hadn't gone far before she headed back through the march to Ressk and Mike bringing up an increasingly distant rear. "No one told you to stop walking," she pointed out as Darlys paused and started to turn. "And you two . . ." Reaching out, she pulled the slate from Mike's hands and snapped it onto her vest. ". . . you'll get this back when we stop."

"You can't," Mike began, glanced at the slate, checked her expression, and spread his hands. Beside him, Ressk wisely remained silent.

"We're racing the additive in the food." Her voice pitched to carry, she knew even Werst and Kichar out on point could hear her. "Sooner or later, we're going to want to sit down and give up, so if we're going to escape, we don't have time to let reprogramming slow us."

"That reprogramming could help us escape," Mike reminded her.

"Please," Torin grinned. "Tech's a crutch. An unarmed Marine in underwear can deal with anything the universe can dish out."

"Vacuum?"

"For that, we'd also need boots."

"So we can die with them on?"

"Pretty much. Since you're back here anyway . . ." She nodded at the club hanging from a loop on his vest. ". . . you've got our six."

When the lights went out, she kept them moving for another two hours on the cuffs. Four hours' sleep would be plenty given that a large part of the day had consisted of standing around and waiting for the rest of the team to inch through the passage in the rockfall.

"Least no one's shooting at us," Werst grunted as he stretched out and flexed his feet.

"Hey!" Mashona reached across Kichar to smack him, her cuff light drawing an arc across the ceiling of the tunnel. "You trying to get your fukking ass blown away? Anyone's short," she grumbled as she flicked off her light and pillowed her head on her arm, "you can keep that to yourself, too."

Without perimeter pins, Torin set half-hour watches. "You two," she added to Mike and Ressk, lit once again by the slate, "are excused, but I want no more than an hour's work before you get some sleep. I'll take third watch to make sure of it." Settling on the floor by Kyster, fully aware Darlys, who had first watch, would spend it staring at her rather than an empty tunnel, she closed one hand around the salvage tag, and closed her eyes.

Mike looked pleased when the lights came back on. Yawning, scratching at the edge of his jaw where the depilatory had begun to wear off, he stood and shot a calculating look back the way they'd come. "Have to admit, I half expected that sleeve to burn out by now."

"Another fine reason to move our collective butts." Torin, who'd been up since just before the lights had come back on, kicked at the bottom of Jiyuu's boots. "Nap time's over, Private."

Curled up on his side, he pulled the edge of his vest a little farther over his face and muttered something unintelligible into Watura's shoulder.

Torin smiled. "Private Jiyuu!"

He was on his feet, at attention, his hair in a fuchsia nimbus around his head before his eyes opened.

"Tell me you only use those powers for good," Mike murmured close enough to her ear to prevent eavesdropping.

"So far. Biscuits while we walk, people." They'd eaten only the kibble while they were by the spring and had water to mix it with. "With any luck, there's a pipe in our future. If we're really lucky, it's fallen out of the ceiling leaving an easy exit. If we're remarkably lucky, the water'll still be working and it'll have dropped a few biscuits before the collapse."

Ressk rubbed a finger up and over his nose ridges. "Why not wish for a VTA and the Navy in orbit while you're at it, Gunny?"

"Gunnery sergeants don't wish for things, Corporal, we make them happen."

"What are happening now?" Presit leaned forward, peering at *Harveer* Umananth. They were close enough in height that she could do it comfortably, and Craig was all in favor of that. An uncomfortable Presit was a bloody pain in his ass, and she was already conflicted about their continued presence on the blasted battlefield. Sector Central News had loved the first story she'd filed so much—definitely considered to be good news—they'd asked her to stay with the scientists for a while—not such good news.

She'd been agitating for something to happen ever since, and an agitated Presit was also a pain in his ass.

Umananth's nictitating membrane flicked over his eyes. He was uncertain. It hadn't taken Craig long to learn to learn the young scientist's tells. Or take a good portion of his—and his colleagues'—money at the poker table. It helped that they went easy on him because he was so clearly mourning. He didn't much like being that obvious, had hoped to be seen just as Presit's crew, but he was more than willing to take advantage of the situation. Salvage was a hand-to-mouth operation, new CO2 scrubbers didn't buy themselves, and, besides, Torin would have appreciated the sentiment. Would have felt that anyone—particularly someone with an advanced degree—who insisted on drawing to an inside straight got what they deserved.

He still felt nothing when he looked out at the gleaming surface. Okay, that wasn't entirely true; he felt appalled at the loss of life, a little sick about how it had happened, but the point was he still didn't feel Torin. Time spent where she'd died hadn't brought her closer. Or him closure.

"*Harveer*!" Presit's voice had risen from sharp to damned near painful.

"We're picking up some strange readings," Umananth admitted reluctantly.

Flashing Craig the signal that he should start recording, Presit leaned a little closer. "When you are saying strange, what are you meaning?"

Umananth brushed a bit of fur off the screen—the heat had the Katrien shedding her plush undercoat by the handful—but otherwise ignored her.

"Are you meaning strange readings are being coming from the glass?" Presit continued, sliding into on-air cadences. "Are you meaning the dead are finally to be telling you their story? Are you meaning . . ."

"I are meaning," Umananth snapped, flicked his tail, and started again. "I *am* meaning that we have several energy signals approaching the system."

One small hand gestured upward. "In space?"

"Yes."

"From where?"

"OutSector."

"What are making them?"

"I don't know!" He half turned and shouted something across the sled in his own language. With other species present, slipping out of Federate meant he was either being deliberately rude or he was a lot more shaken by his unknown readings than it appeared.

Craig'd bet on the second.

As Presit took a moment to recap—moments he could record in his sleep these days—he pulled his slate off his belt and brought *Promise*'s scanners on-line. He made his living finding space debris; odds were that his scanners were at least as good and probably better than anything on a chartered cruiser. Given their position on the edge of Confederation territory, OutSector covered one hell of a lot of space, but at least gave him a direction to sweep.

Not good that the energy signals were strong enough his scanners locked on them almost immediately.

"Son of a fukking bitch!" He thumbed in the code for the cruiser. "Captain . . ." Crap! He'd met the Rakva briefly when Presit had "requested" the use of a shuttle and couldn't remember her fukking name. Good thing there was only one captain up there. "Captain! Suggest you get us all the hell off planet, we've got incoming ships!"

"This one sees them, Mister Ryder. It is certain they are hostile?"

"Anything of ours would ping my scanners. I've got no bloody ping!"

"Shuttle on its way. Please to herd the science team to the landing site, Mister Ryder."

"On it!" He retracted the recorder's tripod. "Bad guys on the way!" he snapped before Presit could object. "We're out of here. Umananth!" The scientist had moved to a screen at the far end of the sled. Ignoring Presit's shrill protests, Craig hurried to his side. "Get your people on the sled, Captain's sending a shuttle."

Umananth's hand hovered over the repeating pattern on the screen, claws nearly touching the surface. "These are hostiles?"

"H'san to a brick!"

The scientist blinked up at him. "What?"

"Yes." Craig took a deep breath. "These are hostiles."

"And they'll attack?"

"Yeah. Seems to be what they do." Craig nodded toward the closest of the half dozen stations surrounding the sled. "Get them in and let's go."

"I can't call them in!" He wrapped his tail around his leg, membrane flicking back and forth so quickly Craig wondered if he could see. "*Harveer* Detalanth is in charge of the team!"

A Niln who Craig thought was one of Umananth's grad students handed the scientist a slate. "I have *Harveer* Detalanth on com."

He stared at the screen for a moment, then clearly came to a decision and began to talk, dropping once again out of Federate.

The grad student gave Craig a look that could only be translated as *when I'm in charge, things will run much more smoothly*, and jumped down onto the glass, tail stretched out for balance as she headed toward the closest station.

Craig turned as Presit's claws dug into the skin of his arm. His reflection in her mirrored glasses looked about as freaked as he was feeling. He usually got to war zones long after the fighting was over.

"No one are telling you to stop recording," she snarled. "If we are having the Others attack, then we are finally having vids worth uploading."

"They're not attacking yet. They're not even in-system yet."

She snorted. "Then what are the reasoning for hurrying?"

"I don't know, maybe because we don't want to be here when they arrive and being at the bottom of a gravity well tends to slow that whole running away thing the fuk down."

"I are not running." The fur on her throat gleamed as she frowned up into a heat-silvered sky. Craig had no doubt that she was trying to see beyond the atmosphere and into space. "I are needing an accurate ETA if I are going to go live. Meanwhile . . ." Her jaw lowered, she directed the frown at him. ". . . you are to be recording the panic of packing up.

"Oh, no, I . . ."

"You are having something else to do?" she asked pointedly.

Fortunately, because most of the research team was Niln, once *Harveer* Detalanth gave the order, packing up the stations happened quickly and efficiently without any of the interspecies complications that often turned the simplest maneuver into a cross between a comedy routine and a turf war. Tripod back up, Presit interviewed each returning scientist and tech about their fear of suddenly being in an active war zone—a couple of responses were going to need editing—while Craig shot background.

As the last of the crates were being loaded, he carefully nudged Umananth and pointed at three rectangular boxes left out on the glass. "What about them?"

"*Harveer* Detalanth says it's better to lose the equipment than the data, and they'll keep transmitting until they're destroyed."

"Fair enough. What about him/her?"

Both sets of lower legs braced against the glass, the Ciptran handed up a piece of equipment a little larger than his/her thorax. The big bugs were bloody strong, Craig would give them that, but he'd never run into one that didn't exude a "get the fuk away from me" attitude. It was actually impressive to see a Ciptran work as part of a team since he'd heard them described as the exception to the rule that only social species developed sentience.

"Dr. Anahnt'c's going to run alongside."

"You're shitting me?"

Umananth shrugged. "He/she is as fast as the sled."

"And he/she are not agreeing to an interview," Presit snarled, joining them. "He/she are keeping a truly unique viewpoint from my public. And you . . ." She unerringly found the same place on his arm she'd dug her claws into before. ". . . are keeping recording in case the Others are coming here faster."

"You know what Torin says the military calls the press?" Craig asked Umananth, removing Presit's hand with as much force as their significant size difference allowed him to get away with. "Range finders."

It took a moment. The *harveer* snickered.

"You are not being funny," Presit growled. "And neither are Gunnery Sergeant Kerr."

One of the ubiquitous grad students took the controls and the sled began to move, rising up on its air cushion and heading toward the landing site at the edge of the glass. Dr. Anahnt'c allowed it to move some small distance away, and then he/she began to run. Carapace glittering green and gold in the sunlight, antennae streaming along behind him/her, four lower limbs moving in a strangely nonrhythmic sequence, he/she seemed to have no trouble maintaining the distance.

"Impressive." Braced against the movement of the sled, Craig zoomed out far enough to get the full effect of the running Ciptran against the glass.

Umananth shrugged. "My species eats more insects than yours. I look at him/her and can't help thinking of an all-you-can-eat buffet."

"I are thinking the same," Presit admitted, bronzed nails absently clawing out a handful of undercoat and tossing it over the side to drift away on the wind.

All the equipment and half the scientists went up on the first shuttle load. To Craig's surprise, Presit didn't try to force her way into one of the seats.

"I are telling you," she snorted. "I are not running. The story are happening here." One hand waved dramatically toward the glass, and Craig took his cue to begin recording. "First, they are destroying our Marines on what are being a molecular level . . ."

Beside him, Umananth's grad student began a protest Presit ignored.

". . . and now they are returning. Why? Are they here to be destroying the glass or to be retrieving it? Or . . ." Her voice dropped to conspiracy levels. ". . . are they here to be chasing off the scientists before there are being results of their analysis? Are the Others being afraid of what we are to be finding in the glass?"

Craig had to admit they were all very good questions.

And none of them stopped him from picking Presit up and carrying her into the shuttle when it returned. As much as he intended to save her life, her shrieked protests, combined with a nasty bite on the hip and four parallel scratches along his neck nearly got her spaced until Dr. Anahnt'c used what looked like pincers on the end of a mid-leg to clamp her mouth shut.

"Gunny."

Torin stopped and glanced down, hearing a hint of the young Marine who'd been tossed out to die in Kyster's voice.

His nose ridges were open and flexing slightly. "Body. There."

"How long dead?"

He shrugged. "Nearly no smell left."

"You sure you're not imagining it, kid?" Ressk's nose ridges were also open. Torin was impressed he'd pulled himself away from Mike and the slate long enough to question the younger Krai's nose.

"I'm sure."

They had no reason to check on a long-dead Marine and every reason to keep moving through the tunnels as fast as possible.

Thumb and forefinger curled into her mouth, Torin whistled twice, the sound carrying far enough to bring Werst and Kichar to a stop. They weren't so far ahead they couldn't have heard her if she'd yelled, but if the Others were still monitoring, she intended to give them as little information as possible.

"Watura . . ." She felt a light tug at her sleeve and, damn it, she knew she had to discourage this kind of thing, but the kid had made the call and he deserved to come along. ". . . Kyster. With me."

Instinct had maintained the Human, Krai, di'Taykan parity although she'd have rather not have justified their presence by taking any of the three di'Taykan.

The cave entrance was high and narrow. All three of them had to turn sideways to fit through, but at least they had plenty of headroom. She sent Watura in before her and Kyster after, not wanting to put more pressure on the young private by trapping him, even momentarily, in a small cave with one of Harnett's ex-goons. He'd probably be fine, but she wasn't willing to bet Watura's fingers on it since he'd be fuk all use without them.

The Marine, a male di'Taykan, lay with one leg bent to the side and his hands crossed one on top of the other on his chest. Pale blue hair had fallen away from a pebbled scalp and surrounded his head like long, discolored, conifer needles. His eyes were closed, but in death they'd have gone pale blue from lid to lid. The skin that clung to the bones as though it had been vaccum sealed had a deep blue tint and the stain under the body looked black.

"Keep your light on his chest, Watura." Dropping to one knee, Torin gently moved the dead Marine's hands.

He'd died of his wounds. Been scooped up away from his fireteam, his squad, his platoon, and dropped here where he'd died. Undiscovered. No way of knowing exactly how long he'd been here, but Torin had seen plenty of dead di'Taykan and that kind of desiccation didn't happen overnight.

Thumb rubbing lightly against the raised crest of his collar tab, she silently filled in what it told her: Corporal, 1st Division, 2nd Recar'ta, 1st Battalion, 4th Armored. No way of knowing his name with his tech off. His vest surrendered a tube of sealant and two filters. If he'd had three sheets of supplement tucked away, they'd have arrived with the same baggage. Almost the same baggage. She snapped the pheromone masker off his throat and straightened.

"Gunnery Sergeant?"

"Had a di'Taykan in my platoon once, di'Stenjic Haysole," she said quietly, eyes on the tech, dialing it back to zero. "He asked me . . .

Squinting into the rising sun, she let the words trail off. Something glittered by the doorway that had led to the third room. Heart pounding, she took a step back and vaulted over the wall. Her boots and legs were covered in a fine coat of gray by the time she reached it. A masker, partially melted and covered in char but recognizable for all that.

". . . he said, if I die, take the masker off before you bag me."

"Did he? Die?" Kyster added when she turned to face him.

"He did."

"Did you . . . ?" Watura finished the question with a noise that could have meant any number of things.

Torin tucked the masker into her vest and smiled. Kyster wouldn't have asked because it would never have occurred to Kyster that she might fail. "There wasn't enough left to bag," she told Watura bluntly. "Just like we can't bag the corporal." Wishing she could spare a mouthful of water, she looked down at the body. "We will not forget. We will not fail you."

"Fraishin sha aren. Valynk sha haren."

"Kal danic dir k'dir. Kri ta chrikdan."

Easy odds that neither of them had ever stood in those positions before. But every Marine knew the words.

"All right, let's go; we're on the clock."

"We can't just leave him."

She felt her lip curl as she turned toward the living di'Taykan. "That's rich coming from you, Private. How many did you drop down the disposal? Leave to die in a cave just like this one? Leave to die, alone?" As a Marine, Watura had seen plenty of death. As a di'Taykan, there were few things worse than being alone. "We'll remember this Marine and take that memory with us because it's all we've got. How many have you forgotten?"

Beside her, Kyster snapped his teeth together.

Hair flat against his head, his lime-green eyes nearly black, Watura stood for a moment, light on the dead di'Taykan's face; then his legs folded and he sat. "I'm staying with him. I only came because I thought if we got out you'd put in a good word if I helped with the escape, but there's no fukking point. It's just more tunnels, and he's been alone long enough."

Torin actually considered leaving him there. Then she sighed. "And Jiyuu?"

"What?"

"Don't even try to tell me that was the only reason you came. You came because Jiyuu came."

"He'll be fine with Darlys. Me, her—it doesn't matter to him."

"Evidence suggests it does."

Watura shrugged.

Fine. So much for the compassionate approach. Plan B. She leaned forward until their faces were so close the air between them began to warm and she could feel her body responding—the near contact overwhelming Watura's masker—but she wasn't planning on holding the position long enough for it to be a problem. "Look at me."

His eyes had started to pale as the light receptors closed.

He'd be reacting to *her* arousal in a minute, so she had to make this fast before it spiraled out of control. Voice too low to be overheard out in the tunnel, she said, "I'd really rather you hadn't come along, but since you did, and since in a moment of temporary insanity I didn't send your ass back to Staff Sergeant Pole, your ass is my responsibility. That means your ass is getting out of here with the rest of us, so stand up and get out in that tunnel and try to convince me that you're worth being considered a Marine."

He leaned back, unable to look away, and tried to focus on her face. "We don't leave our people alone."

"No. *We* don't leave our people behind." Still holding his gaze, she stretched out an arm and picked up one of the pale blue hairs, tucking it into Watura's vest. "Remember this. Now . . ." She straightened. "If the Others catch up because you decided to park your ass, I'm going to be more than just a little pissed! On your feet!"

At the edge of her peripheral vision, she saw Kyster glance down at the body as though he expected it to respond. Hell, she was a gunnery sergeant in the Confederation Marine Corps and if she wanted the dead to rise, they'd damned well do it, but right now she'd settle for getting one pain-in-the-ass di'Taykan moving.

On his feet, Watura looked like he couldn't remember standing.

Torin jerked her head toward the exit, and he moved with the motion, as though a string connected her desires and his actions. Which was, bottom line, the way it worked in the Corps with or without complacency-causing kibble.

As he began to push his way back through the crack toward the tunnel, Kyster closed his hand around her wrist.

Knowing what was coming, Torin dropped back to her knee, one hand resting lightly on the dead Marine's shoulder.

"I can take a part of him out as a part of me," Kyster said quietly, mouth up against her ear.

She'd given him this, a way of making right what he'd had to do to stay alive. She couldn't take it away again. This wasn't about food—although the Krai could get food value out of anything organic—this was about giving meaning to death.

"Do it," she said, picked up another pale blue hair, and stood. She waited until she heard the first crunch, then she worked her way back out into the tunnel, her boots making as much noise as possible against the rock.

Slate held in his feet, Ressk worked the screen with both hands, freeing Mike to lean against the opposite wall of the tunnel and watch her as she emerged. When both brows lifted slightly, she wondered what he saw, wondered if he'd expected more than the carefully blank expression she knew she wore.

The three di'Taykan stood together, bodies touching shoulder to hip, heads bowed, lime-green, fuchsia, and ocher hair interweaving as they studied the line of pale blue crossing Watura's palm.

The weight of Torin's regard pulled Darlys' attention up off the hair. "We didn't know him," she said.

"Yes, you did," Torin told her as Kyster slipped out into the tunnel. "He was a Marine."

A single whistle got Werst and Kichar moving again.

"Ressk."

"Just one more . . ."

Mike reached down before she could reply and pulled the slate from Ressk's grip. "When we stop again, Corporal. Let's get out of here."

They were no more than three meters from the cave when he fell into step beside her and said, "At least we definitely know we're heading toward a pipe."

"I thought the geography told us that."

"They wouldn't have dropped that Marine here if they hadn't expected him to be picked up by the Marines at the pipe."

Torin frowned. "So they're not watching all the time. There've been no other bodies, so they knew to stop using this section of tunnels." Too late for the dead corporal.

"Makes me think the delivery system is automatic."

"Or they were in too much of a hurry to check the situation at the pipe when they left him."

"However they left him."

"Matter transmitter ray?"

"They used a matter transmitter ray in *Pirates of the Back Belt*," Jiyuu offered. "When they needed to get the captain out of the brig."

Mike held out his hands. "That's what I'm saying."

Torin almost smiled. "For shame, Technical Sergeant, pulling a theory from bad vids."

"It wasn't a bad vid, Gunny!"

She did smile at the indignant protest. Her cheeks felt funny.

"Don't the Others just bring the Marines in under cover of darkness, Gunny?" Darlys asked, moving closer. "That's what we always assumed."

"Your lot made a number of incorrect assumptions," Torin reminded her.

"And I am sorry for what I was a part of, but still, there'd be no one in the tunnels at night to hear them," Darlys insisted. "Not with everyone gathered around the pipes."

"Kyster?"

His teeth snapped together. "Never heard them."

"You couldn't be in every tunnel, every night."

"Next cave to the gunny's when she came in. Didn't hear them."

"But if you were in a cave, you might not have heard them."

"Would have."

"But . . ."

"He says he would have, Darlys. That's the end of it."

"Yes, Gunnery Sergeant."

Contrary to expectations, there was more damage in the tunnels the closer the pattern told them they were to the pipe. Cracks and fissures widened, and at one point the lights hung no more than a meter and a half from the floor, dangling on their cables.

"Solid workmanship." Mike reached out, fingers not quite touching the twisted metal. "I'm impressed they're still on."

"I'm impressed you repaired them with a sleeve," Torin told him, stepping over a pile of loose rock. "I'm less impressed by the workmanship of an enemy holding Marines captive."

"Holding a grudge, Gunny?"

"Hasn't been long enough to be considered a grudge, Sergeant." She noted the recon marks on the wall and waved her people over to the right, where Werst had determined the floor was more stable. "Check back in a couple of days."

They caught up to Werst and Kichar at the turn just before the last straight ten meters into the pipe. Werst's nose ridges were slowly opening and closing, and his lips were drawn up off his teeth.

They could all smell it this time, not just the Krai.

Torin shifted her grip on the club and deliberately drew in a couple of deep breaths, letting the smell of rot coat the inside of her mouth and nose. No point in ignoring it, it wasn't going away. Best to get used to it quickly so that it wasn't a distraction. "We go in like we're expecting survivors," she said. "If we're attacked, and it's at all possible, we disable, we don't kill."

"What if it's not Marines we're attacked by, Gunnery Sergeant?" Kichar's dark eyes seemed enormous.

"Disable," Torin told her. "I want some fukking answers."

She wouldn't have allowed an officer to physically lead a team into an area so potentially deadly, but not only wasn't she an officer, she had the most combat experience of the group and would be best able to threat assess the situation. And that put her out front.

Not that it really mattered.

They all knew what the smell meant. Preparing for a threat was the military version of wishful thinking.

The first body lay across the tunnel exit, one hand stretched out toward them. Human, male, his skin as dark as Mashona's, his face haloed by a stain on the stone. Torin held the others in place and carefully, gently, turned his head with the toe of her boot.

"Looks like the blood came out of his nose," Darlys murmured.

"Filters!" Torin snapped.

Whatever it was had killed quickly. With any luck, they weren't slapping on protection just a little too late.

Almost all the bodies were sprawled facing the tunnels, but there was no way of knowing whether they'd started to run because they'd known there was something in the air or because the pipe had buckled. It hadn't pulled out of the ceiling though it had exposed approximately six meters more length disappearing into a jagged hole. Half a dozen of the dead Marines closest to the pipe had been crushed under falling rock.

"All right." Torin let the club hang by her side. "Technical Sergeant Gucciard, get that slate up and running. The rest of you, by twos and by tunnel sections, get me a head count. And stay sharp; at least some of that rock has fallen since the pipe came down."

When the pipe broke, a flood of kibble had spewed out across the node. The edge closest to the water outlet had clearly been turned to mush and then allowed to dry. The five-by-two-meter slab looked like the crust that formed on the top of the manure pile in high summer back on her family's farm, but Torin figured she'd keep that observation to herself. The speed at which the kibble absorbed water had probably kept it from destroying the entire spill—a good half meter of the far edge remained loose and mixed with the occasional biscuit. Given the pervasive smell of rot, she couldn't tell if they'd gone bad, but the Krai would know. And not much care.

The water chute had kinked, but the area around the contact point was damp. Torin pressed it in with her thumb, pressed harder when it refused to give, and finally slammed it with the club. A trickle of water ran over her wrist. She cupped her hands and nearly filled them before the pressure behind the contact pushed it out again. Unable to drink it through the filter, she let it splash against the floor, turning the pale gray dark. It'd be a pain in the ass, but they could fill the canteens.

The living taken care of, she turned her attention back to the dead.

Ninety-seven.

Werst was chewing. *"Cree arac,"* he said shortly. *Cousin,* Torin translated. Or as near as made no difference. "On my father's side. Went MIA about twenty-four maybe twenty-five tendays ago."

The dead were the main course at Krai burial rituals. As a rule, Marines gave that sort of thing up, but then, as a rule, Marines weren't left to lie where they'd fallen.

"There's almost a hundred of them," she said when Kichar expected to start carrying them off to the disposal pit. "We haven't the time. Nor for that," she added as Kyster opened his mouth. The last thing she wanted to cope with right now was the reaction to him suggesting the three Krai act like a memorial unit by eating a finger off each of the dead. Then she turned her attention back to Werst.

"You took off your filter." Carelessness she wouldn't have expected from Werst.

He swallowed. "Heeirc and I were close, Gunnery Sergeant."

He expected to be reamed out for it, but Torin couldn't see much point. The filters were significantly more uncomfortable for the Krai than they were for the other two species, and that likely had as much significance in his choice as his *cree arac* did. That and the additive in the food wearing away his ability to care. "You're our canary, then."

"Your what?"

"Just let me know if you start dying." She scratched at the edge of her filter—damned thing was pulling at the skin of her cheek. "You, Kyster, and Watura start pulling the biscuits out of that kibble on the floor. Grab only the ones that smell like a Human or di'Taykan system could handle them. Jiyuu, Kichar—refill the canteens. You'll need to slam the contact with the club and the water won't stay on for long. Mashona, Darlys—the extras that came in with the Marines have to be in here somewhere. There's definitely going to be something we can use. Ressk, help the sergeant. I want that slate working sooner rather than later."

"When do we get to take the filters off, Gunny?" Ressk shot a resentful glare at Werst.

"If Werst's alive in half an hour, it should be safe." She took a deep breath, closed her eyes for a heartbeat, and opened them again to see all eight Marines watching her. "Don't just stand there with your thumbs up your collective asses! You have your orders; move!"

The question was, what did they do next? Torin had never wanted an officer around quite so much. Good, bad, indifferent, it didn't matter—just someone to deal with the big picture while she handled the details. It was shortsighted of her not to arrange it so that Colonel Mariner sent Major Ohi along. He'd come in with Mashona, he was still functional. He could have functioned for her so that she could function for everyone else.

Sagging back against the pipe, she let it hold her weight as she slid to the floor.

The floor?

Crap.

The pipe rang as she slammed her head back against it. Eyes watering, she forced herself up onto her feet. First Watura, then Werst, now her. The additive in the kibble was definitely beginning to work. She couldn't tell if the pain helped her focus on anything but the pain, but even that was something.

"Gunny?"

"What?"

Mashona was smart enough to take her cue from Torin, wiping the obvious question off her face. "The stuff was all together wrapped in a piece of the smart fabric. Six more filters, another tube of sealant, some leather ties like they used to hold the rocks on the clubs, and some rope."

"Rope?"

There were loops of pale gray draped over Mashona's outstretched hand. "There's about thirty meters."

Wondering why the hell she thought giving herself a concussion was a good idea, Torin nodded. "Good work." A quick glance down at her sleeve and she raised her voice. "Eleven minutes to lights out, people."

"We staying here tonight, Gunny?"

Torin looked past Mashona, past the bodies, out at tunnels. Was there another pipe after this one? And another one after that? Were they right, everyone who'd said there was nothing out there but more tunnels? Mariner and Braudy and Kenoton and Pole . . . More tunnels and no way out?

She didn't, couldn't believe that.

"Yeah, we'll bunk down close to the pipe for the night." Most of the dead Marines, struggling toward the tunnels when they died, were closer to the node's outer curve. "Take advantage of the water, make sure we're all good and hydrated before we start out at first light. We might not get this lucky again. Let's pull some pallets over while we can see clearly."

Crouched by the spill of kibble, separating out the biscuits, Kyster watched the gunny and Mashona pull pallets around to the side of the pipe where the crushed bodies weren't. He wasn't thrilled about staying the night, but there was enough of the food from the pipe that the smell of decaying meat shouldn't be too much of a temptation.

"Gran used to make a killer *greetani krii*," Werst muttered, tossing another biscuit in the sleeve.

"Mine, too," Kyster admitted. It was tricky getting the meat to rot without insects finding it even with technology that tried to guarantee it. The effort was part of what made it taste so good. He turned a biscuit over, didn't like the blotch of color on the back and tossed it in the dubious pile, finding it hard to believe he was actually discarding food.

"This is what she asked for."

He turned to see Darlys standing by Watura holding a pallet, the lower half of her face weirdly out of focus behind the shimmer of the filter. "Who?"

"Gunnery Sergeant Kerr."

"She asked for a pallet?" Watura wondered, standing.

"She said," Darlys told him quietly, "that she wanted to find a pipe with working water that had delivered biscuits before it quit. She asked for this . . ." Balancing the pallet on one edge, she waved a hand at the sleeve Kyster had just filled. ". . . and she received it."

Werst snorted. "She also wanted the pipe to have fallen out of the ceiling leaving us an easy exit. And I don't see that . . ."

The lights cut him off, and Kyster slapped at his cuff.

"She asked for a way out." In the darkness, Daryls sounded as though her faith had been justified.

"What the fuk are you talking about?" Werst demanded.

With the light from Watura's cuff shining up into her face, Darlys' eyes were solid ocher lid to lid. "Look up. The gunnery sergeant asked for a way out." One hand reached out and grabbed the other di'Taykan's wrist, pushing his light down toward the floor. "Just look up."

"Son of a . . ."

Kyster exchanged a confused look with Werst, who shrugged. They both stood, walked to Watura's side, and looked up.

"I don't see . . ."

"Follow the line of the pipe," Darlys told them.

"In case you're missing the point of the exercise, genius, it's too *serley* dark to see anything without . . ."

When Werst's voice trailed off, Kyster frowned and tipped his head back. "But it's just . . . Oh."

At the top of the pipe, where a chunk of the ceiling had fallen, there was light.

NINE

//**IT'S LIGHT," MIKE SAID DEFINITIVELY.** "It's not *a* light."

"So it's a way out?"

They were standing close enough, necks craned back to stare up at the pale pinprick of illumination high above them in the dark, that Torin could feel him shrug. "It's a way into someplace else. Can't promise out."

"Good enough. Werst . . ."

"Not in the dark, Gunny. Not if we don't have to."

"Stop reading my mind, you're still a distance from that sergeant's hook." She frowned, hands flat against the pipe. The smooth surface, even crumpled by the collapse would be a bitch to climb. If Werst said he'd rather not attempt it in the dark, well, it was her choice still on whether it was worth it to try. If their need to haul ass was greater than the risk to the Krai. If waiting until they had light was the best thing to do or merely the easiest.

"Gunny . . ."

"No, you won't either, kid." Werst cut Kyster off cold. "Not unless she orders it. Then all three of us go."

"Stop reading his mind, too," Torin muttered absently, reaching as far as she could and feeling the faint ridge of buckled metal. She gripped it as hard as she could, fingertips only, and tried to lift herself off the floor. No real surprise when there wasn't enough resistance to hold her; she'd need suction cups. "Odds that your patch will hold come morning, Sergeant?"

Mike shrugged again. "It's a sleeve, Gunny. Probably shouldn't have worked at all."

That was helpful. *Make a decision, Torin. Do your fukking job.* "All right. We sleep. Kyster, Werst, and Ressk are excused watch and ready to climb at first light. Sergeant, do what you have to in order to get that slate working, remembering you'll eventually be climbing that bastard of a pipe and that, at least, is one thing the slate can't help with."

She dreamed that night that the pipe led into the shuttle bay of a Navy cruiser. It might have been the *Berganitan*, she didn't see enough of the ship to know for certain. Haysole was there, and Guimond, and Sergeant Glicksohn, and a dozen other Marines she knew were dead. Dead Marines were a part of her life, but Craig was there, too, and when she woke, half an hour before light with the dream still in her head and the edges of the salvage tag cutting into her palm, she had every intention of blaming the fukking kibble for the soppy state of her subconscious.

"Did you sleep at all?" she asked crouching by Mike's side, one hand on a broad shoulder for balance.

"No."

"You sure that's wise?"

He slipped a hand into his vest and pulled out a stim. "If we were always wise, would they give us these?"

Torin touched her vest over the inner pocket where her two remaining stims waited for inevitability. She'd forgotten about them. Another malfunction to blame on the kibble.

"Operating system's up and running." He turned the screen just enough for her to see a familiar pattern. She could practically hear him filtering what he was about to say, dumbing it down for the nontech-inclined. "Another hour, maybe less, and I'll have recovered the first program."

"Which is?"

The shoulder under her fingers lifted and fell even as he continued to stroke data off the screen. "Damned if I know. Could be solitaire. Could be long-distance communications. Could be CMC Mapping."

"I vote for option two or three." She tightened her grip for a moment, then stood. "Good work, Sergeant. All right, people wakey, wakey. Welcome to another glorious day in the Corps."

"Does it count as day when it's still too fukking dark to find your ass with both hands," Mashona grumbled as half a dozen pale circles sprang up on the ceiling, indicating where Marines had hit their cuff lights.

"I'll find your ass," one of the di'Taykan offered. Male. Probably Jiyuu.

"As happy as I am that you're offering to help a fellow Marine," Torin told him, "Mashona's lost ass is her problem. I want us fed and watered when the lights come back on, so let's move."

The pale circles slid down the walls and spilled in darker circles on the floor—a game of connect the dots and find the Marines.

"I thought that was an *if* not a *when*, Gunny."

"I am applying the power of positive thinking, Mashona."

"If you will it . . ."

No mistaking Darlys' quiet murmur.

"I'm going to will my boot in your butt in a minute, Private. Let's move!"

The water still ran at the pipe although the contact point had stiffened further.

"No surprise, given the abuse it's already taken," Torin grunted, smacking it hard with the side of her fist. With her bowl full, she switched it for Mike's and moved out of the way so Watura could fill his and Jiyuu's.

"One minute to light."

They'd make the climb regardless.

"Ten seconds."

Eleven.

Twelve.

"Maybe we're in a different time zone?" From anyone but Kichar, it would have sounded sarcastic.

Thirteen.

Fourteen.

And then Torin realized she could see the pale slash of the pipe stretching up toward the distant ceiling.

"Could be rerouting within the sleeve to handle the load," Mike said thoughtfully.

"You design the hookup to do that, Sarge?" Ressk sounded impressed.

He snorted. "Not intentionally."

It grew light enough to see faces and then expressions. Shadows lingered out among the dead, but by the pipe it had clearly gotten as light as it was going to get. "All right, then, let's . . ."

The vibration was slight. If Torin hadn't had one hand flat against the pipe, she might have denied she felt it. "Technical Sergeant?"

"I don't know, Gunny . . ."

"It feels like standing at the perimeter of the spaceport, watching the ships take off," Kichar said quietly.

"Like the ground is shaking?"

"Yeah."

At some point the ground had shaken enough to bring down a section of the tunnels. Not to mention partially collapse the pipe they were standing by.

Mike nodded. "Small earthquake." He gestured toward the hunks of rock that had fallen from the ceiling, the parts of dead Marines protruding from under them adding emphasis. "I suggest we get the hell out of here."

"Excellent suggestion." The tremors seemed to have stopped. "How do you want to do this, Corporal?"

Head tilted back, nose ridges open, Werst stared up at the ceiling, one palm flat against the smooth metal, fingers spread. "Off shoulders," he said at last. "*Serley* thing's too vertical down here. The higher we start, the better the odds we'll be able to find an angle that'll hold us. Me first, then Ressk, then Kyster."

"But his foot," Kichar began. Cheeks flushing as everyone turned to look at her, she snapped her lips closed, pressing them together until the edges whitened.

Kyster showed teeth, but he let Werst answer.

"Yeah, kid's only got three working limbs which is still one more than the rest of you. If he can't follow up, you lot'll never manage and we'll have to fukking stay down here until we rot."

No one seemed too upset at the thought. Torin wondered if there was a difference between calm acceptance of the inevitable—which Marines were not supposed to excel at in point of fact—and not actually giving a damn.

"There's the rope," Darlys reminded him after a minute.

"It'll help if we get a chance to tie it off." He had it slung diagonally across his body. "You still need somewhere to put your *serley* feet." A finger jabbed at Watura. "You're tallest."

It was actually almost funny to watch Werst climb Watura like a tree until he stood, feet gripping the di'Taykan's shoulders.

"Brace him, I'll have to jump."

Jiyuu and Darlys each took a shoulder and Torin made the third side of the triangle when she set both palms flat against the middle of Watura's back, just below where his neck joined his body. Mashona was almost as tall, but the gravity difference made Torin just a little stronger. Just a little might mean squat, but it might make all the difference.

"On three," Werst growled. "One. Two . . ."

Torin flexed her right leg and braced her left. She could feel Watura readying himself.

"Three."

He jumped with all four limbs spread, fingers and toes scrambling for purchase the instant he landed. Torin tried not to think of how much he looked like a tree frog wearing gray-on-gray camouflage. He slid back about half a meter, then somehow managed to creep right about the same distance and stop his fall. "Here," he grunted. "Catches the edge of where the pipe buckles. *Serley* shadows make it hard to see from the ground."

Watura shifted to the right until he was directly under the point indicated, and Ressk climbed to his shoulders as Werst carefully moved higher. Ressk's jump was significantly more graceful, but then, he knew where he was going. When Kyster jumped, he seemed to use his back foot like a rudder in the air, and if he slid a little when he landed, it wasn't so far that anyone still standing at the base of the pipe was forced to notice.

Then there was nothing to do but watch them climb.

Torin suspected Darlys was praying and only hoped she wasn't praying to her—for she was a vengeful god, or, at the very least, a god who could use a few hour's more sleep and a large cup of black coffee.

All three Krai picked up some speed as they crossed the point where the pipe had buckled and slowed again at the longer, more vertical section following. Werst slid once, and it took both Ressk and Kyster to stop him. He used a few words Torin had never learned and snarled, "Stay left."

"First program's up, Gunny."

Hating to do it, although it was a stupid conceit that her gaze alone held the climbers up, she turned to the technical sergeant and said, "That's amazing."

Mike grinned. "No, it would be amazing if you'd done it. From me, it's business as usual."

"Fair enough. What've you got?"

"High-end translation program. Had to hazard a guess, I'd say major's slate at least."

"A translation program?"

"High end. Probably belonged to one of Colonel Mariner's original staff officers from that diplomatic mission. We know the Others pick up more than one prisoner from an engagement."

"A high-end translation program." It didn't sound any better when she said it.

"Could come in useful."

Torin sighed and raised her voice slightly. "Anyone here forget how to speak Federate?"

The responses suggested not. Even the climbers chimed it with a no, a not yet, and a profane suggestion the slate translated as physically impossible given the way knees bent—although Jiyuu looked intrigued.

Mike's grin broadened. "I'll get to work on the next one, then."

Torin relocked her gaze on the three Marines climbing the pipe as though her attention would make the metal less slippery, as though it would make the curves flatten into a path leading safely to the light, as though they needed her attention to keep them safe.

❧   ❧   ❧

"*I will not fall. I will not fall.*" Kyster knew that non-Krai in the Corps believed his people would eat pretty much anything they could fit into their mouths, which was true although *fit* was a relative word, and that they never fell, which was stupid. A life lived tens or even hundreds of meters above the ground in the living *jourdun* or in the copies tech had built near the spaceports meant falling, or rather impact, and not necessarily with the ground, was the biggest killer of both the young and old.

Krai bone was hard enough and the distance small enough that sliding down the pipe, hitting the floor by the fused kibble, and splatting down at Gunnery Sergeant Kerr's feet would do damage but wouldn't kill him.

He'd die of embarrassment.

The toes of his good foot ached and his bad foot burned, the pain a heated reminder of his disfigurement. He struggled to keep up and snapped his teeth when one of the others too obviously waited for him.

At the point where the pipe rose up into the ceiling, they found places to perch where the metal had buckled. Kyster's fingers actually ached with the effort of holding on, and he squatted gratefully, head back, following the beam from Ressk's cuff up through the rock toward the light. Cables, about as big around as his leg, matte black and impossible to see from the ground, split the crevasse into smaller sections. Once into the crevasse it would be an easy climb. Even for him.

"Six meters to the top," Werst grunted. "Give or take. Not far."

"Tight fit for the sarge," Ressk pointed out.

"Tight fit for the gunny."

"Not going without her," Kyster growled.

The two older Krai turned toward him, teeth bared.

"No one's suggesting that, dumbass." Werst was breathing hard enough his nose ridges stayed open. He lifted his hands carefully off the pipe and, without warning, threw himself up and sideways, just barely hooking the fingers of his right hand over sharply angled stone. Swearing, he hauled himself up and grabbed on with his other hand and both feet.

Ressk slid back about half a meter. Close enough that Kyster could reach out and catch him. Catch him and follow him to the ground. Don't catch him and let him fall on his own. Problems with both choices. Fortunately, he managed to stop his fall a handspan from where Kyster would have had to choose and snarl, "A little warning, you *serley chrika!*"

"Didn't want to think about it too long," Werst muttered absently as he climbed higher, moving faster now he was in the cleft. "Stay there; first cable I cross, I'll send the rope down."

"Don't need the rope!" Kyster shoved his bad foot into a crease in the pipe and shuffled forward. "I'll prove it!" When Ressk grabbed his arm, he barely managed to stop from jerking free and sending them both plummeting floorward.

"Wait for the rope, Private."

"You can't . . ."

Jerking his chin toward his collar tabs, Ressk's lips drew back. "Yeah. I can."

"*Tri keert!*"

The end of rope slapped into the pipe half a meter away, but both Kyster and Ressk had braced at Werst's warning.

"Go on!" Ressk nodded toward it. "You first. If you fall, I'll shove you to one side on the way by so that you don't crush anyone when you hit bottom."

"I won't fall!"

"Yeah, yeah, famous last words. Get your ass up there."

Even with only one working foot, he could go up a rope. Babies could climb before they could walk. He swung up onto the lowest cable and then, at Werst's nod, went one higher.

"Talk to me, Corporal!"

"Couple more minutes, Gunny. We're almost there."

The gunny's voice had effortlessly filled the space. Werst had sounded like he was bellowing. Feeling smug about the difference, Kyster wrapped a hand around the next cable as Ressk reached the cleft and pulled himself up.

"Brakes on, junior!"

"Let him go. How much *serley* trouble can he get into in six meters?"

The weary, superior tone in Ressk's voice made him want to find some trouble, but he concentrated on climbing, on finding the way out the gunny knew was there. He could feel weight bowing the final cable as someone joined him and hurriedly thrust his head out into the light. There was a brief flash of curved walls and fallen rock and then he found himself back down in the cleft, Werst holding a fistful of his combats and snarling right into his face.

"The gunny wouldn't appreciate you losing your fukking head."

He didn't have a hope in hell of freeing himself and he knew it. "There's nothing up there."

"You know that now!"

"Someone had to be first!"

"Shouldn't have been you, dumbass!"

"No loss if I buy it." He had a horrible feeling he sounded sulky.

"Listen, kid . . ." Werst dropped his voice, nose ridges pinching closed. ". . . no idea why, but Gunny likes you. She sits down and gives up, we're fukked. You get killed, I'm not sure she'll keep going. Don't fukking get killed. Understand?"

Kyster felt his jaw drop. "She likes me?"

Muttering profanity under his breath, Werst pushed past him up and out. Kyster pulled himself together enough to follow.

"Gunny wants to know what we've got," Ressk called from a couple of cables down.

"We've got tunnels."

"That'll thrill her."

It looked like the tunnels on the lower level. Same smooth rock, same curved walls; Kyster couldn't see any caves, but a part of the wall had collapsed near where the pipe continued to rise behind the rock. He limped over and took a closer look.

He could just barely see the pipe, but he thought he could reach it. Balanced on a hunk of fallen rock, he stretched out an arm, fingers reaching until they brushed the . . .

"Gunny! Kyster's down! Werst thinks the pipe in the upper tunnel is live."

"Live?"

"Probably a broken cable in the wall making contact with the metal!"

"Go." Mike handed her the rope. "I'll anchor this end."

Down was not dead. Werst would have said dead. Torin had nine people to get out. She wasn't losing any of them. And she really wasn't losing a kid who'd spent all that time surviving injured and alone before she got there.

"One on the rope at a time," she said, slinging her canteen and the sleeve of biscuits. "Minimize losses." Years in allowed her to say it as though those losses weren't listening.

It was hand over hand for the first three meters before there was enough of an angle to bother putting her boots on the pipe. Logic said bare feet would grip better against the slick metal, but logic had never met the soles of Marine Corps boots. They read the pressure and surface under them and adjusted accordingly. Torin had no idea how it worked, but it worked regardless of the power situation so, in point of fact, she didn't give a good Goddamn. Someone had told her once—it might have been Glicksohn way back—that they'd been designed to mimic the pads on the Mictok's eight legs. No, probably not Glicksohn, he'd always been a little freaked about the Mictok.

Died saving one.

Kyster would just be one more name on her personal list.

Except there was never any *just* about it.

Her shoulders were aching and her palms burning by the time she reached the cleft.

"Going to be a tight fit, Gunny," Ressk warned her. "Stay as far left as you can."

The cables had minimal give. The shattered planes of the rock, none at all. Fortunately, flesh compacted.

Over the sound of her skull scraping against stone, she could hear Mashona beginning to climb.

"Foot here, Gunny." Ressk's hand wrapped around her ankle, bending her leg as he set her foot on a higher cable. "And push."

Torin grimaced as she finally emerged into the upper tunnel. It had to be Darlys' whole progenitor fascination that made her think of a birth canal because she sure as hell couldn't remember the original experience.

Kyster lay on his side at the base of the tunnel wall, right hand stretched out, fingers curled in toward the palm, Werst on one knee beside him. When she saw the younger Krai's nose ridges moving, she let out a breath she hadn't known she'd held.

"Still out of it," Werst muttered as she knelt beside him. "Minimal contact, and it blew him back." He nodded across the tunnel at the collapsed wall and the glimpse of metal in the shadows. "Probably would have killed one of you lot or the di'Taykan, but we're tougher."

"You build in the tops of trees," Torin said absently, checking Kyster's vitals. "Damn well better be able to take a lightning strike."

Werst snorted. "And we don't break when we're slammed into rock either."

Kyster's eyes fluttered open and locked on Torin's face. "*Ker sa arratrinigre, sa kai terst.*"

When she glanced over at Werst, he was smirking. "Has to do with his mother and is not something he'd want you to hear if he was in his right mind, Gunny. Be better if he never realizes I heard it."

She'd got the gist of it from the tone, and Werst was right. "Go help Ressk get the team through the cables, Corporal. I'll handle this." Kyster needed to be able to move the moment Mike hit the upper level. No longer wandering through sections of the prison designated for the Corps, they were now where they weren't supposed to be, and surely the Others would try to prevent them from getting any farther. No point in keeping prisoners if they were blithely permitted to escape.

Thumb rubbing against Kyster's palm, she gently worked his hand open, making sure all the small bones continued to be attached to all the other small bones and that they still worked the way they should. A bad hand along with the bad foot was the last thing the kid needed. The fingertips were burned but not badly. Only the second finger had even raised a blister; the others were no more than scorched. His hand trembled in her grip but seemed essentially undamaged.

"You," she said, when she realized the young Marine had actually managed to focus on her face, "are one lucky son of a bitch. If you'd gotten yourself killed, I'd have kicked your ass."

"I'm not dead?"

"You're bruised." She ghosted her hand over the curve of his skull. "And you've got a knot on your head the size of a H'san's balls, but you're not dead."

He licked his lips and tried to sit up. "I'm sorry."

"Did you know the pipe was live before you touched it?"

"No."

"Then it was an accident. No one's fault."

"But . . ."

"Don't argue with me, Private. It makes me cranky." She slipped a hand behind him and lifted him carefully until he was leaning against the wall. "Stay there until everyone's up. Mashona!"

"Gunny."

Torin straightened and nodded to the right as Mashona trotted over from the hole in the floor. "Give me three minutes down the tunnels that way."

"You think it'll be a repeat of the pattern down below?"

"Are we standing in a node?"

Mashona looked around. "No."

"No. So not a repeat. Let's find out what it is." Her head felt clearer than it had since before the rockfall. She might've thought that they'd been wrong about an additive in the food and there was some kind of *complacency gas* being pumped into the lower levels except that she knew exactly when she'd stepped out of the fog. When Ressk had yelled down that Kyster was injured. Adrenaline. Clarity had followed the surge. Which explained how Harnett and his goons seemed to have more get up and go than the rest—their situation had kept adrenaline levels high. It also explained why the stims worked.

If she wanted to keep her people sharp, she needed a series of constant stimulants.

"Jiyuu." A nod to the left. "Three minutes that way."

Fuchsia hair sagged. "I'm tired."

"Get over it."

"You're only sending me because you don't like me."

It seemed he was taking a break from sucking up. "I'll like you one fuk of a lot less if you don't pull your own weight. Now, move!"

He didn't move fast, but he moved.

Mashona got back as the last di'Taykan came through the hole, leaving only Kichar and the sergeant below.

"I went a little farther than three, Gunny. There was a rockfall. Big fukkers this time, but they're like stairs up into another level. Looked like more tunnels," she added before Torin could ask. "Didn't go up, though."

"Good work." Torin turned her head and raised her voice. "Jiyuu! Move your ass!"

"And like magic he appears around the curve," Ressk murmured as the di'Taykan came into sight.

"When you call," Darlys began.

"Drop it," Torin ordered, wondering if maybe shoving Darlys into the hole and smacking her head up against an electrical change would help.

"Nothing that way, Gunny." Jiyuu sounded almost petulant. "Just more tunnel. It keeps curving." He sketched what looked like a sine wave into the air. "But there's no little caves, no nothing."

"We've got access to a higher level the other way," Mashona told him.

The ends of his hair flicked back and forth . . . "Then why did I have to—" . . . and stilled as he caught sight of Torin's expression. "Never mind."

Kichar's cry of pain drew attention back to the crevice.

"Ressk!" Torin dropped to one knee and shone her cuff light along the left wall.

"She hit a charge." Ressk had a foot wrapped around Kichar's wrist and was holding her steady against the rock, her legs straddling the lowest cable.

"Where?"

"Near the top. Not sure which one, but it knocked her ass over tip."

"Kichar?"

"I'm good, Gunny." Her free hand was shaking as she rubbed at the dribble of blood on her chin from where she'd bitten her lip.

"Stay there until you're steady enough to climb."

Her eyes widened. "I can't. The sergeant . . ."

And right on cue, Mike yelled, "What's happening up there?"

Ressk twisted and peered down along the pipe. "Kichar took a hit from one of the cables, Sarge." Then he turned and peered up into the light, eyes closed to slits. "I can keep her steady, Gunny, but I need to know what cable to avoid."

"No argument, Ressk." Torin leaned out over the hole. "Any idea, Kichar?"

"I was reaching . . ." She squinted and shook her head. "Sorry, Gunny. One of the top two, but I don't know for sure which one I touched."

"Volunteer to check for a live cable?"

"I'll do it, Gunnery Sergeant."

"Sit down, Darlys, I was kidding. All right, Kichar, it looks like you'll have to avoid both of them. Ressk, get her over there." Torin shone her light on a cable about three meters from the top of the crevice on the opposite side from the cables in question.

"She can't reach the edge from there, Gunny."

"She doesn't have to reach the edge," Torin told him working her way around to the other side. "She just has to reach me." As Ressk guided a visibly shaky Kichar up to the cable, Torin lay flat on the floor, upper body over the hole. The smooth stone felt surprisingly cool through vest and combats. "Mashona, Darlys, on my legs. Jiyuu, Watura get ready to take her from me when she's at the edge. Come up close beside me and, as long as you're there, a knee on my ass wouldn't hurt; just hold the innuendo in reserve, we don't have time for it right now. Kyster, Werst, make sure nothing shows up to interrupt the party. Technical Sergeant Gucciard," she raised her voice, "climb slow."

He sounded amused. "I can do that, Gunny."

"Ressk, hold her steady. Kichar, lift your arms over your head. Grow another eight centimeters if you can."

"Gunny?"

"Stretch, Kichar."

Bending at the waist, Torin let herself fold in over the edge. Kichar's reaching hands were clammy, so she locked her fingers around the young Marine's wrists, nodding in approval as Kichar, face pressed against the rock, mirrored the grip. Two deep breaths. Hold. And she straightened, back muscles clenched tight, arms taking up the last of the distance as Kichar planted her boots against the minimal footholds in the wall and helped as much as she could.

As her hands came up to the edge of the floor, Jiyuu and Watura reached out and each grabbed a wrist to drag her up the rest of the way.

"Boots!" Torin snapped as one of Kichar's came a little close to her face as the private went by.

"That's not going to work with the sergeant," Mashona pointed out, dragging Torin in from the edge with a handful of combats. "You'll never be able to lift him."

The moment Mashona released her, Torin rolled onto her back and let the knots crack out of her spine. "Won't have to. As soon as he's on the cables, that'll free up the rope. There's seven of us up here. He's a big guy, but he's not that big. Ressk."

"On it, Gunny."

She rolled again in time to see Ressk and the sergeant hit the lowest cable at the same time. It rocked a little, and Ressk sucked air in through his teeth.

"I'm getting a buzz, Gunny!"

"Sergeant, climb two cables and then slide right, hard against the rock. Ressk get the rope and get out of there. You lot," she lifted her head and glared around at the watching Marines, "quit blocking the damned light."

Safest to throw the rope, Krai to Krai—grow up that far from the ground and hanging on was a skill learned early. Torin moved out of the way so Werst would have room to make the catch, then wrapped the rope around her ass and braced herself, Mashona and the three di'Taykan on the rope between her and the hole.

"Gunny, I'm getting more buzz!"

Without boots, Ressk had no insulation from the power surge.

"Climb me!" they heard the sergeant snap.

"What?"

"My boots are insulated, you're not. You can reach the edge from my shoulders!"

"Werst!"

"I'm there, Gunny!"

Ressk surged up over the edge, yanked the last meter by Werst's grip on his wrist. The rope tightened. Torin threw her weight back against it, boots braced, as Mike scrambled up on Ressk's heels. Darlys swore softly and adjusted her grip, but the line held. Odds were better than good they could have managed with a couple less di'Taykan, but Torin was a big believer in hedging her bets—particularly with a life on the line.

"Sarge!" On his knees, Ressk leaned out over the hole. "Keep it tight to the wall! Your body's out too far! Your shoulder's going to . . . Fuk!"

Fortunately, the shock slammed him forward not back. The rope went slack as one of the sergeant's hands slapped up and over the edge, fingers scrambling for purchase, nails scraping along the rock as he began to slide.

Werst grabbed for him and caught the cuff of his combats.

Throwing himself flat, Ressk hooked a hand in under his vest.

By the time Torin reached the hole, there was nowhere left to grab on. Hands held what they could; a bit of vest, a fistful of combats, the strap of his canteen, the sleeve of biscuits thrown over his shoulder. The sleeve gave way. There was a flash, the stink of burning meat, and the clatter of the biscuits bouncing off the pipe.

"Heave!" Torin ordered both hands clutching fistfuls of air, refusing to let herself think the words, *dead weight*. "Come on!"

Gravity defeated, Mike hit the floor hard enough to knock the breath from him in a pained grunt—a welcome sound, the dead neither breathed nor grunted. Torin moved in as Darlys flipped him onto his back, dropping to one knee by his side as his mouth opened and closed, his face growing alarmingly flushed as he tried to speak. Finally, he managed to spit out the word, "Slate!"

"Slate?"

"Off!" One hand slapped wildly at his vest where the slate hung.

"His combats probably absorbed some of the charge," Ressk explained, snatching the slate free. "He's afraid that if the slate didn't get caught in the initial surge, there's still a chance off-charging could be enough to corrupt the data."

"You got all that off two words?" Jiyuu asked as Torin raised the sergeant's torso off the stone to help him breathe.

"Techs don't like to waste words." Ressk ran both thumbs along the screen and frowned. "I think we're good."

"Sergeant Gucciard! Look at me!" Hand cupping his jaw, Torin turned Mike's face toward her, locking their eyes. "Deep breaths. With me. In. Out." If he kept panting, he'd hyperventilate and likely pass out—given the tremors she could feel running through the muscles of his back, she wanted him conscious. Breathing slowly, deeply, forcing him to match his rhythm to hers, she unfastened his vest and slipped a hand inside to press against the left side of his chest. She was almost certain that the charge had been too strong to send his heart into fibrillation, yet given that he apparently believed his combats had absorbed at least part of it, she wanted to be sure.

His heart raced under her palm—but under the circumstances that wasn't too fukking surprising. When it slowed without faltering, when his breathing echoed hers, she sat back on her heels and opened a canteen. "You'll live," she told him as she passed it over.

"Too bad." A little water ran down his chin. "Because I feel like shit."

He was sitting on his own, so she stood. Kichar's eyes still had a tendency to show white all the way around, but otherwise, she seemed fine. Kyster was standing, leaning against the wall but on his feet. Without the med-alerts on a working slate, she had no way of knowing how much damage they were hiding and had no intention of assuming they weren't. The sleeve readouts confirmed they were alive but little else. "Ressk."

When she held out her hand, he put the slate in it. "Still just sysop and translation running, Gunny."

Tonguing the codes that would have connected her own state into the com unit in her jaw, Torin stared at the screen, willing it back to life. Unsuccessfully. "Well, we're up a level and no one died," she announced snapping the slate onto her vest and drumming her fingers against it. As Ressk glared, she moved her hand carefully away. "I'd call that a win. Werst, stay by Kyster. Darlys, with Kichar. Jiyuu, Watura, help get the sergeant up onto his feet. Ressk, you're with me on our six. Mashona, lead the way to the next level."

"You don't think we should explore this level, Gunnery Sergeant?"

"We're not in a vid game, Kichar, we get no points for mapping the level. As long as there's a way up, we take it."

"We get the hell out of Dodge, Gunny?"

It was one of the Old Earth sayings Hollice used to drop into conversation. She shared a look with Mashona, a look that said Hollice might not be dead, and nodded. "That's the plan."

"Dodge?" Kichar asked quietly.

Darlys shrugged. "It doesn't matter as long as the gunny knows."

The observation was accurate enough that Torin let it go.

The tunnel to the right had taken some heavy damage.

"Earthquake," Mike grunted, definite enough that he clearly didn't expect to be questioned.

"So you're a geologist now?" Torin asked watching him weave an unsteady path around the debris.

He turned in Watura's grip far enough to smile in her general direction. "Multitalented. Also, used to test weapons systems. This . . ." A nod toward the crack they were following. ". . . looks natural. Seeing this here, makes what happened below look natural. Earthquake," he repeated, brows rising and falling for emphasis.

"So you're saying we need to haul ass out of here before the Others drug us into compliance and show up to physically try and stop us, or the whole place shakes down around our ears?"

"Yeah . . ." A too vigorous nod nearly tipped him over. ". . . pretty much."

"Good thing we're in the Corps and not the Navy," Torin snorted, "or all that might be a problem."

"You don't think earthquakes might be a problem, Gunny?" Kichar's eyes were huge.

"Give me a break, Private; you don't get to be my age without learning how to make the earth move."

As expected, the three di'Taykan got it first. Drugs and physical deterrents and earthquakes got lost in the raucous comments and blatant speculation. Torin let it continue until they reached the place where the ceiling had collapsed, opening up the next level, and then she stopped it with a word.

The rock had fallen in such a way as to create a crude set of stairs.

"Piece of pie if we had a heavy with us," Mashona noted, prodding the lowest boulder with her club. "Shove this here a little closer, and even the Krai wouldn't have to jump for the edge."

"I think you mean piece of cake," Torin corrected absently. She'd noted the lack of heavy gunners before, had assumed it was just that their exoskeletons had been removed during transport, but, now that she thought of it, heavies had a way of moving defined by the contact points sunk into their flesh. She couldn't remember seeing a heavy gunner by either of the two pipes. "Mashona, Ressk—were there heavies in Lieutenant Colonel Braudy's group."

"Don't think so, Gunny." Mashona looked over at Ressk who shook his head. "Hard to tell for certain without the skels, but none of ours for sure. Why?"

"I'm betting there're no heavies down here."

"Maybe they're in a group by themselves?" Jiyuu offered.

Possible, but Torin didn't think so. Without their exoskeletons their augmentations meant nothing, so why wouldn't the Others have imprisoned them as well? Because they only wanted the basic models of the three species? If so, why?

"Maybe the Others were afraid they'd find someone like the technical sergeant to build them new skels out of kibble and spit and then they'd just smash their way free?"

"You asking, Kichar?"

Her cheeks flushed. "No."

"Good, because that's exactly what the technical sergeant would do." Torin gestured up toward the hole. "Mashona, take a look."

She had to jump for the edge and pull herself up through the floor, but it wasn't far and the Krai could always climb one of the taller species. Again.

"What have you got, Corporal?"

Mashona reappeared at the hole. "More tunnels, Gunny!"

"Oh, joy."

"They are being Others ships?"

"How the bloody hell should I know?" Craig danced the fingers of both hands over his screens, making sure that *Promise* had been powered down to the minimal levels necessary for life support. He knew she had, he'd done it himself, but with three ships of the really fukking big variety orbiting Estee, a little paranoia seemed like the logical response. Torin would be so proud.

"You are going to battles before!" Presit snapped, poking him with a remarkably sharp elbow given the amount of fur padding it.

"No, I go to battles *after,* and make and model is surprisingly hard to identify from debris. But they aren't Navy, I can tell you that."

She snorted. "Please, I are telling you that. Nor are they being press."

"No shit. Methane Alliance?"

"I are not thinking so, Methane Alliance ships are . . ." Her hands sketched blobby shapes in the air.

"Butt ugly?"

"That are being close enough. These . . ." Bronzed nails tapped against the worn edge of the control panel, and Craig only just managed to stop himself from grabbing her wrist. Experience had taught him there were significantly more annoying things she could be doing. "These are not being butt ugly, but are not being familiar either. Being Others, then."

"Because you say so?"

The thin black line of her lips lifted off sharp white teeth. "Yes."

"Okay." He was actually surprisingly comfortable with that. He might freak out about that later. "Why are they here?"

"They are removing the glass and are taking it back to their worlds and are melting it and are reconstituting the contents."

Heart pounding, he turned to stare at her, which was, at least, a change from staring at his screens. "Is your fur too bloody tight? Has all that fluff overheated your brain?"

"It are only a theory!"

"It's a dumbass theory!"

"And you are having a better one, then?"

"Maybe, since they won the fight over this particular piece of real estate, they've just come back to set up camp."

"Then why are they not staying after they won? Why are they giving our side a chance to fortify?"

"We didn't fortify!"

Even including his reflection in her mirrored glasses as part of her expression, she looked smug. "No, but we are having the chance. First they are leaving and now they are coming back; I are not knowing why, but I are betting it are as I said—for analysis of the damage their new weapon are having done."

That, he had to reluctantly agree with.

Tucked up against the nearer of Estee's moons, they watched for just under eight hours as the three ships maintained their orbits. The scientists' chartered ship had fled the moment Captain Yritt had all her passengers on board, but Presit had announced that this was finally a story worth her attention and they would wait until the Navy responded. Craig thought about tossing her in the head and hauling ass out of system, but her curiosity seemed to have infected him.

"But if they spot us, we run."

"If they are spotting us, we are trying for an interview." She'd laughed at his expression and patted his arm. *"I are mostly kidding."*

It was that *mostly* that had him change the security codes on the com.

"You are not trusting me?"

"Not as far as I can throw you." And since she couldn't have weighed more than sixteen kilos, that was pretty damned far.

During the eight hours they'd been watching, the ships had sent no VTAs down to the surface, but with *Promise* powered down, Craig couldn't get a read on how extensively they were scanning. He was more relieved than he let show that they clearly weren't removing any of the surface their weapons had previously fused. Torin would call him stupidly sentimental, but he didn't want any part of her ending up in enemy hands.

Actually, given the number of Marines who'd died down there, it was entirely possible she'd understand.

"Readings are changing!"

Craig swallowed the last of the coffee in his mug and crossed the cabin to peer down at the screens. "They're powering up."

"Being ready to leave?"

"We'll know in a minute." He plucked Presit out of his chair and settled into its duct-taped, familiar embrace as she smoothed her fur and grumbled about respect. Ignoring the grumbling in favor of tracking the enemy ships, he coaxed *Promise* up to the edge of readiness.

"How are we knowing if we are being spotted?"

"Easy peasy. We blow up."

As far as Craig could tell—and it wasn't as if he were set up to register alien tech, so he couldn't be one hundred percent sure—all three ships passed the nearer moon, heading out-system without noticing them tucked up against the edge of the gravity well.

"We are not blowing up."

"Trust me, I'm as chuffed as you are. They've likely read the Susumi portals opening as our Navy rides to the rescue . . ." He tapped the three distinctive signatures on the long-distance scanner. ". . . and don't want to shoot it out." When he reached out to slide the power buildup back a bit, Presit grabbed his arm. Her hand might be tiny, but her claws made her point.

"No. We are following now."

"The hell?"

She sighed and repeated. "We are following now. This are being too good a chance to lose."

"What is?"

Her claws tightened just a little before she released him. Crouching down, she rummaged in the bag by her feet—Craig vaguely remembered her taking it out of the locker and had assumed she'd gone for her brushes—and pulled out her personal recorder. Straightening, she held it out on one tiny hand. "Be breaking the case open. Quickly!" she snapped when he hesitated. "We are not having time for you to be questioning me!"

Frowning, he did as she asked and watched with increasing suspicion as she separated a memory chip from the recorder's hardware.

"When Durgin a Tar canSalvais were following the *Berganitan* through Susumi space to Big Yellow, he are using this program."

"You told me you told the military you didn't know how he did it. They've been trying to reverse engineer it!"

"I are not trusting the military. And besides, I are not lying, I are *not* knowing how. I are not a pilot." She dropped the chip onto Craig's palm. He didn't remember holding out his hand. "But he are doing it with that."

"And why didn't *he* tell the military?"

"Because I are having the equations." As Craig frowned in confusion, she added, "Durgin are not having them memorized, are he? He are not remembering enough to be of any use, and I are having taken this and replaced it with a corrupted chip before we are going onto the *Berganitan*."

Without knowing the Susumi equations that defined the destination, Durgin had locked onto the tail end of the *Berganitan*'s Susumi signature. Staying close enough to lock while simultaneously maintaining enough distance to keep from being swept up in the wake and destroyed was an insanely dangerous maneuver. Pilots had known the theory for years, but Durgin had been the only one to ever successfully emerge with his ship not only more or less intact on the far side but exactly where he'd intended it to be.

Craig slipped the chip into his panel. "These aren't Susumi equations."

"No. These are Susumi adaptations. We are using these to follow the Others home. We are maybe using these to end the war."

"We are maybe using these to die in a new and exciting way."

She grinned, the tip of her tongue visible between sharp white teeth. "We are all being dead someday."

"Fuk it, Presit." But even he could hear that he wanted to be convinced. "I'm clearly not the mathematician Durgin was!"

"No." Her claws were sheathed when she touched his arm this time. "But you are being a much better pilot."

The new tunnels weren't exactly the same as the old. They were wider, and the walls weren't as smooth. Mashona called them lightly pebbled and that seemed as good a description as any as far as Torin was concerned. There were no small caves and the curves had nearly become actual corners.

Kyster and Kichar both insisted that they'd fully recovered. They were young enough and anxious enough to please that Torin didn't believe them, but as they were doing nothing more than walking, surrounded by armed Marines, she let it go. Mike, who'd taken the largest hit, occasionally stumbled and had a tendency to angle off to the right. When asked, he said he felt like shit, and *that* Torin believed. The readouts on his sleeve had defaulted to Ventris norm and his medical readout kept coming up yellowish orange.

Without the darker marks of the caves breaking up the pale gray expanse of walls, it was hard to get any good idea of how far they'd walked without actually calculating time and the average speed of a movitated Marine.

"About twenty-eight kilometers since we hit this level."

"Thank you, Ressk."

"Think we're actually getting somewhere, Gunny?"

"Are we where we were, Corporal?"

"No . . ."

"Then we're definitely somewhere else."

"Somewhere closer to getting out?" Werst asked without turning.

"Yeah. I think so."

"Going to tell us why you think so, Gunny?"

"I expect the belief is based on years and years of experience combined with a number of subliminal clues that I'm not consciously aware of."

"Gut feeling?" Mike asked in the stunned silence that followed her declaration.

"Pretty much, yeah."

Mashona's raised fist halted forward movement and conversation both. They'd come within three meters of their first t-junction—a cursive tee perhaps but a familiar intersection for all that. Passing it after Mashona had scouted ahead and returned with the all clear, Torin couldn't help but think that there were now three possible ways the enemy could use to come up behind them. And, logically, that they had to run into the enemy soon.

Although both tunnels remained empty as she brought up the rear of the squad, she thought she could smell something vaguely familiar. Sweet. Not rotten food, dying comrade sweet but truly sweet; like those horrible red candies given out on First Landing Day that were supposed to taste like cherries, but those who took the dare and ate them insisted there had never been such a flavor in nature.

"Hold up, people." Their small column stopped dead. "You smell it, Ressk?"

His nose ridges slowly opened and just as slowly closed. "Like a bowl of jellied *aln* in the sun? But it's not close. In the distance."

"Everyone back on me; we need some intell."

Head cocked, Ressk's ridges opened again. "I'm not sure which tunnel it's coming from, Gunny."

"Werst, Kichar—give me a quick two minutes each way."

"Gunnery Sergeant Kerr, Kichar's injured," Darlys began, but Torin cut her off.

"Kichar's Recon. Even juiced, she'd do it better than the rest of us."

"Not better than you, Gunny!"

"I wasn't including me, Kichar, now move."

The smell continued up *both* cross tunnels.

"Fine. Right it is, then. Mashona!"

"On point, Gunny."

"Why right, Gunny."

Torin shrugged. "I'm right handed." Then she had to spend a few moments explaining to Ressk why right-handed people tended to turn right if given an option. The Krai were not only completely ambidextrous but ambiextremitied as well.

Six minutes up the new tunnel and around the first of a series of increasingly tight curves . . .

Ressk tapped her lightly on the wrist, his voice low, not intended to carry. "The smell's getting stronger but not from in front of us, Gunny."

She tapped Mike on the shoulder, signaled that they should keep walking until they were around the next bend and wait, and then she flattened against the wall, dropping to one knee. Without a helmet, the best way to survive a head shot was to keep from being shot in the head, and removing that head from where the enemy was aiming was the easiest way to do that.

By the time the sound of boots had faded—deliberately silenced for the benefit of their stalker as all nine Marines waited barely eight meters away—she could hear an almost familiar tapping growing closer. Club in her left hand, knife in her right, she waited.

The bug didn't exactly have a face, so Torin had to assume the way both antennae flicked straight up indicated surprise. Having tossed a grenade at one while sharing the insides of Big Yellow, she'd learned that the sharp smell of lemon furniture polish translated fairly closely to *oh, fuk!* They were the only insectoid species of Others she'd ever fought against and wouldn't have picked them as their jailers if given a choice—mammals knew at least some of the strengths and weaknesses of other mammals.

She'd barely raised the club when the bug pivoted its entire body around the rear clump of its millipedelike legs—hard to see actual numbers under the skirt of its body armor, but there were at least three involved—and took off back down the tunnel. Torin wanted to say it looked terrified but had long since learned that cross-species generalizations seldom came close to what was actually happening.

The question now became did they follow the bug or run like hell in the other direction?

Easy enough to answer; the jailers knew the way out.

"We've got bugs, people. Let's go!"

TEN

BUGS HAD A LOT OF LEGS, BUT THEY WEREN'T particularly long—all that movement down by the floor made them seem faster than they were. While the cherry candy bug might be motivated to get away, Torin's need for answers drove her to close the distance before the odds changed in the bug's favor. She could hear boots pounding close behind her—Mashona and the di'Taykan; the Krai couldn't keep up on the flat and the other two Humans were still shaking off the effects of the current.

They raced through a series of switchbacks where Torin's smaller turning radius allowed to her gain a little ground. When they reached another t-junction and the bug started left, hesitated, and then turned right, she dove forward and got her arms around the abdomen, using momentum to bring them both crashing to the ground. Torin wasn't too concerned about injury, not to herself or the bug—they were both considerably tougher than they looked—she just wanted to slow it down long enough for backup to arrive.

"Gunny!"

"Haul ass, Mashona!" She used her elbow to block one of the under arms, claw bouncing painfully off bone, and twisted away from the other. Her position made her relatively safe from the upper arms where *relatively* meant the bug wasn't quite able get hold of her but was more than willing to raise bruises trying. Its mouth parts clattered, and Torin got a nose full of the sharp, ammonia scent of evergreens mixed with cinnamon. Xenolinguists in the Corps were fond of speculating on how much the bugs depended on scent; did it stand on its own as a language or did it merely support verbalization. Torin's gut feeling said both, just as her gut was saying that cinnamon-sprinkled evergreen equaled yelling for backup. Her head slammed into the tunnel wall, but she managed to tip the bug over onto its side, exposing the vulnerable underbelly and giving the bug something to worry about other than taking her to pieces as it began struggling to get away. Apparently, no one had ever told it that the best defense is a good offense.

Odds were very good she was young and had never fought a mammal before. At least not hand to claw.

The sound of approaching boots got lost between the ringing in her ears and the crack and scrape of bug and Marine against the stone.

"Gunny!" Mashona's warning was suddenly up close and personal. "Hostiles!"

She had a split second to decide. Did she hold onto the bug and use it as a hostage, assuming its companions cared enough about it to stay back, recognizing that in her business, assumptions about alien species usually fell on the *early death* side of stupid? Or did she jump clear, giving herself and her people more maneuvering room?

Shifting her grip, she let the bug get her legs under her again and when she thrust up with her abdomen, Torin used the movement to jump clear, rolling and coming up onto her feet just in front of and between Darlys and Mashona.

"Well . . ." She shoved a tangle of hair back off her face and her fingers came away bloody. That explained why her head hurt so fukking much. ". . . this is interesting."

No point in tracking the bug as she scrabbled back to her companions. It seemed a lot more important that Torin keep her eyes on the three quadrupeds, two other bugs, and four members of a bipedal species she couldn't remember ever fighting. Taller than the Krai but at the low end of Human norm, they were stocky—if she had to guess she'd say muscular—hairless, with ivory skin, thin, almost nonexistent features, and eyes that showed black from lid to lid.

"What do we do, Gunny?" Mike asked quietly.

Not a good idea to glance back. Better to assume they were all there, then. Ten of the good guys. Ten of the Other guys.

"We don't make any sudden moves," Torin said at the same volume.

One of the quadrupeds—the female, the short plush fur on her lower half a tawny gold only a little darker than her eyes—moved slowly out in front of the group, a member of the unidentified species close by her side. They wore dark gray uniforms patterned with black but no helmets. No PCUs. No visible tech at all. No weapons except for . . .

"Werst. On the far left. Is that a sling?"

"Looks like, Gunny."

Made out of what looked like a strip of leather and it wasn't the only one. Now Torin knew what to look for, all the bipeds were carrying. The leather looked identical to the strips that held the rock heads on the clubs, braided to increase the surface area.

The quadruped gestured, vertical pupils in golden eyes narrowed to barely visible lines, and seemed to ask a question.

The biped at her withers swept a flat, emotionless gaze over the Marines and answered.

The quadruped seemed to disagree.

Torin didn't know much about the Others rank structure, but if she had to guess, the two silver lines curving along the front of the quadruped's shoulder signified officer. The pattern the biped wore, however, very nearly matched her collar tabs for complication. Senior NCO.

The biped, dark eyes locked on Torin's face, answered again. At length.

"These aren't our jailers," Torin said, slowly straightening up out of fighting stance. "They're prisoners as well. Stripped-down uniforms. No tech. Weapons created from available resources."

In the silence that followed, she could hear the three Krai breathing in sync.

"You think they know that? That we're not *their* jailers?" Mike asked at last.

"I think the senior noncom there just explained it to his officer."

"If they're not our jailers, then who are?" Kichar wondered.

A snort. Werst probably. Definitely when he started talking. "Not the time, kid. And they're still the enemy."

Torin would have bet her pension that the officer, currently scraping the claws on one foreleg against the floor, had just said the same damned thing. She nearly smiled at the expression on the NCO's face. *Nearly* because it was never a good idea to show teeth across species lines until all parties were clear on the meaning. *Smiled* because given the reaction of the NCO, the odds were good the officer was a lieutenant at best. Or the alien military equivalent.

"Darlys, got a gender on the NCO?" It didn't really matter since sex was unlikely, at least as far as she was concerned, but she liked to have the pronouns straight in her head.

"Male, Gunnery Sergeant." The di'Taykan always knew. They didn't usually care, but they always knew.

One of the other bipeds said something aggressive. The NCO responded calmly.

And the slate clipped to Torin's vest repeated the last few words injecting two *ands* and a *the* in Federate.

Everyone froze. Torin could only see the ten facing her, but she could feel the reaction of her own people, and the silence had never shouted, *"What the fuk?"* quite so loudly.

"Gunny . . ." Mike, moved up behind her left shoulder. ". . . hand me the slate."

Still holding the NCO's gaze, she dropped her left hand, one millimeter at a time, until her fingers were touching the plastic but not obscuring the screen. If he'd spent any time in combat—and experience told her he clearly had—he'd have seen a slate before. The belief that the Others didn't take prisoners might be back on the table, but no one had ever suggested that meant they didn't examine captured tech. When he nodded, she unclipped it. "The translation program?"

"Don't know why it's analyzing," Mike grunted, "but yeah."

"I could have brushed against the screen while I was grappling with the bug. Accidentally activated it."

"Could have." He tugged it out of her hand. "But it's unlikely."

Another terse question from the officer. Another long reply from the NCO. Torin got the impression it was longer than it needed to be. Long enough for the translation program to work out a few more patterns and compare them to languages it had stored. Hell, for all she knew, the officer who'd owned the slate had been working on cracking the Others' common language in his or her spare time and had all relevant recordings loaded. That explained why it had come up with a conjunction and an article so quickly.

"It's running three levels of analysis. Minimum." Mike sounded impressed. "Keep them talking, Gunny."

She wanted to ask just what exactly she was supposed to keep them talking about given the lack of a common language, but they seemed to have plenty of other points of congruence, so what the hell. Touching her collar tabs, she nodded to the other NCO, then shifted her gaze to the officer and came to attention saying, "Gunnery Sergeant Torin Kerr." Her tone made it quite clear that gesture merely acknowledged rank and was not, intrinsically one of respect.

Because she was watching for it, Torin saw an expression that looked very much like amusement flash for a moment across the NCO's face. He, at least, understood the subtext.

The officer snarled a reply, a stiffer crest of hair running along the center of her skull and down the back of her neck, flaring up. She had a set of impressive teeth to go with the claws.

Torin heard teeth snap behind her. One of the other quadrupeds reared. Definitely male given the lack of uniform covering his lower body. Impressively male, actually. His crest was larger, too. Suddenly, there was a snap of leather and a rock flying toward her head. She swung the club without thinking.

The sharp crack of the impact rang out over the shouting—and the pervasive smell of lemon furniture polish—slapping the rock up to shatter against the ceiling between the two groups. For a moment, the only sound came from pieces of rock pattering down onto the polished floor, then Torin and the other NCO filled in the silence.

"No one moves, or you'll have me to deal with before that lot gets over here! Private Kyster!"

"Gunnery Sergeant!"

He was younger by a considerable margin and still not entirely stable.

"Do *not* let that happen again."

"Yes, Gunnery Sergeant! I mean . . ."

"Teeth together and lips over them!"

"Yes, Gunnery Sergeant!"

The opposing NCO had also frozen his people in place and was speaking quietly to his officer, explaining, calming. She was scared shitless, Torin realized, impressed that she'd managed to keep her natural aggressive instincts in check. The quadrupeds she'd faced had been fierce fighters and damned near impossible for a biped to defeat in hand to hand given that it was more hand to hand to two sets of viciously clawed feet and a spine as flexible as a cat's. Given the chance, they weren't averse to using their teeth. If the young officer had chosen to fight, Torin's small group wouldn't have stood a chance, particularly considering that the other two quadrupeds were half again the officer's size.

She finally, reluctantly, turned her attention back to Torin, and her NCO lightly touched her arm, saying, "Durlin Vertic."

The officer inclined her head at the introduction.

"Marines! Attention!"

Torin could feel their surprise even over their trained response as six boots and three pairs of bare feet hit the floor in unison.

The NCO snapped something quickly to the two male quadrupeds who'd shifted their weight back onto their haunches. Durlin Vertic studied Torin's face for a long moment, not old enough to completely hide her embarrassment. She didn't take respect as her due; that was a good sign. After a long moment, she shifted position subtly, bringing all four legs into alignment, the claws still prominent but somehow less obvious. Then she relaxed, and her NCO looked remarkably as though he wanted to pet her flank.

"Marines! As you were."

"Gunny?"

"She held her people in check, Sergeant, in spite of a clear personal preference to attack. That deserves our acknowledgment."

"And now?"

Before she could answer, the NCO stepped into the space between them. He touched the insignia on his shoulder much as Torin had touched her tabs and said, "Durlave Kan Freenim." Then he beckoned one of his own species forward. "Durlave Kir Sanati." The second biped's insignia was similar although less ornate, and it seemed clear that Durlave Kan and Durlave Kir were rank designations. He held up his hand, palm flat and ran a finger over it as though he were writing on a screen and then he waited.

"Front and center, Sergeant," Torin murmured. When Mike drew even with her, they stepped forward together. "Technical Sergeant Gucciard," she said, nodding toward the other Human.

Durlave Kir Sanati looked pointedly at the slate and began to speak, slowly and distinctly.

"Seems like they want to work on the language issue." Mike frowned at the code scrolling across the screen, held up a hand to cut off the flow of words, changed something although Torin had no idea what, and indicated Sanati should continue.

As Durlave Kan Freenim stepped back, so did Torin.

"Let's move things down the tunnel a bit, people," she said quietly, "give these two a chance to work without input from the masses screwing things up."

Durlin Vertic had to smack one of the male quadrupeds to get him moving, but her people seemed to be doing the same thing. Retreat. Regroup. Wait.

"What happens after we can talk to them, Gunny?"

"That depends on what they have to say, Kichar."

"But they're the enemy!"

Torin poked at the cut just above her hairline, examined the blood on her fingertip, and decided it was nothing to worry about. "Might be time to redefine terms."

"You can't just redefine enemy!"

"Don't see why not." Stretching out her legs, she got as comfortable as a polished rock floor allowed. "History does it all the time."

"As near as I can figure, we're in for two and a half, maybe three and a half days. All I know for sure is I'm getting fractions."

Presit shrugged under the movement of the brush. "It are not counting, so it are making no difference."

"It'll make one fuk of a difference if I don't get enough warning to get us out cleanly. Or are you forgetting that the last time you tried this, your ship damned near went to pieces on reentry to normal space?"

A wave of one small hand dismissed that as unimportant. "I are not forgetting, but that are no reason for you to be stopping brushing."

Craig rolled his eyes but continued moving the brush through the fur on the reporter's back. God help him, he was starting to find the repetitive motion and the feel of the long silky hair under his fingers comforting. Grooming was a communal activity for the Katrien, but Presit clearly considered him an acceptable substitute. The last time circumstances had forced her into it, but this time she'd chosen to go to Estee in search of a story without any others of her species. He had no intention of examining her motivation too closely and every intention of believing it had to do with the way she preferred to receive attention without having to return it. Nothing to do with him. Them. Because the last thing they were, was a them.

If everything went well, they'd exit Susumi space in the wake of the Others' ship essentially the same time they'd entered it.

If something went wrong, if even one of the adaptations were off by a single integer, they were screwed. If the Others spotted them before he could get *Promise*'s engines back on-line, they were screwed. If he couldn't work out the equations to get them home, they were screwed.

Why was he doing this again?

For a chance to end the war?

What bloody difference did it make? Torin was already dead.

"Your rhythm are faltering."

"Presit . . ."

She twisted around until he was on the receiving end of a narrow-eyed glare. He regretted dimming the light levels so she could remove her dark glasses. "You are having something better to do?"

As it happened, no.

"At least you've stopped bleeding, Gunny."

"Head wounds bleed, Mashona." They couldn't spare the water to wash the blood out of her hair, but once it was completely dry, she could crumble it out of the clumps. It wasn't her first head wound, not by a decade and a half at least. She'd added a few new bruises to the yellow-and-green remnants of her confrontation with Harnett's goons, but except for a purple-and-black lump rising up on her right elbow that pushed against her sleeve every time she bent her arm, they could be ignored. Having decided that, she refused to acknowledge the ache in her right hip as she stood and stretched before wandering a short distance down the tunnel, stopping just short of where she'd have to acknowledge Jiyuu on watch. She couldn't go to Kyster, it didn't work like that, not in a group this small, but, given a chance, he could come to her.

She'd almost begun to wonder if he would when she heard the distinct step/shuffle of his approach.

"Gunnery Sergeant Kerr."

"Private."

He stood close enough that he could have spoken without being overheard, but he remained silent, shifting in place as if he wasn't certain of what he was going to stay. Torin glanced down at the top of his head, noted that the few bristles were pale against his mottled skin, wondered if he was from the most northern of the Krai's three massive continents, and waited.

Finally, he drew in a deep breath, nose ridges open wide, released it slowly, and said, "I didn't mean . . ."

When she was certain that was all he'd intended to say, Torin nodded. "You reacted."

He frowned. "If we fought?"

"We'd have lost."

"But you . . ." He stared up at her, eyes wide and made a gesture that, given the context, probably meant *could have kicked ass.*

"Not this time. Learn to pick your battles, Private. You know now what'll make at least some of that lot charge forward. Remember it. You may be able to use it some day."

"Yes, Gunny!" He shifted his weight on, and then quickly off, his bad foot. "I'm sorry."

"Good."

❧   ❧   ❧

Torin tucked her half-finished biscuit into a pocket on her vest and stood as Mike approached, meeting him halfway between the bit of tunnel they'd claimed and the neutral zone where he and Durlave Kir Sanati had been working on their communication problem.

"Keep it simple," he said without preamble, "and we're good to go. Talk slow, no abstract concepts, and forget the Artek . . ."

"The Artek?"

"The bugs. They don't speak Primacy."

"Primacy?"

His brows dipped in. "They don't call themselves the Others, Gunny. Their coalition is called the Primacy. I assume that's what their common language is also called."

"Common to everyone but the bugs? The Artek."

"They usually wear translators. Anyway, Sanati's a bit of a linguist, and she manages, the rest just make assumptions and point."

"Sounds like dealing with staff officers," Torin snorted. "Have you uploaded?" She wasn't sure what the base specs were for implants at the technical sergeant level, but she was damned sure that everyone in tech had made upgrades. There'd been rumors of a tech sergeant running a video feed from his implant to his optic nerve—not exactly Corps approved.

"Yeah. It's running good."

"All right. Do me. Seriously," she added when he blinked. "I tried to contact the slate earlier on my own, and it didn't work."

"Wasn't set up for it then." Mike gave her jaw a long look as though he could see through flesh and bone, and work out the system parameters of the tech—which, except for the looking through flesh and bone was no doubt exactly what he was doing. "You know your code? Lots don't," he pointed out at her expression. To her surprise he passed her the slate. "You do the initial input. I don't need to know them."

"You planning on inputting upgrades I won't understand?"

He glanced around at the tunnels and said dryly, "Not likely."

"Then I don't see a problem."

"Security?"

Torin snorted. "If you want to play 'mine's higher,' you'll probably win. Tech's always higher than infantry. Besides, when my last implant burned out, it took my jaw with it; might have been nice if someone'd had the codes to cut the power." The Corps psychologists said the memory of the pain, the memory of smell as her jaw had cooked from within, had been neutered and could in fact be safely taken out and examined without stress. Torin said in response that the Corps psychologists had clearly had their heads shrunk below usefulness—but not where they could hear her.

The new translation program overwrote her old, significantly less complex program and made her jaw itch. *Made you think your jaw itched,* the Corps psychologists corrected. Torin gave them that one.

Durlave Kan Freenim was waiting for her in what had been the tech zone.

"Prisoners?" He gestured past her to where her people waited.

"Yes. You?"

"Yes. Not yours?"

"No."

"We do not take prisoners." He answered before Torin could ask. "There is no honor." Now was not the time to get into that. "Who, then?"

"I don't know." Which was the truth as far as it went; she didn't *know,* but suspicion sat like a rock in her gut.

He gestured at her sleeve. "Your clothing is on. Ours is not."

"You have embedded tech?"

"Very much the same, I think. We have some of it from you." Creases folded into his forehead. "We believed it a good idea."

"How? You don't take prisoners."

"We are not unseeing . . ."

Unobservant?

". . . and we are not primitive. We would like our clothing to work."

Yeah, and Torin would like to be somewhere else, but no one was making that happen for her.

Freenim sighed. "Will you make our clothing work?"

"Can't. The technical sergeant had to leave his tools behind." And currently allies or not, they weren't sacrificing a set of combats so the enemy could gain technical equality. Even if she'd been willing, the odds of Mike being able to link up three entirely different systems were slim to none.

"I understand." But he'd had to ask. Torin got that. "What do we do now?"

The way Torin saw it, they had three choices—continue the war, continue escaping separately, continue escaping together. Spending any longer doing nothing at all was a good way to fall victim to the influence of the food and end up spending the rest of a short life doing nothing at all. Separately, there was a chance one group could get out even if the other didn't, but even though separately they could cover twice the ground, they'd always be watching their backs, aware the enemy was in the tunnels. Together, there'd be new skills and better odds of overcoming whatever their bastard jailers decided to throw at them, but close proximity to the enemy wasn't likely to make anyone happy. If they were betrayed, the presence of the quadrupeds, not to mention the bugs, pretty much ensured her side would lose the fight. And if they took their eyes off the Primacy and were ambushed, that *pretty much* pretty much disappeared, replaced by a sure thing. On the other hand, if they decided to do the ambushing . . .

Torin didn't need to say any of that aloud—even if she thought the translation program could handle it. Durlave Kan Freenim knew their choices as well as she did.

"Now, we go on. Together."

"Yes." Freenim's head wobbled. Probably the equivalent of a nod. "Together. Knowing where the other is, that is . . . best."

Would have been interesting to know why the translation program paused.

"You have no officer? Then Durlin Vertic will lead."

"I lead my people."

"The durlin will lead you."

The durlin was listening, claws on her left forefoot lightly scoring the ground, so Torin nodded and said, "Yes." Lying convincingly had never been a problem.

The Primacy had been following the Artek who'd been following subtle vibrations they could feel through their feet.

✿   ✿   ✿

"So we'll be following the bugs, Gunny?" Kichar's eyes were enormous. "They're allies now?"

"They're Artek and remember, the enemy of my enemy is my friend," Torin told her. She hadn't been surprised when the phrase had translated perfectly. "Although it might be more accurate to say the enemy of my enemy is not currently my enemy though that will change with circumstances. For now . . ." Her expression suggested they not argue. ". . . we'll operate like two squads in a single unit."

"I'd rather have them where I can see them," Darlys admitted.

"That's why you're with us," Werst snorted, scowling up at the di'Taykan.

"United front, people!" Torin snapped. She'd started forgetting the di'Taykan had been Harnett's before they were hers, but Werst never would and she appreciated the reminder. "Fake it if you have to. Our odds of getting the hell out of here just went up, and we need to get moving before . . ."

The tunnels plunged into darkness. From the spot where the ten members of the Primacy had been standing came the distinct scent of sandalwood.

"Never mind."

"We move at one light. The Artek say we are close to the beginning of the vibrations." Vertic's lips pulled up off her teeth. Torin didn't assume she was smiling. "When we meet the ones who hide us here, your people will fight?"

"Yes, Durlin. My people will fight."

"Good. For now, learn what is needed to know." She pivoted on one back foot and returned to the two male quadrupeds, leaving Torin and Freenim alone in the DMZ between the two groups. Although it was difficult to tell given that Torin's cuff light was illuminating the durlin's path and nothing much higher, the males seemed to relax a little the moment Vertic was in arm's reach.

The small group had escaped from their holding tunnels a day before Torin's people. As near as she could tell from her interpretation of the translation program's more idiosyncratic word choices, their prisons had been identical—tunnels, pipes, areas around the pipes under the control of senior officers. The biscuits she compared with Freenim looked the same, but they'd both been around enough to not suggest swapping the contents of their lunch pails.

Everyone in the group but the Artek had been scooped from the battle on Estee.

"We landed in small caves off the big tunnels; lost one too badly injured for the primitive aid available, but the rest of us came together under the durlin. She convinced the seniors to allow her to attempt an escape."

Torin made a note of his expression. Given that he was a senior NCO talking about a junior officer, the way he said *convinced* told her a lot. As backgrounds went, it was heavily edited, but she'd left out a few details herself. No point in giving it all up on the first date.

Her opinion of Durlin Vertic went up.

"The Artek argued on going with us."

"You understand them?"

He snorted. "They are very . . ."

The translation program ran through a number of words that made no sense before settling on unstoppable. Torin ran through a few words herself but figured that persistent was probably the closest. Freenim had also noticed that the older prisoners had stopped caring about escape and had, like Torin, assumed it was due to an additive in the food.

"They are content to be where they are. Except for the Artek. But the body differences are so great, how can they match the drug in the food we all eat?"

Good question. When it came right down to it, mammals were mammals, furred or hairless, two legs or four. And speaking of four . . .

"When I fought the durlin's people, there were riders."

"No Ner were taken," Freenim told her. "The Polint are not happy. All your species are here?"

"All our warrior species." He hadn't asked about the heavy gunners, so Torin didn't fill him in. He'd engaged with the enemy as often as she had, he had to know they existed.

"So few."

"Enough."

He leaned around her to look down the tunnel, Mike and Ressk visible in a pool of light as they worked on the slate. When he straightened, he looked thoughtful. Or possibly constipated. This was the first time she'd ever had a conversation with a member of the Primacy that didn't involve a high-caliber weapon as the primary conversationalist. "There is information you are not telling me."

Torin snorted. "There is information you are not telling me."

She made a note of how his features arranged themselves when she knew he was amused. "Of course."

"I don't like taking orders from an enemy officer, Gunny."

"You're not. You're taking orders from me."

"And you're taking orders from her."

"Officers are officers, Werst. And durlins are lieutenants—I can handle her. The Artek are following vibrations in the floors and the walls and . . ." She frowned as Cherry Bug looped the tunnel just at the edge of the pooled light, running up one wall across the ceiling and down the other. Torin suspected they were too heavy to manage the trick at anything but full speed, far too heavy to actually walk on the ceiling, but she still glanced up, skin creeping on the back of her neck, realized Werst was doing the same, and grinned. "We're not wandering blind any more, that's the main thing."

"And when we get where we're going?" Mike put in on her other side.

"Depends on where we end up and what happens when we get there. We're playing this one by ear, people."

"I admire your optimism, Gunny."

"You're supposed to." And maybe the additives in the biscuits were taking the edge off. Maybe they kept her—maybe they kept everyone—from wanting to continue the fight. Maybe not. Maybe they were all capable of being a lot more evolved about things than anyone suspected. The reason didn't matter. All that mattered right now was getting the hell out of the tunnels.

Next morning they assembled at first light, Durlin Vertic absently clawing at the floor as she swept a narrowed gaze over Torin and her people. Torin had a feeling that the scrape of claws against rock was going to get old really fast. "The Artek lead. We follow. You guard the rear." Then she spun around and moved up behind the three Artek with Sanati. One of the bipeds—Torin really needed to get a species name from Freenim—snarled something the slate missed but her implant picked up. She very much doubted the translation was precise, but then, it didn't need to be.

"We going to have trouble with the history between us?" she asked the other NCO.

Freenim snorted. "Some of both our people are young. What do you believe?"

She snorted in turn. "We'll have trouble."

"Good assumption." He shot her a look that could only be interpreted as long suffering and strode ahead to growl at the younger members of his species beyond the implant's pickup.

Torin barely had time to assign a march order, placing Kichar and Watura at the rear, when the Artek, wafting a scent like buttered lavender, began to move. For the Artek and the Polina it was a slow run. For the rest of them, a little faster. It was entirely possible that the durlin was trying to see what they were made of. It was also possible that this was their standard operating speed, but given the looks Freenim's people were shooting at their officer, Torin doubted it.

"Their durlin's got guts putting us at their backs," Jiyuu muttered.

She did have guts, but Freenim was at their rear and Torin right behind him leading her people, so she likely felt they could handle anything that came up.

"Gunny?"

"Werst." She fell back a few strides. Barefoot, the Krai could handle the pace. In boots, they'd have never done it.

"Any problem with us taking the high road?"

Glancing up, she measured the distance between the edge of the lights, thought about asking if he was sure Kyster could bridge it, and decided he wouldn't have asked if he hadn't been. "You drop if you feel anything that indicates a break in the cable."

"Yes, Gunnery Sergeant."

"Knock yourselves out." The lights ran about twelve centimeters under the curved roof of the tunnel three meters up. The Krai were all around a meter high. "You need a lift?"

"Got it covered. Ressk! Kyster!" He threw the names back over his shoulder. "Going up."

"Gunny?"

"It's okay, Kyster. Just hang back of my position. I don't want any misunderstandings with our new friends." In military terms, *friend* carried less significance than *ally*.

They must have discussed it in the night as first Ressk then Kyster literally ran up Werst's body and jumped for the lights from his shoulders. Then Ressk held the cable in both feet and dropped down holding Kyster. Werst climbed them both. The maneuver cost them a little distance but they quickly made it up, swinging from hand to foot.

Freenim shot her a questioning glance—wrinkles across the pale skin of his forehead standing in for eyebrows—but Krai physiognomy made questions moot. It was pretty obvious why they'd taken the high road. Even with one bad foot, Kyster had no trouble keeping up.

She figured they'd covered about fifteen kilometers at a steady trot, boots beating the distance into the stone, when all three Artek ran straight at a wall. And up the wall. And back down to the floor. Torin suspected that frustration smelled like a wet dog lightly sprinkled with cinnamon.

Hand up, she brought her people to a halt, maintaining the careful spacing between the two groups. Three slap/thuds as the Krai dropped back to the ground, and Torin noted that the three di'Taykan were showing the most effect from the run. No surprise. They'd been down here the longest on questionable rations, no matter that they'd been getting the supplement all along. And she suspected Harnett hadn't been big on PT.

"They say . . ." Sanati glanced at the blank wall as though it could have answers. ". . . the sounds go up here."

"The same sounds they have followed?" Durlin Vertic demanded, claws digging at the floor again.

Sanati waved her hands in the universal gesture for *I don't know what the fuk they're talking about*. "Perhaps."

"That isn't an answer!"

One of the Artek—Torin thought, given the deep brown-on-brown pattern on her exoskeleton, it might have been the one she mentally referred to as Cherry Bug—turned and clattered her mandibles up at the snarling officer, all four arms waving.

"This is so loud," Sanati translated. "If not the same sound, then we not feel the same sound."

"Durlave Kan! Have everyone . . ." Vertic so obviously didn't look back at Torin when her people did, she might as well have been staring. ". . . spread out along this wall. Find a way through to that noise. If it goes up, we're going up."

Freenim turned to Torin. "We need to find the way in the wall."

"Yeah, I got that."

The wall was solid.

Nothing any of the six species present could do made any impression on it. The durlin finally had to snap something out in her own language to the two males in order to get them to stop clawing at the stone. When she was done, Freenim ran up one side of them and down the other. It was amusing to watch—Torin moved Mike and the slate far enough away to allow the dressing down a semblance of privacy—but it didn't get them any farther along. The air was redolent with the smell of wet cinnamon dog.

"Never have a demo charge on you when you need one," Kichar sighed, sagging against the stone and sliding to the floor.

"There has to be a way through to another level that doesn't involve wholesale destruction," Watura moaned, hair limp, lime-green ends barely moving. "What the fuk do these assholes have against stairs?"

"Or a lift tube?" asked a voice from farther down the tunnel.

"A lift tube would help," Torin admitted.

"No, Gunny, I meant there's a lift tube." Kyster stepped back from the dark rectangle that had just opened under his hand in the opposite wall. "Here."

If it was a lift tube—and it was definitely a tube of the correct dimensions, but that was all Mike was willing to commit to without finding some sort of tech—the antigravity wasn't on.

One of the bipeds—species name, Druin—leaned out over the edge and dropped a rock. Since s/he pulled it from the bag of rocks intended to be used with the sling, Torin was just as glad to see it go. So far no one had broken the truce, but missile weapons on only one side of an argument lent an unfair advantage to the side in question. The rock fell far enough that its inevitable landing was barely audible.

"Well, down would be easy," Mike noted dryly.

The rock seemed to have fallen a lot farther than the three levels they'd climbed.

"We have risen four," Freenim said thoughtfully. "But I would guess it fell farther than that also."

"Could be levels of dumbass empty tunnels under," Werst snorted. "Like these up here."

"It's possible," Torin acknowledged. *Dumbass* described these latest tunnels—although pointless and annoying would also be pretty damned accurate. Given the number of turns and cross tunnels and blind ends, they weren't the shortest distance between two points. They just were—the turns, cross tunnels and blind ends leading nowhere. It was like negotiating a particularly futile maze.

"Could be more tunnels above these."

"Could be." She shone her cuff light up and squinted along the beam. "That looks like the upper end." Leaning a little farther, Mike holding a fistful of her vest, she managed to make out two darker rectangles against the inside of the tube between them and the top. "Only two floors up. Eight meters max."

"Might as well be twenty," Durlin Vertic snarled after she'd had a look. "Even the Artek cannot hold a vertical surface so time."

The correct translation should probably have been *for so long* rather than *so time*, but the meaning was clear.

"And there's nothing for the Krai to climb."

Even the pebbled finish was gone.

"No hand grips. What if it's not a lift, but a link tube?" Ressk offered. "And that rock hit the top of a car not the bottom of the tube. All we need to do is call a link!"

Mike waved a hand at the featureless wall. "So call one."

"There's got to be tech in here somewhere. Kyster! How'd you get the *serley* door open?"

Kyster rubbed at the back of his neck. "Was just banging the wall."

All three di'Taykan snickered.

"Banging *on* the wall!"

More banging accomplished absolutely nothing. Kicking merely proved that in a game of rock versus boot, rock won.

"There must be tech!" Sanati almost wailed. Frustration seemed to be creating a bond between her and Ressk.

"Then find it," Vertic snarled. "We cannot spend our lives here!"

Torin was starting to like the four-legged officer.

"Gunny, we have an idea." Darlys moved closer, Jiyuu and Watura on her heels. "What about a low-tech way?"

"I am listening."

"Two people make a base here, standing facing each other at the edge. Watura stands on their shoulders, then Jiyuu stands on his, then I stand on Jiyuu's. One of the Krai climbs us, gets the door open, and secures the rope."

"Volunteering to commit suicide does not impress me, Darlys."

"We're serious, Gunny." She looked more than serious, she looked as if she were seconds away from begging for the chance to do something stupidly dangerous. "We can do it."

"We'll brace ourselves against the side of the wall," Jiyuu put in. The break he'd taken from sucking up seemed to be over. "We're the only ones who can do this."

"Watura?"

He shrugged.

"You have something to say about this?" Torin asked.

Watura glanced over at Jiyuu and shrugged again. "Not really, Gunny."

"It was Darlys' idea, but I came up with the two people bracing the whole thing at the bottom." His eyes a pale pink, Jiyuu looked remarkably pleased with himself.

Torin shook her head. "There's got to be another way."

There was no other way.

"They will not die themselves?" Vertic wondered.

"It's very dangerous," Torin agreed, assuming the durlin had actually meant *kill themselves,* "but it was their idea and physically they're certainly capable of doing it."

"I would not order it."

Good for her. "They've volunteered."

There was one small hitch.

"Are you out of your fukking mind?" Werst demanded. "I'm not climbing your unsupported bony asses to get anywhere."

"It will please the gunny," Darlys told him, eyes dark.

"No offense, Gunny . . ." Werst looked past the di'Taykan. ". . . but I don't give a flying fuk."

"I'll do it. Besides," Ressk added as attention turned to him, "if there's tech up there, and there will be, I've got the best chance to get the door open."

Werst shook his head. "No."

"Not your call," Ressk reminded him.

"It's a fukking stupid idea."

"Got a better one? That doesn't involve wandering around these fukking tunnels until we starve to death?"

"Hey, there's a lot of meat on . . ."

"Werst. And you," Torin added nodding toward Darlys as Werst fell silent, "do not speak for me. Ever. I don't like this idea, but Ressk's right. No one's come up with a better one, no one's found anything else in the walls of these tunnels, and no one wants to sit here with our thumbs up our collective butts until we starve to death. It's Ressk's choice. He chooses to make the climb, we have a go."

"I choose to make the climb."

"I'll let the durlin know."

Durlin Vertic stared at her for a long moment, and Torin, unable to read her expression, would have given half her pension to know what she was thinking. "It is a crazy plan," she said at last.

"Yes, sir."

"Do you understand it will work?" Again with the claws against the rock. The sound was moving from annoying to infuriating. Eventually it would become background, and that couldn't happen soon enough as far as Torin was concerned.

"Do I believe it will work? The Marines involved believe it'll work. I believe in them."

The durlin's ears rotated slightly forward. "There is no better plan."

"No, sir, there isn't."

Widening her stance, she leaned her upper body out over the shaft, twisted, and indicated that Torin should shine her cuff light up toward the door. Twisted again, pointed Torin's arm down toward the bottom. When she straightened, she didn't look happy.

"My people . . ." A gesture toward the golden fur on her flank made it specific rather than general. ". . . do not climb well."

"My people . . ." A matching gesture toward the Krai. ". . . make a kickass net."

"And my people should trust your people in such a position?"

Such a position—suspended in a net over a lethal drop. Torin wouldn't put Kichar alone on the rope that was for damned sure, but the rest had been in long enough that the personal had worn off the war. "Yes, sir."

Vertic took another long look at Torin, another look out over the shaft, and finally said, "It is a crazy, dangerous plan. Perhaps the Artek secretions can help. Do it."

"Yes, sir."

"We didn't need her permission," Torin heard Darlys mutter as she climbed carefully up onto Watura's shoulders. "Not once Gunnery Sergeant Kerr said yes."

Watura's response was too quiet for Torin to hear. She sucked air through her teeth as the di'Taykan shifted his bare foot on her shoulder.

"Remember what I said about inappropriate touching," she growled as Darlys began her climb up Jiyuu. As a general rule there was no such thing as inappropriate touching where it concerned di'Taykan on di'Taykan, but climbing the side of a vertical shaft, held to the wall with the smeared secretions from a sentient insect's footpads was not the time to indulge.

Because they were of a height, she made up the base of the tower with Mashona. Mike, given a male's heavier build, would have made more sense, but he and Sanati were still working on finding tech. Durlin Vertic was all in favor of getting the antigravity turned on before she ended up in a net, hauled up eight meters like a load of laundry. Torin couldn't say she blamed her—and made a mental note that the Primacy collectively knew what an antigravity lift was and clearly used them at times other than when they were attempting to take over a Confederation station. It might be information Military Intelligence could use even given that Military Intelligence was historically held to be an oxymoron.

"I'm in place, Gunnery Sergeant!"

"How can you gain weight on kibble and biscuits and water?" Jiyuu grunted from the middle position.

"Like you've got reason to complain," Watura sniped.

"Enough, people!" The di'Taykan may have been light as a species, but three of them, even with the weight divided between her and Mashona and the wall had her locking her knees and praying to any gods that might be listening in. Mashona's expression suggested she was doing the same. "Ressk! Move!"

He had his hand on her elbow when Mike yelled, "Got it!"

"Got it working?"

"Found the panel and got it open."

Torin snorted. "Go, Ressk! Long odds on them ever getting it working." Breathing shallowly through her nose, she hoped the secretions would be enough to keep the di'Taykan in contact with the wall as Ressk used them like a living ladder. Her right knee felt ready to buckle.

"I'm up. There's a ledge. It's no wider than Werst's dick, but it'll hold me. Door mech seems . . ."

The last word got lost. Darlys shrieked a warning. Torin grabbed Watura's legs. Jiyuu dropped past, arms and legs windmilling, mouth open, screaming. Torin felt something loop around her waist and haul her back as Watura's weight threatened to take them both over the edge.

Jiyuu's screaming stopped abruptly, cut off by a wet crack. Followed a moment later by a muffled thud. He'd clearly hit the side before he hit bottom.

Watura twisted as he fell, got his hands out, and managed to prevent his spine from impacting with the lip of the shaft. Mashona grabbed a handful of his combats and all three of them—four of them, Torin corrected as she identified the dark brown arm folded around her waist as belonging to one of the Artek, who were obviously a hell of a lot stronger than they looked—collapsed in a heap.

"Gunny!"

Surrounded by the scent of cherries, Torin crawled forward. "Darlys?" She was hanging from the lip Ressk balanced on. Torin fought the urge to tell Ressk to hurry, well aware he was moving as fast as he could. Twisting, she looked into Cherry Bug's face. "If I have to . . ." The motion for Darlys falling and Torin throwing herself forward wasn't very complicated. ". . . can you . . ." *Keep me from going over* was a little more complex but she managed it.

Cherry Bug clacked her mandibles together, and a second Artek rushed forward to grab Torin's other ankle.

"All right, then."

Mashona yelled, "Hang on, Darlys!"

Darlys yelled, "Fuk you!" Pale feet scrabbled for something more than mere contact with the wall.

And Ressk yelled, "Got the door!"

"In a vid, we'd have turned the lift on at the last minute." Mike pounded the side of his fist against the wall. "Jiyuu wouldn't have died."

"If life was a vid," Torin muttered, "it'd make more fukking sense." The only bit of bright news she'd had lately was that Watura and Darlys both agreed that Jiyuu *was* dead, that the only scents coming up from the bottom of the shaft were shit and blood. No pheromones. And only death stopped that.

The odds were stacked high against anyone surviving that kind of a fall. Torin moved back to the edge of the shaft and shone her cuff light down into the depths. No surprise when it still wasn't up to the job.

"You want to go down there and make sure." Durlin Vertic moved to stand beside her.

"Yes, sir."

"Even though your own people tell you they are certain he is dead."

"Yes, sir."

"I order you not to."

Torin turned then and looked at the durlin, who returned Torin's regard with a level stare of her own.

"I order you not to—I take the responsibility for this decision."

Torin drew in a long breath and let it out slowly. "Yes, sir." Then she turned again and leaned out into the shaft. "What the hell's taking that net so long, Corporal?"

"Almost done, Gunny!"

Werst and then Kyster had gone effortlessly hand over hand over foot up the dangling rope as soon as Ressk and Darlys had found a way to tie it off, and Werst had bit off a piece of his arm and spat it down toward Jiyuu's body. The three Artek just needed a little of their weight held and had scrabbled up the wall, all four arms working the rope.

The Humans, Druin, and remaining di'Taykan could have gone up essentially the same way, but the Polina needed the net and assistance getting into it. As long as there was going to be a net, better safe than dead.

Like Jiyuu.

One of Harnett's goons and an annoying suck-up.

He was young. Not that youth excused what he'd done.

Watura sat braced against the tunnel wall about four meters from the entrance to the shaft, his knees drawn up and his hair a lime-green curtain over his face.

"It's weird," Kichar murmured, arms wrapped around her torso. "You always think of the di'Taykan and sex, not actual feelings. I mean, not that I don't think they have feelings, it's just they have so much sex that something like a crush is just kind of a surprise."

"Guys his age don't have crushes," Mashona told her shortly.

"Yeah, but Jiyuu didn't . . ."

"Quit while you're ahead," Torin advised as she passed. "And don't apologize to me," she added when Kichar started to stammer.

Watura's hair gave a single flip as Torin dropped to one knee beside him. "She's right," he said. "Jiyuu didn't like me more than he liked any other of us. I was just there for him. He liked that."

"Doesn't change what you're feeling." She laid two fingers against the back of his hand. Touch meant more to the di'Taykan than words.

His hair parted. His eyes were so light that, although he was staring at her fingers, she doubted he could see them. "You didn't like him."

"Doesn't matter."

"You don't like me."

"Doesn't matter."

"We were Harnett's."

"Now you're mine." She maintained the contact until Werst called out and the net dropped.

With one of the two lower ranking Druin up, the heavier of the two male Polina, Samtan Tern Helic'tin volunteered to go up first. "If it can hold me, it can hold the durlin."

"If it can hold you, it can hold me," Bertecnic, the other male, muttered. Since Freenim ignored him, so did Torin. It was an understandable observation.

Helic'tin worked all four legs through the bottom of the net, smoothed down the fur that had been ruffled up in the wrong direction then, holding the net up like a skirt, he walked to the edge, took a deep breath, snarled wordlessly, and nodded.

"He's ready!"

The rope tightened as they hauled in the slack.

"On three," Werst yelled. "One, two . . ."

Stepping off the edge knowing four enemies, one skinny biped, and three giant bugs were all that kept gravity from winning, knowing that there was already a body broken and bleeding at the bottom of the shaft, knowing all that and stepping off anyway was one of the bravest things Torin had seen for a while.

He dropped almost his body length down, then began inching up toward the open door.

"You need to lose a little weight!" Ressk yelled.

"Less talk and more pulling!" Helic'tin snarled.

"Samtan Tern Helic'tin." Torin murmured to Freenim. "Samtan? Lowest rank?" The translation program ignored it, so it could be a rank or a species designation. When the other NCO nodded, she opened her mouth to fill him in on their rank structure and closed it again.

Freenim smiled. "How much to tell the enemy. When we get out of here, the war will not be over."

"Our private equals your samtan." She snorted. "If you can win the war with that information, you deserve to."

There was cursing and claws scrabbling against stone with enough force to fling chips down the shaft when Helic'tin reached the end of his journey but no screaming, so they counted it a win. Bertecnic went up a little easier. Durlin Vertic easier still.

"We've worked the bugs out of the system!" Ressk yelled.

The slate translated bugs as Artek.

The Druin who'd flung the rock earlier swung first, but Kichar didn't hesitate to try to pound the hairless ivory head into the floor. Torin grabbed at a dark gray uniform and hauled the Druin up as Freenim grabbed Kichar and dragged her to her feet.

"Trade?" she suggested.

He grinned and tossed the young Marine toward her, catching his own with the other hand.

Kichar sagged in Torin's grip, blood dripping from her nose, eyes still wild. "He started it, Gunnery Sergeant!"

"And you know why, Private! *You* heard both halves of that translation. Defensive moves would have been enough."

"You always said that the best defense was a strong offense!"

"So you were doing what I would have?"

"Yes, Gunnery Sergeant!"

And the truly frightening thing was that Kichar was probably right. "Then next time, use your head instead of mine."

"Yes, Gunnery Sergeant." She wiped her sleeve across her lower face and frowned at the red blaze on the fabric. "I'm sorry, Gunny."

"If you've got that much energy to spare, get up there and take your turn on the rope."

"I don't . . ." She was going to say she didn't need the net. Torin could read it in the stubborn set of her shoulders, but she reconsidered at the last minute. "Yes, Gunnery Sergeant."

As Mike and Mashona helped her into the net, Torin moved over to Freenim.

"Samtan Everim was not injured, Gunnery Sergeant."

"I'm glad to hear that, Durlave Kan."

"But he knows he will be if he tries something so stupid again." Freenim gave the handful of uniform he still held a little shake. "Doesn't he?"

"Yes, Durlave Kan." Given their different physiognomies, Everim looked no more repentant than Kichar.

Mike went up next with the slate, then Everim, then Freenim . . .

"Your officer is already up there," Torin pointed out when he suggested he should be the last up.

. . . then Mashona.

One hand holding the net, Watura touched the pale blue quills in his vest pocket with the other. "I don't want to leave him, Gunny."

He wasn't talking about the nameless di'Taykan.

Torin reached out and touched the inside of his wrist this time, a more personal touch than the back of the hand. It drew Watura's gaze off the bottom of the shaft and he turned his head to stare into her face, his eyes so dark barely any of the lime green showed. "I give you my word," she said quietly, "that we will come back for him. For him and for everyone down here. We will not leave anyone behind."

"Your word, Gunny." It wasn't a question, so she let it stand. His hair flicked forward. "Have you started to believe what Darlys says about you, then?"

She grinned, more a Krai expression than anything, but left her fingers pressed against his skin. "I believe what the Marine Corps says about me."

"Exiting Susumi space in three, two, one . . ." The sound of the engines changed as the Susumi drive went off-line and Craig's hands flew across the board.

"If we are being right behind the Others' fleet, I are wanting some good high resolution shots."

"Not now," he grunted, shrugging Presit's tiny hand off his arm. He'd expected more buffeting given the dumbass stunt they were pulling, but although *Promise* both rocked and rolled, she'd come through a lot rougher rides. Not to say that he was actually in control at the moment, but they were still in one piece so he was counting it as a win.

Then the proximity sensor went off.

"Is it being the Others' battleship!"

"Worse. It's a fukking asteroid field!"

"Why are that being worse?"

"There were only three ships, and there's one fuk of a lot more . . . son of a bitch!" He still wasn't exactly steering, but the upper jets pushed them down out of the way of a tumbling rock that would have shattered them had it connected. Then the starboard jets. Then the aft port jets. Then he was finally in an area clear enough to control the tumbling.

"Out of Susumi space into an asteroid belt," Presit snorted, adjusting her glasses as the star fields stopped spinning. "That are being too cliché for vids." She was trying to look blasé about the experience, but the drift of shed fur heading for the scrubbers gave her away. "So, where are the Others being?"

"I'm not reading them."

"Are your sensors being broken?"

"No, they're working fine." Ignoring the lines of sweat dribbling down his sides, he waved at the screen. "There's nothing out there."

"They are hiding in the asteroids."

"No, they aren't."

"But we are following them. We are having gone where they are having gone!"

"Apparently not."

"Then you are doing it wrong!"

"Fuk you, too."

Her lips pulled back off her teeth, and her hair puffed. "I are having seen you! You are playing with the screens, with your fingers, when you are making equations."

"So you're saying I sent us careening into the back of Bourke on purpose."

"The back of Bourke?" She frowned. "I are not knowing where that is!"

He looked out at the totally unfamiliar stars and sighed. "That makes two of us, mate. That makes two of us."

ELEVEN

//**FIRIV'VRAK IS SURE THIS IS THE UPPERMOST** level, Durlin."

"Firiv'vrak is sure," the durlin repeated glancing down at the Artek by Sanati's side. "And the other two?"

"Not convinced, Durlin."

The Artek clicked something that sounded distinctly rude, the odds rising when Sanati didn't bother translating. It seemed Firiv'vrak was the actual name of Cherry Bug. Or as close as species with soft mouth parts could manage.

"Until at least two of the Artek agree, or we find the exit, we keep looking for a way up."

"Yes, Durlin."

As Torin moved past, she glanced down at the Artek and found herself staring at her reflection multiplied in the cluster of six black eyes. Both antennae whipped around, sweeping forward over the eyes, down past the mandibles, and back to lie with the tufted tips about four centimeters above the thorax. It looked so much like an eye roll that Torin wondered just how much the Artek understood of the common tongue. Not being able to speak it only meant their mouth parts weren't capable of the shapes; it said nothing about comprehension.

"You know what I miss," Ressk sighed around a mouthful of biscuit. "I miss my gran's *gringern*. She'd get the outside all nice and crispy, but the inside stayed runny and warm. Now that's *chrick*. What about you, Sarge? What do you miss?"

Curious, Torin paused long enough to hear Mike's answer.

"Sarge!"

He glanced up from the slate. "What do I what?"

"What food do you miss?"

"Pizza. Thin crust pie, a minimum meter diameter, sliced pie fashion so it's slightly floppy triangles with about a four-centimeter base, and can be folded over properly. Hot sausage, pepperoni, salami, beef, smooth sauce, with just a hint of sweetness to match up with the spice from the sausage, and a thick gooey cover of mixed cheese." He sighed and stared into the middle distance. "With a big glass of milk on the side."

"You've been thinking about it, Sarge?"

He snorted. "We've been eating fukking biscuits for days. Damned right I've been thinking about it. I'd trade my mama for a slice of pizza right about now."

"Trade mine, too," Ressk acknowledged. The Krai had no trouble digesting the favorite foods of the species they served with. Hardly surprising, Torin admitted, since they could also digest both species. "Got anything else up yet?"

"Think so. Still code to untangle."

"Want me to take a crack at it?"

"Not yet." He dropped his attention back to the screen.

Ressk caught Torin's gaze as she passed and definitely rolled his eyes. Hip-deep in the recovery, Mike didn't want to share. Since he was senior to Ressk by a considerable margin, it was his call.

"How are the rest of your people dealing with the death?" Freenim asked as she drew even with him.

Torin nodded toward Darlys walking ahead as gracelessly as it was possible for a di'Taykan to walk. "I'm about to find out. Yours?"

"There are always those happy to deal with one less enemy."

"Can't say as I blame them," Torin admitted; she lengthened her stride and fell into step beside Darlys and Mashona, a gesture sending the corporal forward to walk with Watura and Kyster.

"Hey, kid, did I ever tell you about the time that the gunny took on three Silsviss in a bar fight?"

Kyster looked up at the taller Marine like she'd just passed over a bowl of Ressk's gran's *gringern,* and that was more than enough encouragement for Mashona to start talking.

She'd almost finished the story, only slightly exaggerated and remarkably accurate considering she'd been in a bar fight of her own in a different part of the same establishment while Torin had been taking on the three Silsviss in question, by the time Darlys finally spoke.

"Gunnery Sergeant Kerr?"

"Darlys."

"It was my fault." Her hair lay flat against her head, and her eyes were so light that Torin wondered how she could see. "My fault that Jiyuu died."

As much as Torin didn't like Darlys, both for what she'd done under Harnett and for the asinine way she'd reacted to the whole progenitor nonsense, she couldn't let that stand. "You didn't push him."

An assumption, but a reasonable one—she wouldn't have done anything to have pissed Torin off to that extent. It would've been much more likely had Watura or Jiyuu pushed her.

"I was the first to fall." Her hair rippled once, front to back "He lost his balance because I lost mine."

"You purposely lost your balance?"

"No." Another ripple. "When Werst stepped off onto the ledge, I shifted too far out of position."

"Intending that Private Jiyuu fall?"

"No!" The ends of her hair flipped up. "But then I was falling, and I pushed off on Jiyuu's shoulders to save myself!"

"Survival is a species imperative, Private. I allowed you to make the climb. Was it my fault that Jiyuu fell?"

"You couldn't have known . . ."

"Neither could you. It wasn't your fault. It was a tragic accident. Nothing more."

"Then you forgive me?" Her eyes had darkened slightly.

"There's nothing for me to forgive, Private. At least not in this particular instance." She might not have killed Jiyuu, but Torin wasn't letting her off for earlier deaths.

They walked half a dozen steps in silence.

"We've left him behind. What will we tell his *thytrin*, Gunnery Sergeant?" Despair made the question less than rhetorical.

"We tell his *thytrin* that we got help and went back for him because that's exactly what we're going to do." She didn't add that she'd given her word to Watura.

"Help?" Darlys waved her hand at yet another length of gray, nondescript tunnels, her hair in constant movement now. "We're never going to get out of here. We're going to die, one by one in stupid accidents like Jiyuu or murdered in our sleep by them!"

Fortunately, Mike and the slate were far enough away and Mashona was still making enough noise that the two closest Druin weren't privy to a translation. Just as well, Torin allowed, no matter how well things seemed to be going, there was no point in giving anyone ideas.

"We should just go back." Her voice dropped to a near murmur, as much talking to herself as to Torin. "Go back where it's safe."

"We're not going back." Although even thinking about it made her long for the area around the pipes and the comfort of being surrounded by Marines. She pinched the flesh between her thumb and forefinger, the pain helping her shake off the longing. "There's a way in here, Private, we're all evidence of that, so I'll tell you a secret that all NCOs learn—if there's a way in, there's a way out."

"Gunnery Sergeant Kerr!" Kichar's voice cut through the ambient noise, so excited, she sounded about twelve. "We've found a door!"

Darlys' light receptors opened the rest of the way so quickly she blinked away tears and her expression suggested that her belief in Torin's godlike powers had been firmly cemented into place.

Torin sighed. "It's all in the timing, Private." She twisted in place. "Technical Sergeant Gucciard! Let the durlin know we've found a door!"

Standing beside what looked like a standard, internal compression hatch set flush with the wall of the tunnel, Kichar looked as though she'd invented the concept of egress. "There's no keypad, Gunny! I think it's just mechanical."

"Good job, Private." A nod to Werst who had, after all, been on point with Kichar. "Corporal."

Werst snorted. "Wasn't exactly hidden, Gunny."

One after another, the Artek pressed their torsos against the hatch, antenna tips brushing over the surface.

"They agree that whatever it is on the other side, it's not vacuum," Sanati said after Firiv'vrak clattered at her for a few moments.

"They can tell that through a compression hatch?" Torin was impressed.

Sanati shrugged. "I'm sure your people have useful skills."

One of her people had died getting them up to this level, up to this door. Torin felt her hands curl into fists, but before she could step forward, she felt Mike's fingers close around her wrist. "Let it go, Gunny." His voice a deep rumble by her ear. "I don't think she meant it like that."

He shouldn't have had to tell her. When she nodded, he released her. It was just the damned sameness of the tunnels and the despondency lurking around every corner, the urge to just say the hell with it and give up. She needed a fight to clear her head. She needed to find whoever was keeping them imprisoned and complacent and kick their collective asses up around what served them for ears.

Breathing a little heavily through her nose, she turned her attention back to the hatch. If the Artek believed that there was no chance of them being sucked out into space, then the next logical course was to get the damned thing open.

The handle was round, old-fashioned looking, about half a meter outside edge to outside edge, and jammed tight. Torin couldn't budge it.

"We're going to need a lever of some kind." Mike wrapped a big hand around the arc of metal and gave it an experimental tug.

"Step aside, Sergeant. Gunnery Sergeant." The durlin sounded slightly amused. "Samtan Helic'tin. Samtan Bertecnic."

The pair of Polina stepped forward as the human NCOs stepped away. Bracing all four feet—*All eight feet,* Torin corrected silently—they each took hold of one side of the circle and on the count of three—*"Onin, tyn, jhord!"*—forced it to turn. Even under masking fabric, muscles knotted impressively in arms, shoulders, and backs. Metal screamed as rust released, both Polina snarling in counterpoint.

"They're very strong," Torin observed quietly.

"They are," Freenim admitted.

Torin glanced down. She'd actually been making the observation to Mike, hadn't heard the durlave move up beside her, and that was just a little more trusting than she was willing to be.

"It is their best feature," he added wearily and she hid a smile at the tone. "The young males join up to prove themselves so they can get a . . ."

The translation program sputtered through *herd/pack/family group,* then hurried to catch up.

". . . back home. They never re-up. Most of them do not survive to finish their first contract. The females, though . . ." He shook his head. "They are used to always making the final word. Have to be officers. Fortunately, they are good at it."

With the latch disengaged, the Polina turned their attention to shoving the door open, claws scoring the tunnel floor.

The Polina social structure sounded a lot like the Silsviss. Not the first time she'd noticed that evolution had a limited number of tricks up its sleeve.

"Should you be telling me this?" Torin wondered, her voice pitched to the same quiet, not-intended-to-be-overheard tone.

"You do not know us. We do not know you. Makes me wonder why we fight."

"*We're* not," she pointed out.

"Because no one has told us to."

She acknowledged the point. "I'll do what I have to in order to get my people out alive. If I have to ally with the enemy to do it, I'm good with that."

"And if it comes down to it, at the end, to yours or mine?"

Torin turned to look at him. "Don't ask questions you know the answer to, Durlave. It's annoying."

He grinned then. Omnivore teeth. But then, so were hers.

There was a soft pop as the seal finally broke, a finger-width of space open at the edge of the hatch by the time Durlin Vertic gave the order to stop.

"Smells stale," Helic'tin growled, broad nostrils flared. "And burned." He slapped his uniform cuff with his left hand. "Still dead."

"Gunnery Sergeant."

"Durlin!" Some requests were so obvious they didn't actually require words. "Technical Sergeant."

"On it, Gunny."

The male Polina moved reluctantly out of the way as Mike moved
his uniform sensors closer to the gap. According to his internal diag-
nostics, the shock back in the crevice had cleared up whatever problems they'd been having. "Station norm. Atmosphere's identical, at
least right inside the hatch." He leaned in. "I can smell the stale but
not the burned."

"Not much nose, Sergeant," Helic'tin snorted.

Vertic reared slightly, claws out. "Open it!"

Mike dove out of the way as the two males surged forward and
threw their combined strength against the door. Torin thought she
heard a Druin snicker and wasn't entirely certain that Vertic, still an-
noyed about the tech imbalance hadn't given the order in such a way
as to purposely embarrass the technical sergeant.

With everyone standing well clear, the Artek went through the
hatch first. Considering how hard they were to kill—and Torin could
personally vouch for that—they were the logical choice. She didn't
like taking Sanati's word for it that a crackle of mandibles and the
smell of rotting vegetation meant *"All clear!"*—but since she suspected the durlin liked having to use a subjective translator a lot less,
she let it ride.

It seemed they'd found a deserted control room; deserted for some
time given the layer of dust. A control panel made up of three individual stations ran along the full width of the opposite wall, the
matte-green surfaces presumably screens. A two-station central unit
sat in the middle of the room. The wall to the right held three large
lockers and the wall to the left was curiously blank. After the constant
gray of the tunnels, the various shades of reddish brown—from the
sandstone pale on the walls and floor to the dried-blood color of the
five stools to the actual panels made up of every shade in between—
almost hurt the eye.

Torin ran a finger through the dust on the edge of the nearest
panel and exposed a bit of worn plastic that had clearly been the place

where the operator had rested a body part while working. Memory provided the image of a similar spot on *Promise*'s panel where Craig rested his heels and she had to fight to keep her hand from dipping under her vest to close around the salvage tag.

"Gunny?"

Given the tilt to Mike's brows, she didn't want to guess what her expression must look like. "Any idea what this was used for?"

"Not unless we get it up and running."

"Can you?"

The brows changed tilt. "Can I interface a barely functional slate with unknown alien tech?"

"Not exactly. We still need the slate for translations. Leave it on the center panel."

"Go in cold?" He pulled in a deep breath through his nose, and let it out slowly. Torin had the distinct impression that by the time he'd finished he'd forgotten she was standing there. "Function requires form—control panels have certain necessary similarities. We start there. Ressk! Sanati!"

Torin left them to it, crossing over to where Durlin Vertic stood by the lockers.

Vertic tossed her head in the general direction of the main panel, the stiff crest of hair fanning out with the motion and then settling slowly back against her neck. "They work on making it functional, Gunnery Sergeant?"

"Yes, Durlin."

"More important than opening these." A more truncated gesture toward the lockers.

Since it didn't seem to be a question, Torin didn't answer.

"Helic'tin. Bertecnic. Open them."

Given the opportunity to risk some cash, she wouldn't have bet against the durlin giving that order. Or against the way the two male Polina simply ripped the doors off the lockers and tossed them aside. She appreciated the efficiency.

The first two lockers held empty boxes. The third held a half-empty box of environmental filters.

Torin reached down and slipped her forefinger under an adjustable plastic band, lifting the top filter out of the box. "Full-face coverage," she said peering through the clear film. "And damned near . . ." A quick glance toward the Artek. ". . . one size fits all."

"There was more than one species here," Vertic agreed. "Or no need for such adjustable gear. They used the other filters when they left. And did they abandon this control room only, or the whole facility?"

The entire prison could have been automated. Start with an air exchange similar to that on the stations, then provide food and other provisions based on a sensor-generated body count. Simple. Toss in a few random items now and then to keep your prisoners guessing. Integrating new prisoners merely meant gassing the areas around the pipes in order to bring them in to the small caves unobserved. Where there was one lift, there could easily be a dozen undiscovered, and the whole program could be based on an if/then statement. If new prisoners arrive, then do this.

Torin turned to glance at Kyster. He hadn't been near the pipes, couldn't therefore have been gassed, and that made a simple solution much more complex.

Gassing every square centimeter of tunnel and cave? That would take time. Still, there was nothing to say that the lights wouldn't stay off as long as the system needed them to, and after the new prisoners were in place the tunnels could be flushed. When the lights were turned back on, time would essentially be reset.

All right. Automated. And every now and then they—whoever the hell they were—dropped into this single control room to check on the system. Not often, given the dust. Unless there were other control rooms and the system wasn't manual at all.

Actually, all that was moot. How the prison was run became relevant only if the information helped them haul ass out of it. If there were other control rooms, then that would be relevant since it meant they were probably being tracked. If they were being tracked, they'd have been recaptured by now. Therefore, no other control rooms.

And they'd abandoned this one.

Who were they?

"Where did they go; that is the question." Freenim pulled another filter from the box.

One of the questions, Torin silently agreed.

"I can answer that, Durlave." Having caught the attention of everyone in the room, Mike reached out and hit a pressure switch.

Turned out, the wall over the control panels was a window. As the blast shield slid down out of sight, all six species crowded forward and stared across a forebidding landscape at what looked to be a landing site for VTAs although the amount of smoke and particulates in the air made it difficult to be completely certain.

"I'm guessing that's the way out," Ressk murmured. "About ten kilometers, Gunny?"

"About," Torin agreed, shifting to allow Kyster in between her and the panel. The Krai were not going to be able to cover the distance without boots. Although there looked to be solid paths among the lava fields, the rock would be too hot for bare feet.

"Definitely a landing site," Freenim allowed as a gust of wind temporarily cleared the air but stirred up half a dozen small firestorms and one large enough to collapse what had looked like a secure rock bridge.

"I don't see a ship." Sniper trained, Mashona had the best eyes in the group.

Werst snorted. "In this weather? Probably parked inside."

Torin lifted the filter she still held. Given the pyrotechnics on the other side of the window, it seemed a ridiculously fragile protection. Given that they hadn't yet found the door . . .

A panel slid down on the left wall, disappearing into the floor, exposing the hatch and the keypad beside it. A light bar running across the top blinked orange and . . . well, Torin saw a shade that looked to be lavender, but the way it shimmered she suspected it was lavender only to Human eyes.

"Technical Sergeant?"

He shrugged. "It was the next switch."

"All right. We need to get this thing open, so concentrate on the keypad. We know what it . . ."

Through the soles of her boots, Torin could feel the same faint vibration they'd felt back on the lower levels.

The Artek went crazy. With all three emitting, the scent of lemon furniture polish was unpleasantly strong. By the time the quake finished, they were tucked into the angle between wall and floor, torsos folded down, both sets of arms holding them into what looked like a painfully compact position.

"If they react that way to little quakes," Torin murmured to Freenim as Sanati tried to talk them into unfolding. "How would they react to a big one?"

"They believe we will have a chance to find out. Soon."

"Soon? The quake damage I saw down below was fairly recent. It should take time for pressure to build up again to something big."

"On a stable landmass, perhaps." He nodded toward the window. "On that?"

"Good point."

"The Artek feel that in a large enough quake, this structure could collapse."

It seemed the Artek enjoyed stating the obvious. "In a large enough quake, any structure could collapse."

"According to Sanati, they have been expecting a large enough quake since we found a section of collapsed tunnel."

Another section of collapsed tunnel. "You think they're overreacting?"

The other NCO shrugged. "Maybe a little." Outside the window another chunk of the landscape fell into a lava pool, sending up sprays of molten rock. "Maybe not."

"Technical Sergeant!"

"Gunny?" He didn't bother looking up from the keypad.

"ETA on the door?"

"No."

"All right, then."

"Gunny, I've found the communications board!" Perched on the edge of a stool, Ressk had all four extremities working the panel.

"Can we get a message out?"

His nose ridges opened and closed. "I, uh, can't actually get it to do anything. I just know where it is."

Torin just barely resisted the urge to slap him on the back of the head. "Try for a little more substance next report, Corporal."

"If the slate was up and running . . ."

"A Marine should be able to control a situation without tech."

He shot her a look over one shoulder and sighed. "It's a tech situation, Gunny."

"We could force the door."

Torin turned toward the durlin, but Freenim was there before her.

"It's an air lock, sir. We will need to close it after."

A drifting cloud of ash hit the window with a noise like tiny claws scrabbling against glass, reducing visibility.

Kichar and Everim were glaring at each other again.

Helic'tin and Bertecnic had their claws out, and Kyster and Werst were showing teeth. A biological response from both species, but it was effect not cause that concerned Torin. And she didn't *care* who'd started it.

It was probably quiet and peaceful back down at the pipes.

"All right, that's enough!" Torin's voice in Federate and in whatever language was spilling out of the slate filled the room, leaving no space for fidgeting or attitude. "We're going nowhere until that door is open, so find a spot, put your ass in it, and turn off your mouth. When the durlin has something she wants you to do, she'll let you know!"

Somewhere around the time the durlin had taken responsibility for not going down to retrieve Jiyuu from the bottom of the shaft, Torin had stopped pretending to take orders from her.

Over by the door, Firiv'vrak clattered something and wafted a bit more lemon polish around the room.

"You can't stop the building from collapsing; it's not your problem," Torin snapped. "Sit!"

All three Artek folded their legs and settled to the floor.

"Durlave Kir Sanati, the control panel."

"Yes, Gunnery Sergeant."

A moment later the only people standing besides Torin, Freenim, and Dulin Vertic were working on tech.

Freenim's expression was admirably blank as Torin crossed the room to stand next to him and the durlin—nothing for him to react to in a senior NCO acting as senior. Vertic looked slightly startled, but she recovered quickly and hid it well.

"Gunnery Sergeant, Durlave Kan; perhaps we should use this time to inventory our supplies. We can shorten the rations, but if we do not find water soon . . ."

"If we assume this control room is some kind of central maintenance station," Torin began.

"Then how were the workers supplied?" Freenim finished.

"Werst!"

"Gunnery Sergeant?" Her tone pulled him up onto his feet, but he made it look like it was his idea.

"Head back out into the tunnel. Take Kichar and Kyster with you; you're looking for living quarters."

"Merinim!"

"Durlave Kan?" The Druin's reaction was a mirror image of Werst's. The Primacy's equivalent of a corporal, then. Torin made a mental note.

"You and Everim go with. Take one Artek, they may can sense . . ." He waved a pale, long fingered hand. ". . . whatever the *xercan* it is they sense."

"*Xercan?*" Torin asked quietly as the six jostled for position leaving the room.

"Leftover profanity from religiously intolerant time," Freenim explained, cracking his knuckles.

"Yeah," Torin sighed, "we've got those, too."

"Corporal?" Kichar moved as close to Werst as she could get without actual physical contact. "Do we watch them?"

"Watch who?"

"Them!"

Kyster turned with the other two Marines. The Druin were checking out the opposite wall of the tunnel much the same way they were—using fingertips and eyes in place of scanners. He had no idea what the big bug was doing. His stomach growled.

"They're doing their job," Werst snorted returning his attention to the wall. "Nothing to watch."

"But they're the enemy!"

"Not right now."

"That's not something you can just turn off."

The older Krai snorted. "Corps tells me to turn it off, I turn it off. Gunny talks for the Corps down here, and she says you turn it off."

"But how can she expect us to do that? How can she do that?" Kichar thumped the wall with the side of her fist. "She's been fighting them longer than any of us."

"She'd be most tired of it, then, wouldn't she?" Kyster flared his nose ridges as they turned toward him but stood his ground. He couldn't tell what the corporal was thinking, but if he was reading the Human signs right, Kichar was going to argue. Yeah, big surprise.

And then the big bug pushed between them to rub its antenna against the wall, claws tapping lightly along the same path.

Startled, Kyster stepped back. His good foot came down on something soft. Before he could recover his balance, a hand closed over his shoulder and shoved him aside. He stumbled, rolled off his bad foot, and cracked his head against the wall.

The big bug was right there, pushed up against him. He grabbed at it, felt air flow over his fingers, and realized it had side gills. Too weird. It smelled like roast *arlin*. Kyster's stomach growled again. Did it taste as good as it smelled?

"Stand down, Private!"

His mouth snapped closed before he realized the corporal wasn't talking to him. Kichar and that Everim were toe to toe. Again.

When Werst reached out to haul her back, the other Druin—Merinim—stopped him. To Kyster's surprise, Werst glanced over at Merinim but didn't even expose his teeth. He shook free of her grip, but that was . . .

Kichar was down!

Kyster charged forward and rocked to a stop, a segmented foreleg hooked diagonally across his chest.

"No biting, Private!"

Teeth closed on air, lips barely grazing the bug's shell, neck kinked from jerking his head up at Werst's command.

Kichar knew a number of dirty moves from ground level. Everim dropped. From where Kyster stood, it seemed the Human was heavier but the Druin more flexible. Bigger didn't always mean squat—people who came up against the Krai learned that all the time—but Kichar was using her size to keep the other guy pinned. As she drove the hard wedge of her fingers into the muscles of his thigh, the point of his elbow caught her in the nose. The spray of blood was amazingly red among all the gray.

"All right, that's enough." Werst had a fistful of Kichar's combats, right up by the neck, and he used the pressure on her throat to haul her up onto her knees. He didn't have the height to get her standing.

Merinim was doing much the same to Everim, and Kyster would have bet his next full meal that she'd said the exact same thing.

Stepping back, Werst's gesture jerked Kichar up onto her feet. "Gunny'd object if we let you beat each other senseless, so that better have taken the edge off."

"I was winning!" Even muffled by the hand pinching her nostrils shut, Kichar sounded pissed.

"Don't care. Playtime's over; let's get back to work. Kyster!"

He jumped. Steadied himself on the bug, who didn't seem to mind. "Corporal?"

"What's your buddy found?"

Found? The bug smelled like a type of candy he remembered Humans sucking back on Ventris and was stroking the wall with her antennae. She sat back on her lower legs—chitin plates clacking against each other—tapped the wall with a foreleg, tapped his head with an antennae—it felt like being hit with a stiff feather—and tapped the wall again. Her hands weren't heavy enough to make much of an impact.

"I think . . ." He frowned, nose ridges opening and closing. "I think she heard something when I hit the wall, and she wants me to do it again."

"So do it again," Werst grunted.

It kind of hurt the second time.

Werst sighed. "Not with your head, Private."

Face flushed, he tapped the wall with his fist until the bug stopped him. She rose up, first and second set of limbs braced against the wall, shuffled left, shoving him back out of the way, leaned back, and fell forward.

A door slid open in the tunnel wall, exposing a small, bright room.

"Good work, Kyster." Werst's hand came down on his shoulder. "You and the bug have found the crapper. Find me a news reader and a cup of *sah* and I'll get you a fukking promotion."

"Want to tell me about it, Private Kichar?"

She'd washed her face and wiped down the front of her combats, but blood remained caked in red-brown rings around the inside curve of both nostrils. Drawing in a deep breath through her mouth, she came to attention. "Beginning at roughly 18:20 by my sleeve, I was involved in . . ."

Raising a hand, Torin cut her off. "You don't have to tell me about it, Kichar. I asked if you wanted to. Do you?"

Her cheeks flushed. "Uh, no, Gunnery Sergeant."

"You learn anything from the incident?"

"That the Druin are bendier than they look, Gunnery Sergeant."

Torin was tired enough she almost smiled. "Not quite what I meant, Private. Don't do it again."

"Yes, Gunnery Sergeant!"

Kichar pivoted on one heel and almost managed to march smartly away. Bruises under the fabric, Torin decided, watching her move, but nothing more serious. The corporals seemed to think it was the kind of fight that could safely be ignored—puppies fighting for dominance—and she trusted the corporals. Well, she trusted Werst. Turning to face him, she said, "Fill the canteens, then see that everyone drinks as much as they can hold. Have our people take it in turns with theirs."

"On it, Gunny. And the actual crapper?"

"Using it won't interfere with filling the canteens."

"That'll make the job a joy." He didn't specify which job.

Torin didn't ask. "Welcome to another glorious day in the Corps."

The sound of claws scraping stone announced one of the Polina behind her. Smelled like Vertic—she was a little less musky than the males.

"The technical sergeant does not have the door open yet." The durlin stared down her long nose at Torin who added another check mark in her *all officers state the obvious regardless of species or affiliation* column.

"No, sir, he hasn't."

"Find out why."

"Yes, sir."

Given that Vertic was standing less than two meters from where the technical sergeant was working, it seemed like she could safely say that the chain of command had been firmly established.

Mike had cannibalized one of the plastic bands from the filters to make tools. Torin'd had no idea there'd been so much small shit in there. She dropped her voice below the level the slate could pick up. "Durlin Vertic is wondering how much longer it's going to take you to make a totally unknown alien tech bend to your will. Anything I can tell her?"

"No."

"All right, then." She passed on Mike's response to the durlin, edited slightly for length, and went back to staring out the window at the landing site, trying to map a route through pools of lava and firestorms, vision impaired by the blowing smoke and ash. If Mike didn't solve the hatch soon, she'd be finding patterns in chaos and that was never healthy.

"Gunnery Sergeant?"

"Private Darlys."

"Is there a way across?"

The wind slapped another cloud of ash against the window, and Darlys' hair snapped back in reaction, falling forward again almost sheepishly a moment later.

"It's ten kilometers, Darlys. You should be able to cover that in your sleep." Not quite the answer to the question. There was a way between the landing site and the prison because there had to be although, with no visible road, it was likely their captors used a variation on a skimmer. Still, even skimmers had trouble over lava pools.

"It'll be dark soon."

"You know when sunset is?" Torin leaned forward and peered up at overlapping layers of burnt-orange clouds. It looked as though the atmosphere was on fire, and until she had intell to the contrary, Torin wasn't going to rule that out. "Have you even seen the sun?"

"Not dark out there, Gunny, I mean in here. If Technical Sergeant Gucciard doesn't get the hatch open soon . . ."

"He'll work by cuff light. He'll manage."

"But if he doesn't get the hatch open . . ."

"He will. It's a hatch, Private." Fully aware that everyone currently in the control room was listening, she raised her voice slightly. A little hope couldn't hurt. "It has a limited range of function—it opens, it closes. The tech may be alien, but it's not complicated."

"But it is alien and . . ."

"Technical Sergeant Gucciard will get the hatch open." Her tone made it clear she'd just said the final word on the subject.

"Got it!" Mike's tone, on the other hand, was triumphant.

Darlys' eyes darkened, but before she could put words to the awe visible on her face, Torin snapped, "Tell Corporal Werst to hurry with the water. We won't be here much longer." Pivoting on one heel, she returned to Mike's side listening for the sound of Darlys' boots moving away. That kind of timing was only going to strengthen the di'Taykan's belief in her developing godhead.

Metal whispered past metal as the hatch unlocked. Mike moved away from the controls and nodded up at the bank of lights now burning a steady pattern of blue and yellow over the door. "Should mean we've got air pressure."

"Should?"

"Alien tech, Gunny." He cranked the handle around one-handed and pulled gently. At the soft sigh of a seal breaking, he glanced down at his sleeve. "Contained atmosphere escaping reads as identical. Do I have a go, Gunny?"

"Durlin?"

Her claws squealed as she scraped a rear foot against the polished stone floor. Torin winced and mentally listed everything they still had to do in order to keep from tying the durlin's feet together. To her credit, she almost managed to hide her excitement as she said, "You have a go, Technical Sergeant."

Mike pulled the door open.

And the earth moved, bucking once, twice, three times. The sound of crumbling infrastructure rolled down the tunnels and into the control room—cracking rock sounding so much like weapons fire that Kichar wasn't the only one to throw herself to the ground reaching for the weapon she wasn't carrying.

Torin, left hand grabbing the edge of the center control panel, unlocked her knees and rode it out. With her sleeve readout turned away from her, and unwilling to loosen her grip, she had no idea how long the earthquake lasted. It felt like fifteen or twenty minutes.

The Krai were still standing at the end of it—their preferred real estate never entirely stopped moving, giving them a highly developed sense of balance. Torin had cracked her knee against the panel but remained on her feet as had two of the Polina—Bertecnic had dropped back onto his haunches, rear legs spread to either side. The position would have looked comical if not for the scimitar curve of ten-centimeter claws fully extended from each foot. Everyone else sprawled where the quake had thrown them. The Artek, tucked back into the angle of wall and floor were—with no danger of misinterpreting their reaction—just one side of hysterical.

The lemon furniture polish smell was nearly overwhelming. Torin rubbed her hand under her nose. Maybe it was the short rations lowering the levels of complacency drug. Maybe the smell was acting like smelling salts. Maybe this most recent burst of adrenaline had burned things off. She felt more like herself than she had since Harnett's death. "Technical Sergeant Gucciard, can you use what you learned opening the inside hatch to get through the outside hatch ASAP?"

He stood, rubbing his left elbow. "I can."

"Do it."

Scooping his tools off the floor, he stepped into the air lock. "Ressk!"

"On it, Sarge."

"Gunnery Sergeant Kerr, we do not know the external atmosphere."

"We know it required filters for whoever manned this control room. We know they required the same rough mix we do—we passed no air locks between the prisons and the upper levels. Logically, we then will manage with filters.

Vertic tossed her head, the short mane flaring. "It would be best if the control panel could be made to function."

As the durlin moved closer, Kyster picked the slate up off the ground and handed it to her remaining by her side, his nose ridges flared—with her if it came to a power play. Torin appreciated the thought, as unnecessary as it was.

"Durlin Vertic, we have run out of time. This facility is on its way to a collapse. We need to get our people out of here before that happens."

She blinked, thick fringe of lashes sweeping up and down. "Of course."

"All our people." Torin inserted the words cleanly into the pause. The durlin had clearly been going to continue speaking and part of the trick was to never appear to interrupt. Plausible deniability was everything.

The durlin stared at her for a long moment then repeated, "All our people."

Torin decided to take the statement as agreement. "So far, our best way off this rock, our best way to get all our people off this rock, is that landing site. We need to pick up the pace. I'll have everyone ready when the sergeant gets the outer door open." The other part of the trick was to sound so confident that an argument appeared to be a petty play for power.

Vertic frowned slightly, reacting to Torin's tone even though the words she actually understood came from the slate with a flat mechanical delivery. "And if there is no ship at this landing site?"

"I'll have the technical sergeant build one."

She smiled, then. A quick flash of teeth, as much challenge as amusement. "Very well. Go ahead."

"Sir." A quick sweep of the room showed Everim already handing out the filters. Freenim was beside him, making sure everyone knew how to achieve a seal regardless of the shape of their skull. They shared a silent moment of communication at the NCO level, then continued with what they'd been doing.

"Durlave Kir Sanati."

The Druin turned from the control panel. Torin didn't want to read too much into an alien expression, but she looked relieved. Given that the panel had surrendered nothing after the blast shield, her frustration level had to be high.

"Get as much intell on the earthquakes from the Artek as possible and make sure they're ready to move out."

They glanced together at the giant bugs still pressed tightly up into the angle between wall and floor. They were no longer clattering like a skimmer with a bolt loose, but they weren't happy.

Sanati snorted, and in the natural light Torin noticed a nictitating membrane flick across the black on black of her eye. "I do not think convincing them to leave will be a problem, Gunnery Sergeant."

"Gunny!"

Ressk's summons pulled her into the air lock.

"Inner hatch needs to be closed to open the outer. And the sarge figures that it's going to whoosh."

"And whoosh would be a tech term for?"

"Whoosh!" He made a broad, sweeping gesture with one hand. "*Serley* thing opens all the way when activated. One unstoppable movement."

Torin glanced over at Mike's broad back, his head bent over the open panel, both hands working. "And you have to open it manually from here."

Since it wasn't a question, he didn't bother answering it.

"Go get him a filter."

"You don't think it would be better to get me a filter, Gunny? I mean, if you're going to lose one of us . . ."

"We're not losing anyone, Corporal. Go." As Ressk trotted out into the control room, she moved closer to the hatch. The light bar blinked orange and lavender. "Time frame, Mike?"

"Five," he grunted. "Ten maybe."

"Make it five."

She had to admit she was impressed by the detail his wordless response managed to convey.

"Durlave Kan Freenim says everyone has a filter but you, Gunny."

The Krai's bare feet made no sound against the heavy rubber floor. Bare feet and lava pits—that would have to be dealt with. Taking the filter from Ressk's hand, she nodded. "I'll be right in. Mike."

He reached back without looking up.

"Put it on," she said, dropping the seal over his fingertips.

"Still five."

"Do it now so it's done." She'd worked with enough tech to know not to leave him to his own devices. He'd remember about the time he was measuring the lack of oxygen in the air, calculating the precipitants, and passing out.

Even with his back to her, she could see his eyes roll, but he slid the band over his head, settled the ear pieces, and activated the seal.

Torin stepped forward and checked it, feeling the seal ease more completely into place under her fingertips.

Ignoring her, he kept working, big hands maneuvering makeshift tools with delicate precision.

"Good thing for us you work hardware as well as software," Torin murmured, touched him lightly on the arm, and left. He neither needed nor wanted her hanging over his shoulder.

She took Ressk with her when she left. "You're operating the inner door," she told him before he could protest. "You're the only other person in here with a hope of reopening it if it locks down. His ass is in your hands."

His nose ridges flared. "Neither of us . . . Oh." The top of his head flushed. "Metaphorically."

"You think?"

With Ressk standing ready at the interior controls, Torin leaned back into the air lock. "Closing the inner door now, Technical Sergeant."

"Fine."

She straightened and pulled the hatch closed, dogging it down.

The lights remained a steady blue and yellow.

"They should begin blinking when Sergeant Gucciard has the outer hatch open, Gunny. And the odds are good that's when the *serley* thing'll lock again."

"That's why you're standing there, Corporal." With Mike on the other side of the hatch, Torin would have happily traded a bag of biscuits for a working com unit. Actually, at this point, she'd happily trade a bag of biscuits for a cold beer and take her chances on starving to death.

"Gunnery Sergeant Kerr?" Freenim stood at her shoulder. "The filters have no seal on the Artek, but Samtan Firiv'vrak is fairly certain they will breathe outside. As long as they move quickly."

"Fairly certain?"

He shrugged. "Sanati's translation. She says they wait for the technical sergeant's analysis, but their species is adaptable for many atmospheric levels and they know what fire requires to burn."

"Good." Torin glanced out the window. Fire was certainly burning. Which reminded her that she had one more thing to take care of before they began the run to the landing site. "Durlave, don't the Polina usually carry another species into battle?"

"Yes. They work together as a team." He offered no more information on how they worked as a team, nor did Torin expect him to. They were allies by chance, once out in the real world, they'd be enemies again. "It was thought strange," he continued, "that there were no Ner in the prison."

No Ner on one side. No heavies on the other. Their captors had some strange prejudices.

"Do you think they'd be willing to carry another species across to the landing pad."

"Not the Artek."

Too bad; she'd like to see that. "No, not the Artek. The Krai."

"Ah. The feet. You have noticed the Polina also do not wear boots."

She swore under her breath, condemning the biscuits and whatever was in them to hell and beyond.

"They cannot walk across open flame and by the end of the journey they may be uncomfortable, but their feet are very tough; the center pad, which bears most of their weight, is covered in a hard and nerveless . . ." The translation program noticeably paused. ". . . shell."

A clear case of "close enough."

"And carrying a Krai? Their bones are very dense." Information exchanged for information. "They aren't light."

He exhaled audibly through his nose. "You can ask, Gunnery Sergeant."

She could ask. He wasn't going to.

Fine.

The quiet tick of claws on stone behind her turned Torin to meet Durlin Vertic who'd nearly reached the hatch.

"How much longer, Gunnery Sergeant."

A glance down at her sleeve as though Mike had given her a definitive time. "Not long, Durlin."

"Good."

The lights over the door began to blink. A moment later they turned a deep, ugly orange.

"External hatch open, Gunnery Sergeant."

"Understood, Corporal."

The control room was silent except for the distinct scent of used cat litter. Torin wished she could ask the Artek for a translation. A moment later, the lights returned to their original color although they continued to blink. A moment after that, they stilled.

"External hatch closed and sealed, Gunnery Sergeant."

It was an assumption, of course, but it seemed a valid one. "Open it up, Corporal."

"Understood, Gunnery Sergeant."

The durlin rolled her eyes and Torin smiled, the way she'd smile at one of the Krai, her teeth covered. If Ressk was laying it on thick enough for an alien species to notice, it was thick on the ground indeed.

"Convenient you have two tech among you, Gunnery Sergeant."

"Yes, Durlin, it is." She responded to the words alone, the way she would with any officer. "I had noticed, Durlin, that when your species goes into battle you go with another."

"We do." A muscle jumped in Vertic's right arm as she went to reach back, then stopped herself.

"The Krai use their feet as extra hands." Inexact, but Torin needed to use words the slate could translate correctly. "They have no boots and . . ."

Vertic cut her off. "And you want to know if we will carry them to the landing site as we would carry the Ner."

"Yes, Durlin."

"Perhaps it would be more sense if they stayed here. Without boots."

"We don't leave our people behind, Durlin."

"We are both leaving a great many people behind, Gunnery Sergeant."

Torin inclined her head to acknowledge the point, to acknowledge the three-hundred-odd Marines still down in the tunnels eating their kibble and filling their time and not caring they were prisoners. And, hopefully, there still were three hundred Marines—the quake that had opened the way to the surface had wiped out an entire node and the last quake had definitely done some damage.

"As you said, Gunnery Sergeant, we need to get all our people out." She glanced at Ressk, working on the locking mechanism. "But we both start small. We will carry your Krai."

"Thank you, Durlin. They aren't light."

The durlin dismissed that observation with a cutting motion. "Neither *freetay* nor *ryrin* . . ."

Mount nor rider, Torin translated silently when the program didn't try.

". . . wears body armor or carries weapons or ammunition or even much in the way of supplies. And, we are strong."

"Under these conditions . . ." A glance toward the window where a firestorm close to the building painted the glass with lurid bands of color. ". . . the extra weight on your feet . . ."

"Our feet are also strong."

"Yes, Durlin." The durlin had been emphatic enough that Torin no longer believed she'd agreed purely for the benefit of the Krai. Sometime, when she had the time, she'd like to have the relationship between the Polina and the Ner explained.

The lights over the hatch stopped blinking, burning a steady blue and yellow. Ressk spun the handle and pushed the hatch open.

"Filter works," Mike said stepping out into the control room. Looking directly at Torin, he slapped at the readout on his sleeve. "Seventy-four point two percent nitrogen, twenty-two point three nine percent oxygen, carbon dioxide six point two percent and neon point zero

seven percent. Everything else, and there's a lot of it, reads trace."
The Krai would be happy with the CO2 levels. The di'Taykan would
not. "Precipitants are mostly ash, but there's other shit this thing's too
basic to read." He sounded personally insulted by the failings of his
uniform tech. "Temperature's up to 39.7 degrees C and that's in the
shade of the building. Closer to the fires, well, it'll be hotter."

At those temperatures, with only basic environmental controls
working, the di'Taykan were going to be very uncomfortable. If Torin
was reading Freenim's expression correctly, the Druin weren't too
happy about it either.

"We can reach the landing site, then, Technical Sergeant
Gucciard?"

Mike shifted his gaze to the durlin, one scorched eyebrow raised,
and repeated, in a tone that wondered why she asked, "The filter
works."

She scraped her rear claws against the floor. "Gunnery Sergeant,
Durlave Kan—get everyone into the air lock. Helic'tin, Bertecnic—
we will carry the Krai."

Torin felt a hand grip her sleeve. "What is it, Kyster?"

"They will carry the Krai?"

"That's what the durlin said, Private."

"On who . . . uh, which, Gunny?"

"Not for me to say."

Teeth carefully covered, the durlin pointed at each Krai in turn.
"You, on Helic'tin. You, on Bertecnic. You, on me."

When Torin looked down, Kyster didn't look happy about getting
to ride an officer across a lava field. "Gunnery Sergeant?"

"You can't walk through a lava field, Private. Say thank you and
mount up." She raised her voice slightly, more for impact than need.
"Filters on everyone." A quick round of the room to check the seals.
Hairless, the Druin and the Krai needed only minor adjustments, the
press of her finger along the band to ease it down the last bit. Other
species took a little more tweaking. Given that the di'Taykan hair were
sense organs—the Corps used hoods for that very reason—Watura
and Darlys both kept fussing until she glared their hands down.

"Is it painful?"

"No, Gunny, but it feels . . ."

"Like crap," Watura finished, the ends of his unconfined hair flipping up and down.

"Lung burn feels worse," Torin reminded them. Their uncovered hair was going to take damage, no way around it. Her own hair was about the same length, and the band settled uncomfortably, sealant seeping through and around it. Her scalp itched. Although, since she hadn't washed her hair for days, there could have been other reasons for that.

Kyster looked unhappy perched on the durlin's withers, clutching the straps on her vest. Ressk looked intrigued. Werst looked bored. They could maintain their hold on a tree in a high wind, Torin had every confidence they'd stay on board. All three Polina seemed . . . not exactly happy, but significantly more *settled*.

The floor bucked once, the whip end of a wave motion, tumbling them together but not actually knocking anyone down.

"Watch your fukking elbows," Mashona growled as she steadied Kichar.

Freenim snarled something the program missed as the Artek charged through the hatch. The last bug into the air lock clicked something back.

Torin understood their need for speed. "Marines, we are leaving!"

TWELVE

//**T**HEY MUST HAVE BEEN KNOWING WE WERE BEING behind them!" Presit paced the width of the tiny cabin, her legs short enough it was actually worth the effort. "I are still saying they are having deliberately ditched us!"

"Not so much *still* saying as *continuously*," Craig muttered, bending over the board. And Presit was delusional. If the Others had been aware of the small salvage ship locked onto their Susumi tail, they'd have destroyed it rather than risk a message with any kind of usable equation getting back to the enemy. No, they'd been ditched out here beyond the black stump because trusting to the Susumi modification had been a fukked idea from the get go—where nothing else was certain that much stood out like a dog's balls. But he'd given up arguing with Presit some time ago, allowing her to monologue uninterrupted.

Her small hand grabbed his forearm, lacquered claws digging in just enough to keep him from jerking free. "Why are we not going back already?" she asked suddenly, suspiciously. "You are working that board since we are being left here, and nothing are happening."

"We can't go back until we know where we are," he reminded her, plucking her hand from his flesh. "Destination equations are dependent on the start point, and I don't have a start point."

"There are being your start point!" She poked an imperious finger toward the view screen and the scattered points of light. "It are not hiding!"

"It's also not in the damned computer!" Sighing, he sagged back in the chair, unable to look at his reflection in her glasses. He'd found one possible reference point—deep space telemetry had picked up what it thought might be the Colvin-Habbes Nebulae—but that was it. Not nearly enough information to anchor a Susumi equation.

"You are saying before it are only a matter of time."

"I lied."

"So you are saying now?"

"That we are totally screwed. Fukked royally. Up the proverbial shit creek without the proverbial pa . . . Ow!"

Presit released the piece of his thigh she'd pinched and stepped closer, peering up into his face, her teeth very sharp and very white between the black lines of her lips. "I are not believing that."

He snorted. "It doesn't matter what you believe. Believe the porky if you want to, but screwed, fukked, shit creek—that sums things up."

"Then we are looking for why we are here."

"Here?"

"Here. Why are they dumping us here?"

"They didn't . . ." Craig stared out at unfamiliar star fields, back at Presit, and sighed. Why not. It wasn't like they had anything useful they could be doing. "Okay, fine, I'll bite. Why did they dump us here?"

She swatted him on the thigh, right where the bruise was rising. "I are not knowing that! But I are suggesting we be looking for real estate with atmosphere we are able to be breathing, then the Others are able to be breathing it, too."

He spent a moment working over the syntax, then said, "How do you figure?"

"Their known space are overlapping our known space, thus we are being at war." She waggled linked fingers at him, claws gleaming. "But that are only happening if we are wanting the same spaces and that are meaning breathable air. The same breathable air. We are not fighting the Methane Alliance!"

She had a point. "So I look for planets around here with breathable air. And then what?"

"And then we are at least not dying up here when the air are being too contaminated for the air scrubbers!" The additional *you idiot* came through loud and clear.

"No drama about that." A fond pat on the edge of the control panel; breathable air he could deal with. "As long as I can find ice, I can keep the O2 levels up."

"Ice?"

"Not exactly rare."

"And food?"

"Eventually, that may be more of a problem," he admitted.

Head cocked to one side, she folded her arms and raked a speculative gaze over him, the points of her teeth showing. "You are being good for many meals."

And he had no doubt that if it came to it, she'd kill him in his sleep and mourn the lack of condiments. Presit took care of number one. "Okay, then, why don't I look for some planets?"

From the outside, the prison looked like a single-story bunker, the walls stained and pitted by the particles on the wind, the single window and hatch the only breaks in the visible sixty meters.

What kind of idiot built an underground prison in an area so geologically unstable? Torin wondered. Just one more thing that made no sense to add to the mental list of *what the fuk* she'd been keeping since she woke up in that cave.

Tucked to one side, in a metal cup that had to be another sixty meters across, was an equally enormous chunk of ice.

"Berg or asteroid," Freenim wondered, eyes squinted against the glare.

Torin shook her head. "No fukking idea."

Just because this part of the planet was on fire didn't mean all of it was. It could, and likely did, have ice fields extending around both poles. But berg or asteroid, the cup explained where the water for the prison came from.

Directly outside the hatch was a covered platform clearly—given the burn marks and the tie-downs—used for skimmers. Unfortunately, there were no skimmers on the platform.

Still in the air lock, Torin had laid out the order of the march. *"The Artek'll head out first, then the Polina—given the environment, there's no reason for them to be held to the pace of the bipeds and a lot of reasons for them to get the fuk out of this mess as soon as possible. Ressk, when you get to the landing site, get the hatch open. Durlin?"* She'd paused, and the durlin had nodded, approving the order. And thank fukking God for that; Torin had been half afraid she'd argue. *"The rest of us will stay together. We will not survive out there in a firestorm, so let's make sure we don't have to."*

"And how do we make sure of that, Gunny?"

"We move our collective asses, Watura. And if you've got something to pray to, you pray."

He'd glanced over at Darlys, then, who was once again staring at Torin like she had all the answers and then some. It was the *and then some* that made Torin want to say, *"Don't be praying to me, dumbass, I'll be out there with you!"* but she decided not to waste her breath.

"Marines, set your environmental controls as low as they can go."

"That's not very low, Gunny," Mashona had murmured watching both di'Taykan fiddling with their cuffs.

It wasn't. Regular combats weren't designed for the kind of heat they'd be facing. But it'd be better than nothing. Not much better but a little.

The Artek had taken off running the moment Mike reopened the outer hatch, looking like nothing so much as giant cockroaches scuttling for safety. Which, technically, they sort of were although no one—and Torin could see more than one set of lips pressed close behind the filters' shimmer—had the bad taste to make the observation aloud.

The Polina had paused for a moment, the males holding back only because they were tucked in behind the durlin.

"Gunnery Sergeant, Durlave Kan. We will meet you at the landing site."

"Yes, sir."

"Gunny . . . !"

Kyster wasn't worried about riding, but she could see the panic rising at the thought of being away from her. "It's just like climbing the pipe, Kyster. Ressk and Werst are right there, and I'll see you at the other end. You'll be fine."

"But . . ."

"I said you'll be fine."

He'd nodded then, holding so tightly to the straps on the durlin's harness, his knuckles were white.

When they ran full out, the Polina moved a lot like big cats. It didn't look comfortable for the riders, but then, Torin had never actually ridden a big cat, so she could be wrong.

It took little discussion to put Kichar out on point with Torin and Everim back on their six with Freenim.

"If this was a vid," Torin muttered, "one of them would begin to fall into a lava pit and the other would save their ass and they'd become best friends forever."

Freenim snorted. "We have those stories, too. In real life, one of them will no doubt shove the other into a lava pit given the opportunity. Best to keep them separate."

The first part of the skimmer path—about a hundred meters out from the platform—could almost be called crushed gravel. The skimmers were at their lowest there, weight and backwash grinding the path to conform to the drive requirements. There'd be a similar hundred meters at the other end. Ten kilometers away.

"Well, at least it's a dry heat," Watura sighed wearily.

No one laughed.

Torin fell into an easy lope, glad to have Kichar beside her because it forced her to shorten her stride to where the four Druin—roughly the private's height—could keep up. Air sucked through the filter tasted of sulfur and ash, but it didn't burn either her eyes or her soft pallet, so the odds were good any taste at all came from her expectations. The air *looked like* it should taste of sulfur and ash and so it did, filter be damned. Some Marines never really got used to working in the smaller filters that sealed tightly over mouth and nose, but Torin preferred them to the full-face versions. It always took her a while to begin ignoring the shimmer just at the edge of her eyelashes, and this time out she didn't have the luxury of *a while*.

The air emerging from skylights over lava tubes would be hot enough to singe hair and bake eyebrows off but easy enough to avoid as the column shimmered—provided Torin could tell the difference between the filter's shimmer and the air shimmering. There'd be no skylights on the skimmer path—unless some had broken through since the last time it was used—but if the wind shifted while they were passing one, there'd be close to the same amount of damage done.

At the end of the first hundred meters, the path got rougher. Loose rock and small fissures forced a certain amount of caution.

"You turn an ankle and we will drag you the rest of the way." Loud enough all nine runners could hear her. "It won't be fun, so stay on your feet!"

Half a hundred strides later, they passed a skylight about three meters to the right. In the absence of any wind, the temperature may have risen a degree or two. Maybe not. It was hot enough a degree or two made little difference.

Torin could already feel the heat on her hands and the back of her neck, skin beginning to prickle and pull tight. Watura may have been joking, but it *was* a dry heat—similar to that generally found in industrial-sized ovens.

"Watura, Darlys—you tell me if the heat is too much. Mashona, Sergeant Gucciard—keep an eye on the di'Taykan."

"You don't think we'd say something, Gunny?" Watura asked.

Darlys wouldn't; not and risk her disappointment. She'd like to think that, now Jiyuu was out of the picture, Watura'd have more sense. She'd like to think so, but she wasn't banking on it. "At these temperatures, you could go down before you're aware you're being overcome."

"If I'm going down, Gunny, I'm aware of it."

The opportunity for innuendo had perked them both up. "Good for you."

When they reached the first large, triangular fissure and the skimmer path swooped right to go around, Torin realized 10K was a low estimate. Ten kilometers as the 740 flew—not that any Marine would want to take a bird out in the abrasive soup that passed for atmosphere—but probably closer to twelve or fifteen at ground level. Still easily doable but that much again more dangerous.

"Stay all the way to the right," Torin barked as they began the by-pass. "We don't know how stable the edges are." The fissure was deep and about six meters across at the widest end, the lava in it deep red and already beginning to develop an insulating skin.

They were warmed up now—and considering they'd be cooked in a little under an hour, that was almost funny—so she picked up the pace. Both the Artek and the Polina were out of sight, but that was more the terrain than the speed the nonbipeds were making.

The Gunny'd said he'd be fine, so he was, but Kyster had grown up in the city, he'd joined the Corps as soon as he was legally able, and neither in the city nor in the Corps had he been expected to ride large animals. Or the enemy. Or an officer.

It wasn't that it was hard; it was just weird. The motion reminded him of the upper walkways in the wind—the ones so high only the Krai ever took them. He hung on to the straps on the vest and the bellyband with his good foot and kept his weight high up on the durlin's withers, centered on her spine, and tried not to think about how it was the durlin's spine. The di'Taykan would be good at this, they liked touching, except their feet would be dangling on the rock and that would kind of defeat the whole purpose.

For the first time ever, he wished he had his boots. If he'd had his boots, he'd be running with the gunny.

They crested a ridge and the durlin didn't slow, bounding down the far side, rear legs sliding sideways in the loose rock as she reached the bottom. She dug in her claws, let momentum center her, and crossed under the first of the massive stone arches without having lost any speed. As they passed, the heat from the wide fissure slapping against his left side like an open palm, Kyster saw scorch marks high on the rock. Not the place to be in a firestorm obviously. He tightened his grip . . .

. . . and nearly lost his seat when the durlin's arm reached back, her hand closed around his wrist, and she shoved down.

Down?

There were a set of straps lower on the vest as well. He transferred the hand she wasn't holding and she released him, slapping him on the thigh as he dropped that hand down as well.

The slap seemed like a good thing. Like approval.

He realized why she wanted him to change his grip a moment later as they reached a steeper ridge and she threw her body forward, using her hands and arms to help claw her—their—way upward.

Her sides were heaving by the time the ground leveled out, the short golden fur darkened with sweat, but instead of slowing, she lengthened her stride. Kyster could feel long muscles moving under his legs. It was comforting in a way. Like being a part of something, something that meant not being alone. The rise and fall of her spine threw him forward and back, reinforcing the similarities to the upper walkways. He found himself suddenly remembering home and wondered if there was less oxygen in the air than Technical Sergeant Gucciard thought.

It hurt to think of home. He'd learned that on his own in the tunnels, so he never did it; except now, he couldn't seem to stop. The light at home was green, not orange, and the breeze in his face would smell of food, not alien body odor. For the first time since Harnett's men had abandoned him, he let himself believe he might be able to go back someday. Gunnery Sergeant Kerr had gotten him this far, he just had to believe she could get him the rest of the way

She believed she could do it; that had to be good enough for him.

It wasn't quite as much of a surprise when the durlin reached back the second time. Both her hands gripped his wrists hard for a second and then let go.

He got that he was supposed to do something, but he didn't know what.

Then he saw the fissure directly ahead of them. The path followed the edge of the fissure half a kilometer, maybe more to the left, over a small arch of the harder, smoother stone then looped back to turn away from the channel almost directly across from where they were.

Helic'tin charged past, yelling a challenge. Then Bertecnic. It didn't look as though either of the males were going to turn.

It didn't feel as though the durlin were going to turn.

Leaping over the fissure would definitely be faster than going to the bridge.

Muscles bunched as she planted her rear feet.

Nope. Not going to turn.

Kyster hurriedly stuffed his bad foot under the bellyband.

Helic'tin launched himself. Landed. A moment later, Bertecnic landed on his heels. Ressk and Werst might have yelled something, but it got lost in all the whooping.

He clamped his nose ridges shut and closed his eyes as the durlin launched herself over the fissure. The blast of heat as they crossed suggested the lava flow wasn't very far down, but he had no intention of opening his eyes to find out for sure. The last thing he needed was to have the fluid in his eyeballs cooked away. He'd heard that kind of thing could happen.

The landing slammed his teeth together, and if he hadn't been Krai, he was sure they'd have shattered. He sucked in a scorching lungful of air with the impact. He could feel the durlin readying her next stride when she began to fall back.

With a crack like breaking bone, the edge of the rock split away, splashing down into the lava flow.

The durlin screamed. Kyster smelled burning hair. Cooking meat. Her hindquarters bucked up. He let the movement throw him forward, over her shoulder. His bad foot caught on the bellyband, but he kicked free. When he hit the ground, he rolled, slammed up against the rough curve of a boulder, and bounced back. Didn't matter. At least the durlin wouldn't have his weight forcing her down.

Another crack.

He looked up in time to see the durlin silhouetted in front of a fountain of red.

She screamed again.

Helic'tin and Bertecnic surged forward and grabbed her arms. Werst and Ressk were both standing, toes clutching the lower straps, reaching out for fistfuls of her uniform.

Another crack.

The two males leaped back, dragging the durlin with them.

And then they were all standing, breathing heavily, a good two meters in from the new edge.

"Kyster, are you hurt?"

"Why?" Kyster grunted, rolling up onto his feet. The rock was hot. Almost too hot against the scar tissue.

"Why? You fell off!"

"I jumped."

"You jumped?" The older Krai exchanged a glance that pulled Kyster's lips up off his teeth.

"She was falling. I didn't want to be too heavy for her." He limped back to the durlin's side, ignoring the conversation going on over his head. The language seemed to include a lot of growling and snarling—he didn't think they were fighting, but they might have been. "She's hurt." There were two ugly burns on Durlin Vertic's right haunch, both deep enough to show charred muscle, both seeping blood, the larger trailing rising lines of white blisters all the way down her leg.

"Even through the filter, she smells *chrick*," Ressk murmured.

Kyster's mouth was watering. He couldn't remember when he'd last had cooked meat. "I don't think they have sealant."

"Good thing Gunny had me carry the one we found, then." Still standing, Werst pulled a tube from his vest. "Already works on three species, and she's bleeding red, so here's hoping we've got enough body chem in common."

Kyster caught the tube, then held it up high enough to get the durlin's attention and mimed spraying it on the burn.

Bertecnic growled a protest. It sounded like a protest. Durlin Vertic growled something back that shut him up and gestured for Kyster to get on with it.

"This shouldn't sting and it should keep the blisters from breaking and it should block the scent a bit, I hope." He kept his voice soft, nonthreatening, the words slurring into each other in a soothing rise and fall of sound.

"She can't understand you," Ressk pointed out.

"Yeah, but she knows where I am." He thought that the bits of burn he'd covered looked less painful. The hair on the lower part of her short tail had curled and turned brittle in the heat. "I don't want to be on the wrong end of those *serley* claws."

She kicked out when the spray hit the deepest burn, but she didn't aim the kick at him, so Kyster figured the talking worked.

"Is it helping?"

"How should I know?" But it looked as though some of the lines of pain had eased in her face.

Ressk said, "Kyster, your feet . . ."

"I'm fine." Most of his weight was on his good foot, keeping the scars off the ground, but he was used to that. He tipped a little sideways, laid one hand against a sweat-damp wither, unsure if he'd be riding from here on in.

The thought barely finished, the durlin reached down, grabbed the front of his uniform and swung him up onto her back. He shifted forward quickly, well up from the burns.

One big hand closed around his ankle and lifted his bad foot. He could only see the side of her face and he had no idea what she was saying, but it looked like she was asking him something.

"I'm fine." His scars hurt, but he was used to that.

She shook his foot gently, patted his leg, and took a careful step forward.

The easy grace was gone. He could feel the stutter in her muscles, feel her heart racing like it hadn't before, not even when she was running full out.

Helic'tin said something quietly and tipped his head back, exposing his throat.

The durlin snarled a response and began to run. Her new stride favored her injured leg and rocked him to the left. He shifted his weight, got a smack on the thigh, and managed to find a position that worked for them both.

"Gunny?"

"Private."

"What if there's nothing at the landing site? No ship, no com board, nothing."

"You're on a 10K run through a lava field, Kichar; you don't think you have enough to worry about?"

"Well, yeah, but . . ."

"One thing at a time, Kichar. First we get there. Then we deal with what we find." Torin could see claw marks scoring the rock heading up to the top of the first ridge and wasted a moment wishing her boots came with retractable pinions. She paused for a moment on the crest to get a look at the downhill path. Downhill was always trickier; visibility was worse, but the urge to speed up so that gravity could do part of the work was nearly irresistible. Accidents happened going downhill. Kichar, to her credit, kept her pace matched to Torin's.

Then her right heel landed hard in patch of scree. Torin slid about two meters, hit solid rock, went over a small boulder, and picked up the pace she'd been setting on the other side of the ridge.

She heard Mike applaud, turned without stopping, and took a small bow. So far, except for the heat, she'd had worse runs on Corps-approved courses.

"Single file here," she called as they reached the first of the stone arches. "Stay up against the rock."

This was the closest they'd come to actual moving lava, and the heat was vicious. Torin could feel sweat running down her sides, and the back of her throat when she swallowed was painfully dry. Instead of the crackle and snap of fire that the heat and the red light suggested, the only sound was the slow gurgle of molten rock against the side of the fissure, the distant howl of the wind, and the rhythmic sound of boots hitting stone.

"Firestorm while we're in here would be a bitch," she heard Mike mutter thoughtfully.

Then the earth moved.

Her left boot made contact about five centimeters before it should have, compacting her knee and hip. She stumbled, recovered, and slammed against the bottom of the arch as the path suddenly tilted about sixty degrees to the right. Caught on a bit of rough stone, her filter crushed her eyelashes for a moment before it pulled free.

She heard one of the Druin cry out.

"I've got her!" Mashona's voice rose over the profanity.

The quake was probably too minor to have been felt inside the prison, but minor inside and minor under a stone arch next to a lava flow was something else again. If the ground had pitched in the other direction . . .

"Sound off by number!"

They were all still up and moving.

"There's an open space up ahead. We'll regroup there."

They'd barely gone three kilometers and the two di'Taykan didn't look good. No point in asking if they were going to make it because they had no choice. Fortunately, for all their height, they were relatively light, and if it came to it, she could sling one over her shoulders and Mike could handle the other.

Those parts of the Druin's hairless scalp not covered by the filter were starting to pink up, but otherwise they were in no worse shape than the Humans. Merinim, the Druin who'd fallen during the quake, had a bleeding scrape on one hand.

"And a bruise that matches that one's fingers on my shoulder," she muttered, nodding at Mashona.

"Learn to walk and I wouldn't have to haul you up off your ass," Mashona answered, grinning.

Torin glared Kichar to silence before she could butt into what was no more than good-natured bitching and the best sign she'd seen so far that their mismatched group had started to work as a unit.

The next ridge was steep enough, the rock loose enough, that a couple of times, Torin used her hands for added security. The rock was hot, not uncomfortably so, but then she wasn't holding on for any length of time. How hot would it be under the Polinas' feet? Or the Artek's? The big bugs looked fragile, but looks were deceptive—not only had experience taught her that they were a bitch to take out in hand-to-hand, but during her years in the Corps, she'd seen more than one blasted landscape where only the bugs had survived.

Given the angle, it wasn't a ridge she'd have chosen to drive a skimmer over—or more precisely up—but they emerged onto a sort of plateau still pointed pretty damned near directly at the landing site. Lengthening her stride, grateful for more-or-less level ground, she jumped two small fissures and realized there was a sizable fissure coming up they'd never get over.

"Bridge, Gunny. To the right, about 100 degrees from Marine zero."

Given the amount of particulates in the air, Mashona's ability to pick a black rock bridge out of a black rock background was nothing short of amazing.

The path turned around a vaguely bovine-looking rock formation and paralleled the lava flow

"Gunny . . ."

"I see it, Kichar."

A piece of the far edge about a meter and a half long had a rough unfinished look, its angles not yet melted to curves.

"Do you think they jumped, Gunny?"

"Odds are good someone jumped."

"Do you think they made it? Should we look?"

Torin remembered hearing once—probably before deployment onto Sart Hellaya, a planet young enough to still be seething with the aftereffects of becoming a planet—that the temperature of lava was around a thousand degrees centigrade, give or take a couple of hundred degrees. At those temperatures, flesh and bone were damned near instantaneously destroyed on contact. "We'll find out soon enough if they made it. No one gets closer than necessary to the flow."

The bridge was a smaller version of the arch they'd crossed under. Natural. Not built. Smooth enough but no more than about a third of a meter wide. Their boots would see to it they had traction, but the two meters actually over the fissure were not going to be fun.

Back inside the control room, they'd watched a bridge very like it collapse.

"At least no one's shooting at us," Torin pointed out when Mashona made that point out loud. "When it's your turn, take a deep breath on this side and do not breathe again until you're across. Watch your feet if you have to, but do not look over the edge. One person on the bridge at a time and move as fast as you safely can."

"One at a time?" Freenim asked quietly, having moved up beside her as they came to the bridge. "Why? It looks like it could hold all ten of us."

"Someone freaks in the middle, I want to keep collateral damage to a minimum."

"You would rather they didn't pull someone over with them?"

"That's what I said. Kichar?"

"Gunny?"

"Go! She's the youngest." Torin answered Freenim's unasked question as Kichar took a deep breath and ran. "Doesn't prove a damned thing if you or I make it over. We could walk across on the lava if we wanted to."

Freenim snorted. "It seems the expectations of Gunnery Sergeants and Durlave Kans are almost the same."

"Almost?"

"They might allow me to run. Everim. Go!"

"Technical Sergeant Gucciard, if you could keep those two from continuing the war on the other side."

"Sanati."

"Mashona."

"Merinim."

"Watura."

Watura stumbled at the center. Recovered. Clearly disoriented, he turned to face back the way he'd come. His eyes were so pale a green they were nearly yellow and it was likely all the light receptors had slammed shut. He swayed.

Torin raced up the nearer slope of the bridge, dropped her shoulder just far enough to catch the swaying di'Taykan in the stomach, heaved him up and over, got in four more long strides, hit solid ground, tripped on his dangling legs and rolled to protect him as she fell.

Strong hands dragged them back from the edge.

"Get some water down him," Torin growled as she came up onto her feet watching as Darlys crossed with Freenim right behind her. "A wet filter's better than a dead Marine."

"You saved him." Stumbling forward, Darlys clutched at Torin's combats, her eyes not quite as light as Watura's, but it was close.

"Part of the job," Torin told her dryly as she mirrored her grip, swinging her away from the edge and lowering her onto a rock downwind of what little air flow there was. Overheated di'Taykan released significantly more pheromone than their maskers could handle. "Technical Sergeant?"

To his credit, Mike knew exactly what she was asking. "With only basic environmental controls on line, that's as cool as I can get them."

"What if there was a way to insulate their combats from the outside temperature?"

"That would help, but . . ."

Unfastening her vest, she shrugged it off her shoulders. "Mashona, we'll need your combats as well."

"Gunny . . ."

"You're tall enough, Mike, but we need your brain functional when we arrive. Mashona and I only have to get there. Besides, women can handle heat better than men and we're definitely more comfortable up close to the di'Taykan when they're in this condition, particularly given that we'll be running.

"Not arguing with that," Mike agreed, shifting uncomfortably.

Freenim exchanged a speaking glance with Everim. "So the rumors are true."

"Why am I not surprised that those are the rumors the enemy has heard," Torin sighed. "Sergeant, get a little distance between these two and everyone with external genitalia and fill the durlave in on some of the truth behind the rumors." The rock was hot under her socks, so she got her boots back on as soon as possible and advanced on Darlys wearing, besides footgear, her underwear and her vest. "Mashona, you're a little taller, so you and Sanati wrestle your combats on over Watura's. Kichar and I will deal with Darlys."

Still disoriented, the di'Taykan weren't a lot of help, but Darlys laid back and allowed herself to be handled, an almost contented smile on her face, while Watura seemed to want to do some handling of his own.

"Gunny, if he grabs my boob again, can I deck him with my club?"

"Only if you want to carry him." Torin left Kichar to finish the seals at wrist and ankle and slip Darlys' vest back on over the double layer of combats while she moved over to give the other two a hand.

"If you deal with this all the time," Sanati muttered, "I can see why you are so fierce when you fight."

Torin checked to be sure Watura's masker was up as far as it would go. "Yeah, well, there's nothing like a little sexual frustration to make you want to kick butt." Her bare legs were already starting to prickle from the heat.

It might have been the water, it might have been the rest, it might have been the double layer of combats, but both di'Taykan were looking better.

"Get them up and get them moving, we've still got a good seven klicks to cover."

"What's good about them, Gunny?" Mashona wondered as Torin tucked the salvage tag in under her vest.

"People where I'm from pay to go places this warm."

Mashona stared at her like she'd grown another head. "Why?"

"Damned if I know."

Moaning low in her throat, noises Kyster would have bet she wasn't aware she was making, Durlin Vertic hobbled the last hundred meters to the landing site and let her upper body sag in against the wall, radiant heat unimportant next to the support it offered. Kyster slid off and moved around her flank until he could see the burns.

Blood had seeped from the more damaged areas, staining sweat-darkened fur even darker, and all but the smallest of the blisters had broken. He pulled out the sealant and emptied the rest of the tube.

The two males had allowed the durlin to arrive first—or had stayed behind her to catch her if she fell, who the hell knew—and now they started crowding in, making low keening sounds. Ressk threw himself flat on Helic'tin's back as she took a swing at him, the blunt claws on her hands drawing a line of red against his jaw.

"That sound like a get the fuk away from me, to you?" he asked as he dropped to the ground.

"And damned convincing, too," Werst growled remaining mounted as Bertecnic danced back millimeters ahead of a second swing. "Get the *serley* door open. Heat's adding hurt. Kyster! Get the durlin to stand still, that'll keep the sealant from cracking."

"How?"

"How the hell should I know? Just do it."

Edging around on her good side, Kyster tucked up close by her front legs and lightly touched the damp fur at the edge of her uniform to get her attention. When she dropped her head and snarled at him, he showed his own teeth in return.

"Yeah, that'll help."

"Shut the fuk up."

"That'd be shut the fuk up, Corporal."

Kyster ignored him. Still stroking the durlin's fur with one hand, he held the other up where she could see it in what he hoped was the universal sign for stop. Unfortunately, there was no universal sign for *stop moving or you'll crack the sealant and let the hot air back into your burns.* There really needed to be.

She stared at him for a long moment, then sighed and let the wall support a little more of her body weight.

He held up the sealant tube, shook his finger at her, pretended to crack it, made a pained face and tapped his butt about where she'd been hit. He didn't recognize the sound she made in response.

"Is that pain?"

"It's laughter, kid." Now Bertecnic had stilled, Werst slid to the ground. "Ressk?"

"No the fukking door isn't open yet, Corporal."

Since the durlin seemed likely to stay where she was and the two males were looking a little crazily overprotective, Kyster stepped back and took a look around.

The landing site, like the prison, seemed to be mostly underground. Seemed like kind of a dumb idea to him, since it looked like most of the planet's underground was liquid rock, but maybe he was missing something. There was a wall, an almost identical door, and some scary scorch marks. Scary because the nearest lava flow was about 300 meters away, and if a firestorm could extend this far . . .

The three bugs were huddled just to the left of the door.

"Are they dead?"

Werst moved closer and poked one.

The durlin barked a command an idiot could have translated. *Don't poke the bugs.*

Kyster limped up behind Werst, rolling onto the side of his bad foot to avoid the blisters, and peered over his shoulder. "Their gills are moving."

"Their what?" Werst demanded.

"The feathery things on their sides are gills," Ressk grunted, shoving the point of his knife under the cover on the door controls pounding the hilt with his fist. "It means they're breathing. Shit!"

Kyster ducked as a shard of obsidian whizzed by. "The knife broke?"

"Give the kid a prize," Ressk snarled, jiggling the three-centimeter piece still jammed in the cover.

Rolling his eyes, Kyster returned to the durlin's side, pointed to Bertecnic—only because the darker male was closer—and mimed claws ripping the cover off the panel. The durlin snorted, and barked a command.

Bertecnic shoved Ressk out of the way and ripped the panel cover off the wall.

"No really," Werst snickered, "give the kid a prize."

"Shut up." Ressk retrieved the point of his knife and peered up into the control panel. "Looks just like the other one."

"Good."

"Technical Sergeant Gucciard opened the other one."

"Less good."

Kyster watched, confused, as one of the bugs slowly toppled over. A second later the ground began to shake.

"Gunny!"

"I feel it!"

And with no more warning, the skimmer path dropped around eight centimeters and angled about thirty degrees left. One off-balance stride later, it snapped back up two centimeters. Those who'd managed to remain standing during the first movement were thrown off their feet during the second.

Nearly deafened by the crack of rock breaking behind them, Torin ignored the bleeding scrape down the length of her right leg and rolled up onto one knee. The blast of heat nearly flattened her again and she braced herself, one hand on the ground, as the landscape settled.

"Fuk."

She took Mike's offered hand and let him haul her to her feet. "You have a way with words, Technical Sergeant."

Six meters behind them, the path came to an abrupt end at the edge of a fissure already a meter across and still spreading, the rock groaning as the heat forced it apart. From the ruddy glow and the sudden rise in temperature, the lava flow was dangerously near the surface.

"Good thing it's behind us," Kichar murmured, rising carefully to her feet.

"The gods are on our side," Everim agreed. His eyes narrowed as Kichar glanced over at him. "Our gods on our side. Not yours."

"We don't need your gods. We have plenty."

"Play nice, children." Torin hauled Darlys upright in turn and leaned her toward Kichar. "Durlave? Problem."

Freenim was still on the ground, crouched over Merinim who was panting and holding her face. No, not her face . . .

"Filter snagged when she went down," Freenim said without looking up. "I patch with ours, but it is not holding in the heat."

"Here." Torin pulled one of their slap-on filters from her vest and passed it down. "Try this; it's a little bigger because of the Krai's nose ridges."

He gazed at the filter for a moment, lying limp over his palm, then up at Torin. "Yesterday, we were enemies."

She shrugged. "And we may be tomorrow. Today, we've jumped out of the same frying pan."

"Gunny, yesterday . . ."

"It's a metaphor, Kichar. Just something we say to remind ourselves that there's a war on."

The young Marine rubbed a hand over the back of her neck. "I thought you'd forgotten."

The look she exchanged with Freenim spoke of what they'd both seen over the years. "Not likely."

"But . . ."

"There's a war on, Kichar, but we're not fighting it today."

Merinim gingerly turned her head from side to side, hand up and ready to pinch the tear closed again. "Holding better, but I would not trust it to sudden moves."

"So we'll move a bit slower." Torin took a swallow of water, sweat dribbling down her side under the vest as she raised her arm and pushed a fold of the filter into her mouth. "It's not . . .

The second crack wasn't quite as loud, but something told Torin that was only because it came from farther away. The echoes bouncing off both higher ridges and the low cloud cover suggested it had been one hell of a noise.

"Gunny . . ."

Torin really didn't like the sound in Mashona's voice.

". . . I think that was the prison."

"Cracking?"

"There's a black line. There." Eyes squinted nearly closed, Mashona pointed back the way they'd come. "Near the corner. It wasn't there before."

Even mimicking Mashona's squint, Torin could barely see the prison let alone a crack. "I'll have to take your . . . Mashona. Look at the sky left of the prison and a bit beyond. What do you see?"

"The light against the clouds is yellow instead of orange."

"The light against the *bottom* of the clouds. Durlave!" Torin whirled in place. Merinim was up on her feet now, one hand against the patch on the filter. "We haven't time to go careful. Get a filter over her mouth and nose! Another over her closed eyes! You and Everim keep her on her feet, she'll be running blind!"

"That is unnecess . . ."

"There's a firestorm coming!"

Merinim took a deep breath, closed her eyes, and ripped open the damaged filter. Freenim quickly slapped the others on.

"To stick in this heat," he began.

"We won't be out here long," Torin snapped, grabbing Darlys' arm. "Let's move people! Spend everything you've got!"

Taking small careful steps across the skimmer pad—walking hurt but standing hurt more as the paving brought up new blisters—Kyster made a wide circle around Helic'tin's back end until he could look up into the Polina's face. Or, given the angle, up into the Polina's nose. His head was back, the wide nostrils were flared, and he was staring along the skimmer path through narrowed eyes.

Curious about just what Helic'tin could smell through the filter—because the only *serley* thing Kyster could smell was his own feet cooking—he took up a position of his own at the edge of the pad and opened his nose ridges. He slammed them closed after a couple of seconds when it felt like his brain had been dehydrated and turned into jerky.

A big hand closed roughly around his shoulder, the two fingers on one side, the two thumbs on the other, and pulled his attention off the packs of jerky he used to be able to buy on MidSector Station.

"What?"

Helic'tin growled something and lifted his other arm to point.

"I can't smell it!"

The second growl needed no translation. He jabbed at the air with one clawed finger.

The skimmer path. Rock. Fissures. Heat shimmer. Orange clouds. Yellow clouds . . . Yellow clouds? Maybe it was what passed on this shithole of a planet for dawn although Kyster wouldn't actually say there'd been a night. It had never actually gotten dark and . . .

The yellow pattern shifted. For a minute, it looked as though the clouds were on fire.

Fire.

"Firestorm!"

Werst met him halfway back to the door. "What are you talking about, kid?"

Mouth open, unable to suck in enough air, he gasped the word again. "Firestorm!"

They turned together to stare at the wall. At the scorch marks well over their heads.

"Fuk! Ressk!" Werst whirled and raced back to the panel. "Get the damned door open!"

"Working on it!"

"Yeah, well, work faster! If I'm going to be roasted, I want to be eaten after!"

Still standing at the edge of the platform, Helic'tin made a noise that spun Kyster back around. The nearest ridge had gained what looked like a fringed edge. And the fringe was moving.

"I see them! The others!"

"Where?"

It took Kyster a minute to realize why Werst was staring up into the sky. "Not those others, our others! There! On the path! Hey!" He waved both hands above his head. "Over here! Gunnery Sergeant Kerr!"

Sucking air through her teeth, amazed that it could actually be hotter than it was, Torin concentrated on putting one foot in front of the other. She'd stopped sweating, and that was bad, knew she was dehydrating but couldn't let Darlys go long enough to grab her canteen. The di'Taykan was still moving her feet, but Torin and Kichar were holding most of her weight.

At that, she was doing better than Watura whose feet were dragging, boots scraping against the rock in a rhythm that suggested he was still trying, still conscious, but only just.

She could hear Freenim calling cadence as Merinim ran full out with her hand locked in the back of his uniform. That was trust. The Druin were out in front now, the distance widening enough that space between Freenim's voice and the slate and her implant were becoming a distraction.

Stop thinking, Torin. Run!

"Ressk!"

He slapped Werst's hand away. "Stop fukking distracting me!"

With all three Krai grouped around the panel, Kyster's head pivoted between the path and the door. He could hear the roar of the approaching firestorm. Tried to convince himself he could hear the pounding of boots on gravel. Couldn't even though they were close enough now he could make out separate people. Or separate clumps of people.

"Ressk! If that door isn't open when they get here . . ."

"We'll all roast together!" Ressk's snarl cut Werst off although he kept his eyes locked on the panel. "I know! Shut up!"

Helic'tin twisted to look back over his shoulder and yelled something. The durlin yelled back, and Kyster didn't need to understand the language to know she'd told him that whatever he'd said first was a dumbass idea.

Then the durlin yelled again as Helic'tin spun around one rear foot, charged across the skimmer pad and shoved Ressk and Werst aside, rearing back . . .

He was going to slash the panel.

Kyster could see it as clearly as if it was happening in front of him.

He was going to slash the panel and destroy it and the door would never be opened and they'd all die. The gunny would die.

What would the gunny do?

He threw himself in under the raised forelegs, and punched the Polinta as hard as he could in the balls.

Helic'tin screamed and twisted back on himself.

The blow landed just under Kyster's shoulder, lifted him up and flung him high enough in the air that he had time to twist and see the ground approaching before impact.

The door wasn't open.

And Torin could feel the heat behind them raising blisters on the backs of her bare legs. "Mike, go!"

"I've got him, Sarge!" Watura dipped sideways as Mashona took his weight and, relieved of the burden, Mike began to pull ahead, arms pumping, boots digging.

Darlys was still more or less on her feet, but Watura was going to collapse and take Mashona down in another minute.

"Take him, Gunny," Kichar gasped. "I can . . . hold her . . . until Mash . . . until she gets here."

Moving up alongside, Torin got a good two handfuls of Watura's combats—actually, Mashona's combats—and yelled, "Mashona, switch!"

As he fell toward her, she ducked forward and lifted him up across her shoulders wondering when the gravity had gotten stronger. "Fukker's gained weight!"

Mike was almost at the door. They still had a chance.

✧   ✧   ✧

Kyster struggled to sit as he heard boots pounding across the skimmer pad. Arms flailing, his hand hit something solid, and he used it to pull himself up, realizing too late it he'd been lying tucked between the durlin's front legs and was holding a handful of damp fur. Then Technical Sergeant Gucciard raced past, stumbling to a panting halt next to the control box.

"Sarge! It won't make the connections!"

"Won't?" The sergeant gasped.

"Won't," Ressk insisted, "there's something missing!"

Bracing himself with one hand flat against the wall, the sergeant stared into the panel. "Oh, that's not good!"

"We are almost with no time!" the durlin yelled.

The slate! Technical Sergeant Gucciard had the slate on his vest, Kyster realized as more boots pounded across the platform and the four Druin arrived. Kyster turned to see Mashona and Kichar carrying Darlys, Gunnery Sergeant Kerr with Watura over her shoulders right behind, and behind her . . .

"Sergeant! The firestorm!" Kyster thought that was Sanati.

He didn't believe it could get hotter, but it had. If the sergeant didn't get the door open, they were all going to die.

It was light, really light suddenly, and Kyster saw the sergeant straighten, close his eyes for a second, then reach into the panel.

The door opened.

Torin saw the door open as she hit the edge of the platform, Watura a dead weight across her shoulders. No, a limp weight. Not dead. Not so close.

Durlin Vertic grabbed Kyster by the collar and hauled him through the door, keeping her body between him and the firestorm.

When she got a moment, Torin really had to ask about the whole ride/ridden relationship

Freenim thrust Merinim inside, then he and Everim each grabbed an end of an Artek and tossed them in. Sanati and Ressk grabbed another.

Werst flipped the last onto its back and dragged it.

As soon as the Krai were in, Helic'tin and Bertecnic charged over the threshold.

Mashona, Darlys, and Kichar were at the door.

Then she was at the building.

On the threshold.

Turned.

Mike's teeth were clamped so tightly together a muscle jumped in his jaw. His eyes were open. He had his far hand braced against the building, most of his weight on it in spite of the angry, painful looking red the skin had turned, blisters erupting in the heat of the firestorm. The hand thrust into the control box was a twisted mess of bone and char.

"Mike!"

He lifted his head. Sucked a breath in through his teeth. Focused on her face and straightened, lifting his hand off the wall, snapping the slate off his vest. He nodded, once. Tossed the slate at her, then threw his body to the side, forcing his arm around, turning the ruin of his hand.

Torin threw herself backward, Watura's heels knocked hard against her thighs by the closing door, the slate bouncing off his ass and clattering against the floor. On her knees, she could hear people breathing all around her. Rough rasps of air sucked through dry mouths and throats. Damaged, but alive.

Watura rolled off her shoulders, grunted when he hit the floor and, with that question answered, she crawled forward. Hands and knees. Not enough left to manage on knees alone.

Even through the filter she had no energy to remove, the inside of the door was cool against her cheek.

She couldn't hear Mike burn, not through the door.

Except . . . she could.

THIRTEEN

WHEN RESSK CRAWLED INTO HER LINE of sight and pulled himself up onto his feet by the control panel, frantically pawing at the cover, Torin roused herself enough to lightly touch his shoulder.

"He's dead, Ressk."

"You don't know that!"

"I do." The filter hadn't moderated that final blast of heat and her lower lip, baked dry, split as she forced it to form words. "The firestorm hit as the door closed." She nodded at the line of char that marked the edge of the opening. "Concentrate on getting the inner door open."

"But . . ."

"He's dead," she said again, tasting blood. "Technical Sergeant Gucciard gave his life to save ours. He knew he was dead the moment he closed that connection." She'd seen that knowledge in his eyes; he'd chosen the manner of his death, sold his life for the highest price possible.

It was the kind of sacrifice Marines got medals for.

Posthumously.

"I should have gotten the door open!"

"Sarge said a piece was missing." Werst.

Torin turned and slid down the door until she was sitting, back against the barrier Mike had used to save them, broken blisters on her knees weeping fluid. "He said there was a piece missing in the controls?"

"Yeah."

Werst was on his feet, and Torin realized that he and Ressk were probably in the best shape of all of them. They'd gotten a ride from the prison. Kyster . . . Kyster was tucked in the cradle of Durlin Vertic's front legs but she'd deal with that in a minute.

"He looked into the panel," Werst continued. "Said there was a piece missing. When time ran out, he shoved his hand in."

"Sounds like you couldn't have gotten the door open, Ressk."

Behind the shimmer of the filter, his nose ridges were opening and closing so quickly they seemed to be fluttering. "It could have been my hand!"

"And then we'd be mourning you." She met Werst's gaze and knew they were both remembering another time, another life given. "Sucks to be the ones moving on without him, but he gave us that chance and we're not going to waste it. Go get the inner door open."

"But, Gunny . . ."

"That's an order, Corporal." She didn't wait to see if he obeyed, heard him move across the air lock as she sucked air through her teeth and dropped back onto her knees so she could reach Watura and flip him over onto his back. "Werst, I need a reading on the air quality."

He snorted, finally noticing her lack of uniform, glanced down at Watura and Darlys, and then down at his sleeve. Frowned. Slapped the fabric a time or two. "Uh, mine never worked, Gunny."

Right. She knew that. "Kichar?"

"I'm sorry, Gunny. It's fried."

"Wonderful. All right . . ." Watura's pulse was thready, but his heart was beating and his lungs were filling and he was alive. The rest would have to wait. It was only cool in the air lock in comparison, but it was enough to bring the di'Taykan some relief. ". . . help me get my uniform off him. His sleeve had protection for roughly half the distance, it might still work. Durlave, if you and Everim could strip Mashona's combats off Darlys."

"I've got it, Gunny." Mashona sat up and gasped. The blisters were less evident on her much darker skin but they were just as present.

"Let me." Freenim touched her lightly on the shoulder as he knelt by Darlys, Everim moving around to pull off her boots. Merinim sat slumped against one of the side walls blinking rapidly, the filter off her eyes but still covering her mouth and nose.

As Torin slid Watura's arm out of his vest, Kichar reached for the fasteners of his combats. "I've got it, Gunny."

Torin let her have it. Bracing one hand against the inside of the door, she stood and walked in a more-or-less straight line across to Durlin Vertic. Besides the damage to exposed skin, her back felt twisted, the ache radiating down into her right cheek, and it hurt to breathe deeply. "Sir. You're injured."

"Burned. Painful, but I will live."

"And Private Kyster?"

Her hand stroked Kyster's shoulder; it looked like she was petting him. "He stopped Helec'tin from destroying the control panel."

Helec'tin's claws scraped the floor as he shifted his weight, but Torin couldn't read his expression at all. She settled for demanding, "Why the hell would you want to do that?"

"I thought it would open."

"He did not think at all, he reacted," the durlin snapped. "It is a problem with our males! I should have been watching more closely!"

If Vertic wanted to take the blame, Torin wasn't going to stop her. She hissed out a breath as she dropped to one knee by Kyster's side and gently turned his head so she could get a better look at the bruising coming up on one side of his face. "You stopped Helec'tin? How?"

"He reared and I punched him in the balls." Before Torin could ask why, he added, "It was what you would have done."

Given their respective heights, probably not, but it was a sweet thought. His eye was likely to swell closed and from even a cursory examination of the damage, had he not had the Krai's nearly unbreakable bones, impact would have smashed his skull like a melon. "What can't I see?"

"He cannot lift his right arm."

His nose ridges flared. "I can!"

The durlin snorted. "It causes him pain to lift his right arm," she amended dryly. "See to your own injuries, Gunnery Sergeant. I will watch him."

"I'm not . . ." Actually, she was. "Yes, sir." As she started to straighten, Bertecnic was there, bending at the waist, a hand shoved under her arm. She didn't even begin a second protest, just let him help her up. Mashona was already standing and in spite of exhaustion, Torin didn't blame her—it was the only position where the blisters touched nothing.

This lock, like the other, was big enough for a skimmer, but with nine of them in there and two of them still flat on the floor, there wasn't much room to spray sealant.

"The Artek?" she asked as she pulled their second tube of sealant out of her vest.

"I believe they are dormant." Sanati knelt by Firiv'vrak, her ear pressed against the chiton. "I believe they chose to do this in order to survive."

"Can you wake them up?" She stepped over Darlys to get a better angle on Mashona's legs.

"No. I believe they will wake when conditions are favorable."

"Define favorable." When Sanati looked confused, Torin shook her head and tried another angle to get at Mashona's burns. "Never mind."

"Give it here, Gunny." Werst stood as Kichar peeled Torin's combats down Watura's legs. "I don't have to bend."

With the sealant on and air no longer hitting the broken blisters, the pain dropped to ignorable levels. Torin accepted her combats from Kichar, considered what would happen as they rubbed against the burns, and decided against putting them on.

"Besides," Mashona pointed out as she refused hers, "they reek of pheromones, and I'm in no shape to start an orgy. You owe me," she added, poking Darlys gently in the side with the toe of her boot.

The di'Taykan managed a weary obscene gesture. "I'm lying down."

Werst snorted and lifted Watura's arm. "Got a reading, Gunny. Same as at the prison, but CO_2 levels are rising."

"It's an air lock," Torin sighed. "They're notoriously underventilated. Ressk."

In answer, there was a hiss of air pressure balancing, a few eddies that didn't stink of sweat and blood and sulfur, and the interior door slid open.

Freenim held up a hand for silence and leaned just far enough out to peer up and down the corridor. "Empty." He started to pull the filter off and snarled out a string of words neither the slate nor Torin's implant bothered to translate as the band remained firmly attached to his skin.

Grunting as muscles pulled, Torin reached back, dug her fingers into the soft seal between the band and her skull, and dragged it off. "The hair probably helps to break the seal," she muttered, frowning at the amount of hair turned brittle in the heat that had broken off with the filter.

"Then it's just your hair, Gunny." Mashona had three fingers from each hand digging at the band, but it didn't budge.

It seemed that only Torin's came off easily. Even Merinim's with the actual filter hanging in tatters around the edges of her face seemed stuck tight.

"You checked each seal, Gunnery Sergeant," Durlin Vertic reminded them. "Perhaps they keyed to your touch."

"Then, if I may, Durlin . . . ?"

She inclined her head, giving Torin access to the back of the band. It didn't come off easily and a chunk of the Durlin's pelt came with it, but it came off.

"Fukking alien tech," Werst muttered as Torin tried to keep as much of his scalp as possible attached to his head. "Good thing you didn't cak it, Gunny or these fukkers'd be permanent."

"Hang on to them," the durlin ordered, tucking the filter into her vest as the two males helped her to her feet. She touched her right foot down, took a step, snarled, and curled the leg up against her belly. "We do not know what we will face in this building."

"I'm guessing tunnels," Werst snorted, rubbing his head.

The corridor outside the air lock looked like it could have been in any one of a hundred stations Torin had visited during her time in the Corps. There were two doors sharing the wall with the air lock entrance, another almost directly across from it, and one to the right of that.

Werst snorted again. "Or not."

"Ressk, get to work on that door." Torin nodded at the door across the hall. They needed to go deeper into the building to find the landing bay and that seemed to be the only route. "Mashona, Kichar, help Darlys and Watura. The rest of you make sure to move the Artek out of the air lock before the door closes and we can't get it open again."

"When will they wake up?" Kichar asked as she draped Darlys' arm across her shoulders.

Lifting the end of an exoskeleton, Freenim shrugged. "Because they keep so much to themselves, the details of their species are not well known even by those who also serve."

"But they will wake up?"

He grunted a little at the weight. "Probably."

"If they don't," Werst began.

"Allies," Torin reminded him. No need to be more specific; she knew exactly what he'd been about to say, and the Krai's eating habits were best kept within the Corps.

Before Werst could respond, the door across the hall opened.

"Fast work, Ressk." She crossed toward it, followed by Durlin Vertic, who waved everyone else back. Kyster followed anyway. Torin wasn't entirely certain if he was following her or the durlin.

Ressk shot a look of contempt at the control panel. "It wasn't locked, Gunny. It's just a pressure pad. Just had to get the cover off, then it doesn't get anymore straightforward. It's like we've got this far, and they've stopped messing with us." He smacked the side of his fist into the wall. "Too late for Technical Sergeant Gucciard, you bastards."

"Let's not punch inanimate objects until we've got a better idea of what's going on here," Torin suggested. "Don't forget what happened on Yenal's Five."

"What happened to you on Yenal's Five?" Durlin Vertic asked, and Torin remembered that the Polina had been among those they'd faced—although she hadn't known their species name at the time.

"A frustrated tech punched a hidden detonator and every piece of abandoned equipment on the field blew."

"Good."

Torin had to admit that was fair; they were her side's hidden detonators after all. Fair, but a bit tactless. "We lost a lot of good people there, Durlin."

"As did we."

The background noise dropped as they stared at each other for a long moment.

"No one wins," Torin said at last.

The durlin nodded. "Not that I have seen, Gunnery Sergeant."

They turned together to look through the open door.

Another control room. Similar but simpler than the one in the prison—fewer of the matte-green surfaces they'd assumed were screens and stools for only three operators.

"If there is a blast shield over that wall . . ." Durlin Vertic waved a hand at the apparently blank space over the main control panel. ". . . we need it down. We need to see what is in here."

"Ressk, Sanati."

"The sarge opened the other one."

"Corporal."

"Gunnery Sergeant?"

She jerked her head toward the control panel—partially because she didn't trust her voice and partially because she had nothing to say. Ressk was right, but Mike was dead, and they marched on because that was what they did.

No one wins.

Not that I've seen.

Her stomach growled, and she tried to remember the last time she'd eaten. They had half a biscuit each remaining although the water situation should have just reset. "Those stools say crew, and where there's crew there's facilities. We've already proved that once, people, prove it again."

The door to the left of the air lock opened onto crew quarters. Three lockers, two bunks—there'd be someone on watch at all times, and they were clearly hot-racking although Torin didn't see why, they had plenty of room. *Could include a species that sleeps standing up,* she thought checking the lockers. Empty. An interior door led to the head.

"Put the di'Taykan on those beds until they recover . . ." Neither di'Taykan managed innuendo and that, in and of itself was reason enough to get them lying down. ". . . then get the canteens refilled." She drank the last of the lukewarm fluid in hers and passed it over. They wouldn't die of thirst, but starvation was a very likely possibility unless they returned to the prison for more supplies in the next couple of days. "Splash a couple of bowls of water on the Artek, see if that brings them around." Then something occurred. "They don't melt or anything do they, Durlave?"

Freenim grinned. "Not as far as I know, Gunnery Sergeant."

"One Artek at a time," she amended.

"Gunny!" Ressk's voice was only just audible from the control room. Torin spent another moment missing her PCU before heading out of the crew quarters. Apparently everyone in their mismatched little squad had gotten a promotion recently since everyone but the di'Taykan and the Artek followed her. "Thought you might want to be here for this," Ressk continued as they entered the room, and he twisted what looked like an old-fashioned, delineated knob.

The blast shield went down—just as it had at the prison—exposing a window—just as it had at the prison. But the view . . .

Standing between Ressk and Sanati, Torin, Freenim, and Durlin Vertic leaned on the edge of the control panel and looked out.

"That's a landing bay."

Sanati nodded. "It is."

And looked down.

"That's a ship."

Ressk nodded. "It is."

Given the alien configuration—and Torin had to admit she was a little impressed by that given the constraints atmospheric entry put on ship design—it was impossible to tell what kind of a ship. Or even, from above, how large it was.

Torin took a deep breath, stomped down hard on the little voice that cried they were saved because they'd determined nothing of the sort, not yet. They'd be saved when they were unloading back on MidSector only to discover Finance had screwed up their back pay. She raised her voice to fill the room and spill out into the hall, the translation from the slate rising in counterpoint. "New job, people! Find the way to that ship!"

It didn't take long. Nothing they did worked on the door to the right of the control room, but the door to the right of the air lock opened onto a broad set of gray metal stairs. If Torin had to guess, she'd say they ended five floors down—and that was using floor as a measure of distance, not suggesting there were five actual floors. There were forty-two steps on each of the two spans they could see clearly, and they looked just a little higher than Human norm. The lights seemed dimmer than they did on the upper level, but that could have been the result of distance and tired eyes.

"As no one is looking forward to going down those and return-ing again," the durlin said from the doorway, "I suggest, Gunnery Sergeant, that you take those you want with you when you examine the ship. You may have Corporal Ressk and leave Durlave Kir Sanati working on the panel; the others are up to you."

"Yes, sir. I don't suppose you have a pilot with you?"

"Not that I am aware of."

"I believe Firiv'vrak has said she is a pilot, Durlin."

All heads turned toward Sanati.

Who shrugged. "When she told me, it did not seem relevant given our position underground without a vehicle."

"As I said . . ." The durlin's front claws twitched against the floor, but with her weight on only one back leg, she couldn't dig in the way she wanted to. ". . . not that I am aware of. Unfortunately, until Firiv'vrak regains consciousness, it would not matter if she were a *hydnograte,* so I fear the answer is no, Gunnery Sergeant, I do not currently have a pilot."

"Then there's no need for anyone but Ressk and me to make the climb."

"Durlin Vertic!" Everim pushed forward. "There should be one of our people there as well."

Vertic twisted her torso around until she could see him. "Why?"

"They could break the ship!"

Torin had a feeling the translation program missed sabotage al-though the more simplistic *break* was accurate enough.

"And also strand themselves? I do not think so."

"If he's going, Gunny, I'm going." Kichar shouldered her way through to Everim's side and glared at him. She wasn't tall for a Human, and he was the tallest of the Druin, so the shit-eye was happening on the level.

"Neither of you are going unless the durlin orders it," Torin snapped. "The slate stays here, and it'll create fewer misunderstandings if those heading down the stairs can understand each other."

"I agree." Arms folded, Durlin Vertic swept a flat unfriendly stare over those assembled. "Gunnery Sergeant, you and Corporal Ressk get started. Durlave Kan Freenim, I am certain that you will find plenty for these others to do."

"Yes, sir."

"But, Gunny!"

Torin sighed. "Do as you're told, Kichar."

The steps were wide enough that they could walk side by side. With no railings, Torin took the side nearest the wall. As a Krai—and a Krai who'd ridden over from the prison rather than run there on his own two bowed legs—Ressk was significantly less likely to fall. And a lot less comfortable given the depth of the stairs and the length of those legs.

"Gunny, do you mind if I take a short cut?"

"Be my guest. If it's actually shorter, I may follow you."

He flipped over the edge and began to descend under the stairs, swinging hand to foot from step to step.

"Or not." It was certainly faster. "Wait at the bottom before you try anything."

"I could start on the door."

"Wait." Not a tone he could argue with. She couldn't be positive he wouldn't take stupid risks, thinking that Mike's death meant he had something to prove. She could understand where he was coming from, sympathize even, but she sure as hell wasn't going to indulge it.

There were five floors. Forty-two steps per span. Two spans per floor. Eighty-four fukking steps per floor. The sound of her boots slamming down on the metal treads set up a complementary pounding in her head. Her knees were aching, the muscles in her calves were tight, and she wasn't entirely positive that she hadn't sweated the sealant right off the blisters by the time she reached the bottom. It sure as hell felt as if someone had rubbed salt into open wounds. The only bright side was that the air felt cooler against her exposed skin.

Ressk was standing by the door, hands locked behind his back, staring at the control panel. "It's not a pressure plate," he said without turning. "But I don't think it's much more complex."

"Good. Get the door open, then." Torin sat on the second step up, trying not to make it look too much like a controlled fall just in case Ressk turned. The metal was cool under her ass, separated from her skin by only by a thin layer of underwear, her combats having been abandoned on the end of Watura's bunk. Between the burns and the di'Taykan pheromones, she hadn't wanted them anywhere near her. Besides, without knowing what was under Durlin Vertic's vest, she was still one article of clothing up on her. Hell, three if she counted her socks. Five if she counted her boots. She'd won poker games with worse odds.

"Gunny?"

Ressk's voice shook her out of her reverie. The door was open.

It had been a mistake to sit. She had to pull the club from its loop on her vest and use it to push herself up onto her feet.

Standing just back of the threshold, Torin looked into the launch bay. She could feel the air moving past her, swirling around her legs. It was warmer than the air in the stairwell but not by much. It wasn't outside air, that was for damned sure. A quick glance up showed the top of the bay closed off with some kind of force shield.

"I wonder what's powering that?"

"Best guess," Ressk said dryly, "geothermic."

"Well, they've got enough of it. Smell anything on the breeze when the door opened?"

He snorted. "Nothing personal, Gunny, but all I can smell is you."

"How can that possibly not be personal?"

He frowned. "You don't smell edible?"

Her turn to snort. "Small mercies. Come on."

There were another forty-two steps leading down from the door onto the floor of the landing bay. Torin's boots seemed to get heavier with every step. As they reached level ground, she pointed over at the link waiting with open doors. "That's how we're getting back up."

"If I can make it work."

"It goes up and down, Ressk. How hard can it be?"

Looking at it on the level, the ship wasn't particularly large and had the charred look of a vessel that had been brought in through atmosphere more than a few times. Backs against the wall, they moved slowly along the starboard side. Except for the sounds of their footsteps and the distant hum of the roof, the launch bay was completely silent.

"I don't see anything that looks like a Susumi drive, Gunny."

"No. Neither do I. Doesn't mean there isn't one, though."

"The drive the Primacy uses looks a lot like ours."

"This isn't a Primacy ship."

Fortunately, the exterior hatch was open, or neither of them might have recognized it.

Before Torin could step on the ramp, Ressk pushed past her and walked halfway up it.

"Doesn't seem like security's enabled, Gunny."

"Pull a dumbass stunt like that again, Corporal," she told him tightly as she caught up, "and tripping an automatic security system will be the least of your worries."

His nose ridges closed. "I just . . ."

"I know." She gently touched his shoulder. "Don't do it again."

Toes of her boots just about to the edge of the hatch, Torin tossed her club into the air lock. The inner door was open, and there was nothing to indicate that the ship was using power in any way, but then again there was nothing that indications of power usage were mandatory. The club bounced on the deck, rocked a few times, and stilled.

It seemed safe.

The interior was unique but familiar enough to determine function. Two rows of six, three-meter benches standing up on their ends filled the main compartment. Enough light spilled in through the open hatch to examine the closer of the dozen benches. The deep gray surfaces weren't particularly well padded, but the dangling deep red straps suggested a safety harness, which suggested in turn that this was passenger seating.

"Check what's behind the hatch at the back," Torin said, heading up to the front of the compartment to examine the pilot's control panel. The narrow window above the single meter-by-two-meter panel let in enough light for her to see that the console looked nothing like the one on the *Promise* although there might be similarities a pilot could spot. The two stools, however, were identical to those in the control rooms. Stools told her that the ship used internal dampers. The pilot's console told her nothing at all. And Ressk told her that the space at the back of the ship was an empty cargo bay.

"So, no Susumi drive."

"I'm sorry, Gunny."

"Why? Did you remove it? You have nothing to apologize for."

"But we can't . . ."

"I know. And in no galaxy is that your fault." She ran her hands back through her hair, feeling more of it break off. "Does the ship even have power?"

Ressk examined the console, nose ridges opening and closing. "I don't actually want to touch anything."

"Yeah, well, neither of us wanted to get dumped on this burning shithole of a planet, so suck it up. We need to know."

"There might be an easy way . . ." He turned and headed out of the pilot's compartment.

"Ressk?"

"Hang on, Gunny. We'll know in a minute."

In less time than that, the lights came on. The ship had power.

"Good." She nodded as Ressk came back through the hatch. "If nothing else, maybe Firiv'vrak can figure out how to fly us back to the prison."

Ressk stared at her for a long minute. "Back? Why?"

"It's where the food is."

"If the bug gets into orbit . . ." He stared at her for another long moment, then shook his head, nose ridges closing. "No. Probably not." The bulkhead boomed, hammered by the side of his fist. "No way they'd have dumped us somewhere fukking convenient. Technical Sergeant Gucciard died for nothing."

"He died saving eighteen people from a firestorm."

"So we could die later."

"Later is always the preferred option, Corporal." Torin lightly touched the edge of the console where a bit of the shine had worn off. "Technical Sergeant Gucciard died buying us time."

"Gunny, if you're about to add that where there's life there's hope, please don't."

It hadn't occurred to her. It wasn't hope that kept her going, it was just that not going wasn't an option. She almost wished it was. Still, a few days catching up on her kibble consumption and it would be.

On the way out, Ressk paused by the air lock and the lights went out. When Torin threw a questioning glance in his direction, he reached up and slapped the wall to the right of the hatch. The lights came back on.

"There's a switch just inside the air lock?"

"There is."

"Well that's just . . ." Frowning, she slapped the spot and the lights went out. ". . . unoriginal."

"It's where every biocular sentient race installs it, Gunny. Everyone except for the H'san," he amended. "I saw a vid that told how they like to have the switch on the floor."

"Handier if you're carrying groceries," Torin agreed dryly, leading the way down the ramp.

"Do you think that's . . ." He ran to catch up. "Never mind."

The bulk of the ship kept them from being able to see anything but the upper corners of the window into the building's control room.

"You feel like they're watching you?" Ressk asked, scratching at a bit of peeling skin on the back of his head.

"They are watching us, Corporal." The link looked like it was functional. All the right lights were on. There was, however, only one way to be sure. She stepped in and waited. "Ressk?"

"I don't know, Gunny." A flick of his finger dislodged the dead skin from under his nail. "I mean, two buttons, one for up one for down and only two places it could go; it seems simple, but I gotta say, I don't trust simple."

"Four hundred and twenty stairs, Ressk. Counting those . . ." She nodded toward the forty-two at the end of the bay. "Four hundred and sixty-two. Against gravity. Each step a little higher than Human norm and one hell of a lot higher than Krai norm."

He shook his head, sighed, and stepped into the box. "Untried alien tech, Gunny. This is nuts."

"Four hundred and sixty-two steps," she repeated sagging against the burnished metal wall. "Do the honors."

Nose ridges flared, Ressk pushed the upper button.

Nothing happened immediately, then the light in the link flickered, and the door very slowly began to close.

"We could still jump out."

"Yes, we could."

They didn't. Ressk shifted his weight from foot to foot as they waited, but Torin didn't have the energy even for that. She couldn't remember the last time she'd been so tired. Or the last time she'd slept. Or, for that matter, the last time the lights had gone out.

Fuk!

First day here, she'd taken a stim and then forgotten about them. There was always a chance that the heat outside had destroyed their effectiveness, but there was equally a chance that the inner pocket in her vest had offered enough protection. Being able to pry them out of the packaging was a good sign. So was the familiar bitter flavor. Unfortunately, except for a nasty taste in her mouth, she didn't feel any different.

"Gunny?"

"What is it, Corporal?"

"When this is over, if we get out, they'll be the enemy again, won't they?"

The words in her mouth were *of course* because whatever happened between her Marines and certain members of the Primacy on this burning shithole of a planet had no effect on anything off this burning shithole of a planet. But the words that found their way out were, "Not mine."

"Gunny?" He didn't quite understand.

She wasn't entirely certain she did.

The door finally closed. The burnished metal box vibrated slightly.

"Just because it looks like a link," Ressk muttered, "doesn't mean it is one. It could be a decom chamber."

"Then we're clean."

"Or an oven."

"Then we're cooked."

"Or a disintegration box for garbage."

"Then we're dead." The doors opened onto the upper corridor. Torin pushed herself off the wall and stepped out. "But it's a link."

"There was no way you could have known," Ressk muttered, following her.

Torin turned just far enough to raise an eyebrow in his direction.

"Except that you're a gunnery sergeant," he amended. "Now what?"

"Now we tell the durlin that it appears to be a functional VTA, and while we might be able to get into orbit, without a Susumi drive that's the extent of our travel plans."

"I are not believing that you are finding seven planets out there and there are only being one with an atmosphere."

"They've all got atmosphere," Craig muttered as he ran the orbital equations one more time. "There's only one with a *breathable* atmosphere."

"And when you are saying breathable, you are being too generous."

"If you can go outside with only a filter, that counts as breathable in the larger scheme of things."

"Larger scheme." Presit folded her arms, sagged back against the bulkhead, and snorted. "I are not going outside in a filter. And I are not going outside and be cooked. That kind of heat are being very bad for the fur. You are needing to find another. There are being billions and billions of stars, so you are needing to create the equations to the next one."

The argument was old. The last bit about the equations, that was new.

"I need to what?"

She sighed, jumped down off the bunk, and crossed to stand beside him. "I've been thinking about the problem."

That worried him. That and the sudden use of Federate syntax.

"You are having long-range sensors, right?"

"Right."

"So you are gathering all the data possible and you are creating an equation for a very, very short jump. No farther than your sensors can see." A small black hand waved dismissively at the planet below. "If there are not something better than this, then you are doing it again."

Slipping in and out of Susumi space in small jumps . . . No pilot in their right mind would try something so fukking stupid, but if *Promise* could see the destination, then it wasn't exactly an open-ended equation because math worked in two directions. If he could describe where they were going, he could work the equation backward to determine where they were. "At that distance, we'd have nothing more than the grossest details." He couldn't believe he was actually considering it. "We wouldn't have the faintest fukking idea of what we'd jump out into."

"The Susumi wave would be pushing small stuff out of our way," Presit reminded him.

Craig snorted. "Some of that small stuff could be ships with other people on board."

"Enemies." She waved a hand dismissively, fur ruffling in the created breeze.

"How do you figure?"

"We are here because we are following Others' ships. So this are being Others' space. So ships are belonging to the enemy."

"That doesn't mean we can just destroy them."

"Excuse me, but I are believing that is exactly what enemy are meaning." She frowned, the silver pattern on her forehead folding into a stylized *M*. "I are believing you used to be a gambler. Did Gunnery Sergeant Kerr have your balls when she are dying? What are the worst thing that could happen?"

His chair creaked as he shifted his weight. "We die."

Presit shot a scathing look out at the planet. "I are not seeing much potential for a long life staying here."

She had a point. Actually, she had a number of them, and they were digging into his arm again. A hand around her wrist, he lifted her claws free and stared down at the seething mass of clouds below them.

Fuk it. He'd rather die in space. "All right."

"And that are meaning?"

"*You're* right." A flick of a finger brought the long-range sensors back on line.

She snorted. "And if you are realizing that sooner, we are being so much closer to home now and I are being so much closer to filing my story and— What are that?" Shoving past him, a bronzed claw tapped one of the screens where an equation flashed. "Are there a ship out there?"

"No, sensors are still locked on the planet. I hadn't redirected them yet."

"There are a ship on the planet?"

"No."

"You are not knowing what's on the planet?"

"I know." There wasn't enough air in the cabin. There wasn't enough room in his chest. He could actually feel himself start to sweat. "It's a salvage tag. It's one of *my* salvage tags."

Either the stim had worked on some level, or she was just too tired to sleep. Torin stood at the back of the control room, not so much watching Ressk and Sanati trying to work out the panel as staring over their heads into the launch bay. If they could get the force field open, and if Firiv'vrak ever woke up, they could use the VTA to hop back to the prison and get food. Then Firiv'vrak could take it up above the cloud cover and find out where they were. Maybe send a message if they could figure out the com system. Of course, the message would take years to get anywhere regardless of where it was sent, and figuring out the com system was a pretty big if.

Back to the prison for food seemed to be the best they had going. She'd lost two people getting this far and what had it gained them? Sweet fuk all. If they'd stayed in the prison, Mike and Jiyuu would still be alive. Maybe Ressk was right. Maybe Mike had sacrificed himself for nothing.

"I think the Artek are rousing." Freenim stepped into place beside her.

"You think?"

He shrugged. "They are large bugs. It is hard to tell for certain, but two of them seem to be breathing faster. And there is some leg movement." One set of fingers waggled patterns in the air. Torin didn't bother trying to interpret them. "Or not. Everyone else is asleep."

"Good."

"Your Private Kyster is lying with the durlin. I think she is taking him like her Ner."

"That's a pretty strong bond?" Torin guessed. Not exactly a long shot considering.

"Very strong. Although in this case, I think it is habit and wishful thinking. He was bonded to you?"

"No. Not like that. He'd been through some stuff and doesn't like to be alone."

Freenim shrugged again. "Who does? Why is your chest glowing?"

"Pardon?"

He pointed. "Your chest is glowing. It comes up through the neck of your vest."

Torin ducked her head but couldn't see anything. If her chest was glowing, there could be only one reason. Well, one reason she felt able to cope with. Frowning, she caught hold of the cord for the salvage tag and dragged it out. In the harsh light of the control room, it was just barely bright enough to see and still cool to the touch when she closed her fingers around the familiar shape. "I accidentally activated it a while ago. It's probably just playing out its program."

Torin? Can you hear me?

She didn't realize she'd sat down until she found herself on the floor, legs folded, staring down at the tag.

"Gunnery Sergeant?"

Torin? I'm reading your tag! Answer me, damn it!

Her hands were steady, but her tongue was trembling as she activated her implant. Had she been asked, she'd have said that tongues didn't tremble. Had she been asked, she'd have said that Craig Ryder was half a universe away. "Craig?"

The silence continued long enough that she started to think she'd imagined she'd heard him.

Then . . .

You're alive? His voice sounded like it had been shattered and badly reassembled. She wouldn't have imagined that. It had to be him. It had to be real.

"Gunnery Sergeant Kerr?"

Freenim, Ressk, and Sanati stood in a half circle, staring down at her. Reminding her that she was Gunnery Sergeant Kerr and not someone who'd just heard a voice she'd never expected to hear again. There'd be time to indulge that other person later. She took a deep breath, closed her fingers around the tag, and watched the light leak out between them. She sounded like Gunnery Sergeant Kerr. Mostly. "I certainly hope I'm alive because this would be one fukked afterlife if I wasn't. There's a ship in orbit," she added, having gained enough control of her expression to look up. Before her more immediate audience could speak, she held up a hand to cut them off. "You are in orbit, aren't you?"

They told me you were dead.

She could hear another break. Hear it hastily repaired. "Understandable mistake. We always believed the Primacy didn't take prisoners."

The who?

"The Primacy, it's what the Others call themselves. We always believed they didn't take prisoners."

"We do not," Freenim pointed out. Interesting that a "what the fuk" expression remained so similar regardless of facial features.

"Gunny's listening to her jaw implant," Ressk said slowly, nose ridges snapping open and snapping closed. "There's a ship in orbit."

"A ship?"

"A ship." He blinked, and his nose ridges stayed open. "Holy fuk! There's a ship in orbit! We're saved! We've got to . . ."

Torin reached out, grabbed a handful of his combats, and jerked him to a stop, shaking her head. When things seemed too good to be true, in her experience they usually were.

So the Primacy took you prisoner?

"No. The Primacy doesn't take prisoners. We're in a prison with the Primacy. Some of the members of the Primacy. Soldiers. Like us."

But who . . . ?

"No idea."

Okay, not the Primacy. There's a third side to this war?

"Space is big." She should probably stand, but she wasn't sure she could trust her knees. "What the hell are you doing here, Craig?"

They told me you were dead. Torin, the rock . . . the rock where you were standing was fukking melted. We went there, to Estee, to the planet where they said you died . . .

"We?"

Presit's with me.

No, you are being with me, or you are not getting to the planet where the gunnery sergeant are believed to be dying at all.

Fukking great. She was on an open com. "You went to the planet where they said I died," she prodded.

Yeah, we went, but . . . fuk, it was glass, no DNA, no nothing.

Glass? "How much glass?"

I don't remember . . . uh, thirty square kilometers, give or take. Why?

And just like that, Torin realized that she'd assumed the rest of Sh'quo company was alive. That Mashona and Ressk had been scooped up with her, but the rest were still on Estee, still fighting. "How many dead?"

The pause went on a little too long.

"Craig?"

Over seven hundred.

Her turn to sit silently. The others in the control room hadn't heard Craig's answer, but they'd heard her question. They knew what her reaction meant.

Torin?

Time enough to mourn later. Always time enough to mourn no matter how little time there was. She took a deep breath and let it out slowly. "You were on Estee. How did you get here?"

Three of the Others' battle cruisers showed up. We hid up behind the moon, and when they headed home, we used those suicidal equations Presit's old pilot worked out—remember them?—turns out Presit had hung onto them and lied to the military.

I are not needing to give them full disclosure.

Presit sounded sulky, and Torin had to close her teeth on a laugh that would have sounded hysterical.

Anyway, we hitched a ride on their Susumi trail. We got dumped in-system, though. No idea where the ships ended up.

"Are you out of your fukking mind?"

She heard him snicker; pictured him sitting back in that ratty, old control chair, heels up on the edge of the board. *Possibly.*

"So it's you and Presit in the *Promise*?"

Yeah.

Even if they could get to the *Promise*, two people in the cabin had to be more than a little friendly. Eighteen people, seven species, became a dirty joke.

The edge of the salvage tag cut into her palm. "You have to go get help, Craig."

Fuk that. You're not getting rid of me so easily. We're in uncharted space. There's no way of writing the equation that'll get us home.

She was almost glad to hear that. One small corner of her mind had played with the suspicion that the Elder Races were somehow involved and the prison was tucked away in an unfrequented corner of the Confederation. "There's no matching star charts in *Promise's* memory?"

None. I haven't the faintest fukking idea of where we are. I'm coming down.

"No!" That brought her up onto her feet so quickly abused joints screamed a protest and one of the blisters on her calf made a sucking sound as it detached from the floor. Grounding *Promise*, a ship with Susumi but no VTA capability would end everything. "We have a shuttle!"

A VTA? A way into orbit? So this prison you're in . . .

She felt his smile against her skin.

. . . is not exactly holding you?

They had an alien VTA locked behind a force field. Their only pilot was a comatose giant bug. In orbit was a two-person vessel, already holding two people, lost and unable to return to known space. "Not exactly," she agreed dryly. "Presit, do you have your camera?"

Of course I are having my camera!

"Good. Because, if nothing else, we have a story to tell."

We are being too far from a transmission satellite, Gunnery Sergeant. You may be telling your story, but there are no way to have it being heard."

"Craig can pulse it on *Promise's* emergency beacon."

If you are wanting just anyone to hear it, Presit snorted.

"I am." She wanted the whole fukking universe to hear it. "Freenim, get Durlin Vertic."

"You hear him in your jaw implant?"

"Yes, sir."

"Are you sure you hear him?"

"Yes, sir. If I were imagining his voice," Torin added when the durlin indicated she needed more convincing, "he'd be in a battleship and he wouldn't be lost." Nor would he be traveling with a reporter, particularly not Presit a Tur durValintrisy, the recurring fuzzy burr in Torin's butt.

"Then I believe you, Gunnery Sergeant." Eyes on Torin, vertical pupils nearly closed, Vertic's right hand worked the fur under the front edge of her vest. "Do you know what the odds are?"

"Sir?"

"The odds of this male arriving here, out of all the places he could have been in a vast universe, arriving with one who can record our last words. We have a saying among my people, space is big."

"We have the same saying, Durlin."

"We also say coincidence should be left to poets." She shifted her weight to scrape her claws against the deck, sucked a breath in through her teeth as she remembered the injury just a little too late. "He said the battlefield was glass?"

"Yes, sir."

"My people dead as well as yours."

Thirty square kilometers of glass made that likely.

"There was rumor of a weapon, untested, that . . ." A glance at the slate made it clear the pause was a search for a translatable term. ". . . unmade matter. The result was very like glass. The rumor was that a high number of the council were against ever using it."

"Seems like it got used."

"Yes."

"Your people dead as well as mine."

"Yes."

"It's past time this war ended."

Lips drawn back off her teeth, the durlin nodded. "Long past."

The lights flickered.

"Gunnery Sergeant Kerr! Durlin Vertic! We have the force field . . . Oh, fuk!"

The lights flickered again, then steadied.

"Down! We have the force field down!"

"Well done." The durlin moved slowly back out into the corridor, still on three legs. "Now, we need a pilot."

Firiv'vrak rose unsteadily onto her feet and swayed in place for a moment struggling to lift her antennae up off her body. She shuffled forward a few steps, got tangled in her own legs, and toppled into Sanati's arms. After Sanati, clicking sympathetically, set her back on her feet, she turned and swept the feathered tips of her antennae slowly just under the edge of the upper chitin plates of the other two Artek. One of them kicked out and made a noise like a malfunctioning pressure suit. The other didn't move.

Grief smelled like burning spices—pungent and unpleasant. Species with nictitating membranes used them, the rest wiped watering eyes and watched as the two living Artek dragged the third into the stairwell, away from prying eyes, and devoured her.

"They shouldn't get to eat it all," Kyster muttered, clenched fist rubbing at his stomach as Kichar handed around the last pieces of biscuit and everyone but the Krai tried not to hear the faint crack of chewed chitin.

"It is how the Artek honor their dead," the durlin told him.

"It's how the Krai honor our dead, too. If Darlys dies, can I eat her?"

"She is not Krai."

"It doesn't matter," Torin answered before Kyster could. "We do what we must to stay alive."

Head cocked, the durlin looked from Torin to the Marines sitting beside her. "Is that what your Corps believes?"

"It's what I believe."

Kyster stared down at half a biscuit. "I don't want to be last, Gunny. I don't want to be alone again."

Torin had nothing left to give him.

"Don't worry about it, kid." Werst dropped a chunk of biscuit into his bowl of water and glared at it until it began to dissolve. "I have every intention of being too fukking tough to die."

Kyster seemed to find that comforting.

A giant bug? Weren't they trying to kill us last time we met?

"That was then. She's the only pilot we've got."

And what am I?

"In orbit."

Right. She listened to him breathe for a few minutes, the sound inside her head like it was a part of her. *They told me you were dead.*

Torin wiped blood off on her vest from where the edge of the tag had cut into her palm. "I know."

"Who is he?"

"Jealous, kid?"

Kyster showed teeth.

"Thought so," Werst snorted. "He's a Civilian Salvage Operator. Guy who found Big Yellow by screwing up a Susumi equation."

"And now he's here."

"Gunny says he is." Werst's tone suggested that was good enough for him.

"You don't find that weird?"

"Bit."

"Maybe it's love."

They glanced up at Mashona together. "Love finds a way," she said as she passed. "That's what the songs say."

"What songs?" Confused, Kyster turned his attention back to Werst. Who snorted again. "Humans. Who the fuk knows?"

Firiv'vrak seemed neither impressed nor particularly intimidated by the VTA. She wedged her abdomen between the two stools and began tapping her upper four limbs and both antennae over the screens. Once or twice she flicked a switch and just as quickly flicked it off again.

Either determination smelled like singed insulation, or one of the switches hadn't been shut off quite quickly enough.

When she finally got the pilot's console on-line, it gave Ressk and Sanati access to whole new sections of the control panel.

"If Firiv'vrak can get it off the ground, we can reverse those equations and use them to dock her again."

Down in the docking bay, the VTA roared, rose up about a half a meter, and dropped again. Torin could feel the vibration through the soles of her feet.

"If she can get it off the ground," Ressk repeated, picking at the flaking skin on his jaw.

"How far can she drop that thing before she does some actual damage?"

"No idea, Gunny." They winced in unison as the bow rose, fell, and the whole ship rocked. "But it seems pretty sturdy. She says the design's damned near idiot proof."

The stern rose and fell.

"Did something just go *poink*?" Torin asked. "Because, generally, that's not a good sound."

I met your father. At Ventris.
Torin thought about that for a minute. Tried to imagine the meeting. "You get along?"
He didn't believe you were dead either.
Of course he didn't.

They were completely out of food by the time Firiv'vrak got the VTA up into the air. Where completely meant they'd fed the handles of the stone clubs to the Krai, remembering finally that Harnett's people had made them out of the kibble

Torin fought the urge to yell over the roar of the VTA's main engines kicking the cloud cover around about a hundred meters above the building. "She's on her way."

Joy.

"Just get Presit and her equipment down here. This is important."

What about me and my equipment?

"We need *Promise's* emergency pulse to broadcast."

Nice to be needed.

Torin could hear his grin. He thought she was kidding, but sex was the last thing on her mind. Presit, she expected to show up uninvited, but Craig—that was still a bit surreal.

"I know what you're doing, Gunny." The whites of Mashona's eyes had gone yellow. Torin couldn't remember when it had happened. "You're sending out our last will and testament, aren't you? Letting the Corps know how we died."

"We're not dead yet, Corporal."

But they both knew it was only a matter of time. Only Darlys continued to watch Torin with hope. Even Kichar had decided her time was better spent scowling at Everim.

Presit peered out the hatch at the undulating tube attaching the *Promise* to the VTA and crossed her arms with enough emphasis they compacted the fur under her HE suit and disappeared into a fold in the orange fabric. "I are not going into that."

"It's exactly the same tube you used to get off Big Yellow," Craig snarled. He briefly considered tucking her under one arm but decided he'd rather survive the trip.

"And Big Yellow are such a happy memory!"

"You're about to break a story about a third force in known space, a group that's imprisoning our people and the Others—no, the Primacy—and you're worried about what?"

Under the faceplate, her lip curled. "Nothing." She pushed herself forward, sliding headfirst down the tube as though she actually knew what she was doing in zero G.

Maybe she did.

Picking up the camera, Craig adjusted the bag hanging off his shoulder, and followed.

They still didn't know where the fuk they were, and they still had no way to get home—even for enormous fukking values of *home*. They were entering a VTA designed by unknown and evidently unfriendly aliens piloted by a giant bug who, last time out, had been trying to kill them. They were about to land on a surface that was the fukking poster planet for unstable geology with no real plan for leaving again.

But Torin was alive.

So who the fuk cared about the rest of it?

They'd been on minimal calories for a while. Even with sufficient water, that made a difference. Torin gave the di'Taykan, who hadn't completely recovered from their collapse after the run between buildings, two tendays. No more. The three surviving Humans, maybe another tenday. Maybe not. None of them had been carrying extra body fat when they arrived. The Krai, with their flexible definition of food, would live the longest. As for the others, Torin had no idea, but the teeth on the Polina seemed to suggest a willingness to crack bone for marrow. Except Durlin Vertic had lost her fur about five centimeters around the burns, and the skin underneath it was an angry red and hot to the touch. She had a chance if it didn't go septic. If it did . . .

Kyster spent a lot of his time limping between the durlin and the taps, bringing her water and shoving the two males out of his way—he'd acquired status with that punch in the balls. Once again, some things were universal.

Kichar and Everim were fighting. Yelling about old battles, the slate between them and the soldiers around them taking no side in the fight. Eventually, yelling would escalate to shoving and someone would break it up. Torin wondered what would happen when no one bothered. A broken body at the bottom of the stairs would keep the Krai alive longer.

When Firiv'vrak got back, they'd send her to the prison for kibble.

And biscuits. And maybe they'd all go back to the prison. Presit could reach the *Promise* just as easily from there.

"Incoming!" Ressk and Sanati were the only ones left showing any real interest in the world around them, and their focus had tightened to discovering the mysteries of the control panel.

The building began to vibrate.

Torin moved over to stand beside them.

"You sure you want to be so close to the window, Gunny?" Ressk plucked at her vest. "We're only mostly sure we've got the landing sequence worked out."

"I'm sure."

FOURTEEN

THE SEATS WERE BENCHES PROPPED up at an angle. A couple of the straps on the safety harness were more than a little suggestive of possible alternative uses, the kind that involved slick and a willing partner. The actual pilot's console looked vaguely familiar and, all things considered, that wasn't right.

Teeth exposed, Presit spent most of the trip trilling at their pilot in Katrien. The pilot had less chance than a boil on a bug's arse of understanding her—hell, Craig'd been spending more time shepherding the reporter around the universe than he wanted to think about and he didn't understand her—but at least one of the patterns those antennae were making in response was definitely rude. Turned out some gestures really did cross species lines.

Gravity took care of getting the VTA back into the atmosphere. It wasn't exactly rocket science; rocks did it all the time. Landing, though, landing became a bit tricky if survival got taken into account. And he needed to survive this.

Torin wasn't dead.

She was Gunnery Sergeant Torin Kerr; she didn't just fukking die. He never should have doubted that.

And the little voice of reason that kept saying, *well, this is just fukking wonderful, mate, now you two can die together,* was easy enough to ignore.

Mostly because the odds seemed good the landing was going to kill him.

"Hey! Uh . . . Firivak! Not that I'm criticizing, but we're coming in a bit steep! And fast! And . . . holy crap!" He clenched his teeth before he bit off the end of his tongue. The last time he'd had a ride this rough, there was a set of twins involved.

"You okay?"

Torin's voice in his military surplus PCU sounded distant. Flat.

"Rough ride," he growled without relaxing his jaw.

"You're thinking about the twins, aren't you?"

"Might be." That had sounded more like Torin.

"Relax. The landing bay is guiding you in."

"Landing bay know there's meat on board?"

"Oh, please, you are not to be talking about your penis again!"

"I didn't quite catch that."

Craig shot Presit a look that made her snicker. Definitely time to work up a new intimidating expression. "It was nothing."

"All right, then."

Except *all right, then* sounded more like *whatever*. Torin fighting her way out of an impossible situation and taking her people out with her, that was business as usual. A Torin who didn't much care, that was wrong. It was true what they said about coming back from the dead—it changed a person.

The shield came up over the window automatically as the VTA hit the brakes, filling the landing bay with smoke and flame. On the single screen they had functioning, the bay looked a lot like the surface of the planet. Smoke and flame.

Torin?

"Coolant, then force field, then the air lock opens. You know the drill."

Yeah, okay, anxious to get out of this antique torture implement but mostly just making sure you were still there. Hate to have come all the way from the back of Bourke and crushed you during that fukking disaster of a landing!

He was shouting by the end, probably so that Firiv'vrak could hear him.

"You all right?"

Fine.

She thought about calling him on the lie. Didn't. "Firiv'vrak?" No need to ask about Presit. If the reporter had sustained any damage, Torin would hear about it.

*Who? Oh, right, Frivark, hang on. Oh, crap . . . *

Not a situation where an expletive followed by an extended pause was likely to be good news.

Torin? She's lost a leg.

"Lost it?"

Yeah, it's lying there on the deck. Not much blood, though, and she seems to be . . . Ow! Hey, watch it with the snapping claws, I'm helping here!

The shield came down as the smoke cleared. Torin caught one quick glimpse of the VTA, scorched but intact, and then the bay filled with billowing clouds of white vapor.

"Sanati, Firiv'vrak has lost a leg."

The Druin leaned toward the window, as though she were trying to peer through the coolant and right into the VTA, then turned to frown at Torin. "How did she lose it in the ship? It is not that large a ship."

"Not misplaced. It's no longer attached to her body."

"I understand—removed!" Sanati nodded, pleased to have worked it out. "If the trauma to her body is not great, in time the leg will regrow."

Cross-species definitions of trauma aside, Torin doubted Firiv'vrak had the time. Given that she had no more time than any of them.

"After there are being the all but crash landing of an alien spaceship," Presit muttered stepping into the link, "why *not* be taking the risk of yet more alien technology."

Craig shuffled to the back of the elevator and tucked the duffel he was carrying into the corner, giving Firivert as much room as possible. "You want to climb five flights of stairs, knock your furry self out."

"I are not wanting to climb," she snorted. "I are just saying that this are being a stupid way to die, all things being considered."

❊   ❊   ❊

They'd tell the universe that prisoners had been taken from both sides. They'd tell that during the escape, enemies had become allies. Mashona was wrong. Torin didn't want the reporter to broadcast a last will and testament, she wanted Presit to send out a warning.

Once that was done, she could . . .

She stared down at her hands as she walked out into the corridor. Curled them into fists. The skin stretched across her knuckles split, clear fluid seeping from the wounds.

Just get the warning out.

Nothing else mattered.

The link opened onto a corridor that could have been on half a hundred stations. Firivink scurried out—and fuk political correctness, bugs scurried—then Presit moved to stand in the open door. And waited.

Craig's palms were sweating inside his HE suit. Nothing else, just his palms. He couldn't seem to make his legs work. Torin was dead. This was some sick joke the universe was playing on him.

"I are not waiting forever while you are getting your head out of your ass," Presit snapped, flipping her hood off and sliding her dark glasses onto her muzzle. "Move!"

He didn't seem to have any other options.

As he stepped forward, she glanced over her shoulder and her lip curled. "Camera! It are not being carried for decoration!"

Ah. She wasn't waiting for him; she was waiting for her close-up.

He lifted it to his shoulder, hit record, picked up his duffel, and followed her out of the lift.

Firverk had gone to join another giant bug. There were two species he'd never seen before—three of a cat/Human combo and four bald, black-eyed, squishy-faced bipeds. So that was the enemy. They didn't look like much. Three Krai—one of them with a swollen eye sticking pretty close to the cat/Human alien who seemed to be injured. Two di'Taykan who looked like shit, like part of their fuk-king hair had been melted, and three Humans. Torin and two other women.

Torin and one of the squishy-faced bipeds were the only ones standing. The others weren't so much sitting as in various states of collapse against the wall.

Torin.

Alive.

Thinner. Obviously thinner given she was wearing her combat vest over boots and underwear. The broken blisters weeping on the reddened skin of her arms and legs explained the lack of clothing. Wouldn't want to put clothing on over that. How the hell had she got them in the first place, though? There was also a pattern of scabs about three centimeters across down the entire length of her right leg. She didn't seem to be in pain, but then, she never did. Her hair looked fried. Frazzled.

There was fresh blood on her lips but old shadows under her eyes. She was staring at him. She was alive. But in some weird way that had nothing to do with her injuries, she didn't look like herself. She looked . . . beaten.

Grateful she couldn't see his fingers trembling inside the gloves—because she'd never let him live it down—he flipped the shoulder catches open and pushed his helmet back.

It could have been anyone in the HE suit. Well, anyone willing to wear a ten-year-old design with a gray patch on the right shoulder and a stain on the left knee he refused to explain. That narrowed the list, admittedly, but still, it could have been anyone.

Then he or whoever it was, reached for the shoulder catches and pushed the helmet back.

Craig had blue eyes. Really amazingly blue—not gray or blu*ish* but summer sky on a planet with a decent O2-level blue. When she'd seen him last, he'd just shaved off his beard—it came and went according to whim—but the reddish-brown scruff on his jaw had moved beyond stubble, so maybe he was growing it back. It was long enough she almost couldn't make out the dimple in his chin.

He was staring.

What the hell was he doing *here*?

He gone to see where she'd died—she'd deal with that later—and then used Presit's hello-I'm-a-suicidal-egomaniac equations to follow three of the enemy's battleships into Susumi space, got ditched, found this planet, and, finally, found her by way of a salvage tag she'd accidentally activated.

What the hell was *he* doing here?

Didn't matter how she asked the question, she didn't like the answer.

At all.

She was a Marine. She didn't fukking believe in coincidence.

Craig heard Presit's narration voice droning on in the background without really listening. The scent of unwashed bodies filled the corridor, unwashed bodies with a faint underlay of burning apples and cinnamon.

He had more brains than to gather Torin up in his arms and murmur sweet nothings into what was left of her hair. That wouldn't end well. And he hadn't expected her to run toward him in slow motion or some such shit, but he had expected more than the thousand-yard stare that had greeted him.

Sort of. When he hadn't expected her to be dead after all and him the butt of a cosmic joke.

Then Torin's eyes narrowed.

Her chin rose.

Her shoulders straightened.

Her upper lip pulled back off her teeth.

He knew that expression; she was pissed.

He didn't know what she was pissed about, and the odds were good he'd catch shit later for grinning like a shot fox in response, but he couldn't help it. Pissed was good. Pissed meant Torin was back.

"Listen up, people! I want those filters in a pile." Torin yanked the one she'd worn across the lava field out of the loop on her vest and threw it to the floor. "Right here."

"Gunny?"

Mashona asked the question. Torin looked at Kichar as she answered it.

"Because it takes a certain minimum mass before the fukkers start thinking."

Kichar's cheeks paled. "Major Svensson's arm."

Exhaustion and hunger toned down Mashona's eye roll, but she gave it all she had. "You want to fill the rest of us in, Kichar?"

When Torin nodded, the younger Marine took a deep breath and rubbed her palms against her thighs. "The aliens, the ones that were Big Yellow, the ones that they've been looking for inside the Confederation, they were in Major Svensson's arm on Crucible. Gunnery Sergeant Kerr had his arm cut off . . ."

The Polina and Werst looked as though they approved.

". . . Dr. Sloan said there weren't enough pieces of the alien in the arm to be a person, so they had to wait until more oozed out of his body."

"Which is why I want the filters in a pile," Torin finished. "Now!"

No one had the energy to actually jump, but the pile of filters began to grow. Although they remained nothing more than a pile of filters.

"Torin?"

She looked at Craig then, really looked at him. And thought seriously about destroying an entire species because it had placed him in danger. "This . . ." A hand wave between them. ". . . this isn't coincidence. Before you showed up here, with her, this place made no sense, but we didn't expect it to. But you being here, with her, that sort of shit doesn't just happen." Using the edge of her boot, she shoved a filter closer to the rest. "This is a setup."

"You're saying Big Yellow set this up? Built a prison, built a landing site, brought you here, brought me and her here?"

"That's what I'm saying."

He snickered, raised a hand when she glared. "No, it's just that your father suggested something remarkably similar to High Tekamal Louden and she shot him down."

"My father and High Tekamal Louden?"

"At Ventris, when we went out for a drink. We thought you were dead," he reminded her. "He's . . ." Suddenly realizing they had an audience, Craig backed up a step. "We've got a shitload to talk over,

Torin, but right now tell me why you think Big Yellow would set something like this up."

"Why?"

"Yeah."

"That's what I intend to find out."

"You are finding out from filters?" Presit snorted, circling the pile as though daring it to be newsworthy. "I are thinking this terrible, *terrible* experience are affecting your mind."

Torin reached out, wrapped a hand around the camera, pointed it away from her face and back down at the pile, then addressed her response to Craig. "You found the plaque in General Morris' office because the aliens reacted to you. I could fit the filters when no one else could."

He shook his head. "You have more experience."

She glanced over at Freenim. "Not really, no. And they're the only things from this place we carried from the other building. They were there to keep an eye on us while we crossed."

"Uh, Gunny. The bowls . . ." Kyster held his up. "They're from here, too."

The slight pressure of the bowl tucked in under her vest had become so familiar in such a short time she'd forgotten she was carrying it. "You're right."

Kyster preened. Kichar and Darlys glared down at the top of his head. That both the Marines and the Primacy carried identical items only made Torin more convinced. She didn't have to look to know this new bit of information had convinced no one else, but that didn't matter. "Throw the bowls in. And the rope."

The pile grew. And remained a pile of filters and bowls and a coiled length of rope.

"Torin . . ."

"Wait!" She felt more than saw Craig flinch. She'd deal with him. With that. With them. Later.

"Gunnery Sergeant Torin Kerr are exhibiting signs of stress induced by . . ."

"Unless you'd like to exhibit signs induced by my boot making contact with your ass," Torin snarled, "you'll limit your reporting to what's actually happening."

Presit smiled, showing a mouthful of sharp, pointed teeth. "Nothing are actually happening."

"Technical Sergeant Gucciard." Ressk offered. "He was wearing his filter, it's still out there. So's his bowl"

"We ate the ties that held the rocks to the clubs," Kyster added, glancing over at the Druin. "And the slings."

"I don't think that's it." Torin glared down at the pile, as though she could force it to change by the power of her mind.

Of her mind . . .

"Twenty-seven percent of the polyhydroxide alcoholyde in the major's arm has migrated—primarily to his nervous system."

There were two gray tear tracks running in narrow lines from the inside corners of the major's eyes down toward the corners of his mouth, the tracks ignoring the way gravity worked on liquid.

When Torin looked up again, Kyster covered his teeth and took a step back into the circle of Durlin Vertic's arms.

Torin didn't want to know what part of her expression had frightened him. "Get out of my head!"

"Torin . . ."

The concern in Craig's voice nearly undid her, but she pushed past the need to reassure him. Teeth clenched, breathing heavily through her nose, she squeezed her eyes shut and then opened them again. She knew she was right and, hopefully, that would be enough to move them. "Get. Out. Of. My. Head!"

"She are having lost it." Presit nodded in a satisfied sort of way, as though she'd expected this to happen all along.

"No, she's . . . she's crying." But the tears were gray. Thrusting the camera at the reporter and operating on muscle memory alone because every brain cell in his head was dealing with the two lines of gray slowly moving down Torin's cheeks, Craig struggled to pull the HE suit open so he could get his arms free. More specifically, get his hands free of the gloves.

When he reached for her, she shook her head—a minimal movement that caused both lines to wobble slightly. "Not me. Them."

She was furious. And she was terrified. He doubted anyone else could see it—he doubted anyone else had been allowed to see as far past the gunnery sergeant although Werst was staring at her in a way that suggested he might suspect.

As the lower edge of the lines reached Torin's jaw, Craig touched the skin just below, ignoring the way his fingers were trembling. The slightly thicker drop at both ends simultaneously rose up, touched him lightly—he had the damnedest idea that they were confirming his identity—then, in a movement almost too fast to follow, wrapped around his fingers, the ends sliding out of Torin's eyes.

When he touched his fingers together, they merged—again, too fast to follow—into one gray lump on the index finger of his right hand—slightly warm but not large enough for him to feel the weight.

His skin crawled. The urge to flick his hand while yelling *"Get it off me!"* was strong.

Torin stared at the gray band around Craig's finger. That had been in her brain. In her brain and possibly influencing her actions since she'd been sucked through the floor on Big Yellow. The ship—or rather the aliens that had made up the ship—had used her memories to run her recon team through its tests, but no one had ever suspected it had left something behind.

When it became known that the aliens had infiltrated the Confederation, when Craig and Presit had finally convinced the Corps of the existence and subsequent disappearance of Big Yellow's escape pod, when the geek squad had announced that Big Yellow and therefore its escape pod were not actually things but were made up of a polynumerous molecular species that was essentially a sentient organic plastic, then all active members of the military had been among the first tested for the molecular disturbance that indicated they'd been probed by the alien. Torin had no idea how many members of both branches had tested positive, but she did know that the brains of her recon team, Werst among them, and the brains of everyone on the *Berganitan* had contained a specific protein marker. Given that it was known their memories had been adjusted so that they'd forget the escape pod existed, a logical assumption was made that the memory adjustment was what the marker indicated.

Torin, who remembered, did not have the marker although she did have a different marker that the science team had assumed correlated to being deep scanned.

Seemed that marker was actually a diversion. Or the marker was the alien and the molecular disturbance only occurred if it had been and left. Who the hell knew at this point?

It also seemed that while the alien was on the move creating intraneural connections, it was a lot easier to spot. Made sense; troops on the move were easier to see than troops dug in. A polynumerous molecular species engaging in aberrant molecular activity was easier to spot than than a polynumerous molecular species just sitting around and shooting the shit with the original brain cells.

Point was, it had been in her fukking brain!

"Torin?"

The only sound she could hear was the durlin's labored breathing. "Put it in the pile."

"You don't want . . ."

. . . to do it yourself? So obvious what Craig had been going to ask. She wanted to walk it out the air lock and drop it off into a lava pit. She wanted to watch it burn. She wanted to destroy it. All of it. Not just this piece. But especially this piece. Her hands were clenched so tightly she could feel her broken fingernails trying to dig into her palms. "You do it."

The lava fields were evident in her voice.

"Why don't we just destroy the fukker?"

"No." She wanted answers more than revenge.

He nodded grimly. "After, then." Bending, he flicked his finger at the pile.

"Like an economy-sized booger," Mashona observed as the gray blob slapped against the side of a bowl, slid down the curve, and disappeared.

Everim began to snicker, then cut it off short as Kichar turned to glare at him.

"Is that . . ." Darlys drew in a deep, rattling breath and tried again. "Is that why you didn't give up? Because that . . . was in your head?"

"She didn't give up," Werst snarled before Torin could respond, "because she's a gunnery sergeant. They don't know what give up means."

"But . . . that was . . . in her head."

"Yeah, and it's probably been drawing hazardous duty pay."

"There." Freenim pointed to the center of the pile where the edges of the bowls were beginning to fold in. "They are melting."

"Not exactly melting," Torin growled.

The actual change happened too fast too make out each individual metamorphosis. One moment there were bowls and filters, the next moment their shapes became indistinct, and the moment after that there was a gray mass ebbing and flowing but not actually defining itself in the place they'd been.

"If it can be anything, why does it choose to be gray?" Watura's voice sounded as though he'd been gargling knives, but he was on his feet and glaring down at the alien. The parts of his hair still able to move were flicking angrily back and forth.

"Gray is neutral," Merinim offered.

"Nothing fukking neutral about those things," Torin snarled.

"Is that enough to make it a person?" Kichar asked.

"It should be."

There was more alien gathered together here, all in one place, than there'd been on Crucible.

"What are it waiting for?" Mulitple peaks rose and swiveled toward Presit as she stepped in for a closer look.

Good question.

The floor touched her chin. It felt cool. She couldn't smell anything but the smoke she'd inhaled before she got the filter on. Since she couldn't move her head, she stared into Ryder's eyes. They really were the most remarkable blue. Pity his nose was running into all that facial hair.

"I wasn't the only person to go through the floor in Big Yellow."

All eyes turned with Torin's.

Craig shook his head. "I was scanned. I was one of the first scanned and they found the protein marker."

"The same protein marker they found in me."

"Yeah, that said we'd been deep scanned."

"The geek squad thought it meant we'd been deep scanned. Maybe it did." Taking Craig's jaw in her hand, barely aware of the warmth of his fingers closing around her wrist, she stared into his eyes, looking past the roiling mix of emotions he wasn't trying to hide and said, "Out. Now." She didn't raise her voice, she didn't imply consequences, she merely left no space around the words for the possibility of not being obeyed.

"You are also having aliens in your head!" Torin felt Presit's ruff brush against her thigh and knew without looking that the reporter was leaning in between them, trying to get a better angle at Craig's face. Since the camera's angle remained fine, Torin didn't move to give her room. "I are telling you that you are messing with the panel before we jump, but you are not believing me. And I are right."

"Just make sure you record this." Craig's mouth barely moved as the gray swelled out of his tear ducts and the fingers around Torin's wrist tightened past the point of pain. No problem. She'd cope with a few more bruises.

"Please. I are knowing how to do my job," Presit reminded him with a disdainful sniff. A small, HE-clad finger poked Torin's hip. "You are better getting that before it are reaching his beard."

A small part of Torin had to give Presit credit for maintaining attitude in the face of truly fukking weird. She lifted the hand Craig still held, letting his breath slide warm across her palm for just a moment, then lifted her other hand to the other side of his face and mirrored what he'd done—one finger to the end of each of the lines.

She half expected them to feel wet, like actual tears, although experience said they wouldn't. She expected them to feel different from the last of the aliens that had poured out of Major Svensson. They'd been a part of Craig for a lot longer. They didn't feel wet. They didn't feel different. They didn't feel like a part of Craig. They felt like nothing at all.

Blisters protesting as the skin shifted, Torin squatted and stretched her finger toward the roiling mass on the floor. One of the peaks elongated. Then it flicked forward too fast to really see, and the gray glob on her finger was gone.

Hands slapped against uniforms as, behind her, everyone reached for the weapons they weren't carrying.

"I fukking hate tentacles," Werst muttered.

Sucking air in through her teeth, Torin straightened. "Presit."

"I are recording."

"Give the camera to Craig."

"You are not telling me what to . . ."

"You went through the floor on Big Yellow as well."

This time the silence was so complete the only sound was a barely audible swoosh that had to be coming from the alien's movement. Another tentacle rose and was reabsorbed. Werst mimed shooting it.

Presit broke the silence with a snort. "Oh, no. I are not having that thing in my brain. I are having . . ."

"The same markers Craig and I had."

"Yes and no. I are tested." She handed the camera off to Craig but then stepped back quickly and flipped the hood of her HE suit back up. "You are having aliens and he are having aliens in your brains—being lovers who are reuniting and are discovering the way to be saving the day. Very romantic. I are not having aliens in my brain, so you are getting away from me! I are not having . . ." Her back impacted with Mashona's legs, and the Marine took a firm grip on her shoulders.

Torin crouched again so she could get up close and personal with the reporter's faceplate. Behind it, she could see her reflection in the mirrored glasses Presit hadn't taken the time to remove. "Helmet off," she said quietly. "You're not reporting the story anymore; you're a part of it."

"I are not a part of this!"

"Take the helmet off, or I'll take it off you, hold you upside down, and squeeze the fukking aliens out of your head."

"You would not be daring!"

Torin allowed just exactly what she would dare to show on her face.

Presit flipped the helmet back down and with trembling hands—the movement visible even through the HE suit—reached up and pulled off her glasses. "This are exactly why my people are arguing against allowing the Younger Races into the Confederation," she muttered. "If it are soaking into my fur, I are never forgiving you!"

"That's fair."

This time the alien didn't emerge from tear ducts but appeared as a faint gray film over the dark gleam of Presit's eyes. As Torin moved her index fingers carefully in toward the curve, she thought it looked as though the reporter had gone temporarily blind. Couldn't have, though, or they'd have all heard about it. The Katrien as a species didn't tend to suffer in silence. The gray film rose out toward her finger like tenting fabric then, with a faint sucking sound, came free.

Not bothering to combine them, Torin flicked the two new pieces of alien—the two new collections of a polynumerous molecular species—into the waiting pile.

The pile sank down, flattening into a disk about a meter and a half in diameter, the edges fluttering like the propulsion unit on one of the more showy species in the Methane Alliance. Maybe it was telling them something, but Torin suspected it was merely regrouping and sharing information.

"So what do we do now?" Craig was a warm, solid presence by her side.

She needed him to move away. Needed him to not stand so close that he was a distraction. Needed him to move because she couldn't. Couldn't tell him that either, so all she said was, "We wait for it to tell us what the fuk is going on."

"What makes you think it's going to?"

"It's still there. If it didn't want to talk to us, it sure as shit wouldn't have stayed around. This stuff is fast, and it can break into pieces too small for the naked eye to see."

"It's still not talking to us."

"Give it time."

"Gunny, on Crucible you had Iful make the alien a voice."

"Yes, I did, Kichar, but it wasn't necessary. Evidence is that these things can mimic cellular structure so perfectly they can't be found on scans, so they can fukking well make themselves a mouth and ears. It's not like there's a shortage of design options."

"What are making you so sure it will do what you are saying?" Presit's voice was a little shaky, but the glasses were back in place and her posture suggested she'd take out the knees of anyone who dared comment.

"Part of it was in my head," Torin reminded her.

"Oh, and that are enough!" the reporter snorted. "You are apparently not being so special; part have been in my . . ."

"Gunny? You want me to shut her up?"

She jerked forward, out of Mashona's grasp. "You are not able to be silencing the . . . Oh."

Sliding through the spectrum and then fading back into gray, the alien mass rose in the middle, rounded the crest, extruded two short arms, and created a vaguely bipedal shape. Given the mass it had available, it wasn't tall and the minimal features made it look like a cross between the Krai and the Druin.

Forming gray-on-gray eyes, it blinked twice and locked its gaze on Torin's face. "We have sufficient data." It spoke both Federate and Primacy—echoing itself the way the slate had been echoing every word spoken since Mike had gotten the translation program working.

Torin passed the slate back to Ressk. "Block the thing's input; we haven't time to listen to translations of translations." Then she turned her attention back to the alien and snarled, "You have sufficient data on what?"

"The interaction of life-forms we have encountered."

"Interaction?" Another piece fell into place. "You used the war to gather subjects to study."

"Yes."

Arms behind her, at parade rest. Easier to hide the way her hands were trembling. "This isn't a prison, it's a laboratory."

"In the manner you understand laboratory. Yes. We built this area to observe reactions in a more controlled environment."

"There was something in the food."

"There was."

"But it didn't affect me."

"Because you engineered an escape?" The ripple that passed through the gray rearranged its mass slightly, its facial shape picking up the longer lines of the Polina. "So, too, did Durlin Vertic. We have been gathering data for a very long time. For generations of your species. There have been other escapes. Others whose chemistry fights the control. And then there is new data. The tunnels challenge. The technology challenges. Meeting those considered the enemy challenges. The planet itself challenges."

"But we would have heard about escapes," Vertic growled.

"No one *escaped*," Torin corrected. She could feel her heart pounding against the inside of her ribs. She could hear the sound of nineteen people breathing. She could feel the back of Craig's hand lightly brushing hers. She could fortunately smell nothing of the mix of seven unwashed species. The Human nose was smart, it shut down when things became too much for it.

She was seeing red. Blood was red. Iron-based blood. Technical Sergeant Mike Gucciard's blood. Private Jiyuu's blood. Staff Sergeant Harnett's blood. The Artek's blood was copper-based. If they understood what was going on, Torin was pretty goddamned sure they'd be seeing green. "If this prison was created to observe in a more controlled environment, then you had to have also been observing in a less controlled environment. You didn't infiltrate the Confederation after Big Yellow. When we chanced on Big Yellow, you used the escape pod to add new parameters to the experiment. One fuk of a lot of people have died over the last few centuries but not, as they believed, in a war. In another laboratory."

Torin didn't remember moving, but Craig had hold of her arms and Werst had shoved his shoulder up against her hips, stopping her blind charge. The alien had to have retreated or, judging by how far down the corridor she'd come, she'd have stomped right through it, scattering it into pieces. As it remained whole, she felt as though she'd scattered herself to pieces instead.

Strangely, it was Presit who pulled her back together.

"I are wanting to be hearing from . . ." Her glasses shifted as she frowned. "From the Gray One now. The one that are being gray because it are choosing to, not because it are filthy," she expanded with a sneer.

Torin nodded down at Werst, and he moved aside. She shrugged out of Craig's grip, felt his touch linger, and said, "We're all waiting to hear from the Gray One." A gesture directed its minimal face toward the camera. "Explain."

It actually cocked its head. Torin just barely stopped herself from kicking that head off its shoulders. "It takes time to collect sufficient data on new species. Creating extreme situations erases all but essential behaviors and shortens the duration of the study."

"Did that fukker just say they started the war so they could simplify us?" Ressk asked over the rising murmurs of protest.

"We began the conflict to shorten the duration of the study. We continued the conflict until we had sufficient data."

"You continued the conflict?" Ressk was shouting now. "You kept us fighting?"

This time, perhaps because the question was directed specifically at it, it answered. "We did what was necessary to maintain the research parameters we required."

Torin grabbed Darlys' combats as she charged by and swung the nearly hysterical di'Taykan easily into the circle of her arms. "There's no point," she murmured against the singed ocher of her hair. "You can't touch it if it doesn't want you to."

"It destroyed the diplomatic ships! It kept the war going! I have lost *thytrin!*"

"Yeah, so have a lot of people." No point in adding that the Marines Darlys had helped Harnett kill had *thytrin* as well. Here and now, facing the reason so many had died, that was barely relevant. Breathing shallowly through her mouth, contact jacking arousal up to uncomfortable levels, she eased Darlys back into Watura's arms. He swayed but managed to stay standing.

The sound of claws against the floor shifted Torin to one side as Durlin Vertic staggered closer, one hand braced on Kyster's shoulder. She drew in a deep breath and visibly shook herself free of the pain. "Now you have sufficient data, what do you intend to do with it?" she demanded.

"The data must be analyzed."

"And then?"

"We will know when we analyze the data."

"Not good enough."

It shrugged. It copied the Human motion better than the Krai. "We will know when we analyze the data."

"On a more personal level," Torin growled. "What the fuk were you doing in my head?"

"Analysis requires context. You provided context."

"Only if you get out of here alive, you little fukker." Craig moved closer to Torin.

"You also provided context."

"Yeah, no shit."

Durlin Vertic cut any further comment off short. "Gunnery Sergeant Kerr."

"Sir?"

"Is there a way to destroy this . . . creature?"

"Yes, sir. Very high temperatures will cook the organic components." If the durlin gave the order, Torin would do her damnedest to follow it.

"It would be an entirely pointless gesture."

"Yes, sir."

"Let's keep it in reserve."

"Yes, sir."

Kyster shifted more of his weight off his injured foot as the durlin shuffled around to glare down at the Gray Ones, her grip on his shoulder tightening. Torin had to remind herself that the Krai were a lot stronger than they looked.

"Why have you decided to end your experiment now?"

"We have sufficient data."

"I know what sufficient means," the durlin snarled. "And it doesn't mean that the experiment came to an end."

It blinked again. Only the second time, Torin realized. Creepy little fuk. "There was some indication we were discovered."

"Yeah, well, a disappearing escape pod gets noticed," Craig snorted. "Should've wiped our memories, too, mate."

"You needed to retain your memories."

"Oh, yeah, to give you *context*." He said context like it was a new form of profanity.

"The memories brought you here. All of you. Although that was not the indication we referred to."

"It was back on Big Yellow," Torin began slowly fitting the final pieces together. "You intended to add new experimental parameters inside the Primacy, too. More context. You deep scanned some of the Artek, but they couldn't get off the ship in time and their Command destroyed their own people rather than let us take them . . ." She turned just enough to see her reflection in Firiv'vrak's eyes. "Did your people know?"

Her antennae dipped, and the air briefly smelled of pepper. Mandibles clattered.

"They suspected," Sanati translated incredulously.

"Then they were smarter than we were."

"Then they never reported their suspicions," Durlin Vertic growled.

When the pepper scent grew sharper, and Firiv'vrak spoke again, Torin held up a hand before Sanati could translate. "They reported," she said. "They weren't believed."

Almost funny how she could share a moment of total understanding with a giant bug. Almost. But not.

"Gunny!"

The durlin started to topple away from Kyster. Torin slipped a shoulder under her flailing arm and eased her to the floor as her legs crumpled. "Durlin Vertic! You still with us, sir?"

Her smile was more of a grimace. "As long as I can be with you from the floor."

Gray-on-gray eyes blinked a third time. "You have been damaged."

Torin reached out, grabbed a handful of Kyster's combats and hauled him back before his fists made contact. "I just remembered, sir. The Krai can digest the alien."

The grimace grew fiercer. "With no harm?"

She pushed the struggling Marine into the durlin's arms. "Not to the Krai."

"Good to know."

"Gunny?" His nose ridges were open and his lips were all the way off his teeth.

"We'll hold it in reserve, Kyster." She gripped his shoulder lightly. "For the moment, you keep supporting Durlin Vertic. Looks bad when the CO faceplants during negotiations. Get up here, then," she added as the male Polina made whining sounds. "There and there." As they settled in flanking positions, she straightened, grateful Craig knew enough to let her do it herself no matter how obviously he wanted to reach out and help. Officers could fall over. That was why there were gunnery sergeants.

"You are ignoring the Gray Ones," Presit pointed out sharply. "They are not going to be happy about that!"

"I don't give a flying fuk if they're happy." Torin twitched her vest back into place before turning to face the aliens. "All right. You were in my head—our heads—to give your data context. Is that why I was saved, plucked off the battlefield when so many others died?"

"We take those who would have died before they die so they are not missed."

"They're missed, you gray son of a bitch."

The pain in Craig's voice pulled Torin closer to him.

"That is also context."

"Fuk you!"

"So it was just chance that you grabbed one of your deep scan contextual subjects?" Torin was a little impressed she had enough energy left for sarcasm. "Save the data before the meat sack dies?"

"Dying would not damage the data. It would give us further context." As Craig growled, it turned a distinctly disapproving expression on the durlin. "Remaking the matter would destroy the data. Their weapon would damage the data. That is why you were saved and brought here. You meeting those you considered enemy gave us the last of the necessary context."

"He says context again and I'm telling Werst to eat him."

Torin closed her hand briefly around Craig's arm, the momentary contact as much as she could handle. "Good thing he listens to me, then. So our escape . . ." She let a gesture that encompassed all seventeen of them finish the sentence.

"You were each acting as your nature demanded. We had no part in it." It turned to look at Werst. "Hazard pay is an excellent suggestion."

"Did it just make a joke?" Mashona wondered.

"With sufficient data, we called in the rest of those researching."

"You were in contact with the . . ." There weren't words. ". . . bits in Craig and Presit's brains."

"We are in contact."

"All the bits?"

"Each."

"Great. A polynumerous molecular *telepathic* species. That makes you omnipresent and damned near omnipotent." Torin had to consciously relax her jaw to keep talking. "Why don't we just call you gods and cut out the middleman?"

"We do not care what you call us."

"Lucky for you," Craig snarled, " 'cause I can think of a few things . . ."

He wasn't the only one.

Torin let the yelling go on for a bit and then raised a hand, cutting it off.

The alien's gaze followed the gesture and seemed amused. "Damned near omnipotent," it repeated.

"Gunnery Sergeant," Werst snorted.

"Progenitor," Darlys added.

"Not. About. Me." Torin's tone promised consequences if anyone else piped up with an opinion. "What," she demanded of the alien as the resulting silence stretched and lengthened, "happens now?"

"The data must be analyzed."

"No, that's what happens next. What happens *now*?"

"That is not up to us."

"How do you figure? Because it looks like the whole fukking thing has been up to you for some time now."

"If you are bringing us here," Presit snapped, "then you are sending us home!"

"No."

"No? What are *no* meaning?"

"What it has always meant."

"You are one smart-ass comment from being an entrée," Torin told it. It was fast, sure, but the Krai were hungry and a hungry Krai was a motivated Krai.

"Our part is over. It is time to leave."

"You're going nowhere without . . ."

Given the way nerves were stretched, Torin wasn't surprised when the sudden shrilling of an alarm from Craig's slate caused Kichar to haul off and slug Everim with everything she had left. As Craig snapped the slate off his belt, Freenim let Everim take his swing then pulled the two youngsters apart, tossing one at Mashona and one at Merinim.

"Six ships just came in-system. Three of ours. Three of theirs. Theirs," Craig qualified jerking his head toward the durlin. "They're some distance apart, doesn't look like they've spotted each other yet."

"I thought you said this system was off the charts?"

"It is."

"Then how . . . ?"

They turned together toward the alien.

The alien was gone.

Torin fought the urge to vomit. She'd have known if it had reentered her. She had to have known. "Presit?"

"There are a blur on the recording." Presit peered over her glasses into the camera's monitor. "Then nothing."

"Fukkers!" It could have been any one of the watching Marines. It could have been all of them.

"No argument. No time either." They were context, sure, but they were also witnesses. It would be stupid for the alien, the Gray Ones, to keep them alive to tell both sides how they'd been screwed over. "Craig, upload everything you've recorded to *Promise*'s distress beacon, then pulse it. No matter what happens next, everyone hears what just went down."

"What if they don't receive?" Craig asked, but he was slaving the camera to his slate so she let it stand.

"It's a distress beacon. They'll receive. Our side will want to save us; theirs will want to take advantage."

"But, Gunny . . ."

"We're on the same side, Kyster." She turned and swept a weary glare over Kichar and Everim. "That's been the whole fukking point of the exercise."

"Gunny! They're taking the . . ." The roar of the engines finished Ressk's sentence. When they got to the control room, when they got the shield down again, the VTA was gone.

"Not enough of them to become a ship this time," Craig grunted.

"Unless they were also the VTA," Ressk pointed out.

"Thanks, mate. Didn't need to hear that."

"They did not go far. Not even into orbit." Sanati smacked a screen with her palm. Against all odds, the static cleared just long enough to show the VTA on the roof of the prison.

"They're pulling out." Torin rested her fists on the edge of the control panel. If her fists were holding her weight, it'd be easier to keep from punching something. "Gathering the rest of their . . . bowls."

It didn't take long before the VTA was lifting again, but they all knew how fast the Gray Ones could move.

"Fastest bowls in known space," Werst muttered as the screen gave way to static again.

Sanati frowned down at the board. "They have left the atmosphere."

Torin hadn't seen any weapons on the VTA, but in a universe where the species running things hung out as bowls, that meant absolutely nothing.

"They are still moving out."

"Perhaps they do not care that we know what they have done," Freenim said quietly. "Perhaps they want us to bear witness as the fastest way of ending the war they started."

"You honestly think they care?" Torin asked him.

The durlave shrugged. "I honestly think they do not care, and that is why they are leaving. Going back where they came from to analyze their data."

"Yeah, well, given the holiday camp atmosphere on this shithole of a planet, I'm just glad they took the time to build the structures out of something other than themselves." Mashona patted the wall beside her.

"You absolutely positive of that?" Ressk asked her.

She stepped away from the wall. "Oh, that's just fukking great. How do we know if they're all gone?"

Torin shrugged when all eyes turned to her. "We don't. We just do our jobs the way we always have."

"It can't be that easy, Gunny."

Fulfill the mission objectives and get her people out alive.

"If it was easy, Mashona, they wouldn't send in the Marines."

Smiles at that. At the expected among the unknown. That was part of her job, too. Be the one thing they could count on no matter what. No matter how much she wanted to beat her head against a wall and scream.

It had been there, in her head. In her head and in Craig's head. She glanced over at him, wondering if the thing between them, the thing she was not going to name, not yet, wondering if it had ever had anything to do with the two of them, or if it had been arranged from the moment she'd dropped through the floor of Big Yellow and nearly flattened him.

He smiled, lifted a hand toward her, glanced around the room, and settled for shaking his head. "No."

"No what?"

"No, they aren't responsible for us. For you and me."

"I didn't . . ." She hadn't had to. And maybe that said enough. Now her fists on the edge of the panel were keeping her knees from buckling. "Okay, then. So what do we do while we wait to see if we survive this next bit?"

"What next bit, Gunny?"

"The bit where we see if those six ships destroy each other or us."

"But not in that order, right, Gunny? Because if the six ships destroyed each other, then they couldn't destroy us. Well, they could if they launched planet splitters before they blew, but . . ." Kichar's voice trailed off. Suddenly the center of attention, she flushed.

"They are not destroying each other." There was a chance, albeit a small one, Presit intended to sound comforting. "Gunnery Sergeant Kerr are having ended the war. The Gray Ones are telling us we are pawns, puppets, *ser ka bingh me.* Gunnery Sergeant Kerr are letting everyone know it. Forcing everyone to take a good hard look at what are happening. And she are doing it in her underwear."

Torin did not glace down at her bare legs. "And my question still stands, what do we do while we wait?"

"We could eat."

The jaws Torin could see dropped. Ressk brought his teeth together with a snap so loud Firiv'vrak clattered something in response.

"The duffel I dropped by the elevator has a couple dozen field rations in it," Craig continued a little sheepishly. "I ran everything organic I had through the mess kit."

"There's food?"

"Yeah, it's . . ."

"Mashona!"

"On it, Gunny."

Werst, who'd started moving at the mention of food, rocked to a stop by Craig's hip, turned, and glared up at her. She ignored him. No way in a hundred hells was she sending one of the Krai out for that pack. Corps training might be the best in known space, but it only went so far.

"I hope you are happy, Gunnery Sergeant, there are no food left on the *Promise*." Presit finally kicked free of the HE suit and began to run her claws through her fur.

"The VTA's gone." Torin nodded toward the window and the empty landing bay, barely visible through the new scorch marks. "You can't get back to the *Promise*."

"He are not knowing that when he are coming down here."

"No, he didn't." She raised a brow in Craig's direction. If he'd come dirtside with some romantic notion of dying with her, she'd kick his ass.

"*Promise* can't hold everyone here even if we just took the Marines actually in this building . . ." He raised a hand before Torin could protest. ". . . which I know you wouldn't allow anyway, and I also knew you weren't leaving unless everyone did—and I wasn't leaving without you. I lost you once already, and had no intention of doing it again. I'd planned to live out my life down here if I had to."

Werst's nose ridges clamped shut. "That's so touching I think I'm going to puke."

Torin tried not to look as if he agreed with him. Living together on this burning shithole came perilously close to dying together.

"I are not given a choice," Presit snarled. "I are perfectly willing to lose you again."

Craig shrugged. "We wouldn't have lived long enough to get home anyway."

"I are not dying here!"

"Good." Torin squared her shoulders. "Neither am I. Pulse the recording again."

"It was quite the transmission," Captain Carveg said dryly. "There might have been a bit of a problem believing it except that all six ships jettisoned an escape pod just after we received it the first time."

Torin stared at the wall over the captain's left shoulder and tried not to think about how much the healing blisters on her thighs itched where the newly issued combats rubbed.

"And when I say all six ships jettisoned an escape pod," the captain continued, "that's exactly what I mean. No one gave the order. And then, funny thing, it turned out that all six ships still had a full complement of escape pods in spite of what we all saw, and in spite of what was on the computer records. Then, when the escape pods . . ." Her hands rose in air quotes, and that was a weird enough gesture from a Krai that Torin actually dropped her gaze to the captain's face. ". . . combined and, according to long-range scanners, joined up with your VTA, well, let's just say it was a good thing the shooting had done minimal damage until that point."

"So there were Gray Ones on the ships, on all the ships, on both sides, and now they're gone?"

Captain Carveg's lips pulled back off her teeth. The three other officers in the room mirrored the action although none of them were Krai. "I think we can all agree they were here and that they were fukking around in, well, let's say our Susumi equations for a start given that we suddenly found ourselves emerging into a brand-spanking-new section of space, but as to whether or not they're gone, I don't know, Gunnery Sergeant Kerr, because, apparently, there is no fukking way to tell. So, if you have some more insider information you'd like to make the rest of us privy to . . . ?"

The initial debriefing down on that slag heap of a planet had been just short of brutal. Had Torin not shared a history with Captain Carveg, she doubted that she and Craig and Presit would have ever been allowed onto the *Berganitan*. The Primacy captains had been more willing to take their people off although they had kept weapons aimed at the Marines while they loaded their VTA.

Durlave Kan Freenim had been the last to leave.

"It is unlikely we will meet again."

"Stranger things have happened," Torin reminded him.

"Truth. Whatever happens . . ." He waved a hand in the general *direction of a war that wasn't a war that was still going on. ". . . I have always believed that I would have more in common with certain members of the enemy than I do with some of my own people."* He held out his fist and Torin touched her knuckles to his.

The blood on both their hands had made the contact sticky.

Once Captain Carveg had been convinced her ship would be in no danger from bringing them aboard—and Torin had no idea what it was that had finally convinced her—the Marines had been taken to Med-op, but Craig and Presit had been scooped up immediately by Intell. It was news to Torin that the Navy even maintained intelligence officers on their destroyers. She'd closed her teeth on the nearly irresistible comment and assured Presit that vivisection was unlikely.

"Gunnery Sergeant Kerr?"

"I have no further information on the Gray Ones, sir. But I believe they're gone."

"All of them?"

"Yes, sir."

"You believe?"

They said they had sufficient data. She lifted her chin, just a little. "Yes, sir."

"And that should be enough, should it?"

She was still a gunnery sergeant in the Confederation Marine Corps. "Yes, sir."

Torin had a private room in Med-op while the *Berganitan's* doctors checked her over. Her injuries were superficial—burns, bruises, a bit of malnutrition—which allowed them to move right to scanning her brain without having to bother pretending that wasn't their entire interest. Since the Corps' scans hadn't found a damned thing previously, she figured the odds of the Navy finding something now were slim to none, but she kept that opinion to herself. A couple of the doctors looked as if they might consider vivisection to be a good idea.

They wouldn't let her see Craig.

When one of the doctors tried to remove the salvage tag, she convinced him to let her keep it.

"What's that old Human saying?" Captain Carveg snorted as two corpsmen carried the doctor out. "Physician, heal thyself? You get into a fight with another member of my crew and I'll have you on charges so fast you'll think you've got a Susumi drive up your ass. But this one . . ." She reached out and gripped Torin's shoulder for a moment. ". . . this one you get to win."

Torin waited, fingers wrapped around the tag. Captains didn't visit gunnery sergeants to tell them they weren't to be brought up on charges.

The captain's nose ridges closed, her grip tightened for a moment, then she let her hand fall back to her side. "The prison collapsed. It looks like earthquake damage. We're reading working tech but no life signs."

There were three hundred Marines down there, maybe more, and at least that many members of the Primacy. There were six destroyers in orbit maintaining a reluctant peace. Room for everyone.

"Gunny?"

"Everyone, sir?"

"I'd like to say there's always a chance, but . . ." She shook her head. "We have teams bringing out the bodies. No one will be left behind."

Torin thought of Jiyuu at the bottom of the elevator shaft and her promise to Watura and of Mike burning as he held open the air lock door. "Thank you, sir."

After the captain left, she slid out of bed and paced the length of the room, seven paces there and seven back. There and back. There and back. No point in testing to see if they'd let her leave. She'd seen the two burly, well-armed sailors standing outside her door. Sure, she could take them, but eventually sheer numbers would beat her down.

"Gunny?"

"Kyster. How did you . . . ?"

He shrugged and limped a little farther into the room. "They didn't see me. I'm good at not being seen. Did they tell you?"

"About the prison?"

He nodded.

"They told me." She let her back hit the wall and slid down it until she was sitting on the floor. Major Kenoton. Lieutenant Myshai. Staff Sergeant Pole. Lance Corporal Divint. Private Sergei. Private Graydon.

"Do you think . . ." His nose ridges opened and closed. "Gunny, do you think the durlin is okay?"

"She's with her people, Kyster." Colonel Mariner. Second Lieutenant Teirl. Lieutenant Cafter. Lieutenant O'Neill. Major Ohi.

"But do you think she's okay?"

He was still very young.

Torin opened her arms. The impact nearly cracked a rib, but she held him the way Durlin Vertic had, in the circle of her folded legs, held him while he sobbed and murmured what Krai words of comfort she knew.

"Are you certain you've made the right decision?"

Torin stepped off the end of the ramp and held Craig in the open air lock with a raised hand. He didn't look happy about it, but he stayed where he was, arms folded and glowering. "Mashona, Ressk, and I are all that survived of Sh'quo Company." Captain Rose. Lieutenant Jarret. First Sergeant Tutone. Sergeant Hollice.

"There are other companies. And a war that's been fought for centuries doesn't end . . ." High Tekamal Louden's mouth twisted into a humorless smile. ". . . without a fight. It's not going to be all politics and diplomacy and no hard feelings no matter what the H'san seem to think."

The Elder Races had issued statements simultaneously insisting that they'd never been under anyone's control and that they'd always said the war wasn't their fault. The actual statements were significantly longer and filled with the kind of bullshit rhetoric that Torin had come to expect from the Elder Races, but that was the gist of it. She tried not to enjoy the fact that their more elder than thou attitude had been shattered by molecular-sized bits of organic plastic. She tried not to wonder if they were lying.

Only the H'san had apologized, but even they'd been vague on what they were apologizing for.

The war went on, but diplomatic efforts to end it were now being managed by the species involved in fighting it. When the Elder Races had protested, both branches of the military had diplomatically told them to fuk off. Or as Presit had pointed out in her award-winning interview with the Mictok's parliamentary representative: *"The Elder Races are being the ones who put weapons in their hands. Were you seriously thinking you are always being able to control where they pointed them?"*

Things were changing.

"I've been compromised," Torin reminded the commandant.

"We've all been compromised," the commandant snorted. "We move past that or we self-destruct. As it is, we face the threat of civil disobedience turning into civil war. Even the Methane Alliance seems to have their fringes in a knot. We could use people who can get the job done."

She couldn't. Or she didn't want to. Six of one, half a dozen of the other. She hadn't had to say it to Craig; he'd seen it on her face, in her eyes. Felt it in her touch maybe. She sure as hell wasn't going to say it to the Commandant of the Corps.

"You can use people who don't remind everyone that they've been compromised," Torin snorted. Even months later, the recording of two gray lines running down her face still ran daily on at least half the available vid channels.

"We know you're clear. Hell, if we know anyone in the Corps is clear, we know it about you. There isn't a part of your body that hasn't been mapped at the subatomic level. There isn't a memory in your head we don't have on record." The commandant's eyes flicked up the ramp toward the air lock. "Yours and his."

"Knowing is one thing. Believing, that's something else."

Pale eyes narrowed. "If I didn't believe, you wouldn't be leaving."

"If you'd really wanted me to stay, you wouldn't be letting me leave."

The pause stretched. Lengthened. Torin settled her weight back on her heels and waited. Wondered when the ambient noise at Ventris Station had grown so loud.

"Granted," the commandant admitted at last. "Gunnery Sergeant Torin Kerr is a little bit too much of a distraction with the situation the way it is right now. I'd like to think we could work around that, but—bottom line—I'm a realist. And you still haven't answered my question."

Was she certain she'd made the right decision?

"I'm certain."

"Good enough." She held out her hand. "Good luck, then."

"Thank you, sir. You, too."

"We'll need it. We're short a gunnery sergeant." When Torin lifted a brow, High Tekamal Louden grinned. "Yes, well, that sounded a lot less lame in my head."

"You're certain about this?"

"Oh, for fuk's sake, Craig, not again." Torin got up off the bunk, crossed the cabin, and poured herself a mug of coffee. "I'm certain. If you're having second thoughts . . ."

"I'm not."

"Because I've heard the Senior Ranks' Mess is running book that I'll stuff you out the air lock within the first three months."

"What kind of odds?"

"Even." Even over the sound of the Susumi drive, she heard him stand and take the three long strides that put him directly behind her. She could feel the air warming against the bare skin of her back and then his skin against hers. "But it's twenty to one you'll stuff me out an air lock before we reach Paradise." She wanted to see Craig interact with her father. Laugh together. Share embarrassing stories. She wanted her mother and her brothers to meet him and know she'd made the right decision. She was clearly growing stupidly sentimental in her old age.

"Before Paradise, eh?" A burly arm wrapped around her waist. "They should have more faith."

"Some of them have worked with me."

"Good point. Why twenty to one, then?"

"I'm not just going to let you do it, now am I?"

Reaching past her with his free hand, he snagged the second mug and held it up for her to fill. "I got a message from Werst just before we went into Susumi space. He says there's a rumor going around that the last visit by the Commandant of the Corps means she's sent you off on a secret mission to deal with the Gray Ones."

"She didn't."

"But if we run into them . . . ?"

Twisting in his hold, she turned to face him. "Space is big."

"Apparently not as big as we thought." Craig dropped his forehead against hers. "Torin, if we run into them, do you have orders?"

"No." She smiled. Made it as reassuring as she figured he'd believe. "I'm out of the Corps. If we run into them, they'll just have me to deal with."